Praise for BRAS & BROOMSTICKS

● ● ● ● ●

"Screamingly funny."
—*Kirkus Reviews*

"A very fun book."
—yabookscentral.com

"Fast-paced, entertaining."
—*Jewish Book World*

"Fast, funny, and original. . . . Extremely hard to put down."
—teenreads.com

"This is one magical romp you won't want to miss."
—*Discovery Girls* magazine

"The first in a series, the novel is a bewitching lure for fans of chick lit looking for supernatural twists on the theme of girl-meets-world."
—*The Bulletin*

"Plenty of laughs and some deliciously complicated predicaments."
—*Publishers Weekly*

"This isn't just another breezy teen read. Mlynowski has a real ear for dialogue, and she displays a keen understanding of teen mores as she pokes fun at high-school cliques."
—*Booklist*

"An extremely funny and pleasurable read."
—*Lake* magazine

"This book is so funny, I read it twice."
—girlposse.com

Praise for FROGS & FRENCH KISSES

• • • • •

"A creative, frolicsome tale of high-school life,
with a bewitching twist."
—*New York Post*

"This frothy sequel to *Bras & Broomsticks* is just as sweet
and funny as its predecessor. . . . Mlynowski's sassy text
surpasses a chick-lit label by being wonderfully fast-paced
and clever. A surprise ending will have fans eagerly looking
forward to Rachel's next adventure."
—*Booklist*

"Humorous and lively."
—*The Gazette* (Montreal)

"Rachel and her bewitching family return, and this time
there's romance in the air. But adding a little magic to the mix has hilarious results. [This] sparkling sequel to *Bras & Broomsticks*
proves Mlynowski [is] a serious contender for the Cabot crown."
—*Publishing News*

sarah mlynowski

magic in manhattan

INCLUDES BOOKS 1 AND 2

bras & broomsticks   frogs & french kisses

EMBER

Bras & Broomsticks copyright © 2005 by Sarah Mlynowski
Frogs & French Kisses copyright © 2006 by Sarah Mlynowski
Cover art copyright © 2012 by Shutterstock
Cover imaging by Ericka O'Rourke

All rights reserved. Published in the United States by Ember, an imprint of Random House Children's Books, a division of Random House, Inc., New York.

This edition is comprised of *Bras & Broomsticks* and *Frogs & French Kisses*, originally published separately in hardcover in the United States by Delacorte Press, an imprint of Random House Children's Books, New York, in 2005 and 2006.

Ember and the E colophon are registered trademarks of Random House, Inc.

Visit us on the Web! randomhouse.com/teens

Educators and librarians, for a variety of teaching tools, visit us at randomhouse.com/teachers

Library of Congress Cataloging-in-Publication Data for *Bras & Broomsticks* and *Frogs & French Kisses* is available upon request.

ISBN 978-0-385-74232-0 (tr. pbk.)

RL: 4.7

Printed in the United States of America

10 9 8 7 6 5 4 3 2

First Ember Edition 2012

bras & broomsticks

For Aviva, my baby sister.
And yes, she'll always be my baby sister, even when
she's seventy-two and I'm seventy-nine.

(Fine, Aviva, seventy-eight and a half).

acknowledgments

Thanks to the power of a billion to:

Laura Dail, my extraordinary agent, who loves Rachel and Miri as much as I do; Wendy Loggia, for her superb guidance and never-ending enthusiasm; Beverly Horowitz, Isabel Warren-Lynch, Tamar Schwartz, Gayley Carillo, Emily Jacobs, Jennifer Black, and everyone else at Delacorte Press who worked their butts off for my book; my mom, Elissa Ambrose, for adding many of the jokes and most of the punctuation; Lynda Curnyn, for always answering my emails Re: IS THIS LINE FUNNY?/Re: DOES THIS MAKE ANY SENSE? within half a second; Jess Braun, for reading everything I've ever written since we were nine, and because she would never in a million years try out for the fashion show; Robin Glube, for all her help; for their love and support, Bonnie, Ronit, Jessica D., Vickie, John, Dad, and Louisa (my SM—in this case stepmom, not step-monster); and Todd, my STBH (Soon To Be Husband), for making every day magical.

BETTER THAN RUBY SLIPPERS

1

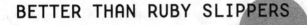

I've wished for lots of things in my fourteen years . . .
a boyfriend, world peace, cleavage. But none of my
wishes have come true.

Until now.

I'm standing by my locker, zipping up my black puffy
coat, when I notice the sneakers.

They're the green suede designer ones I admired at
Bloomie's last week. My mom said I couldn't have them
because they cost more than our TV.

And they're on my feet.

"But how—" I mumble, blinking in confusion.
Where are the beaten-up black boots I always have on?
"I mean, when . . . ?"

Did I accidentally swap shoes with someone after gym? Am I a thief?

Impossible. The only time I ever took anything that wasn't mine was when I inadvertently wore Jewel's retainer. Gross, yes. But criminal? No.

My heart starts beating erratically. This is so weird. How did these shoes get on my feet?

Wait a millisecond. Maybe my mom bought them to surprise me? Not that she normally does stuff like that, but I have been on my best behavior lately (after being grounded for something completely ridiculous, don't even ask) and she's big on rewarding good deeds.

I guess I must have laced them up this morning without even noticing. Lame. But I went to bed really late last night, and I'm always zoned out when I'm tired.

That still doesn't explain why I didn't notice I was wearing them until now though. I glance back down. The shoes are a luminous green. Sparkling, even. They're practically *screaming* at me to notice them.

Whatever. New shoes! The ideal accessory for my awesome after-school plans. I smile like someone who just got her braces off.

"Can I borrow your phone?" I ask Tammy. She's busy rummaging through her satchel. The least I can do is thank my mom—maybe she'll cave on a cell phone for me next.

"Cool shoes," Tammy says, glancing down. "When did you change?"

"I . . . didn't. I've, uh, been wearing them all day." Haven't I? Now I'm totally unsure again.

2

Tammy gives me a thumbs-up sign with her right hand and passes the phone with her left. She uses finger signals to indicate her thoughts. She learned to scuba dive with her family last year in Aruba and now frequently communicates by underwater mime. Thumbs-up means "Let's get out of the water," which means she wants to hightail it out of here.

My mother answers on the first ring.

"Mom, thanks for the sneakers. They're perfect! Sorry I didn't notice them this morning."

Pause. Then muffled static.

"You still there?" I ask, tapping my heels together. Who knew green suede could look so glam? "I can't hear you."

There's furious whispering in the background, and then a loud "Shhh!"

"You need to come home," my mom tells me.

"What? Why?" I ask. My stomach free-falls.

Another pause. More furious whispering. "I have something to talk to you about," my mom says. Her voice sounds uneven. "Something extremely important."

"But I have extremely important after-school plans!" My destiny is waiting for me at Stromboli Pizzeria! This is a complete and utter disaster. "And when I called you an hour ago you said I could go!"

"Things have changed," my mother says, her clipped words ruining my life. "I want you back at the apartment."

My down-filled coat starts to feel like a furnace. "Can't we talk about whatever is so earth-shattering later?"

3

My mother heaves one of her why-must-I-carry-the-weight-of-the-world-on-my-thin-shoulders sighs. "Rachel, enough."

"Fine." I sigh right back. I have a sigh of my own, and it's just as martyrish. In a small triumph, I press the pink End button before she can say good-bye.

"I can't come," I tell Tammy, handing her the phone. My cheeks feel all blotchy. Why couldn't I have just thanked my mom when I got home?

Tammy adjusts her light brown ponytail and makes a fist in front of her chest, her "low on air" sign, meaning she feels bad for me. Tammy is an excellent sympathizer, as well as smart and reliable. She's always there when I need someone to talk to, and more important, when I unintentionally sport poppy bagel seeds between my teeth, she immediately and covertly lets me know by tapping her lips. She's a great friend. It's just that—okay, I hate to play favorites—I like Jewel more. But the way Jewel has been treating me, I might as well be walking around with an I-just-got-dumped sash across my nonexistent chest.

Sigh.

Over the past four months, since she strutted her stuff for the JFK fashion show tryouts and got in, Juliana Sanchez (Jewel for short, Bee-Bee for shorter/longer) has morphed from my sidekick and best friend into a card-carrying member of the inner circle. Yes, she made the A-list. Except for a few minutes in math class, I hardly ever get to talk to her anymore. I miss her.

Going to Stromboli's would have been a step toward

reclaiming our Bee-Bee status. (Sorry for the cheddary Best Buds acronym, but Jewel and I have been using it forever.) The entire cool crowd will be there. I was lucky even to have been asked. Mick Lloyd invited Jeffrey Stars, who invited Aaron Jacobs, who invited Tammy, who invited me. And you don't go if you don't get an invite. You can't. You wouldn't know what pizza place/coffee shop/parentless apartment the A-list selected, so you wouldn't know where to show up. If only they would just choose the same place every time, like they did on *Friends*. Monica never showed up at a new coffee spot, The *Not-So*-Central Perk, wondering where everyone was.

Down the hall I see Raf Kosravi at his locker, pulling out his coat. A strand of his midnight black hair falls into his matching dark eyes, and he brushes it away with the back of his hand.

5

Heart. Beating. Erratically. Not. Because. Of. Shoes.

Sigh. Because of my mother, I will potentially be missing out on precious flirting time with Raf, the boy I'm in love with.

I am also in love with Mick Lloyd. Yes, I know it seems strange to love two boys at the same time, but since I've never spoken more than two words to either of them ("Happy Holidays!" to Raf and "Excuse me" to Mick), I'm not concerned about my divided heart. Mick Lloyd is the cute, blond, all-American type that's cast on every dating show. Big smile, dimple in each cheek, great hair. Raf is more mysterious-slash-sexy. He's not too tall, only around five foot six (which is still much, much taller than me at five foot one—I'd *better* still be growing), and has a lean, fit body like a champion tennis player or an Olympic swimmer (not that I've ever watched professional tennis or swimming). Raf is also in the fashion show with Jewel.

Ah, the fashion show. It's *really* a dance show with a catwalk and designer outfits. Or so I hear. Since I'm only a freshman, and the show is in April, I've never seen it. And since a former JFK student who's now an It Guy Hollywood director launched the idea ten years ago to raise money for the prom, it's always been a cool thing for guys to do. Like football or baseball. There is an overlap of boys who play football with those who are in the show. Unfortunately for the school trophy case, the quarterback is a better dancer than he is an athlete.

Mick isn't in the show, but he does play on the JV baseball team, the only sports team at our school that doesn't always lose. And—impressive residence alert!—he lives in a massive brownstone. Since his mom and dad are frequently out of town, he throws a lot of wild parties (not that I've ever been). Raf and Mick are both very, very A-list. But that isn't the reason I like them.

Raf buttons up his coat and slaps one of his friends on the back.

Sigh.

I am such a liar. *Of course* that's why I like them. I don't even *know* them, so why else would I like them? They're hot and cool—as in sexy and popular—and if either of them were interested in me, I would actually have a real kiss to brag about. (I claim my first was with a Texan named Stu who I met on a cruise. This is a to-tal lie. Although there was a boy named Stu from Texas, he was seven.) Plus, I would instantly be pro-moted from the B-list (B+ on an excellent hair day) to the A-list.

I really want to be A-list. Yes, I know I'm being colos-sally pathetic, and I've seen enough movies to know that popular people always get their comeuppance. And be-ing A-list in high school doesn't guarantee you'll be cool in college. But . . . like blondes, the A-list always seems to have more fun.

I ask you: Is it so wrong to want to be happy? Is it so wrong to want to be liked? Is it wrong to want my life to be like a soda ad, with lots of laughing, jumping, and high-fiving?

Aaron, otherwise known as Tammy's connection to the A-list, waves to her from across the hallway.

Tammy doesn't believe it, but Aaron has a thing for her. Aaron isn't quite A-list, but he went to junior high with Mick and is friends with Mick's best friend, Jeffrey, so sometimes he gets invited through a few degrees of separation. Tammy says that if Aaron liked her, he would have asked her out by now. Instead they've be-come "friends." They IM every night. Tammy claims she doesn't like Aaron, but I don't buy it. She giggles around him *and* her hand signals go into overdrive.

"Ready?" he asks, bundling his scarf like a helmet around his neck and over his ears. He looks like one of the evil sandmen in *Star Wars* who try to kill Luke.

Yikes. Only a freak would allude to *Star Wars*. How

7

am I ever going to achieve cool status when I'm such a loser?

I need to start laughing and jumping. Maybe if I raise my hand, Tammy will give me a high five?

Not.

Instead, Tammy gives Aaron the scuba OK, which conveniently happens to be the universal okay sign, an O with the thumb and index finger. This has always mystified me. Where's the K? What if you just want to say Oh, as in Oh, Raf, why don't you notice me? Or, Oh, at least I have cool new shoes.

"See you tomorrow," she tells me.

Oh why oh why do I have to go home?

I turn the corner onto Tenth Street and run the last bit to my apartment building—I hate to do this to my virgin new shoe soles, but I have no choice. My earlobes have frozen into blocks of ice, and now the doctor will probably have to amputate. Seriously. That's what they do with frostbite. Just call me Van Gogh.

I press the Up button to call the elevator. To pass the time—what's taking it so long?—I make a mental list.

Possible Extremely Important Topics Mom Insists on Discussing Today of All Days

1. Maybe her travel agency, HoneySun (they specialize in honeymoons, wink, wink), has folded.

Maybe she's going to tell us that we have to start saving money. Tighten our belts. Cook more, eat out less. Cancel call-waiting. Return the new shoes.

2. Maybe Miri, my twelve-year-old sister, saw a mob hit man butcher someone and the DA wants her to testify and we're joining the witness protection program and moving to Los Angeles. California would be awesome. Except that everyone in L.A. has implants. Who wants something foreign in her body? Braces were bad enough—they made me look like a robot. (Although, I have always wanted a robot. Particularly one programmed to fold the clothes that are currently carpeting my bedroom floor.)

3. Maybe my mom's gay. Tammy's mother came out four years ago. Since both Tammy's biological parents remarried, now Tammy has three mothers— one biological and two steps. As if one mother isn't annoying enough. Nah. My mother isn't gay. I've seen her bat her long eyelashes and twirl her hair whenever she runs into Dave, the twenty-seven-year-old hunkalicious fireman who lives on the second floor.

4. Maybe, bite my tongue, my mother or sister has a terminal disease. But Miri is always hungry. Are you hungry when you're terminally ill? I think no. Not that I've ever hung out with someone who was that sick. I've never had the occasion. But in a TV movie I saw a few weeks ago, two boys made fun of this poor kid with leukemia because he was losing his hair, and it fully pissed me off. If I ever knew someone who was dying, I would be extra nice to

9

her. My mother *is* looking pretty pasty, so maybe—omigod—she has cancer. Although her pale skin tone could be because of her ridiculously unhealthy eating habits.

Honestly, she eats marshmallows for breakfast. And not the good kind in Lucky Charms—she eats the white ones out of a bag. And she packs herself one lousy bagel for lunch. And then we have tofu-crap for dinner. She refuses to cook meat. Even my sister is a vegetarian now, so it's two against one. Obviously, I don't think anyone is really sick, or I'd be hysterical. And if someone *were* sick, I would have detected it. I notice stuff. Like my mother's birth control pills. Fine, I found them in the secret side compartment of her makeup case—yet another reason I know she's not gay. I don't know why she takes them; she hasn't had a date in two years. I tried to sign her up on an Internet dating site, but she freaked out when she caught me Photoshopping her eye wrinkles from her picture and made me delete her entire profile.

This is turning out to be a really chaotic list. No wonder I never make lists. I'm so bad at them. They're too restrictive, like tights. Miri loves them. (I'm talking about lists, not tights—we both hate the latter, especially itchy wool ones.) I'm the disorganized, last-week's-socks-still-under-my-bed kind of girl, but Miri types and pins her *Things to Do Today! Packing List for Dad's! Reasons Why I'm Anal!* (just kidding on that last one) memos to the massive bulletin board above her desk. The rest of her room is covered in Tae Kwon Do certificates. She's a brown belt, which is two levels away from black. How nuts is that? She's only four and a half feet tall and she can beat up my dad. Okay, fine, she probably can't beat up my dad. Definitely me, though. I went to a class once, but all the kicking, bowing, and focusing required was exhausting. Never mind the impossible no-talking rule—

I notice the sign on the building elevator: OUT OF ORDER.

Groan. I guess the stairs will be my exercise for the day. For the week, actually. All right, the month. I fly up the first flight. I stride up the second. By the fourth I almost black out.

Maybe I should have stayed in Tae Kwon Do. Then I wouldn't be so out of shape. I'm not one of those girls who obsess about the size of their thighs, but it's kind of sad that I'm so young and out of breath.

Maybe there's a sports team I could join.

Nah. *Puff, puff.* Exercise. *Puff, puff.* Is. *Puff, puff.* Too. *Puff, puff.* Hard.

By the time I insert the key in the lock of the front door, I'm gasping.

I hang up my coat in the front closet. "Hello?"

"We're in here," my mother calls from her room.

I wipe the bottoms of my funky new sneakers, turn on the kitchen lights, and pour myself a glass of water. Then I pass my room, my sister's room, and the bathroom and then enter the warden's. She and Miri are sitting side

11

by side on the bed, their legs hidden under a faded purple comforter, their backs against the headboard. Both are in their usual sleepwear: oversized concert T-shirts.

"Why does it reek of smoke in here?" An ashtray overflowing with cigarette butts is stationed between the humps I assume are my mother's feet. What's going on? She hasn't smoked in more than a year.

"Minor relapse," my mom says with a hangdog expression. "Won't happen again. Sit down. We have to talk to you."

Uh-oh. I try to forget about the revolting butts and focus on the issue at hand. This must be really bad. If we'd won the lottery, she'd have greeted me with a smile and champagne. Fine, probably not champagne, since that stuff's pretty pricey. But maybe chardonnay. Occasionally she lets me have a small glass of wine with dinner. Says she'd rather I try it with her than at an unsupervised party.

Not that I've ever been to an unsupervised party. (But if anyone *does* invite me, I'm game. You can call me on my home [not cell] phone or e-mail me at—)

"Oh, Rachel," my mom says. "Where to begin?"

Miri's eating from a bag of sunflower seeds. Watching her is disgusting. She sucks one seed at a time, licks her fingers, then sticks her grubby, nail-bitten hand (a habit she picked up from my mother) back into the bag. One wet seed is clinging to a frizzy strand of her shoulder-length brown hair. Very appealing.

"Want some?" she offers.

Ew!

"Are you wearing shoes in the apartment?" my mother asks, peering over the edge of her bed.

"No." I'm about to thank her for them again, but curiosity about what they need to tell me takes precedence over manners. So I untie them and place them neatly on the floor. Then I slide, baseball-style (see how made for each other we are, sweet Mick?), stomach first onto her bed. "This had better be important."

Instead of responding, my mother lights up.

"Hello? Enough with the smoking," I say, but she has the nerve to ignore me, so I turn to Miri. "Why are you still in your pajamas? Didn't you go to school? Don't you have Tae Kwon Do?" She gets to skip class when she's not even dying?

"I stayed home all day," she says, exposing mashed-up seeds. "Mom and I had stuff to discuss."

"Don't talk with your mouth full," I say. Being the big sister, I try to give Miri constructive criticism. Often.

She closes her lips, swallows, then says, "Don't give me orders when I'm eating."

My mother rubs her fingers against her temples, almost setting fire to her bottle blond hair with the tip of her cigarette. "Girls, please. I can't handle fighting now."

I get nervous again. "Is everything okay? What's going on?"

A smile spreads across Miri's face. "Everything's fantastic." She peeks over the edge of the bed, eyes my new shoes, and giggles. "Amazing!"

My mom shoots Miri a warning look. "Looks can be deceiving, Miri. I meant what I said before."

13

My family is more confusing to interpret than Tammy's underwater mime techniques. "What are you talking about? And if things are so great, why am I here?"

"Rachel." My mother takes a deep breath. "Your sister is a witch."

MY SISTER TAKES ANIMAL RIGHTS A TINY BIT TOO FAR

2

"Excuse me?" I ask, shocked.

My mother repeats herself. "Your sister is a witch."

"She's not *that* bad, Mom," I say, in a hushed voice, coming to Miri's defense.

"No, you don't understand. A witch-witch."

Miri nods. "Think Sabrina. Hermione." She squinches her forehead, thinking. "Or like that sixties TV show, *Bewitched?*"

My mom frowns. "That really isn't the best example."

Tell me, what is a teenage girl supposed to do after her mother says something so crazy? "I think you should consider returning to therapy" is what slips out of my mouth. I mean, *come on.*

My mother bites her chapped lip. "Remember what happened yesterday? With the dead lobster?"

Okay, let me backtrack for a moment.

Last night my father forced Miri and me to have dinner at the home of his future in-laws, the Abramsons of Ridgefield, Connecticut. Yes, in-laws. On April 3, he's marrying STBSM (Soon To Be Step-Monster), referred to as STB for short.

We call her Jennifer in person.

There is also an STBSMM (Soon To Be Step-Mini-Monster). In other words, STB has a five-year-old daughter, Priscilla, which is a ridiculous name. Miri and I call her Prissy for short.

Abramson family dinners go on *forever*. The adults don't care; they don't have biology homework. Plus, they go through a minimum of three bottles of wine, so they're all smashed, and unlike my mom, they don't let us have any. And since Prissy is seated next to Miri and me, we are forced to cut her food and listen to her nonsensical five-year-old questions and ramblings about anything that pops into her head. ("Today at school Ms. Kimmel gave us Popsicle sticks, did your teachers ever give you Popsicle sticks? Mine was broken and it was sunny . . .")

Anyway, when Mr. and Mrs. Abramson's housekeeper, Miss (yes, they call their forty-year-old married Filipina housekeeper *Miss*—don't even get me started), put a full lobster on my sister's plate, eyes and all, I thought Miri was going to hurl.

On the one hand, I was upset. Dad *knows* that Miri is

a vegetarian. Why didn't he tell the Abramsons? Actually, STB knows too, and they're her parents, so she's even more to blame. The whole situation exposed the total disrespect STB has for my mother and the way she raised Miri and me.

On the other hand, *yes, lobster!* I'd had lobster only once, and it had been the most delicious few moments of my life. Since I hardly ever get to have it, my mouth automatically salivated when I spotted the heated butter and shell crackers.

Miri turned an odd shade of lime green. Her gaze washed over the creature that had been prepared for her culinary pleasure. And that was when things got weird.

Her dead lobster moved. Yes. Moved. As in, it came back to life. Can you say *Pet Sematary*? The antennae started quivering, the eyes flickering, the claws snapping. Mr. One-Pound Special began migrating toward her water glass.

I was in the happy process of squirting my own lobster with lemon when I noticed the resurrection on the plate beside mine.

"Ahhhh!" I screamed, shivering.

"Ahhhh!" STB screamed.

"Oh my!" Mrs. Abramson (occasionally referred to as STBSG—Soon To Be Step-Grandmonster) screamed.

"It's alive!" Prissy screamed.

We were in the audience of a horror movie.

The lobster knocked over Miri's glass, flushing our side of the table with water. My father jumped out of his

17

chair, grabbed the sea creature, ran to the front door, and threw it into the yard.

Some neighborhood Fido was going to get his nose clamped off.

Total chaos ensued. Miri started crying, Prissy started crying, I started crying, and Mr. Abramson spit what he was chewing into his napkin.

"Miss! Miss!" Mrs. Abramson yelled.

Miss, looking startled, poked her head into the dining room. "Yes, Mrs. Abramson?"

"Why weren't the lobsters cooked properly?"

Miss fiddled with her apron in confusion. "They were, Mrs. Abramson."

"No, they weren't! One just walked off the table!"

Luckily all the lobsters except Miri's remained dead, and after a few minutes everyone resumed their normal drunk/boring/rambling dispositions.

Except Miri. She spent the rest of the night staring wide-eyed at her empty plate. Miss hurriedly brought her a tomato salad, but she refused to eat.

Later at home, Miri pushed the bathroom door open while I was peeing. She still had that freaked-out look on her face.

"Do you mind?" I hate when she does that. Why does she have to follow me everywhere? "What's wrong with you?" I asked, wrapping the toilet paper around my hand, bandage-style.

She leaned against the towel rack and nibbled the skin around her thumbnail. "I made the lobster come back to life."

I laughed. "You're funny."

"I'm not kidding." Her eyes filled with tears. Uh-oh. I felt my own eyes liquid up. I can't help crying whenever someone else cries. Like how some people retch at the sight of puke. I'm like that with tears, especially my baby sister's. Cute at three, highly embarrassing at fourteen. I blinked back the waterworks and tried to focus on how ridiculous she was acting.

"I felt so bad for him," she whispered, "lying on my plate like that. I told him in my mind to come back to us. And he did."

I laughed again. "You can't *will* things to come back to life."

"But I did. And it's not the first time. What about Goldie?" Goldie lives in a small glass bowl on top of the refrigerator because that is the only spot in the apartment Tigger, our cat, can't reach. "Do you know any other goldfish that has lived for ten years?"

"No, but we take good care of it," I explained. Then came the tricky part: attempting to pull up my undies without Miri getting a peek at my downtown hair. I'm very self-conscious about my body in front of my sister. Mostly because hers is far more developed than mine. Case in point: even though she's two years younger than me, she wears a B, one entire cup size larger than I do. When she rubbed her teary eyes, I made a grab for my panties. Success!

"No," she insisted, still rubbing. "He keeps dying and I keep resurrecting him."

"You've been studying too hard," I said soothingly.

19

Ever since Robyn, Miri's best friend, moved to Vancouver, Miri hasn't made much of an effort to find new friends. All she does is study, go to Tae Kwon Do, and hang out with my mom. Oh—and make lists.

I felt bad for her, but explaining to my sister that she wasn't the Messiah was *not* my responsibility. "Mom!" I screamed through the bathroom door. "Can you please clarify the workings of the universe to Miri?"

I thought that would be the death of the resurrection rigmarole.

Obviously not.

My mother takes another deep breath, this time with the cigarette still between her lips. "I was hoping I'd never have to have this discussion with you." She turns her head and exhales toward the window. "Witchcraft is hereditary, and it blooms during puberty."

Obviously, my mother is crazy. I debate calling 911, but decide that my best bet is to humor her. "And who did she inherit this witch stuff from? Dad? Is he Harry Potter in disguise?" I say in my best patronizing voice.

She shakes her head, unamused. "From me. I'm a witch too."

If I didn't know better, I'd worry that she's been smoking something besides tobacco. I pat her hair. "You should take a nap."

"Rachel, I know this is difficult for you to understand. The powers Miri and I have are very special. They've been passed down through the bloodline, from mother to daughter."

"Mom, you know you're Jewish, right? I don't think there's such a thing as a Jewish witch."

"Being Jewish has nothing to do with being a witch, Rachel." She gives me yet another weight-of-the-world sigh. "I know this is going to be difficult for you, honey. That's my fault for shielding you from the truth for so long. But I wanted you to have normal childhoods. I was hoping that if I didn't nurture the powers, they'd remain dormant."

Normal? I won't even go there.

Her eyes fill with tears. Like me, she cries at the drop of a (pointy) hat. Must be hereditary. Just like this so-called witchcraft.

"These powers aren't always gifts, Rachel," she says in a tremulous voice. "I hoped you both might be lucky enough to escape them. You didn't seem to gain any of my higher consciousness at puberty—"

"Gee, thanks, Mom."

"—which thrilled me. Because all I ever wanted for you was a regular life. But now Miri . . ." She trails off into sobs.

"It's okay, Mommy. Don't worry about me," my sister says, stroking my mother's hand with suck-up circles. "I'm happy about it. I finally understand why I've always been different. Everything makes sense."

Apparently, both my mother and sister are delusional. I scoot closer to the phone on the nightstand, in case I have to call an ambulance to take them to the cuckoo's nest.

My mom wipes her cheeks with the back of her hand and manages to give Miri a smile. "But now your powers have awakened. It's my responsibility to explain the changes in your spirit. We'll start training this weekend."

21

"We're going to Dad's tomorrow," Miri reminds her, her shoulders sagging with disappointment.

Mom pats her knee. "Then we'll start on Monday."

Wait a second. This is an early April Fools' joke. Or maybe I'm an unknowing contestant on a new reality show—*Win a Million Dollars If You Can Make a Fool of Your Eldest Daughter*. Don't they know I hate reality TV? I scan the ceiling for protruding cameras.

My sister pops another handful of sunflower seeds into her mouth. "See?" she says to me. "I *knew* I brought the lobster back to life."

"It's amazing you were able to do that without a spell," my mom says, shaking her head. And then, taking the prank to a whole new stratosphere of ridiculousness, she leans over to the nightstand and heaves a heavy book onto the comforter. From its earthy green cover, the book appears normal size, but then I notice that it's at least two feet deep. My nose wrinkles. The book looks and smells as if it's been left underwater for a few hundred decades.

My mom thumbs carefully through its thin yellowed pages. "According to the spell section in *The Authorized and Absolute Reference Handbook to Astonishing Spells, Astounding Potions, and History of Witchcraft Since the Beginning of Time*, resurrection is very advanced. The version here calls for rose petals, frankincense resin, and—"

"Tell me you didn't bring props." How long have they had this practical joke planned? Does she think I'm that naive? Couldn't she come up with a less preposterous name?

"It's Miri's spell book," my mom says, giving my sister a protective-looking smile.

Miri's eyes widen to the size of DVDs. "Really?"

"Every witch has one. My mother gave me mine when I first came into my powers."

Grandma just rolled over in her crypt. I can't *believe* she's bringing her deceased mother into this absurd prank! "What about Aunt Sasha? Let me guess—she was a witch too?" My mom and her sister got into a huge fight years ago, and we haven't seen her since.

My mother ignores me. "What's amazing is that Miri didn't even need the book. I never had that much raw will when I was her age."

"Raw will? Is that like the Force?" I laugh. Ha-hee-ha. See that, camera? You're not ruining my sense of humor! Oops. That was another *Star Wars* allusion, and even worse, it was caught on film. I slouch down, hopefully out of prime camera view.

To my surprise, my mom keeps the ruse alive. "Yes. It is." She turns back to Miri. "Honey, as impressed as I am with your ability, you mustn't do magic in front of non-witches. Exposing yourself to the masses leads to nothing but trouble."

I've been reduced to the masses? That's so much lower than the B-list.

"I'm sorry. I won't do it again," Miri says, licking her palm. "Trust me, I didn't even know I had it in me. I'll have to learn my limits."

"Exactly. Which the book will teach you." My mom flips through the pages and squints at the headings. "It's been a long time. . . . I'm a bit out of practice. But I

23

estimate your training will take at least a year. From what I remember, section one traces the history of witchcraft. Section two covers the ethics—"

That's it! I've had enough. I'm not going to sit here while my mom pretends to train her apprentice. "This is great fun and all, being the butt of your practical joke, but I'm going to meet my friends now." I hop off the bed and stomp toward the door. Then I realize I forgot my sneakers. And that's when things get creepy.

My shoes float off the floor.

One foot, two feet. Three feet high.

No one is wearing them, touching them, or commandeering them in any way.

My brand-new green suede sneakers fly through the room until they are six feet above the bed, eclipsing the white porcelain ceiling lamp. My shoelaces, which were previously hanging limply, contort themselves into a triangle. And then a square.

And a pentagon!

A hexagon!

A heptagon!

"OOOOHHHMMMIIGAAAAAAAAAAAWD!" I scream, heaving my back against the door. I peek in terror at my mom. Her eyes are closed tightly, her lips are pursed, and she's reciting something under her breath. *What is she doing?* Why is she making her putting-on-lipstick face while my shoelaces morph into haunted polygons? Why is it so cold in here? *What is going on?*

Suddenly, my sneakers crash back to the floor with a thud.

Oh. Oh my. Omigod.

Miri's eyes are wide, but she doesn't look like I do, which is scared stiff. The hairs on my arms are standing up like cactus needles.

My mother is a witch.

My *mother* is a witch. My mother is a *witch.*

My mother is a witch.

And my vegetarian, socially inept little sister is one too.

ANYTHING MY HEART DESIRES

3

"I didn't mean to scare you like that," my mother says, looking sheepish. "My magic is a bit rusty. I was trying to make a heart."

My intestines start playing street hockey and my throat constricts like a broken straw. I feel nauseous and I can't breathe properly and my legs start trembling. How can this be?

No one speaks. The only sound is my mother inhaling on her cigarette.

I sit back down on the edge of her bed in case my legs give out.

"Someone say something." My mother reaches under her comforter and pulls out a pack of cigarettes, then lights a fresh one. I watch the smoke slither across the ceiling.

Miri peers over the edge of the bed again. "The sneakers *are* really cool. Do you like them, Rachel? I can't believe it worked! Those are the ones you wanted, right?"

My mind is blank. "What?"

"The sneakers. I wanted to put you in a good mood. You know, for when you found out that I'm a witch and you aren't."

She what? And I'm way too busy having a heart attack to be in a good mood. "What about . . . is it . . . are you . . . are you going to get warts all over your face?" is all I can manage.

My sister's hands fly to her chin.

"She most certainly won't," my mother says tartly. "Nothing is going to change. Our noses won't grow and our hair won't turn to black straw. Those are myths."

My sister's eyes widen again, and her long lashes touch the base of her eyebrows. "Does Dad know?"

My mother shakes her head. "I never told him. I decided in college that I didn't want to be a practicing witch. When I met your father, I was embarrassed that I was different." She crosses her arms. "I chose to repress the parts of me he wouldn't understand."

"An excellent basis for a marriage," I say. "No wonder you're divorced." Omigod. Omigod. My sister is a witch. My mother is a witch. It's impossible.

It's true.

Omigod. Wait a sec. "What do you mean you didn't want to be a practicing witch?"

"I preferred, and still do, not to use magic in my life. I excommunicated myself from the witchcraft community."

Suddenly, the impact of this entire conversation hits me as if I've just been whacked with a broomstick. "But . . . why not?" Is she crazy? She can have anything she wants. *I* can have anything I want. Zit-proof skin! A flying carpet! No hair on my upper lip!

"Magic isn't all ruby slippers and castles," my mom says sternly, as if she's reading me a warning label. "There are consequences to every spell. And as I told you, I wanted you girls to grow up having normal childhoods."

Of course I'm not listening. Instead, my mind is whirring. Seven-day weekends! School? So yesterday. Knowledge will be automatically downloaded into our brains!

But . . . where would we meet boys?

"What was your childhood like?" Miri asks my mom, interrupting my happy fantasy.

She sighs and looks down at the comforter. "Different. Difficult. One day I'll tell you everything, I promise."

A time machine to see what our parents were like in high school! So we can make fun of their clothes!

Miri's face scrunches up. "So I shouldn't tell Dad? Did your father know?"

We never met our mother's parents. They both died before we were born. "He knew," my mom says. "My mother told him. But he didn't deal with it well." She bites her thumbnail. "You'll have to make the decision about whether to tell your father. It's your choice."

28

My mouth feels sandpapery. "Can one of you poof me up a glass of fruit punch?" This witch thing is going to make my life *a lot* easier.

My mother shakes the burning part of her cigarette at me. "No way. This is exactly what I was talking about. Laziness is no excuse for magic. Trust me," she says, and gets a constipated look on her face. "I've seen the consequences, and I don't recommend Miri use magic to do homework. Or to ace tests. Or to get fancy clothes or toys."

What toys? Am I seven? Did I ask for the deluxe Barbie Corvette?

Although I wouldn't *mind* if my mother or sister poofed up a *real* Corvette. A red one. Convertible. And a driver's license. "What consequences? What's the big deal?"

29

"We don't need to talk about everything tonight," my mom tells us. "But am I being clear, girls? Miri is not allowed to use her spells for trivial matters."

I'm so confused. "What *is* Miri allowed to use her powers for?"

My mother stubs out her cigarette. "Every witch has to decide what's right for her. Including Miri. That's why I'm training her; so she'll be able to make an informed decision. I've chosen not to use my powers. Some witches take advantage of them for personal gain. Others use them to illuminate a path, and show people the way to goodness. A witch could try to make the world a better place by putting suggestions in people's minds to end various wars. The problem with that is that sometimes a spell meant for good ends up causing unintentional disastrous consequences. One witch I knew once tried to end an African heat wave and ended up causing an ice storm in Kansas City. After Miri's training is complete, she'll have to decide for herself whether or not she wants to pursue her witchdom. And if she does, I'm hoping she'll take the altruistic route. Carefully, of course."

"Mom." I tut-tut, shaking my head. "Is it fair to make a twelve-year-old feel responsible for world peace?"

My sister smiles serenely. "I understand what Mom means. If I choose to use magic, I can will people to do good deeds at school and stuff. Maybe if a bully is about to beat up a smaller kid, I can mentally *suggest* to him how he would feel if the tables were reversed. And then maybe he won't be mean."

I eye Miri warily. She *so* isn't going to make the most of this. This is a girl who does all her homework *on the day it's assigned*. Magic will be wasted on her. Like boobs. She's not even excited—I'd be bouncing off the floor like a basketball. She's definitely going to need some sisterly steering. "Hello? Miri, can you get psyched, please? You have *magical powers*."

She shrugs her small shoulders. "I am excited. But I always suspected something was different about me. Like how Tigger always obeys me, and why no one ever found me during hide-and-seek."

Tigger always listens to Miri. She says, "Tigger, I'm freezing. Will you bring me a blanket?" and the fat fur ball digs his pointy little teeth into the purple afghan and drags it across the room. And me? Nothing. I can call "Here, Tigger, Tigger" for centuries and that cat won't even blink. He'll squat on my biology textbook despite my waving my arms and screaming that I have a test the next day. Does he care? Does he move? No. I assumed cats just didn't like me. I didn't realize Miri could communicate with them.

And now that I think about it, I could *never* find her during hide-and-seek. I would cover my eyes, count down from twenty, then look in the traditional places: under the bed, between the coats at the backs of the closets, behind the couch. No Miri. Not even my father could find her. My friends couldn't. Dave the fireman couldn't. (Although my mom might have asked him up just to ogle his hotness.) "Where did you hide?"

"In the bathtub. But I would *suggest* to you not to look there, and you wouldn't. See? I always wondered what was different about me, and now I know. And anyway, I've had some time to let the news sink in. Mom and I talked about this all last night and today."

Excuse me? "You knew this since *yesterday?* Why didn't anyone tell me?" I heard them talking, but I thought they were discussing pollution or something, not anything *important*.

My mom puts her arm around Miri. "I wanted to see how she felt. And emphasize that she's not allowed to use any magic at all, until she's fully trained."

She said that will take at least a year! Reading my mind (*really* reading my mind?), my mom gives me a serious look. "I didn't want anyone to tell her otherwise."

"But . . . you zapped me up new shoes," I say feebly.

"I did that when you called to ask if you could go for pizza, before I knew the rules," Miri admits. "I wasn't sure it would really work. Mom said you were excited that you were invited, and I thought I'd give you something to show off."

I guess that's why I didn't notice them all day. They only appeared on my feet after French class.

"Miri didn't tell me what she had done," my mom clarifies. "So when you called back to thank me, I couldn't have you run around the city in magic shoes. What if they disappeared and left you barefoot in the restaurant, or on your way home? The sidewalks are cold." Then she shook her head at Miri. "I knew we needed to talk."

Miri picks up a sneaker and squeezes it like an orange. "Seems fine."

"Still," my mom reminds Miri and me for the hundredth time, "no more magic until you've finished your training."

She can remind me five zillion times. There is no chance I'm waiting 365 days to test out Miri's magic! Obviously, I'll have to have a word with my sister in private. My stomach grumbles. "So conjuring up cupcakes from Magnolia Bakery is out, too?" They're delicious.

"No Magnolia Bakery," my mother says, exasperated.

"But they don't deliver!"

Miri is shaking her head in disbelief.

I narrow my eyes. "If she starts *suggesting* to me that

32

we switch rooms, that's completely unfair. I'm older and I'm entitled to the bigger one."

My mother and Miri sigh in harmony.

"Good thing Miri is the one with the powers," my obnoxious mother says.

So now it's three in the morning, and I can't fall asleep. I keep flipping my pillow over, trying to find the cold side, but both feel like chairs that have just been sat on.

I prop myself up on my elbows and stare at the pyramid-shaped reading lamp on my night table.

Reading lamp . . . turn on!

Nada.

Reading lamp . . . make it light! I wiggle my fingers at it.

Stupid lamp.

I know the witch stuff sounds insane, and I wouldn't blame anyone for not believing me. If it weren't my own crazy family, I wouldn't buy it either.

But . . . it *is* my family. And the more it sinks in, the cooler it is. With Miri's help, I can have movie stars on my speed dial. A Jacuzzi in my closet. A boyfriend. She'll zap my room clean. (Who needs a robot?) Give me bionic hearing. Poof me up a new wardrobe. The possibilities are endless. Endless!

And I'm not waiting a year. Nice try, Mom. I got Miri

33

to watch the Lord of the Rings trilogy with me four times in a row during my Tolkien phase; surely I can convince her to whip me up a spell or two. Where to begin?

Hmm.

Watching them fly around on Halloween will be nerve-wracking. But this is the most kissed-by-a-prince/win-the-lottery/so-amazing-it's-unbelievable type of thing that has ever happened to me.

Ahhh. I lie down and pull the covers over my head. Then, for the first time, realization washes over me.

It's not the most amazing thing that has ever happened to me. It's the most amazing thing that has ever happened to . . . Miri.

Witchcraft, an ability normally passed from mother to daughter, has skipped me. As with breasts, nature has decided I don't qualify.

34

By four thirty I still can't sleep, so I decide that my mother shouldn't either.

Her ghastly early-morning breath wafts over me as I poke her in the shoulder. Unfortunately, that's a trait I did inherit. I'm sure my future husband will appreciate it.

"What's wrong?" she asks, sitting up. She's still in her ratty concert tee. You'd think a witch could spruce herself up a bit. Give herself a free makeover or fake nails. Get her roots done. She has a blond ring orbiting her brown roots, as if she's Saturn.

I crawl into bed beside her. "You owe me an explanation. Why can't I resuscitate lobsters? Do any witches get magic later in life?"

She switches on her bedside lamp. "Normally magical powers appear during puberty, but some witches come into them when they have their first child." She narrows her eyes. "Don't get any ideas."

"Mom!"

"Just saying. Anyway, one woman I knew traumatized herself and her husband when she levitated their baby right out of the crib."

A balloon of hope fills me. "So it can still happen?"

She nods. "It can."

Fantastic!

And then she adds, "But it might not. Some daughters never become witches."

My balloon pops and sags lifelessly to the ground. "That's so unfair. Why does Miri get powers and not me? She didn't even finish the first Harry Potter and that was the shortest one. I read them all!"

"Honey, I know you think witchcraft is all fun and games, but it comes with serious responsibilities. Maybe when you're more mature and responsible—"

"What do I have to do?" I whine. "Keep my room clean and make hundreds of useless lists like Miri?"

"It's not about specific actions. It's more of a mental state."

"Oh," I say, not sure whether I want to pout or cry at the unfairness of it all.

"Miri looks up to you, and I expect you to help her

35

deal with the changes in her life and to guide her to do the right thing."

Help Miri, guide Miri, blah, blah, blah. Miri gets everything.

I rest my cheek against the pillow and look at my mom. "Remember in fourth grade when all the girls in my class were invited to Krissy Backer's sleepover and I wasn't?" I ask, feeling sad at the years-old memory. Then indignation fills me. Looking like a dork with those braces? Totally unnecessary. That haircut that had total strangers gasping with pity? Completely avoidable. I blink back tears.

My mom studies me. "I know what you're thinking, honey."

"Well, why didn't you?" I blurt out. "You could have made my life a zillion times better if you had only used a smidgen of magic!"

My mom smoothes back my hair. "I understand how it could seem that way to you. But trust me, magic isn't all that it appears to be. I wanted you and Miri to experience *life*—with all its joys and its sorrows—not some artificial world that I created to make you happy." She kisses my forehead. "I love you, Rachel. More than you'll ever know."

"I love you too, Mom," I say, sniffling. After a few minutes of witch-daughter bonding, I sit up. "Did Miri use magic to give herself boobs?"

She smiles and shakes her head. "I developed early too. You take after your father. He didn't have his growth spurt until he was seventeen."

Life is so unfair. "So I guess you can't put a spell on me to become a witch."

"Afraid not," my mom tells me. "If you're meant to be one, you will be."

I get up and walk to the door with a sigh. "Well . . . can I at least keep the shoes?"

My mom hesitates, then smiles. "I'll make an exception just this once."

With that victory in hand, I drag my bare feet back into my bed. But instead of sleeping, I spend the next two hours trying to levitate my duvet.

Unsuccessfully.

37

FLY, MIRI, FLY!

4

It's only quarter of nine on Friday morning and the day is already a disaster.

First, I cornered Miri in the kitchen, begging her to zap away my horrendous under-eye circles.

"Did you listen to a word Mom said? No!"

"I was up all night digesting *your* witch news. Take some responsibility!"

But noooooo.

Then, she borrowed my new sneakers without asking, and since my black boots have been MIA since the switcheroo, I had to wear my smelly gym shoes. If she ever takes them again without my permission, I'm fully dropping a house on her.

Except she's the one with the powers, so I can't even do that.

Third, because I'm still in a trance from yesterday's news, I tripped between the third and fourth floors and banged my knee on a metal stair. The bruise ain't gonna be pretty.

Fourth, Tammy went on and on about how fantastic yesterday's pizza excursion was for the entire twenty minutes of homeroom, and she made me miss all the announcements.

(I'm getting so much better at these lists. Maybe now I can have my powers?)

39

"I really had the best time at Stromboli's," she says, for the eighty-seventh time, while unsnapping her lock. Her locker is right next to mine, because we're in the same homeroom and our last names both start with Ws. I'm Weinstein and she's Wise.

"So who was there?" I ask.

"Everyone."

She must see the look of dismay on my face, because she quickly wrinkles her nose, which makes it look big (I'll admit it's a bit on the large side, even though I always swear to her it isn't), and adds, "I mean, not *everyone*. It wasn't a big deal. You didn't miss much." She wobbles her right hand, which is her so-so signal.

I don't need psychic abilities to know she's trying to make me feel better. "Was Jewel there?"

"Um . . ." She pulls her green binder off her top shelf. "Yeah."

"And Raf? And Mick?"

She bows her head. "Mick was. We sat at the same table."

Ouch. An oversharpened pencil spears my heart. "He would have been at my table if I'd been there," I moan.

"I hadn't realized he was such a nice guy," she says, intensifying the chest stabbing. "I stuck my elbow in tomato sauce and he was the first one up to get me a napkin."

So unfair. It should have been *me* staining my shirt.

"Maybe I'll find out where they're going tonight," she says.

"No point," I say, and sigh heavily. "I have to go to my dad's."

The most annoying part of having divorced parents is spending every second weekend on Long Island. I love my dad, and I want to spend time with him, but the packing, train taking, and missing out on all the weekend festivities are a massive disruption to a fourteen-year-old's social calendar.

Of course, if I have an important event—bat mitzvah, school function, shoe shopping—I can stay in Manhattan, but then I burn Miri by making her go to Long Island alone. My sister says STB nags her more when I'm not around. ("Stop biting your nails!" "Don't pick at your food!" "No practicing your karate in the house!") I don't doubt it. STB never nags when my dad is there. She pulls a Jekyll and Hyde every time. When he's there, she's supersweet and helpful: "You're so creative, Rachel!" As soon as he walks into the next room, she instantly becomes evil: "Why are you such a slob?"

My dad hates when we miss a weekend. But now that he has STB, he can't switch dates easily. She's always got something up her wrinkle-free sleeve—dinners, theater tickets, trips to the Caribbean.

We never went to the Caribbean when he was married to my mom. We never even went to the Jersey shore. To be fair, he wasn't a partner in his law firm then and didn't have as much money. We drove to Florida twice and took some weekend ski trips to Stowe, but we never left the country (unless you count World Showcase in Epcot). Those car rides were long. We'd play Geography, the game where you name a city/state/country that starts with the final letter of the place last named.

"Vermont," I'd start.

"Texas," my dad would say.

"Salem," my mom would complete.

And I thought it was her travel career that gave her the unfair advantage.

All the signs were there. I just didn't speak witchcraft.

Maybe one day my dad will take us to an island. Miri and I could learn to scuba dive and then I'd be able to better communicate with Tammy.

Hmm. Maybe not. Aren't witches allergic to water?

41

The wicked witch in *The Wizard of Oz* melted when Dorothy drenched her. Does Miri have to stop bathing now? Super. Something else to look forward to.

Tammy eyes me with pity. "I'm so lucky my moms and dad all live in the city." She is surprisingly well adjusted regarding her mother/stepmothers situation. On Mother's Day she even buys three cards. "Tomorrow, all of them are coming over for Valentine's Day dinner. Can you believe they all get along?"

"You're lucky." Since my parents' divorce, I don't think they have even volunteered to be in the same room. It's not that they fight—they're always civil—they're just awkward. I get the feeling that, to them, being in proximity to each other is like listening to nails scraping against a blackboard.

I guess I should be grateful that they don't fight. They never fought. My dad just realized he was no longer in love with my mom. They had gotten married young, the day after they graduated from college, before he knew what he wanted. For weeks after they discussed divorcing, he stayed in our apartment until they worked out the financial arrangements and he found a place of his own. And not even during those weeks did I hear them argue.

"You spending Valentine's Day at your dad's?" Tammy asks me, interrupting my trip down Divorce Lane.

"*Mais oui*. Unfortunately. No hot date for me." No potential change in my Frenching status this romantic holiday.

Tammy gives me a comforting shoulder pat as

we head toward math. "Let's stop at the bathroom," she says.

"I have to ask Ms. Hayward something before class," I lie, and continue walking before she has a chance to renege.

Explanation: I'm ditching Tammy in case Jewel gets to class early and saves me a seat. Math is the only time she's nice to me these days.

Okay, okay, I'm a horrible person.

But if it weren't for accelerated math, I'd never spend any time with Jewel. And I see Tammy all the time because we have practically every class together.

Enough said.

As I follow the stairs up to the third floor, I try to talk myself out of my traitorous behavior. Why should I be nicer to Jewel than Tammy? Forget it! Jewel can sit alone for once.

I open the classroom door. Jewel is in the back row, her furry pink pencil case on the desk next to her, saving me a spot. She waves me over.

So what am I supposed to do? Not go? I can't be *rude*.

"Hi, sweetie!" she sings as I slide into the plastic chair beside her.

"Hi," I say, admiring her gorgeous, frizzless mahogany curls perfectly perched on top of her head with two silver hair sticks. (I'd feel stupid with chopsticks in my hair, but they look great on Jewel. She's tall enough not to have to worry about poking out someone's eye.)

She's tried to teach me her frizz-busting technique ("comb it in the shower, insert gel immediately post

43

gentle towel dry, scrunch and diffuse within ten minutes or all is lost"), but I can never get my boring brown just-past-my-shoulders hair to look right. It's not straight, not curly. Just wavy. I'm an ocean head. And as I sit down, a single hair stands up straight to the ceiling.

Jewel giggles.

I lick my finger and rub the strand, trying to encourage it to stay with its friends. "Remember when we used to rub balloons on our heads to make our hair staticky?" I say. I like to remind Jewel about our shared past in the hopes she'll remember we're supposed to be best buds.

"Mmm-hmm," she says, and opens the magazine on her desk.

Jewel and I have been friends since preschool, when we wore matching pairs of white leather sandals. During playtime we discovered we could attach our bands and pretend to be contestants in a three-legged race.

I'm dying to tell her about Miri. She would freak out. I'm freaking out. It's all I can do not to stand on my chair and scream at the top of my lungs, *"My sister's a witch!"*

I know, I know, it's not my secret to tell.

If I were a witch, I would blab to the world. Although . . . then everyone would know I was putting spells on them. Where would the fun be in that?

I'm also dying to tell Jewel because it would give us something we could bond over. It would be just like old times, the two of us whispering secrets. We always had other friends, but we were the team. Occasionally, the three-legged team. Maybe one day we'll be a team again. It's not as if we had a fight, I remind myself as she flips a page. She's just really busy with her fashion show friends.

I spot Tammy at the front of the room, looking for me. I motion hello, but the thing is, the seat next to me is already taken. She finds a spot two rows ahead of us, next to Janice Cooper. Janice hardly ever talks in class, and she always looks very serious when she takes notes. Tammy is friends with her, and she sits with us at lunch. She wears her straight long brown hair half-up in a gold barrette every day. She's a bit geeky, but that's all right.

"Which do you like better?" Jewel whispers twenty minutes later while Ms. Hayward is explaining the surface area of the polygon on the blackboard. She slips me a stack of glossy pages ripped from months' worth of magazines. All feature A-list-looking models in barely-there designer dresses.

45

Jewel doesn't pay much attention in math class. Why should she, when she knows I can explain it all to her later?

I'm really good at math. I mean, really good. Geometry, trigonometry, algebra, whatever. Numbers make sense to me. I get a little rush when I crack a problem. And I always get the highest grade in the class. I know I always get the highest grade, not because I ask my fellow students what they got, but because Ms. Hayward always makes a big deal of it. I'm not sure if she does it to be nice or just to embarrass me. "And once again, surprise, surprise, the highest grade in the class goes to . . . little Miss Back-of-the-Room, Rachel Weinstein."

Ms. Hayward is not one of my biggest fans. Mostly

because I spend her entire class passing notes instead of listening to what she has to say. I still get the highest marks. What's the point in paying attention? Everything she says is plagiarized directly from the textbook.

On the other hand, she can't seem to help showing the tiny nugget of respect she must feel for me. She can't hate her prized pupil. Who else will she send to the state math competition?

All right, yes, I went to the state math competition in November. And—geek alert!—I placed in the top five. I came in second. I am going to kick serious butt on my PSATs.

My dad wanted to know why I didn't come in first. He won a math competition in high school and lets me keep his triangular silver trophy in my room at my mom's. He draws immense pride from his theory that while other daughters wasted their time playing with dolls, I entertained myself by playing with his calculator.

Which is true. Except that I was playing a game I used to call Barbie's Office, and the calculator was used solely as a prop.

Since my dad never had a boy, he tries to use me as a replacement for traditional father-son activities. It worked for *Star Wars* and calculators. Not as much for baseball.

"You throw like a girl!" he'd yell at me in Central Park.

"I am a girl!"

Maybe one day, Mick will be able to teach me. Sigh.

Anyway, I hate when Ms. Hayward focuses on me.

That's why I don't participate in class. Who wants to look like a know-it-all? (Answer: Doree Matson, a fashion show annoyance who unfortunately is in most of my classes—not this one thankfully—always sits in the front row, and has her hand permanently stapled to the ceiling.)

So instead of paying attention, I flip through Jewel's fashion options. I point to a knee-length dress in electric blue. "This one." It's a dress by Izzy Simpson, who is my absolute favorite. Not that I own anything designed by Izzy Simpson. Her designs are way too expensive. Jewel's family isn't rich, but her mom always buys her the best clothes.

She raises a thick, perfectly arched eyebrow. "Yeah? Maybe."

"What's it for?"

"Spring Fling."

She's already shopping for Spring Fling? I don't even know when it is, let alone have a date.

Every year JFK throws four dances: Fall Ball, Winter Mixer (apparently the administration thinks that rhymes), Spring Fling, and the prom. But the prom is only for seniors and, of course, the hot freshman, sophomore, and junior girls who the senior boys want to hook up with.

These dances are big deals. Major big deals. And no one goes without a date. But that's not a school rule. The administration makes a point of telling us again and again that no dates are necessary, but the unwritten mandate is no date, no go, which I am well aware of.

47

Fall Ball: The fashion show tryouts were two weeks away. Watched *Star Wars* trilogy with Jewel (who had yet to be let through the gates of high school coolness). Popcorn! Pedicures! Pajama party!

Winter Mixer: Jewel had a date. New friend Tammy had strep. Me, home alone, with Miri.

Spring Fling: Me at the dance. Cinderella-style, I will gracefully sashay into the gym, professionally blown-out hair swaying over my strapless, sparkling, dewy shoulders. I will dance, I will dip, I will dazzle. I will have a handsome A-lister on my arm. Preferably his name will be Mick or Raf.

I'm going to Spring Fling. I am *not* missing another dance. I don't care who I go with, but this time someone will ask me. I know, I know. I should ask someone myself. But what if I ask and he says no? I'm not being antifeminist. Just chicken. But do you know what I'm even more chicken about?

The dancing part. Did I inherit witchcraft? Oh, no. I've inherited my mother's *total lack of rhythm*. Jewel used to spend hours with me, trying to show me how to move my butt without looking as if I were being electrocuted. Nothing worked.

But people don't really dance at dances, do they? Besides the slow ones, of course, which I can do. That's all about the sway. The school dance is more about the outfits, gossiping, and making out. Dancing is completely secondary.

"Do they know the date yet?" I ask.

"Will told me"—

I blink. Jewel is on a first-name basis with the school president? To Tammy and me he's William Kosravi, the gorgeous and unapproachable senior, and president of the student body. He's also the older brother of Raf, aka one of the Loves of My Life.

—"that it's April third, the night after the fashion show. The Saturday kicking off spring break."

Oh, no. No, no, no. "That's the night of my dad's wedding."

Jewel looks disappointed—for a millisecond. Her lips make an O. "Well . . . it's just a dance." This coming from the girl who has already put together a portfolio of clothing options. "I'll show you my pictures," she says as a consolation.

"What time is the dance?"

"Nine."

I'll never make both. The wedding starts at six, but the torture will carry on until at least midnight. And it's in Port Washington, Long Island, which is at least a thirty-five-minute train ride away.

Ms. Hayward says in a loud singsong voice, "Rachel, I know you don't feel that paying attention in class is worth your while, but perhaps you could stop yapping so your fellow classmates might benefit from my instruction?"

Then she winks at me. See? It's a love/hate relationship.

I space out for the rest of the class, but this time it's because all I can think about is that way back in October, before Jewel forgot we were best friends, I invited her to

49

the wedding (my dad said I could invite two friends) and she said she'd be there.

Guess she forgot that, too.

As the bell rings, I pile my books. "What are you doing after school? Want to come over?"

Jewel carefully inserts her pen, purple calculator, and bunny-shaped eraser back into her pencil case. "Can't. I'm hanging out with Liss." Liss is Melissa Davis, my red-headed, snobby A-list replacement. Her nose is so turned up, I don't know how she sees where she's going. Her mother choreographs music videos, so—do you have to ask?—Liss automatically gets to be in the fashion show. "But definitely another time," Jewel promises, squeezing my arm. And then she takes off.

And that, ladies and gentlemen, is me getting a first-class burn.

A burn that would have been more pronounced if I'd given her the bumblebee-shaped "Won't you bee my valentine?" card that has her name on it in my schoolbag.

I swear it's not as pathetic as it sounds. When we were nine, Jewel threw her flip-flop into a beehive and we each got five stings. We spent the day crying and consoling ourselves with ice cream.

Okay, it's pathetic.

Tammy, at least, is waiting for me at the front of the classroom.

I can't believe I am going to miss Spring Fling because of my father's horror-show wedding. I spend the entire train ride to Long Island freaking out. Which might be slightly premature, considering I don't even have a date yet, but what if someone asks me?

It's completely selfish to prefer an inane high school dance to the celebration of my father's nuptials, but . . . but . . . STB is annoying and she doesn't love him as much as my mother did.

"Spring Fling is just a stupid dance. Get over it." Miri's a tad annoyed that I keep interrupting her reading. She's been hunched over her grotesque-smelling encyclopedia of a book since we got on the train.

"Wait till you're a freshman. You'll see," I tell her. "And I'll stop obsessing if you let me look at the magazine you're not even reading." On the glossy cover is the gorgelicious face of Robert Crowne, the new twenty-one-year-old singer/songwriter. His single, "Sixteen Shades of Love," is on the radio 24/7.

Miri rolls her eyes. "I need it to disguise *The Authorized and Absolute Reference Handbook to Astonishing Spells, Astounding Potions, and History of Witchcraft Since the Beginning of Time.*"

"Are you going to say the entire name every time?" I yawn. "It's putting me to sleep."

"What should I call it?" she asks. "*Authorized and Absolute?*"

"A-squared. That sounds cooler." I gaze at the cover. "Where did that book come from, anyway? Is there an Amazon.witch?"

"Noooo," she enunciates. "Mom put a spell on hers

to produce one for the next generation. But I like the new name. A-squared."

"Let me see it."

"I'm reading." Miri lets out an amazed giggle. "It even updated the language to be appropriate for a young, twenty-first-century witch."

"Fine. It's not like I care." Yeah, right. I spent all day attempting to kick-start my magical powers, whenever my thoughts weren't otherwise occupied with my Spring Fling obsession.

Like when I willed my combination lock to revolve itself.

Believe me, if it had worked, I would not be on this train.

And then later, when I spotted Raf in the cafeteria line, spooning mashed potatoes onto his plate, and I willed him to park that cute butt of his beside me.

He sat next to stuck-up Melissa Davis. She already stole my best friend; did she have to hijack Raf, too?

"So," I say. "How was school? Put any spells on your teachers?"

"Noooo. First of all, I don't know how to use any of the spells, and second, for the hundredth time, I'm not doing any magic until I've finished my training."

Blah, blah, blah. If I were her, I would have made dear old Liss choke on her celery sticks. "What a waste. You could bet I'd use my powers if I had any."

"Maybe that's why you don't."

Look what witch has already become a diva. "What's that supposed to mean?"

Miri leans back in her seat, holding her ticket. "Mom says that some people get them when they're ready for them. Maybe you're not ready."

"Excuse me, Miss Maturity." I push her book and magazine out of her hands, and they tumble into the aisle.

She rolls her eyes. Does she think *she's* the older sister?

I bet she used her powers to make me do that just to illustrate my immaturity.

"You up?" I ask Miri.

My father has enough money to build a pool and sauna in his new house, but not enough for Miri and me to have our own rooms. STB decorated ours in yellow. She thought it was cute. I feel like I'm drowning in a lemon meringue pie.

"No."

I throw a sunflower-shaped pillow at her. "If I were a witch, I would never sleep. I would zap myself perma-awake and spend the night flying around."

She sighs. "Maybe I'll zap myself asleep so I can stop staring at the ceiling."

"Hey, there's a full moon. You want to borrow STB's Swiffer for a quick spin around town?" I giggle.

"Ha-ha."

"Can you fly?"

I see the outline of her head shaking in the dark. "No."

"So you've tried?" I say, psyched to have found her out.

"Mom told me that flying is a myth."

"And you believe her?" I tsk-tsk. "You can bring lobsters back to life, make yourself invisible when playing hide-and-seek, but you can't fly?"

She sits up and her eyes glow in the dark. Not in a creepy way, but because it's dark in here and she's always had really white eyeballs. She can do tricks with her eyes, too, such as crossing them, and making both eyeballs look outward. Mom hates when she does that, and is always warning her that one day they'll stay like that and she'll have only herself to blame.

"I don't get how I did that lobster thing," Miri confides. "And I didn't make myself invisible. I projected my thoughts on you."

"Does that mean I have a weak mind?"

"Maybe."

"Shut up."

She throws the sunflower pillow back at me. "I don't think you're weak minded."

I feel creepy crawlies up my spine. "Do you make *suggestions* to me a lot?" Fantastic. My own mother and sister constantly control my thoughts, without my even realizing it. How do I know what I'm really thinking and what they're telling me to think?

Is Miri telling me what to think right now?

"I'm not telling you what to think."

"Omigod! You're reading my thoughts! Stop it!"

"I can't read your thoughts, moron. You're slamming your palm into your forehead."

I pause in mid-slam. Oops. "I'm on to you, young lady."

STB calls Miri young lady. Miri once called her old lady in retort, but that didn't go over well.

"I don't know what I can or can't do," Miri admits. "I have to start my training. And study the spells. And I've decided not to tell Dad. At least for now, until my training is complete. So don't mention anything, okay?"

"Of course not," I say, distracted. I wonder if I can use one of these spells to make Liss roll around naked in poison ivy. "Will the spells work if I say them, too?"

"I don't think so. Mom says it's not the spells themselves that work. They need to be performed by a witch."

That is so unfair. Witches get everything. Ruby slippers, talking cats, flying brooms, their own TV shows.

I have an idea. "Stand on the bed."

"Why?"

"Just do it."

She kicks off her covers and stands up on her bed.

"Now jump off," I say.

"Why?"

"Just do it."

She swings her arms back and jumps. She lands with a thud on the floor.

Maybe I *do* have the power of suggestion. Or maybe I'm just a big sister whose little sister listens to almost everything she says.

55

Miri massages her right ankle. "Ouch. What was that for?"

"I wanted to see if you could fly."

"I told you I couldn't! I'm not Peter Pan."

Hey. Wait a sec. I feel a rush of cold air, and suddenly my pillow is raising my back, as if I'm in the dentist's chair. Now it's . . . it's . . . moving away from under me and floating into the air! It's smacking me on the chin! On the head! On the shoulders!

Miri's eyes are closed and her lips are pursed, and she's attacking me in a magic pillow fight.

I try to grab the top two corners, but they wiggle out of my grasp like a wet bar of soap.

"Stop it!" I howl. Smack. "This is so unfair!" Smack. Now the sunflower pillow is in on it too, slapping my legs.

Pound, pound. Uh-oh. Someone's at our door.

"Yes?" I say in my most ladylike voice. Smack. Giggle.

Miri's eyes widen, and the pillows drop lifelessly into my lap. She doesn't have time to return to bed, and the door opens while she's splayed across the carpet.

STB is wearing her silk cleavage-exposing bathrobe, and an eye mask is dangling around her neck. "Miri, I'd appreciate it if you got back into bed. Other people are trying to get some sleep."

"Sorry."

"You girls will be exhausted for your fitting." We have dress fitting number 738 tomorrow morning for our horrifically ugly pink powder-puff bridesmaid dresses. STB is batting her eyes furiously, as if looking at us is making them tear. She has gorgeous eyes. They're wide and warm and a kaleidoscope of blues and greens. The rest of her is okay. I mean, she's definitely pretty. She has smooth blond hair that rests on her shoulders, creamy perfect skin, and straight, Liquid Paper–white teeth. She's slim and always dressed in tailored designer blouses and pants. But her eyes are incredible. I bet that's why my dad fell in love with her.

How can someone with those eyes be so horrible?

Miri snorts. "We'll certainly need to be well rested to stand there like mannequins."

I laugh.

STB does not. "Enough with the mouth, young lady. And I wish you would leave those dingy T-shirts at your mother's and wear the Gap pajamas I bought you. Now please go to sleep."

The door makes a loud cracking sound as she slams it. We hear a nasal moan from the room next to ours. "Mo-mmmmmmy, the door woke me up."

We giggle for a few minutes before trying to fall asleep. I'm hoping to return to the dream in which I'm voted the most popular girl in the universe at the school dance.

And that's when a plan bursts in my brain, like a kernel into popcorn.

Miri just did magic. She is therefore willing to break the rules. All I have to do is give her a worthy reason to do it again.

Our dad's happiness = worthy reason.

Like me, Miri wishes our father would find his real

soul mate and live happily ever after. And the only way to make that happen is to put a spell on him.

We have to act now. If we wait until the end of training, it will be too late.

We must use magic to stop him from marrying STB.

Yes! Yes to the power of three! Yes X yes X yes!

Of course . . . since my calendar will be clear, there's no reason she can't whip up a quick potion for something minor . . . like making me the most popular girl at JFK. Jewel will be my Best Bud again and someone will ask me to Spring Fling.

A tiny snore escapes from Miri's nose.

My nose starts to twitch.

My creativity + Miri's magic = the end of STB + the A-list for me!

GLINDA, THE GOOD WITCH OF LONG ISLAND

5

Today is the worst Valentine's Day ever.

"STB doesn't actually think this is nice, does she?" Miri whines. She's standing, legs spread a foot apart, as Judy, the middle-aged dressmaker (she's at least twenty-five), contorts the heinous pastel pink material around Miri's overdeveloped body.

I shake my head. "Of course not. She *wants* us to look like pink doilies. That way she's the only one who looks good." And she will definitely look amazing. She spent ten thousand dollars on her wedding dress. I heard her bragging about it to one of her friends.

Miri looks seriously fed up with being prodded. "I bet Prissy doesn't have to wear this. Hers is probably adorable."

"Actually," Judy says, taking a pin from her mouth and making us realize she is listening to our conversation, "her dress is a miniature version of yours. Your arms are so toned, Miri. You must be an athlete."

"She's a brown belt in Tae Kwon Do," I brag. "She'll probably be a black belt within a year." She could be one tomorrow if she wanted to. Wait a minute. With Miri's help, *I* could be one tomorrow!

Miri squirms. "Why are there rods in the material?"

"It's boning to shape the dress over your breasts."

"How can anything shape this getup? It's so ugly."

The bells on the door chime and STB and mini-STB glide inside. STB normally stops to get her morning iced coffee en route, but because we were running late, STB dropped us off first and then doubled back to Starbucks. (I was trying to figure out how to use STB's blue liquid eyeliner and ended up making squiggly lines all around my lids. The removal required multiple washings. Naturally, STB waited until we were in the car and out of my dad's earshot before she yelled at me for ruining her schedule.)

"How are we in here?" she asks now. She's asking Judy, not us. She doesn't care how Miri and I are doing. Since I'm still in my jeans, I'm enjoying myself. The more annoyed Miri gets at STB, the better chance I'll have that she'll go for my Making STB Disappear plan.

"I look revolting," Miri tells her.

Yes!

STB almost chokes on her coffee. "What kind of thing is that to say? How can you insult Judy like that? Judy, I apologize."

Personally, I think it was the material Miri was insulting, not the craftswoman, but hey, why defuse a situation that's working in my favor?

Prissy is sitting crossed-legged on the floor, caressing the bottom of Miri's dress. "It's so pretty and pink and pink is pretty and my friend Nora has a pink dress and a purple dress and . . ."

STB motions for Prissy to be quiet and then turns to me. "Let me guess; you're not happy either."

Actually, I'm in a terrific mood. "Hard to tell before it's finished," I say diplomatically.

Miri gives me the evil eye in the full-length mirror. She'd better not retaliate and *suggest* I fall on my butt.

"But," I add, "I'm not sure if I'm crazy about the material."

Both Judy and STB gasp. "What do you mean?" STB asks. "It's lace and raw silk. The material alone for each dress cost three hundred dollars."

Three hundred dollars? For doilies?

"Money," Miri says, "which could have been better used in Somalia to help feed starving children."

Or to purchase an Izzy Simpson dress.

STB ignores her and fingers a swatch of the material. "Rachel's right. You can't judge the dress before it's finished. You'll both look adorable. Like dolls."

Does she realize that doesn't help?

"I have sixteen dolls," Prissy pipes up, and then starts counting on her fingers. "Sandy, and Mandy, and Randy and Dandy and Princess." When she runs out of fingers, she stops reciting and remains quiet, contemplating her dilemma.

61

"Fantastic," Miri snaps. "I've always dreamed of look-ing like Barbie."

I wouldn't mind that. Barbie has excellent mea-surements.

STB takes a long swig of her coffee, then places it down on a table. "Miri, how are your fingers?"

Miri clamps her hands shut. "Fine."

STB picks up Miri's right hand and pries it open. She does another one of her gasps. With all her heavy breath-ing, you'd think she was on the StairMaster. "What am I going to do with you?"

Miri shakes her off. "They're my nails, and I can bite them if I want to."

She's getting angrier by the second. This is amazing! My sister doesn't dislike anyone the way she does STB. Before my dad started dating STB, I don't think I ever heard Miri tell anyone off.

STB and Miri embark on a stare-down worthy of a Hollywood action movie. Neither blinks.

Meanwhile, Prissy has finally stopped talking to her-self and is now doing what she always does when she thinks her mother isn't looking: carefully picking her nose. It's kind of cute to watch because she has such small fingers. You'd think STB would be more concerned with that than with Miri's nails.

Suddenly, I feel the newly familiar rush of cold, and I look back at Miri and notice that her lips are doing that pursed thing. Uh-oh. I twist my head back to STB as her iced coffee slowly rises from the table beside her. Yikes! I leap toward the plastic cup and haul it down to safety be-fore anyone can see.

The stare-down is over, because everyone's eyes are now on me.

I take a long sip. "This is delicious," I say while narrowing my eyes at my blushing sister. "My turn to change now, right?" And then, before anyone can respond, I hurry to the dressing room.

Crisis averted. And minus the STB cooties, the coffee was tasty.

I take off my jeans and drape myself in my very own pink life-sized doily. Despite the hideousness of the dress, the truth is I'm finding the whole from-material-to-dress process intriguing. Maybe I'll learn to sew. How awesome would that be? I'd be able to make anything I want, rip off all the hottest designs. People would think I spent hundreds—no, *thousands*—on my outfits. I gingerly kick off my shoes so I won't step all over the material. I could even make my own labels—*Rachel*—and sew them inside. Or on the outside like all the expensive designers do. *Rachel* would come to mean chic. *Vogue* would feature my creations, and I would become internationally famous. Jewel would beg to be included in my televised prime-time biography.

Ouch. It feels as if I just stepped on a pin. Ouch, ouch, ouch. That killed. I hate anything that pricks the skin. How am I supposed to become a world-famous seamstress when I hate pins?

Maybe I'll get Miri to poof up the designer clothes for me, since magic is practically flying out of her these days. But I suppose she'll want to share the glory. Fine, we'll call the label Michel. I step outside, careful to avoid more pin foliage.

63

Miri gives me a sheepish smile as I pass her.

She's definitely almost primed for the plan.

"Arms out," Judy says when I stand in front of her. I comply like a scarecrow. The truth is, I'm relieved to report, my reflection isn't that scary. The dress makes me resemble Glinda from *The Wizard of Oz*. I look kind of pretty. Except for a small zit above my eyebrow, my complexion is relatively clear. My nose is small. My eyebrows have a nice arch. I wiggle them in the mirror. My eyes are pretty big. Too bad they're boringly brown. My teeth are straight and white, so despite my too-thin lips, I have a niceish smile.

"We don't need boning for you," Judy comments, interrupting my critical analysis.

"We don't?" I ask, watching myself purse my lips. That's how I'll look when I'm finally kissing someone. Or casting a spell when my powers kick in. "Why don't we?"

STB sighs. "Because you don't have breasts."

Well, I never! "But I might have breasts by the time of the wedding."

STB snorts. "Rachel, it's in seven weeks."

"These things happen fast, you know. One day you're flat and the next day, boom, you're bursting out of your double-D bra. Do what you think is best, but don't get angry at me if we have to scrap the dress and start again at the last minute because of my inevitable blossoming." These people need to have some faith.

STB throws up her hands. "Give her boning."

"Can I have some too, Mommy?" Prissy asks. "I want boning!"

"Yes, sweet pea, you can have whatever you want."

If she gets breasts before I do, I'll use the boning to make myself a noose.

The nails argument resumes the moment we're in the car.

"I want you to try that special polish again, the kind that tastes bad," STB tells Miri.

I'm sitting next to STB in the front seat, Prissy is singing some highly inappropriate pop music lyrics to herself in the back, and Miri is sitting behind me, staring vacantly out the window. "No," she answers. "It doesn't work."

"If you stopped biting, it would. I don't know how you nibbled through that polish."

It was pretty gross. Well, I had to try some, didn't I? I just put a drop on my thumb and licked it. And then again on my pinky, in case size affected taste. "If she stopped biting," I explain with forced patience, "then it wouldn't need to work." Come on, STB, you can be meaner than this. "But it's not just the biting that's the problem," I say, goading her. "She rips them too."

STB gasps. Miri kicks the back of my seat.

"You rip them? They're not old checks; they're your precious hands! This has got to stop."

Miri stays silent for a few seconds and then explodes.

65

"Why do you care so much? They're my nails! Mine! And I can do whatever I want with them!"

Yes!

STB reaches over her seat and wags her finger at Miri. "No, you can't. You don't always know what's in your best interest."

Since Miri could turn STB into a toad at any moment, STB obviously doesn't know what's in *her* best interest.

"You can't tell me what to do," Miri grumbles. "You're not my mother."

Ah. The infamous not-my-mother line. Silly, Miri. Turning her into a toad would be far more original.

When we return to the house, Miri runs up to our room and slams the door. I'll give her some space to seethe privately. Get her really worked up. Maybe a half hour or so. And then I'll strike with Part One of The Plan. (Insert evil laugh. I would do one, but I've tried it and I sound like a constipated frog. My dad can do a great one, but this is hardly the time to ask him, and anyway, he's at the office, even though STB hates for him to work when we're here. She hates having to entertain us all day without him. Not that she'd ever tell him that. Oh, no, she prefers to fume silently as though it's our fault.)

I decide to give Miri thirty minutes, tops, of solo stewing time. Maybe I'll watch some TV. I plop myself onto the couch in the living room and turn on the tube. Flip. Flip. Flip. Nothing but infomercials, reality TV, and reruns. Hey, maybe *Bewitched* is on. I'll be able to give Miri some pointers. Nope. Just *Buffy the Vampire Slayer*.

Forget that. I don't want to give her any dangerous ideas. What to do, what to do? I guess I could start my homework. I have an English assignment for Monday. I'm supposed to analyze Yeats's poetry for techniques such as alliteration.

Dull, dreary, drudgery.

Plight, plan, plot.

I know it's been only six minutes, but honestly, I think Miri has had more than enough time alone. I enter the room to find her lying on her bed, legs at a right angle straight up against the wall, A^2 propped upright on her lap. I know this is a weird way to read, but we've both been doing it for years. It does seem a little batlike, now that she's a witch.

"I can't believe Dad is marrying her," she complains as I lie down beside her.

Perfect. She's primed for Part One. "He doesn't *have* to marry her," I say in my casual voice.

She smirks. "Then when will we wear our pink doily dresses?"

Aha! Here's my opening. "If the wedding is canceled, we will never have to wear them. Ever. Except on Halloween, if we're so inclined. You can dress up as Glinda, the Good Witch of the North."

She raises an eyebrow. "And why would the wedding get canceled?"

When I was seven, I begged my mom to let me dress up as Glinda for Halloween, but she insisted that the Glinda costumes were all sold out and that I'd have to settle for going as a fairy princess. At the time I

67

believed her. Now I know different. She was afraid that if I dressed like a witch, I would somehow *will* my magic into being. I can't believe she tried to thwart my powers! I can't believe a lot of what my mother did. Or didn't do.

She's a witch. She could have cast spells to make me happy. Like the time I wanted to get tickets to a concert at Roseland, but they were sold out. She could have whipped up two more. Plus backstage passes! She should have stopped me from ever getting hurt! She could have stopped my dad from divorcing her. The back of my neck stiffens. I haven't forgotten that early morning conversation about experiencing the good and bad, but still . . . why not make life picture-perfect?

"Because," I say now, taking a deep breath, "we're going to put a spell on Dad." If my mom wants to ignore the tools available to her, then that's her problem. Not mine. And not Miri's, if I can help it.

Miri raises the other eyebrow. "We're?"

She has to rub it in, doesn't she? "Fine, *you* put a spell on Dad."

"How did I know that would be your solution?"

"Because you're psychic as well as a witch?"

"Or because Mom warned me that you'd try to get me to use magic." She shakes her head. "No. I can't do it. I can't use spells to manipulate our father. It's not right."

Strike out.

Okay, no need to panic. Obviously, a goody-goody like her needs time to let the idea seep in.

And plenty more STB aggravation is sure to come.

I don't have to wait long.

Later, when we're called downstairs for what we assume is dinner, STB and Prissy are sitting, arms perfectly crossed, on the white suede couch. My dad is sitting in a chair, wearing a hideous red and brown striped shirt. He has the worst taste in clothes. He always asks us how he looks, and we all say fine, because none of us wants to be the first to tell him he has bad taste.

"What's going on?" I ask. They're acting creepy. I swear, if they tell us they're witches too, I am seriously going to lose it.

"Miri," my dad begins, rubbing the shiny bald spot on the back of his head, "please take a seat."

My eyes meet Miri's and we sit down. Uh-oh. Did they hear me scheming? Did Miri inadvertently put a hex on STB? Is she no longer able to speak, but capable only of high-pitched ribbits now?

"We are very worried," my father says, his forehead crinkling in actual concern, "about the health of your fingers."

Miri flushes bright red. I laugh. It's a nail-biting intervention.

"Chewing your fingers," my father continues, "can lead to damaged cuticles and infections. Not to mention all the germs you allow into your mouth because they were on your hands."

69

I bet STB looked that up on the Internet and scared my dad. The woman will stop at nothing to get what she wants.

Miri's eyes are quickly filling to the rims with water, like clogged toilets.

"I want to help you, honey." At this point he pats my sister on the head. "We've considered treatments, and Jennifer has come up with an excellent plan." He points his chin toward the coffee table, where a box of Band-Aids lies.

STB runs her perfectly manicured nails through her coiffed blond hair, then says, "We're going to wrap each of your fingers so you don't bite."

That is *so* embarrassing. Perfect! God, I really hope Miri can't secretly read my mind.

Miri opens her mouth, then closes it. I think she's too upset to speak. She's looking like Drew Barrymore in *Firestarter*, and I'm getting nervous that she might set the house aflame telepathically.

Prissy rocks back and forth in her spot. "Miri, biting your nails is yucky." She fans out her little French-manicured fingers. "Don't you want pretty nails like me?"

It's too much. Too awful. I have to help. "Dad, I hardly think these drastic measures are necessary."

"Don't start, Rachel," he says, shushing me. "They are. Now, Miri, give Jennifer your hands so she can wrap your fingers."

STB smiles a toothy victory smile. "And I don't want to see you picking them off."

"Dad," Miri whines, "I don't think—"

"But I do," he says. "And I want you to start taking the B-complex vitamin biotin, which strengthens nails." Did I mention that my father thinks vitamins are the cure for everything? "And I'm your father. I *can* tell you what to do."

Oh, burn. STB totally told on Miri.

STB opens the Band-Aid box and grabs Miri's hand.

"Could be worse," I whisper, rubbing Miri's back. "At least they're plain. She could have listened to Prissy and bought the Disney Princess ones."

After dinner, Miri and I are lounging in front of the TV when I flip the channel and realize that *Star Wars, Episode IV,* the first one ever made, is just about to start. "Dad!" I shout. "*Star Wars* is on television! Come watch! Dad! *Star Wars!*"

"This is awesome," Miri says.

My dad runs down the stairs, full of energy. "It is? Make room for me, girls." He squeezes in between us on the couch. I unfold a multicolored blanket and toss it over our legs. He puts an arm around each of us and we lean into him.

When the electric blue words come on-screen, we all recite, "A long time ago in a galaxy far, far away . . ."

Then we hold our breath. Wait for it. . . . Wait for it. . . .

We belt out the music as loudly as we can, like we always do.

STB, followed by Prissy, marches down the stairs. "What are you doing? Why are you making so much noise? Daniel, I thought we were going to review the wedding place cards tonight."

"We can't," my dad says, not taking his eyes off the screen. "*Star Wars* is on."

"But we have the DVD. Can't we do the place cards first and then you'll watch it later?"

"Watching it on DVD isn't the same as watching it on TV," I explain.

"She's right," my dad says. "We can do the place cards tomorrow. Come watch with us." He pats the space next to me.

STB shakes her head. "I was never into this movie," she says, and then disappears up the stairs.

How can he possibly marry her?

My dad waves Prissy over and she sits on his lap. "What movie is this?" she asks, bouncing. "Who is that? Why is she wearing cinnamon buns on her head? Why—"

"Shhh," my dad says. "No talking except during the commercials."

Prissy tries watching for a few minutes, but then starts to squirm and heads back upstairs.

And it's just the three of us. The way it should be.

The second our father deposits us onto the train back to the city, Miri rips off the Band-Aids.

"She"—thumb off—"is the"—index finger off—"most miserable"—middle finger off—"woman"—fourth finger off, no idea what that one's called—"in the"—pinky off—"entire world!"

"She is quite evil," I happily agree. "Too bad it's about to become official. If only there were something we could do." La, la, la.

Miri stares steely-eyed ahead. Then she nods. "Okay. You're right. We need to get rid of her. I can't have Band-Aids applied to my fingers for the rest of my life."

Yes! Part One in motion!

I give her a nice big sisterly squeeze. She's so tiny. Not that I'm so huge. Maybe after we're done rescuing our dad, I'll get her to make me taller, like five foot two. A giant!

I pull A² from her bag, and she promptly starts biting her thumbnail. What, does she think I'm going to drop it or something?

Plop. Oops. I pick it up off the grimy train floor. "Sorry." Tee-hee. "Here you go. Start looking for an anti-love spell." I put the book into her freshly bitten hands before either of us can do more damage.

She flips through the pages. "I don't know if there are anti-love spells. I haven't finished the first section yet."

"Isn't there an index?" There must at least be a glossary.

"No."

73

Sigh. "What you really need is the spell book on CD-ROM."

Miri taps me on the head. "Can we focus here? We need to get that witch out of our lives."

Witch, huh? I can't stop the grin. "You'll have to learn to watch your word choice. You can no longer use the word *witch* as a negative description."

She slaps her hand over her mouth.

"How can I help?" I ask. I won't even bug my sister for the popularity spell today. I'll let her concentrate.

"Just let me read."

I should start my poetry homework. But first I'll read about Robert Crowne's new tour. Then poetry. "I'll leave you alone so that you can work your . . ." What's the word I'm looking for here? Oh. Right. "Magic." Tee-hee. I really crack myself up.

She taps me on the shoulder. "What we're about to do is a big deal, huh?"

We lock eyes. "Huge."

"Giant," she says.

Maybe she *can* read my mind.

PROJECT POPULARITY + GREEDY SISTER = MORE CHORES

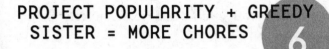

6

As soon as I find a seat in homeroom, I frantically begin my poetry assignment. *Autumn is over the long leaves that love us.* I have no clue what that means.

"Morning." Tammy slides into the empty chair next to me.

"Hey. How was your weekend?"

"All right. Hung out with the moms."

"Nothing from *Aaron?*" I mouth his name in case anyone is eavesdropping.

"No." The edges of her lips droop, but she quickly pulls them up. "No card. Or date. I called to see what he was up to, but his mom said he was at Mick's party—"

There's a roaring in my ears. Mick had another party

that I wasn't invited to. And it was probably the most incredible party ever because it was Valentine's Day weekend. Lights dimmed, romantic music, candles, chocolates . . . the entire A-list.

That's it. I have to get Miri working on the popularity plan pronto. I wonder if I can page her at school. No, she'd hate that.

I'll probably miss another party tonight. I'll probably miss one at lunch.

I'll worry about it later. If I finish this poetry assignment before math, I can have the period free to chat with Jewel. I don't want to waste lunch on it, and it's too obvious to do in bio or gym. I hate gym. I have to wear my uniform puke green sweatpants and too-long puke green T-shirt. This month our phys ed instructors are teaching us meditation and yoga. They think it'll teach us to concentrate.

Now, what was I doing? Oh, right. Poetry!

I find Miri lying on her stomach across the kitchen table. Pages of printer paper covered in scribbles are piled next to her. Our mother is still at work. Ever since two years ago, when she and her friend Bonnie started HoneySun, she doesn't get home until six thirty at the earliest. At least she likes her job now. She especially likes being her own boss. I can relate. I wish I didn't have anyone telling me what to do.

I have to ask Miri. Today. I can't take not being popular anymore. Calm down. I have to wait for the right time. I climb onto the table so I can see what she's up to. "What are you doing?"

"An anti-love spell isn't going to work," she says, bursting my one dream of happiness. "I can't do it. It's too advanced."

"Don't try. Just do," I say.

"No, I'm serious. See the five broomsticks next to this spell?"

I see five miniature icons of broomsticks. "Yesssssss."

"That means it's advanced. One broomstick is for beginners. I don't think the first spell I try should be a five-broomer. And this one looks particularly intricate. I'd need a black candle, a small cauldron, Dead Sea salts, and something called *Achillea millefolium*. Oh, and a lock of the person's hair."

"Dad doesn't have any to spare." I chuckle. "He's pretty bald."

"That's another problem."

"You can do it." This is the same girl who figured out that if we suspended a hanger over our television, we could get thirty-two channels and not have to pay for cable. I'm sure she can figure out a teeny-tiny anti-love spell.

Miri shakes her head. "I don't want to start with a five-broomer. When we tried snowboarding in Vermont, we started on the bunny hill, not the advanced. What if it doesn't work?"

"Then you'll turn Dad into a rabbit?"

Miri doesn't laugh. "Not funny. Really, it's too advanced. And I don't even know what *Achillea mille-folium* is or where to get it. Is it a food? A spice? A lizard? And anyway, the anti-love spell is temporary. It only lasts a few weeks. Most of the spells that have to do with people's emotions are temporary. So eventually he'd snap out of it and reschedule the wedding."

"You don't know that. Maybe by the time the spell wears off it'll be too late," I wishful think out loud. "He'll have figured out that he doesn't love her after all. Infatuation isn't love. So, for a while you'll remove the blinders, and once he sees the truth, he'll never go back." I sigh. I can tell that Miri isn't buying my reasoning. "So what are you saying? Don't tell me the plan is off." No, no, no!

"I'm trying to find an alternative."

Phewf. "You're so good. And smart. I bet you could do anything you set your mind to." Here it comes. The moment of reckoning. The witching hour. I give her my big-eyed-little-girl innocent look. "I bet you could even find me a tiny little popularity spell while you're searching."

She snort-laughs. "Nice try."

"Oh, come on! Please, please find a popularity spell for me? Please? Please, please, please?"

She shakes her head. "There is no make-me-popular-in-high-school spell."

"Why not?" I flip onto my back, leaning my feet against the apple-patterned wallpaper to get comfy. I probably should have taken off my shoes. Oops. Do black smudges come off?

"Because the book was transcribed in 1304," Miri says, leafing though the pages. "High school didn't exist."

"It doesn't have to be *high school* popularity, precisely," I say reasonably. "Is there a spell for winning popularity among the peasants? Can't you whip up something that would make the knights and vicars think I'm cool?" I hop off the table in search of a cleansing solution. "I thought the book was modernized!" The footprints on the wall would lead one to believe that I can walk sideways. Hey, how awesome would that be?

"It's the language, not the content, that's modernized," Miri says. "Do you even know what a vicar is?"

"You're the one doing the research." Must I do everything? I begin to swipe at the telltale smudges.

"Fine, I'll keep an eye out, but I make no promises."

Yes! "Thank you, thank you, thank you!" I give her a big wet kiss on the cheek and then continue cleaning.

You'd think she could offer to zap the stain. Which leads me to a pertinent question. Why do witches have broomsticks? Can't they just raw-will the dirt away?

Two hours later Miri opens my door. "I got it."

"Don't you knock?"

"Don't you want me to get rid of you-know-who?"

I'm stretched across my pink carpet, doing my math homework. The carpet used to be orange before Tigger managed to bring fleas back from wherever he runs to when we hold the door open too long. At first, we didn't even know we had fleas. All we wondered was why we had small red bites around our ankles. The whole experience was pretty vile. Anyway, the exterminator left my blinds open by mistake and the sun bleached my carpet. Now my room fully clashes. I have a sherbet orange dresser, comforter, and desk, and a cotton-candy carpet. The various pairs of jeans and sweaters that hang over every available item of furniture don't help the décor.

Miri shuts the door behind her. She presses her finger against her lips as a warning to be quiet, as Mom is in the kitchen cooking spaghetti and tofu balls. Miri sits down next to me, the book in her lap.

"You figured it out?" I ask, excitement rising. "Did you figure out a popularity spell, too?"

"Forget about your cool spell for now, okay? I'm concentrating on Dad's issue. And I half figured it out. Since we can't put an anti-love spell on Dad, we have to use a spell that will make him realize how awful STB is so he'll fall out of love with her on his own."

Perfecto. "What kind of spell?"

She shrugs. "That's all I got."

"That's it?"

"I had homework, and Tae Kwon Do to practice, too," she huffs. "Besides, I can't come up with *all* the ideas."

Now is not the time to argue. "Well . . . what can STB do that can make Dad stop wanting her? What if she robs a bank?"

"Should I wish for a pistol or a machine gun?" Miri gives me a you-left-your-brain-at-school look. "I'm trying to make the world a better place, not more dangerous."

Maybe that was a bit much. I rub my thumbs against my temples. "Let's think. What does he see in her?"

"He's attracted to evil?"

"Get real, Miri. He's attracted to her looks. Those eyes, that skin, the smile . . ."

Miri claps. "That's it! We hit her with an ugly spell."

"But is Dad that superficial?"

"He must be," Miri says. "What else could he possibly like about her? He's blinded by her"—she pretends to gag—"beauty, and he can't see what an evil person she is. The spell will cast her in a new light. We're looking after his best interests. What happens when she gets old and her face sags? Is he going to get divorced? If he's remarrying, he has to love the woman for who she is inside, right?"

Wow. That was some speech. "Right."

"So, let's do it," she continues excitedly. "I saw something that might work." She flips frantically through the book. "Here it is. It's called the Mask of Repulsion.

81

Sounds good, huh? Let's make a list of the ingredients we need." She jumps up, ready for action.

Does having magical powers excite Miri? Oh, no. But making a list? Be still my heart!

"Mir, we don't have to do it this second," I say, remembering my math homework. "We're not going back to Dad's until next weekend."

She narrows her eyes. "Do you think it's going to be easy to locate these ingredients? I don't have a clue what *Taraxacum officinale* is. And we have to practice."

Scratch, scratch. Scratch, scratch. *Meow.* "Your groupie is trying to scratch his way into my room," I say. Wait a sec. "Who are you practicing on?"

She winks at me.

Is she crazy? "No way! You are *not* using me as your ugly-spell dummy. I can't be A-list looking like an ogre!"

She opens the door a crack, and Tigger dashes inside and plops himself directly on A^2.

The halogen bulb in my brain flicks on and I see my next play. "I understand that you're nervous," I say, backpedaling. "You could turn STB into a tree by mistake. So . . . why don't you practice doing another spell on me? Like say, perhaps, a popularity spell."

She waves her arms like white flags in defeat. "All right, fine. Whatever you want. I'll find you a popularity spell. But for the record, you're being pathetic."

Touchdown! "Yes, I'm pathetic. Pathetically happy!"

"And," she says, smiling, "you're going to owe me. Big."

Ah, the witch turns mercenary. Isn't that always the case? "What do you want?"

She whips out a typed list from the spell book. Apparently, she's been waiting for just the right moment to spring it on me. "For the next two weeks you will, one, set the table and clear the dishes." My mother has us on an alternating schedule of setting and clearing the table, so we're both only supposed to have to do one each day. I wonder if dear old Mom will notice if I take over both duties. Probably not. "Two," Miri says. "You're on trash duty."

"Sure, sure, whatever." It's not as if anyone can tell whether I recycle properly. I can cut a few corners without her catching me.

"And you can't cut any corners with the recycling."

I give her the evil eye (essentially squinting with my right eye while raising my left eyebrow) to ward off future mind-intrusion spells. "I'm on to you."

She ignores me. "Three, you have to come with me to the peace rally on March twentieth in Washington Square."

"Can't Mom take you?"

"I'd rather go with *you*. It'll be fun," she pleads.

"I doubt it." I hate rallies. My mother has dragged me to a slew of them. All you do is stand there and freeze your butt off. "You sure you don't want me to take you shopping? We can go to Bloomie's. I'll buy you that every-day-of-the-week underwear you've always wanted," I add, dangling the only carrot I can come up with under the circumstances.

83

"Peace rally. Final offer."

Any way you add it up, it's worth it. "Deal."

We shake on it. Hip, hip, hooray! I'm going to be popular! I do a little victory dance.

"Don't do that. You look like you're drowning."

Humph.

"And you can't ever tell Mom we traded," she adds.

Is she nuts? "We can't tell her about any of this. She'd turn us both into frogs. Or cats." I nudge Tigger with my foot. "Maybe she had another daughter before me. And she did magic. And Mom turned her into a cat. A male cat, just to be mean."

Tigger meows.

"Why would she turn her into a male cat only to have her neutered?" Miri asks.

"Girls!" my mother hollers from the kitchen. "Time to set the table!"

It's Monday and therefore . . . my turn. But it's worth it. Every time I doubt that, I'll just think of my name at the top of the A-list.

Tigger follows me into the kitchen and almost trips me while I'm taking the plates down from the shelf. Hmm. Who knows? What if I wasn't far off about Tigger? What if he really used to be human and was cursed by my great-grandmother to spend eternity as a not-too-bright feline? Creepy. Especially considering how many times the perv has watched me change.

My mother licks tomato sauce off a wooden spoon while she checks the garlic bread in the oven and stirs the pasta. When she makes dinner, she looks like the

Tasmanian Devil. She's an excellent multitasker. She's the same at work. I've seen her type, fix the jammed fax machine, make coffee, and book a trip to Costa Rica on the phone simultaneously. And that's without using magic. Imagine if she did—her clients would all have sunny, turbulence-free vacations. She's crazy for not using it. What's the point? Why not? Why not be happy? Why not have a perfect life?

When she was married to my dad, she used to take better care of herself. She used to get manicures and visit the hair salon. Now that she's so busy working, she seems to have decided that she'd rather spend the energy on her new agency, and on us of course, rather than on what she looks like. But why shouldn't she have it all? "Mom," I blurt out, "why not use your magic to have great hair?"

"Why are there black smudges all over my kitchen walls?" she asks.

"Tigger's been acting up."

Tigger meows, wraps his body around my leg, and tries to bite me. Bet you wish you were still life-sized so you could tell on me, big sis (or evil nemesis of my great-grandmother).

"Bad Tigger," my mother scolds, waving the wooden spoon at him. "Will you clean him off? He must have stepped into mud on the stairwell. And I told you," she says, and waves the wooden spoon at me, "magic isn't a game, Rachel. I won't use it unless it's absolutely necessary."

You'd *think* saving her marriage to my dad would

have been absolutely necessary, wouldn't you? Maybe it's minor in the grand scheme of witchcraft, but still. You'd better believe I would have kept him around. (And poofed him up some hair and clothes from this decade.)

I open my mouth to tell her what a mess she's made of our lives, but then close it. Because it seems kind of stupid. Why am I angry at her when my dad's the one who left? Because she could have stopped him and she didn't? It's his fault. He should have stopped himself from leaving.

I pick Tigger up and carry him to the bathroom. He starts circling the sink as I turn on the water. Cats hate water, right? Not Tigger. He'll jump into the toilet bowl if it's open. He's also been known to dig his teeth into the end of the toilet paper and make a run for it, tee-peeing the living room, kitchen, and all three bedrooms.

I know I keep joking that he used to be human and female, but it might be true. What if Mom meant to put a prosperity spell on us, and it went horribly wrong? Maybe tee-peeing our apartment is her—now his— revenge. What if Miri's currently unknown popularity spell goes wrong? What if I become Tigger's feline emasculated pal?

I take a deep breath to calm myself down. That's what we learned in gym today—deep breathing. Miri won't screw up. Inhale. She won't. Exhale. The yoga's not working. I bet the technique is only for people living in rural areas with fresh air.

I wash Tigger's already clean paws (thankfully my mother didn't check them) in the sink, then let him down. As soon as his feet hit the ground, he lunges for the toilet paper, bites into the end, and makes a run for it out the door. Stupid cat.

I hope my younger sister has more sense than my older one.

TWO BOYS ARE BETTER THAN ONE

7

A week later, I'm in the middle of a truly fantastic dream in which Mick and Raf are fighting over me at Spring Fling, in a *Matrix*-y slow-motion battle with lots of 360 turns and backflips, when I feel a poking in my cheek.

I open one eye. Miri is hovering over me, shoving her index finger into my face. I close the eye. "Do you mind?"

"Trying to wake you," she whispers.

No kidding. I open the eye and see that the clock says 5:07. 5:07! Did she bump her head on a cauldron? "Why are you waking me at five-oh-seven?"

"Here, take this," she says, and shoves something into my mouth.

I sit up, suddenly energized. "Is that my popularity potion?"

"No. A breath mint."

Humph. "If you don't like my morning breath, don't wake me in the morning. Or in this case, the middle of the night."

"Do you want me to make you a spell or not?"

Yum, peppermint. "So, lay it on me. What did you find?"

She shakes her head. "I don't think I'll be able to do a popularity spell."

"What? You promised!" I kick my comforter off and sling my feet over the side of the bed. What kind of witch is she? She can't do an anti-love spell, and she can't do a popularity spell. She can't even do a spell that will take care of chores—why else would she have to make that deal with me? What good is being a witch if she can't do anything fun? "I don't appreciate you waking me in the middle of the night for no reason except to give me more under-eye circles."

Miri takes a step back and pouts. "It's not my fault. There is a popularity spell, sort of, and it's only two brooms, but it would need me putting dried cinnamon into the entire student body's water supply. I don't have a clue how to do that."

"That does sound tricky," I admit, scooting over. Miri sits down next to me.

"We don't want to get caught putting anything in the Manhattan water supply."

"True." I sigh with disappointment. "So what now? Nothing?" Are my dreams over?

89

"That's the best way for mass popularity. The other way is to collect hairs or nail clippings from everyone in the school—"

"Seems unlikely." I can't see myself running through the halls with hair and nail scissors. Unless I opened up a makeshift salon in the cafeteria and offered free manicures and haircuts. As if people would let me near them with scissors. Anyone who went to middle school with me would remember the time Jewel and I decided to get rid of our bangs and I played barber. Not a pretty sight. "There must be another way."

"I found a love spell, if you want to try that instead."

Now we're thinking. "Tell me more."

"It's only three brooms. And all I'd need are a few minor ingredients."

That could so work! Awesome! If Mick or Raf falls for me, not only will one of the Loves of My Life be my boyfriend, but I'll become A-list by default. Yes! "How long does it last?"

"I'm not sure. A few months, tops."

"Maybe by the time it wears off, he'll be madly in love with me, anyway. He'll realize I'm smart and fun and cute and—"

"Full of yourself?"

Ha-ha. "By the time it wears off, at least I'll be firmly rooted in the A-list." This is an outstanding plan. Instead of becoming popular to have a boyfriend, I'll get a boyfriend to become popular.

I bounce on the bed and let out a scream.

"Shhh," Miri whispers, and tugs at my ankle. "Mom will kill us both if we wake her up. We were up really late last night doing my training."

"Oh yeah. How did that go?"

"Great. Do you know that witchcraft has been around for over twenty-five thousand years? When there were cavemen, there were witches. Later this week we're going to talk about the spread of witches across Mesopotamia and then Europe . . ."

My eyelids start to feel like bricks, and I lie down. "You're putting me back to sleep here."

"Sorry. Oh yeah, the reason I woke you up was to tell you that if you want to do a love spell, you have to buy some yogurt and borrow something that belongs to your guy. Like a piece of clothing."

Oh, is that all? "How am I going to do that?"

She shrugs and climbs in beside me. I move over so she can share my pillow.

"Tell him you're cold and ask to borrow his sweater," she says.

Sweet, naive Miri. "Why, hello, Raf. Chilly today, isn't it? Would you mind taking off that woolly sweater?" He'd think I was a psycho. Although . . . within a week he'd be in love with me anyway, so maybe it doesn't matter. But a pencil would be easier. That I could swipe when he's not paying attention. "Can it be a pencil? Or a notebook?"

She sighs. "Rachel. What happened when you didn't have the right ingredients to make chocolate brownies and you made them anyway? Remember when you used

91

baking soda instead of flour? And they tasted like sawdust?"

"True." But has anyone eaten sawdust? For all we know, it's delicious and tastes like brownies. Or not. "Guess we shouldn't take chances on this first one."

"We don't want to end up with the pencil falling in love with you. Or writing on you." She giggles.

I giggle too. "Or turning me into a pencil." I do love the feeling of a newly sharpened number two poised over a math quiz, though.

We pull the covers over our heads so we won't wake our mother. I can't believe I convinced Miri to put a love spell on anyone. She must be really antsy to test out her magic wings.

At 7:02, I wake up freezing, with sunlight spearing my eyelids. I open one eye and see Miri waving her hands at my window, her eyes closed and her lips pursed.

"What are you doing?" I ask. The left side of my blind is pulled up and the right side is hanging diagonally, still covering the window.

"Using magic to open your blinds. But I screwed up and now one half is stuck."

She's more antsy than I thought. She'd better figure out what she's doing before it's my turn to go under the wand.

In homeroom, I vary the plan slightly. Why have just one boy fall in love with me when I can have two? If I can get my hands on clothing belonging to Mick and Raf, then they'll both fall head over heels in love, and just like in my dream, they'll fight over me. How romantic! I'll open my locker and find two love notes. They'll both want to help me with my coat, so I'll let each of them remove one sleeve. Mick will piggyback me to class while Raf carries my books.

When the bell rings, I hurry back to the second floor so I can stalk the boys and analyze their attire for something to steal. Raf's locker is right by Mr. Silver's classroom. I spot Raf's handsome frame as he snaps his locker closed and heads to class. He's wearing a blue button-down, jeans, a brown belt, and brown shoes. I nibble my lip. If he were wearing a sweatshirt, maybe he'd take it off, but a button-down? I don't think so. And I can't think of any reason he would take off his jeans or belt. Unless he has gym this afternoon. Yes, gym! I can break into the boys' locker room after he's changed and . . . I'll get caught and the entire school will think I'm a perv. If only Miri could whip me up one of those Harry Potter invisibility cloaks. No, wait, I've got it! I can just borrow his gym clothes from his locker. Brilliant! All I need to do is catch him opening his locker and scope out his combination.

I miss him after second and third periods, and then I finally spot him in action just before lunch. Freshmen and sophomores have lunch from eleven to eleven forty-five. Tell me, who's hungry at eleven? It's ridiculous. That's why

93

I'm looking forward to junior year. Not because I'll get my license. Not because of prom. Because I can't wait to eat at twelve like a normal person.

Anyway, Janice, Annie Banks, and Sherry Dollan are congregating by Tammy's locker. They all know each other from middle school, where they were a foursome. Now it's Annie and Sherry, me and Tammy, and Janice is kind of on her own.

"I'm starving," Annie says, peering into her lunch bag. Annie is in our homeroom class, but always sits next to the door, because she supposedly has an extra small bladder and has to go to the bathroom at least once every class. She also has long brown hair and the biggest breasts I've ever seen. Honestly, they must be at least a triple-D. At the moment, she's wearing a red turtleneck, and they look like two beach balls. If only she could share the wealth.

Sherry's in our English class and is Annie's best friend. "Hi-ee girls!" she says now, while chewing a lock of her blond hair. "How is your day-ee?"

Her tendency to add the sound *ee* to every word gets ver-ee annoying. And the fact that she sucks on her curls grosses me out. But she is very friendly and has decent opinions in class. So I try to overlook these things.

I focus on Raf. All he has to do is move over a little and I'll see his locker. Come on, Raf. Your wide manly shoulders are blocking my view! He snaps the lock open and I've missed my chance. He puts on his jacket, gloves, and hat. Maybe he'll drop a glove on his way out for lunch and then, presto, my work here is done.

Raf goes out for lunch a lot. And it's never with other fashion show people. He's also friends with some football players and some sophomores who are in a band called Illuminated. Such random friends.

Tammy and I never go out for lunch. We always eat with Annie, Sherry, and Janice in the cafeteria, on the left side of the room, fourth table from the back.

Until I can sit with the A-list (table at the back near the window), this crew will have to do. Not that I'd drop Tammy. I would do my best to make sure she'd have a seat right beside me. Jewel on my left, Tammy on my right, and Raf and Mick directly across from me. A trapezoid of happiness.

Raf manages to hold on to his gloves. And then the redheaded, ever-annoying Melissa blocks his path and whispers something to him. If only I had superhuman hearing. Is that too much to ask? One measly power?

He says something, and Melissa points down the hall at three other A-list fashion show girls, who are buzzing around, manicured hands waving. In my steal-clothes excitement, I've missed whatever crisis is taking place in fashion show land. Last week the Eiffel Tower that the student set designers were building cracked in half and the cast members were all in a tizzy. The theme is Citygroove, which means that each number will feature a different city. According to Jewel, the Eiffel Tower is for the freshman and sophomore formal wear number. The song is "Come What May" from *Moulin Rouge*.

I'm distracted again when Mick saunters through the hallway. He's wearing jeans and an untucked sweater. I

95

follow him so I can see better. He approaches his locker, places his fingers on the lock, slowly turns the dial . . . seven . . . twenty-two . . . eighteen . . . bingo!

Seven, twenty-two, eighteen! Seven, twenty-two, eighteen. Seven, twenty-two, eighteen. Seven, twenty-two, eighteen. Why don't I have a notepad to scribble this on? Seven, twenty-two, eighteen. I open my locker, rip out my geometry textbook, and write the combination on the cover.

Yes!

"Rachel?" Tammy asks, linking her arm through mine. "When you're finished stalking, do you want to come for lunch?"

Busted. "I was just—"

She laughs. "Daydreaming. I know. He's hot. But I'm starving."

Since I can't confide in her, I nod and secretly plot my next move. I'll have to take five minutes during class, when the hallway is empty, sneak back here, borrow Mick's hat or his puke green gym shirt, hide it in my locker, and then run back to class. The obvious choice is to miss English, since I'm in advanced and therefore supposedly know what I'm doing.

But French is boring.

*

I can barely keep my eyes open.

One of the reasons French is so boring is that I have no friends in the class. Tammy and Janice are in accelerated; Jewel and Sherry are in Spanish. Annie is in regular too, but she's in another class.

"Je parle, tu parles, il ou elle parle, nous parlons . . . ," Doree Matson recites. As usual, she's sitting in the front row and answering all the questions.

When she finally gets to the end of her conjugation, I decide it's now or never. *"Excusez-moi, je dois aller à la toilette."* I hear a few titters from the peanut gallery in the front. They're so childish. I hope I didn't ask if I could pee on the floor.

Did I?

Madame Diamon nods and asks if anyone would like to conjugate *parler* in the conditional tense.

Doree raises her hand.

As I exit the class, I wonder what it's like to teach a language all day that no one understands. To have to listen to people sounding like morons. Staring at you as if you're not making sense. Asking if they can pee on the floor. I couldn't ever become a second-language teacher. Partly because I barely speak a second language. But mostly because I don't think I could teach.

Not that I have a clue what I *do* want to be. A businesswoman? A rocket scientist? I don't know what a rocket scientist does, but how fun would that be? To say you're a rocket scientist. "It's not rocket science," a sexy stranger at a cocktail party would say. I'd lean in closer, allowing him an eyeful of my extraordinary cleavage (this is way down the line, so glistening cleavage is very plausible, if not likely). "Actually," I'd say, "I *am* a rocket scientist," and gasps would ensue. *Mon dieu!*

Must concentrate on covert mission. James Bond

97

music plays in the background. I really should have worn all black today instead of jeans, an orange sweater, and sparkling green shoes. How un-covert can I get?

I skip down the stairs from the third floor. First stop, my locker. I need my geometry book. (When this spell is done, I should ask Miri to find one to improve my memory. I'd better write that down in case I forget.) Hmm. I probably should have noted which locker is Mick's. They all look the same. Metal and narrow.

I close my eyes and try to remember where he stood. Four to the left. No, five to the left. Six. Definitely six. This would be so much easier if I were a witch. I could purse my lips and make his locker glow.

I purse my lips. *Make the right locker glow!*

Nothing glows.

98

Must remember. I think I was right the first time. Four to the left. I peer down the hall to make sure no one is coming. All clear. Peer down the other side. Also clear.

I look at my textbook and see the seven, twenty-two, eighteen, then position myself in front of the fourth locker to the left. Here we go. I take a big breath and turn the dial to the right. Seven. Left, twenty-two. And then a quick eighteen. And . . .

No go.

I turn to the right. Seven. Left, and around once for good luck. Twenty-two. And then a slower eighteen. And . . . nope.

Maybe it was the fifth locker over and not the fourth. If only my brain were like a TiVo and I could skip back to the last episode. I try the fifth locker. And then the next one. And the next one. And the entire row. It isn't working. I need to concentrate.

I slide to the floor, rest my head against the locker behind me, and breathe just like we learned in gym. In. Out. In. Out. Am I turning too fast? Do I have the wrong code? Why isn't my plan working? Why is it so hard to steal a piece of clothing? Maybe I'll tell Mick that I'm doing a project on shoes, and that I need to borrow his. Or maybe I'll stand really close behind him and cut out a piece from the back of his sweater. It wasn't tucked in. He'll think he caught it in a door. Yes, that's what I'll do. I'll try to catch him when the bell rings. But right now I'm tired. So very tired. It's Miri's fault for waking me up so early. Maybe I'll just close my eyes for a second. They're so heavy. Yes, that feels good.

The next thing I know, I'm being tapped on the shoulder.

I open my eyes to see Mr. Earls, JFK's vice principal, looming over me.

"Taking a nap?" he asks. His eyebrows are too close together, like Bert from *Sesame Street*. I've seen him at assemblies and lurking in the hallway corners before, but I've never had the pleasure of being this close to him until now.

"Just thinking," I say. "I'm on my way back to class. Sorry, sir."

"There will be no thinking in the hallway on my watch. And I don't think you were thinking. I think you were napping. And skipping class." He scribbles

99

something on his notepad and throws it at me. "Detention today after school. You can think then. But no napping."

What? Detention? Me? I've never had detention before. Ever. "Oh, please, sir. I was only here for two seconds."

"Do you want detention again tomorrow? That's what you get for arguing with me."

Gulp. Someone's on a power trip.

Blinking back tears, I walk to French. Mr. Earls doesn't realize who he's messing with. One day I'll have magical powers and then he's so going to be morphed into a cat. A neutered cat. Yes, Mr. Earls, do you understand? One day people will call you Fluffy.

As I return to my lonely seat in the back of the class, I feel a heaviness inside my lungs, like when I wake up some mornings and realize that Tigger is sitting on my chest. Life is so unfair. My mom has magical powers. Miri has magical powers and boobs. My dad has STB. Jewel is popular and has a new best friend. Tammy has . . . well, Tammy has Sherry, Janice, and Annie.

And I have nothing. Nothing at all. Nothing . . . but detention.

DETAINED

8

I am such a detention novice that I don't even know where to go.

I head to the school office on the first floor. "Excuse me." I address the secretary. She's staring at her computer screen and doesn't appear to notice me. "Where do I go for detention?" Is it like prison work? Do they chain us evildoers together and force us to mop the gym? Repaint the halls?

"Room one-oh-four," she says without looking at me. "Next to the events board."

I was hoping she'd cry out, "Rachel Weinstein? A sweet freshman like you couldn't possibly have done anything to deserve this awful punishment! Don't be silly! Whoever gave you detention will be dismissed from his post! Go home and don't worry your sweet self for one more minute!"

I guess I'm dreaming. She wouldn't know who I was unless she checked out the trophy case outside the office. When I ranked second at the math competition, I had mixed feelings about my placement being showcased. On the one hand, anyone who passes it will see my engraved name. On the other hand, winning math competitions is more likely to be the ticket to a Star Trek convention than to the kingdom of coolness. But I quickly realized that it didn't matter. My name is barely even visible. The trophy was shoved into the back, behind the bowling club's trophy. Yes, the bowling club. I would have assumed a math competition would be considered worthier than a bowling match at a high school, but what do I know?

Anyway, the secretary doesn't know who I am. She doesn't care that I'm not the type of girl to get detention. Not that I can blame her. I don't know her name either. "And, um . . . what am I supposed to do in detention?" I ask.

"Homework."

I slither toward Room 104. Boring. The only thing keeping up my spirits is the possibility of a supremely hot rebel guy sitting near me in detention, à la the eighties movie *The Breakfast Club*. I'll be Molly Ringwald, all princessy and serene, and he'll be Judd Nelson, with that who-cares attitude. He'll be wearing ripped jeans and a stashed cigarette behind his ear. At first we won't speak.

We'll just eye each other. And then he'll say something rebel-ish, like "Do you think we can smoke in here?"

I'll say, "I don't smoke." And then before the hour of detention is over, we'll be hooking up. I'm not quite sure how we'll get from my retort to the hooking up, but I'll let him figure it out since I've already done more than my share of the planning.

I hold my breath and open the door. Except for a scrawny teacher I recognize from the science department, the desks and chairs are empty. He looks up from his grading. "You're Rachel?"

At least someone knows my name. I sit down in the back row. "Yup." I watch the front door for the rebel. I keep watching. Five minutes later, I raise my hand. The skinny teacher is scribbling all over the paper of some poor student and doesn't notice. I wave again. I'd like to call out, but I don't want to get another detention. I cough. Loudly.

He looks up, annoyed. "Yes?"

"I was wondering where everyone else was."

"You're it." He looks back down at his papers.

I'm it? I was JFK's worst student today? The biggest school rule that was broken in the last twenty-four hours was no napping in the hall? Where are the drugs? The weapons? The kids who skip class? The rebel caught smoking in the bathroom, who still has the audacity to stash a cigarette behind his ear?

Bet this Mr. Science Teacher hates me. If it weren't for my detention, he'd already be at home in his pajamas.

La, la, la.

I would have closed the door if I had thought I was the only one coming. I wonder if I'll get a bad-girl rep if anyone sees me in here. I'll have to dye my hair pink and get a tongue ring.

In an attempt to suck up, I pull my bio homework out of my schoolbag. We have an assignment due on Friday.

Twenty minutes later there's a rustling of voices outside the door. "They're not going to be able to find anyone," a girl's voice says.

"But we have no choice," says someone else. Someone who sounds like . . . Jewel?

"Putting these posters up is such a waste of my time."

If I were just a fraction farther up, I'd be able to see them. I try to covertly scoot my desk up an inch. Nope. Another inch. One more. Five more.

Science Man glares at me.

I smile.

I spot Melissa's long red hair. Melissa and Jewel are outside my detention room.

"Stop whining, Bee-Bee," Jewel says.

Bee-Bee? *Bee-Bee?* I feel nauseous.

"If they weren't good enough to get in the first time, they're not good enough to get in now," Melissa snaps.

What are they talking about? The *click-clack* of their shoes tells me they're about to pass my door, and I quickly scoot my desk backward so they won't see me.

I must see that poster.

The remaining thirty-five minutes of detention takes at least three hours. Finally, *finally*, the hands of the clock above the door say 4:00. Freedom! I grab my bag and launch myself like a rocket from the chair into the empty hallway. In the distance I hear the muffled voices of students with far more energy than I have.

As soon as I see the poster, I feel giddy, fizzy, like a soda can that someone shook and opened.

freshman replacement dancer needed

tryouts friday after school in the caf

citygroove

So that's the crisis. Someone dropped out. Or broke a leg. They're missing a dancer. Whoever the new dancer is, she'll receive automatic A-list status. She'll be able to hang around Jewel. She'll be able to hang around Raf. She'll definitely have a date for Spring Fling.

My heart pounds in my chest. I want to be in the fashion show. I want to have automatic A-list status. I want to hang out with Jewel and Raf. I want to be so cool that I don't have to capitalize.

I'm going to try out.

I clap with glee and do my hooray dance (which looks a lot like my victory dance) in honor of my new plan. In mid-twirl I trip and fall on my behind.

So what if I have six left feet and the show is primarily a dance show?

I know someone with a cure.

105

RUB-A-DUB-DUB, GREEN SLIME IN MY TUB

9

I poke my head into Miri's room. "Are you finished yet?"

She throws her pencil case at me and nails me on the head. Since she's started martial arts, her aim is much improved. "If you'd stop harassing me every four seconds, I would be. Can't you just sit on the bed and wait?"

"Miri, it's been two days. The tryouts are *tomorrow*." I close her door behind me so Mom won't see the trouble we're brewing in here. And I mean brewing, literally. Between Miri's smelly feet is a white plastic bowl. They make her go barefoot in Tae Kwon Do, and I wouldn't let her waste any time showering until she finished the spell. "What are you doing now?" I ask.

"Mixing." She's sitting on her deep-green carpet, leaning against her bed.

The blinds are closed. Wow, she's even more paranoid than I am. Does she really think the sixty-year-old woman and her eight cats who live directly across from us care what we're up to?

Funny, the neighborhood watch would definitely peg her as a witch before Miri.

I peek over the bowl's edge to see what she has going on. The mixture is a weird orangey green. "You're using the popcorn bowl? Gross."

"This *was* the popcorn bowl. It's now a cauldron."

"Guess I'll be having chips for a snack tonight. You should probably buy a new popcorn bowl."

"You get it, then. I'm doing this for you, in case you've forgotten." She points to the spell book. "I need you to help with something. What is eighteen twenty-fourths of a cup?"

"Three quarters," I answer automatically.

"Perfect." She fills her mixing cup with some sort of crushed fruit. "The spell book is like a deranged math test with all these fractions."

I take a sniff. Yum. "It smells like an orange."

"It is. And a cup of crushed pistachio and two-fourths of a cup of butter, which is a half, right?"

I nod. I got the math gene while she got the magic gene. Not fair.

"And," she says, dumping in the final cup, "ground red pepper."

Hmm. That actually sounds tasty. I do love pistachios. "Need any more help?"

107

"I'll call you when it's ready."

I find my math homework. I'm suddenly in the mood.

While I'm clearing the table after dinner (of course I'm clearing the table—these days I'm always setting or clearing the table. "Where's Rachel? She must be in the kitchen setting or clearing the table"), Miri sneaks up behind me. "It's done," she whispers, and hands me the bowl, which is now greenish brown.

"Am I supposed to eat this?"

She laughs. Actually, it's more like a cackle. Something I've noticed as part of her repertoire lately. "Only if you want major indigestion."

Witch humor? "So what do I do with it?"

"Bathe in it."

"Are you insane?"

She puts her hands on her hips. "That's the dancing spell. If you don't want to do it, don't."

"I'm just kidding, Mir," I say, feeling guilty for giving her a hard time. "Thank you. I appreciate your cooking it up for me."

"You're welcome. Want to test it out?"

I smile. "Definitely. So that's all I have to do? Bathe in it?"

"Yup."

"Do you think Mom will wonder why I'm taking a bath for the first time since I was six?"

Worry clouds her face. "Good question. What should we do?"

I have a plan. I finish putting the dishes into the

108

dishwasher, then knock on Mom's door. She's under her covers, her face peeking out, reading a romance novel. My mother loves romance novels. I think she's waiting for Prince Charming to magically appear.

She *could* have him magically appear if she wanted to. Just poof him up. Tall, strong, and a cleft in his chin. Why not, huh? What's wrong with her?

"Mom," I say, "can I take one of your pills? The robo whatever? My back is killing me."

She rests her book against her stomach and waves me over. For a second I think she's on to me, but then she asks, "Did you pick up something too heavy?"

"Um . . . yeah. My desk." Why in the world would I pick up my desk? I am useless at coming up with believable lies.

She sighs. "Rachel, you only get one back in life."

"Thanks for the advice, Mom," I say in my earnest voice. Under normal circumstances I would make fun of her for being such a cheeseball.

"The pills are in my medicine cabinet." She resumes her reading.

"Thanks." And now for the epiphany/performance of a lifetime . . . hands caressing back . . . eyes light up with an idea . . . eureka! "Wait a sec. Do you think taking a bath would help my extremely sore back muscles?"

"Good idea," she says, already lost on a beach with Prince Charming and no longer paying attention.

Mission accomplished. I back out of the room, making sure to close the door behind me, and then I run back to Miri.

"All set. Pass me the bubbles."

"They're not bubbles," she says, and hands me the popcorn bowl.

I open the bathroom door and try to shut it behind me. She pokes in her hand.

"Do you mind?" I ask.

"I have to come in with you."

"I prefer my privacy."

She crosses her arms in front of her chest. "Without my incantation you're just bathing in fruit salad."

I let her in. "Lock the door. And stay quiet. If Mom sees you're in here, she'll know something's up." I sniff. "Gross. It smells like smoke. She's been smoking in here again. Why does she think she can hide it from us? It's so obvious."

Miri shrugs. I don't know why she doesn't care about the smoke as much as I do. She never has. I was the one who used to cry myself to sleep because I was convinced my mom would die of lung cancer. I was the one who, when I was seven, found a pack of her cigarettes that she was hiding from my dad and broke each one in half and flushed them down the toilet. Miri never gets mad at Mom. They're always on the same page. I'm more like my dad. Maybe that's why I never get mad at him. How can I get mad at someone who's just like me?

"What do we do for the spell?" I ask.

"We fill the tub with water, add the mixture, then I recite the spell."

I turn on the hot water. Miri shakes her head and twists the knob. "The spell book says the water must be cold. Probably written before indoor plumbing and hot-water tanks."

cold. Probably written before indoor plumbing and hot-water tanks."

"I'm supposed to sit in a freezing cold bath in the middle of winter?"

Miri shrugs. "That's the spell."

I'm going to get sick for sure. "Let's get this over with."

She sits on the edge of the closed toilet seat and opens her spell book. Then she dumps the concoction into the bathwater and waves her hands over the tub.

I pass her my toothbrush. "Do you want to use this as a wand?"

She shakes her brown hair. "No."

"Maybe a pointy hat? I can make one out of the tissue box."

"What I need," she says, "is for you to be quiet so I can concentrate and access my raw will." She closes her eyes, purses her lips, and gets a constipated look on her face. After a few moments of quiet (as quiet as you can get in New York with the constant honking and car alarms in the background), I feel the familiar cold rush as Miri chants:

111

> **From Heaven to Earth,**
> **From America to France,**
> **Let this potion**
> **Make Rachel dance!**

She opens one eye and peers at the water.

"You've got to be kidding me." I burst out laughing. "That's the spell?"

"That's what it says."

"That's the worst spell I've ever heard! Ever hear of alliteration? And it barely even rhymes. No Pulitzer for whoever wrote that one. And how come you didn't say abracadabra?"

She gnaws on her thumbnail. "Will you just get in the bath?"

"Can you leave now?"

"I've seen you naked a million times. We've taken baths together since we were born."

"First of all, Mom will find it odd if we're both in here. Second, there are some things you stop doing as you mature," I say haughtily. "Such as biting your nails, for example."

"Fine, I'll leave if you're going to be such a baby."

"How long do I have to stay in here?"

"At least a half hour," she snarls, slamming the door.

I lock the door behind her and then undress. I decide to start small. I hesitate before dipping my right big toe in. Ahh! It's colder than snow. I take a deep yoga breath and drop my entire foot in. Ahhh! I whip it back out and then thrust it back in. Ahhhh! Does the thirty minutes count from now or from when I'm immersed? Slowly I put both feet into the water. And then my calves. And then my knees, my thighs, my butt, my stomach, my nonexistent breasts. Teeth are chattering. Lips shaking. Fingers turning blue. My skin is tingling as if it's asleep, but I can't tell if it's from the spell or the frigid temperature. The water looks as if it's been mixed with green slime, and it feels sandy against my skin. Am I supposed to dunk my head? I want my head to have rhythm. I want to be able to swing my hair side to side. I'd better do it. I dunk, keeping my eyes tightly closed.

Cough, cough. Sputter, sputter. Oops. I bet I was supposed to close my mouth.

Miri pounds on the door. "You okay?"

Cough, sputter. "What happens if I swallowed some by mistake? Will my colon do the Macarena?"

"You'll be fine. You can get out now, if you dunked your whole body."

"I thought I was supposed to soak for thirty minutes."

"I lied. You were being annoying."

I quickly rinse off, bolt out of the bathtub, and grab a towel. When my shivering subsides, I empty the grossness out of the bath, rinse it out, and return to my room and my sweats. Then I pull my hair into a bun and tie up my running shoes. I turn on the radio and position myself in front of the full-length mirror on my closet door. *"Me against the music . . ."*

When I try to do the Harlem shake, my shoulders wobble. Without rhythm. Like they always have. I try a body wave. Nothing. A simple butt groove?

Nope.

Abraca-rip-off! I storm out of my room and into Miri's. "What's wrong? Why isn't it working?" My voice is rising and I'm starting to sound hysterical. I took the bath, didn't I? I can still feel pistachio remnants where the sun don't shine. What else must I be subjected to? What other indignities await? The madness must end.

113

Miri rolls her desk chair away from her computer and searches through A². "I don't know. . . . Maybe I didn't do it right. . . ."

"Don't say that. What's going to happen to me? What if you made my arms become snakes, or elastics?"

"Hold on," Miri says. "There's a footnote. XI. Let me find XI. . . ." She looks up at me. "It says that the spell might take up to half a moon turn to take hold."

"What does that mean? A half a month?"

"I think it's twelve hours."

That's not too bad. It's eight now, so that means the spell will be up and kicking by tomorrow morning. "Are there any other footnotes you forgot to read? Like how my skin turns to scales?"

"I don't think so. But guess what."

"What?"

She rolls back to her computer desk. "I just got another wedding update e-mail from STB. This time telling us all about the song list." She groans.

STB sends out weekly wedding updates to all of her guests. About the caterer, the flowers, the anticipated weather. Like anyone cares. All they do is clog our in-boxes.

I check my own e-mail on my computer. I don't even bother opening the wedding e-mails; they go right to the trash. Jewel still hasn't e-mailed me back about the last e-mail I sent her, two weeks ago. Tammy's on IM, so I instant message with her for a half hour, then decide just to call her.

"What's up?" she asks. I imagine her giving me the scuba thumbs-up.

"Nothing." I wish I could tell her!

"The bio assignment took me forever."

Whoops. Forgot to finish that one. After the call I return to my desk, and then at ten thirty, I decide to hit the sheets early. Unfortunately, it takes me forever to fall asleep because I'm too excited. Just as I'm about to nod off, I give my behind a little shake to see if it's gotten its rhythm yet. Hard to tell.

At seven thirty the next morning, I bolt from bed. I shower, get fully dressed, flick the radio on, and return to my spot in front of the mirror.

"*Me against the music . . .*" Again. I feel shivers down my back, like hundreds of ants formed a conga line on my spine. That must be a sign. What are the chances of the same song being played?

So for the second time I try the Harlem shake. And my shoulders move. I mean *really* move. Then I try the body wave. And my body twists in a way it never could before. And then, finally, I shake my butt. And let me tell you, it gets down. All the way down. Touches the pink carpet, back up, and then back down again.

Oh. My. God. Omigod. My arms are flying, my head is soaring, my behind is grooving, and I do not look like I'm being electrocuted. I look like I know what I'm doing. Abracatastic!

"Miri!" I yell. "Miri, come here!"

She runs into my room. I do the Macarena and even *that* looks good. She claps and jumps up and down. "I can't believe it!" she shrieks. "You can dance! And I did it!"

"Girls?" my mom asks from her marshmallow breakfast in the kitchen. "Okay in there?"

"Fine!" I say. "Use your indoor voice," I tell my sister. "Be calm."

But I can't be calm. Because I am good. So good. So good I could be the backup dancer in a music video. Hey, I could *star* in a music video. "How long does this spell last?"

"For good. Only emotion spells wear off."

If it's me against the music, I'm kicking the music's sorry butt.

ROCHELLE/RACKELLE/RUTH

10

Tammy keeps looking at me strangely, as if I'm wearing my jeans and scoop-neck black top inside out.

"What?" I ask as I moonwalk into world civ.

"Why are you jumping all over the place?"

I try to stop the rhythm flowing through my body, but it's tough. I'm like the Energizer Bunny. "I'm not."

"Yes, you are. You haven't sat still the entire day." We claim two desks on the side of the room, right under the map of the ancient world that looks as if it may fall and smother us at any given moment. "Is everything all right?"

"Everything's terrific," I drawl.

"Want to come over after school?"

"I can't. I have a *hmphsh*." I mumble the last part and wipe my hand over my lips as if I'm removing a milk mustache.

"You have a what?" she asks.

"I'm trying out for the fashion show," I admit.

Her mouth pops open 180 degrees, exposing her very narrow, very tall teeth. Her entire body is narrow, tall, and straight. Except her nose, which is wide and a bit crooked. Last month we tried to use some of my mom's makeup to shadow it, but she ended up looking as if someone had punched her. "Why would you do that?" she asks.

"Because I want to be in the show?"

"No, you don't. You said that the show was elitist and materialistic, and that it objectified women."

"I never said that," I lie. I may have said that. But that was when I couldn't dance and had zero shot of getting in.

She raises an eyebrow. "So why didn't you try out last time?" It's amazing that Tammy can already see through me. We buddied up on the first day of ninth grade, when she warned me that I had a blue line on my face. Apparently, my new pen had leaked all over my hand, and unaware, I had scratched my upper lip. Would you believe, an exploding pen on the first day of high school, which led to a gorgeous Hitler mustache? Before our next class, Tammy led me to the bathroom and helped me scrub it until it was less noticeable. Slightly less noticeable, anyway.

"I've decided I need to get more exercise," I say. "To be healthy."

118

Now she raises both eyebrows simultaneously. "Healthy? Since when? You just polished off a movie-sized bag of M&M's after demolishing two slices of pepperoni pizza for lunch."

What, does she keep records of everything I eat as well as say? "And *that's* why I have to start working out."

She shrugs. "I didn't know you could dance."

"Well, I can." As of this morning.

"Lucky. I can't. But I'll watch you try out. For moral support. You know, Annie and Janice are trying out too."

Yes, I know. They've been talking and practicing all week. I was trying to be low-key, so no one would ask me to show them my moves until I was magic-ready.

Annie's bustline hasn't helped my self-esteem. I sneak a quick look at her sitting by the door. I don't know how she dances, but I'm sure she'd be an asset if there's a swimsuit number.

When the bell rings, I rush into the bathroom one last time. I've gone in between every class to confirm that my booty can still move. I now check again (still moving), fluff my lame wavy hair, scan my outfit (these aren't just *any* jeans I'm wearing; they're my Perfect Butt jeans), then apply black mascara to accentuate my brown eyes (if only I had my sister's superhuman eyelashes), and pink lipstick. My heart feels like a crazed yo-yo. Ready.

Tammy is waiting for me outside the bathroom. I grab her hand. What if I bomb? What if the spell just makes me think I look good? What if I make a complete fool of myself?

119

"Rachel, you're not breathing," Tammy tells me at the top of the stairs. "Remember what we learned in gym? In, out, in, out."

I breathe in too quickly and end up hiccupping.

"Deep breath," she says, holding my hands in the air. "When I'm diving, I have to always remember to breathe. Deeeeeep breath. Deeeeeeep breath. Otherwise you could panic, pass out, and get mauled by a shark."

Is this how she tries to comfort me? I cling to her arm and slowly descend the three flights of stairs to the cafeteria. Maybe I'll get lucky, and except for Annie, I won't have any competition.

Wrong. A line of fifty wannabe dancers snakes along the wall toward the caf's entrance, which is being monitored by suck-up Doree. She counts off the first five girls in line, ushers them into the room, and then closes the door so we can't see inside. I recognize most of the waiting girls, and I wonder who the *real* competition will be. Besides Annie, of course.

I remember the last tryouts. I came with Jewel and stood outside the door, and she was so nervous that she shook. A lot of the girls here today were at the first round, too.

The music starts inside (*boom, boom, boom*), and I can't help it; my feet start tapping. Tammy looks at me as if I'm nuts. The music stops, the five girls are let out, and Doree escorts the next five girls in. A few minutes later she leads in another five.

Janice joins us. "Ready?" she asks, looking very

120

serious. I so can't picture her letting loose and feeling the rhythm.

I nod. Deeeep breath.

Tammy engages Janice in conversation instead of me. Obviously, she realizes how nervous I am. Five more girls go in. Why is no one coming out? Are they dying of humiliation inside?

I'm in the next group. Even if I'm the best dancer here, I still might not get in. What if I'm too short? What if they just don't like me? What if I'm not fashion show material? A few of the girls behind me are whispering about Laura Jenkins, the girl who dropped out.

"I hear she was failing all of her classes and her parents made her quit," someone says.

"I'm not surprised," another girl answers. "She's already in remedial everything." I couldn't care less why she dropped out. I'm just happy she did.

The music stops.

"One," Doree counts, tapping Janice on the head. "Two. Three." I'm three. "Four." She taps Tammy.

"Oh, I'm not trying out," Tammy says. "But can I watch? For moral support?"

Doree gives her the once-over. "No."

Tammy squeezes my arm and backs away. "Good luck!"

As I pass through the cafeteria doors, I see the girls who just tried out exiting through the back door, and I feel nauseous. At the front of the room, the tables have been moved so there's a space for us to try out in. The eight freshman cast members (there are nine in all, but

Doree's playing host) are sprawled on top of the remaining tables, waiting to watch us. Jewel and Melissa are next to each other, giggling over a magazine, too busy to notice me.

I have never felt more ridiculous in my life. It's like that dream when you're sitting in homeroom and you realize you forgot to put on your pants. Five masking tape Xs mark the cleared area, separated from each other by a half foot.

"Please stand on the third X," Doree tells me without even a hint that she's in almost all my classes.

We line up, all five of us trembling, as if we're about to beg for our lives in front of a firing squad. *Don't look up,* I tell myself. Don't look up, don't look up. I look up. Raf is on a lunch table all the way in back, lying on his sexy stomach, possibly doing his homework. I think I might puke.

"Please tell us your names," Doree says.

"Janice Cooper," Janice says, since she's first in line. Her voice catches on the *p*, and the firing squad snickers.

Poor Janice.

"Ivy Lions," says the girl next to me. She's wearing high-waisted jeans, glasses, and a plaid scrunchy. I know without a doubt there's no way she's getting in. Two fashion show seniors whisper and laugh, and I can feel Ivy's humiliation radiate from her cheeks. I want to cry for her. I can't decide if she's gutsy or just stupid.

"Rachel Weinstein," I say. Jewel's eyes jump up from the magazine at my name. I smile shyly at her.

"You didn't tell me you were trying out," she mouths, looking slightly panicked. For the first time it occurs to me that she might see me as another Ivy. After all, she's seen me dance.

"Surprise," I mouth back.

"All right, girls," says London Zeal, one of the two producers. Every year two seniors who have been in the show previously are elected to produce. They're responsible for choosing the ten freshmen, ten sophomores, ten juniors, and eight other seniors who will participate. Half are guys, half girls. And just because someone gets in one year doesn't mean he or she will make it the next. Everyone still has to try out. Usually the same people make it year after year, but last year one of the sophomore dancers, Kate Small, hooked up with London's boyfriend behind her back. Guess who got cut this year?

123

Mercedes Redding, London's cohead, is sitting cross-legged on a yoga mat. She is the skinniest person I have ever seen. Honestly, her jeans must be a size zero. Of course, all the guys think she's hot, even though she has the body of a ten-year-old. Or used to think she was hot. She chopped her long blond locks to her chin over Christmas, and the response has not been favorable. Mercedes is a great dancer, but she doesn't talk much.

London, on the other hand, never shuts up, and you can hear her coming down the hall from a mile away— her voice is so nasal it sounds as if she's holding her nose when she talks. You can also see her from a mile away. She dresses head to toe in one color. Today she's wearing purple. Purple tank top, purple skirt, purple fishnets, purple high boots. Purple-tinged sunglasses. She's also lined the rims of her eyelids with purple eyeliner. It's very striking.

"Now, girls," she says. "I'm going to show you a sequence of moves from one of the dances that you would be in, and you're going to attempt to keep up. Then we'll invite some of you, or none of you, to come back for second rounds, which will be in about an hour. The show is in less than two months, so we have no time to waste. The rest of the cast has been working together since October. So whoever we choose has to be better than good. She has to be . . ."

Magical?

"... amazing. So, if you're wasting our time, just leave."

The five of us stay frozen in our spots.

London snaps her fingers and someone starts the music.

I can do this. I can do this. I did it this morning and I can do it now (*boom, boom, boom*).

London positions herself right in front of me. "Five, six, seven, eight! Left arm up, right arm up, twirl, groove, bend, kick ball change . . ." She goes on. And on. The moves get more and more complex. She looks like a mosquito trapped in a small room, zigzagging perfectly in sync with the music from wall to wall.

We're supposed to remember all this? An eternity later, she stops, turns around, and gives us a big fake smile. "Your turn."

I steal a quick glance at the other contestants. They look as if they're going to cry.

"All right then. Let's see who can keep up." She turns her back to us and sings, "Five, six, seven, eight! Left arm up, right arm up, twirl, groove, bend, kick ball change!"

And I'm right behind her. Following her every move. The girls on each side of me aren't doing too well (Janice keeps flapping her arms), and they're all smashing into each other like bumper cars, but I'm in the zone. My arms and legs and butt are in sync and can feel the music. Not only am I following London, I'm kicking higher, swooping lower, and shaking faster.

I'm on fire.

For the first time ever I am totally lost in the music. All I feel is the piercing beat and the liquid movement of my body. When the sequence is over, I realize that everyone is staring at me. Not only London, Mercedes, Jewel, and Raf, but the entire freshman cast as well as the other contestants.

I look up at Jewel. "Wow," she mouths.

London crouches beside Mercedes and whispers. Then London stands up and says, "Rochelle, we'd like to see you at callbacks at five. The rest of you can go."

Rochelle? That's me. Yes!

I wander the hall for the next hour. Wendy Wolcott, a freshman with short black hair that frames her face, is also wandering. We're walking in opposite directions and keep crossing paths in front of the second-floor water fountain. We don't speak to each other, neither wanting to get too close to the competition.

At 4:55, I return to the caf.

Jewel tackles me the second I walk in. She has a huge smile on her face. "When did you learn to dance like that?"

I smile back, mostly because it's the first time in forever that she's voluntarily spoken to me outside of math class. "I've been practicing."

"No kidding. You were amazing. Like, superstar amazing."

"Thanks."

"Good luck," she says, and pats me on the back. "Not that you need it."

In the corner, Wendy is tying her shoelaces. Annie walks in. I wave. I wonder if she has to wear a sports bra for dancing. All the boys in the show stop what they're doing and stare. The three of us line up.

London motions to the cast to find their seats. "First we want to see you dance freestyle. Second, walk. Third, interact with your partner for the formal."

Walk? I have to walk? I didn't ask Miri for a walking spell. What if I don't know how to walk?

"Mercedes and I make all the casting decisions, but we're allowing the freshman dancers to help us decide since they're the ones who have to dance with you. So first, freestyle."

She snaps her fingers, and the music pumps through the room. (How does she do that? Is the room set up with the Clapper? Is she a witch too?)

I start to move. My feet move, my knees move, my butt moves, my arms, my neck. I feel rubbery and alive and I couldn't stop myself if I tried. Wendy and Annie dance beside me, but they're watching yours truly out of the corners of their eyes.

When the music stops, everyone applauds, looking at me.

"Very good," London says. "Now, all of you please pretend you're on the catwalk and walk toward me." She shuffles backward and beckons to us, as if she's a father teaching his kids to ride a bike. Heel, toe, heel, toe. I remember reading that in a teen mag. I hope I don't need training wheels.

"Very good. Now, Rackelle and Anna, please sit down and let's see how Raf looks with Wanda."

127

My heart leaps into my mouth. Raf! Why on earth did Laura quit the show when Raf was her partner? Who cares if she was failing school? And who in the world are Rackelle, Anna, and Wanda? Oh, right, that's us. London's way too cool to remember our names.

Annie/Anna and I sit. I try to keep my back straight and model-esque by imagining a ruler against it.

Raf jumps off the table and joins Wendy/Wanda. She's only an inch shorter than he is, not a half foot, like me, and my heart sinks. They look adorable together.

"Give her a twirl," London instructs.

He gives her a twirl.

"Now a dip," she says.

If only I could purse my lips or twitch my nose and

make him drop her. Miri? If you can hear me, toss her to the floor like a pair of discarded socks.

London whispers something to Mercedes, and Mercedes nods. "Thank you, Winnie. That was excellent. Ruth, you're up."

That must be me again. I stand and try to heel-toe my way to the center of the room. Heel, toe, heel, toe. Or is it toe, heel? And that's when it happens. I trip. I stumble and fall forward onto my hands.

Everyone gasps.

"I'm fine!" I sing, trying to keep my voice light and fluffy. I force myself to laugh. "No problem. Must have tripped on something." Unfortunately, I realize that I tripped on my own untied laces. Stupid magic shoes.

"You okay?" Raf asks, arriving by my side. Our eyes meet. I know this sounds like something out of one of my mom's romance novels, but I can't look away. His eyes are liquid midnight. It's as if I'm drowning in them. He offers me his hand and I let him help me up, and his touch is hot, like the side of a whistling teakettle. Omigod. I'm so in love. Really and truly this time.

When I've regained my balance, he lets me go. Damn. Maybe I should fall again. Or not. Everyone is staring at me. Just what they were praying for—a klutz who will trip on her own two feet during the show. Perhaps even fall off the stage.

"Let's see a twirl," London tells us. Raf takes my hand again and I twirl into him. Please don't let go.

"Now a dip."

I lean back in his arms. I could stay like this forever.

His lips are only a few inches away, and he smells so yummy. If only he'd lean in a bit closer and kiss me. That would be so romantic . . . or not. My first kiss in front of the entire fashion show cast?

"Thank you, Randy."

That's it? Why didn't I get an excellent like Wendy did? Despair overwhelms me like a wave in the ocean. I'm not going to make it.

While the boys gape at Annie's assets, I wonder how many weeks I'd have to set and clear the table for Miri to break both Annie's and Wendy's legs. Kidding. Kind of. What a terrible thing to joke about. I guess that's why Miri got the powers and not me. I'm an awful person. I must have the worst karma. My aura must be a revolting brown-green for trying to sabotage my father's wedding alone.

Annie's not a bad dancer. But I don't think she and Raf look like a match made in heaven or anything. She's too tall.

"Thank you for coming," London says after Annie is done. "The results will be posted on Monday. Try not to obsess all weekend."

What? On Monday? I have to wait the entire weekend?

See? I knew I had lousy karma.

129

PASS THE BENZOYL PEROXIDE

11

On the train ride to my dad's, Miri doesn't even pretend to care about the tryouts. All she wants to talk about is the spell for STB. "He's going to take one look at her and run the other way," she says gleefully. "And then she'll finally be out of our lives."

"Finally," I repeat. Even though we can't perfectly imagine what life would be like with a single dad—he and STB were an item after six months of him being separated from my mom—those six months without her were much better than the time with her. We were the priority. He lived in the city in a building called Putter's Place. It's a popular building for Manhattan fathers when they leave their wives. On Sundays I'd see half the kids in my grade with their suitcases in the lobby.

Maybe he'll never remarry. Maybe he'll miss us and come home. The backs of my eyes prick. Maybe I should think about something more fun. Like the fashion show. "And speaking of finally, on Monday I'll know if I made the cut. Do you think that my tripping screwed my chances?"

"Uh-huh," Miri says. She's obviously not paying attention, because the proper response would have been "No! Of course not! Don't be stupid!" She pulls her new spell notebook out of her schoolbag (she's now making lists of her attempted spells and her observations in a navy blue spiral book that she doesn't let out of her sight), as well as a foot-long, inch-wide glass beaker filled with light orange guck. "We have to get this cream on STB's skin."

131

"Where did you get that beaker? It looks like something from science class."

"That's where I got it."

"You stole it from your science lab? I thought you were a good witch, not a bad one."

She flushes. "I'll return it on Monday."

"Sure you will." I shake my head with exaggerated disappointment. "Two weeks and you've already gone over to the dark side."

She pouts until I stick out my tongue and wag it up and down. As usual, my silly face makes her laugh. She crosses her eyeballs in response.

"So how are you going to get the concoction on STB's skin?" I ask. "Hug her?"

"I would if that weren't completely out of character. She'd know something was up."

"Why don't you mix it in with her moisturizer? You know the two hundred dollar mini-tube she special-orders from France and hides on the top shelf of their bathroom?"

"If I mix it with that, she'll get a rash every time she uses the cream."

"Is that what's going to happen? She's going to get a face rash? We could have just put poison ivy in her room."

"It's supposed to cause the ugliest of ugliest face conditions. Which I'm guessing means boils or maybe even jaundice."

"It's not going to hurt, is it?" It's one thing to make her temporarily ugly, but I'd feel horrible if we caused her any physical pain. (I was just kidding about breaking Annie's and Wendy's legs. Sort of.)

"No. And I added horseradish, which is supposed to make any spell temporary, so it should only last a few days. Just long enough to make Daddy snap out of his fascination with her and cancel the wedding." Miri stares into the beaker. "Keep your fingers crossed."

As soon as we step off the train, we spot our father.

"Hi, Daddy," Miri says, and throws her arms around him.

I feel a lump in my throat, like I always do when I first see him. It really sucks to have divorced parents. I know

I'm supposed to be mature about it (I'm lucky to have two parents who love me, et cetera, et cetera), but sometimes I can't help feeling sorry for myself. I don't want to be a hypotenuse stretched between two divergent parents. I don't want to see my dad only once every two weeks. I see my gym teacher more often than that. Is that normal?

My dad hugs me, and my throat slowly de-lumps. He takes our bags, and we follow him to the car, where STB and Prissy are waiting. STB waves as soon as she spots us. Prissy squishes her face against the back window.

STB turns her head to see us when we climb into the back, then gives us a big fake smile. "Hi, girls, how are you?" There's no way she likes these weekends. Why would she? Who wants to take care of two teenagers?

"I get to sit in the middle," Prissy says, settling back into her booster seat.

STB faces front again, admiring her reflection in the sun visor mirror. "Did you have a good two weeks?"

"Yup," I say. I bet she won't be admiring herself after tomorrow. And I bet as soon as my dad's out of earshot, she won't be this nice.

"That's great," she says. "Really great."

As if she cares how our weeks went. Two can play that game. "How were your weeks?" I ask.

She sighs. "Long. Weddings are so difficult to plan, aren't they, honey?" She reaches over and pats my dad's bald spot. If she keeps touching it, it's going to get even bigger.

"And we'll have three more weddings to plan after this one, since we have three daughters," my father says.

It weirds me out that Prissy lives with my father. At least she doesn't call him Dad. I wonder if she'll start to after the wedding. Her father lives in L.A., so she only sees him a few times a year. I wonder why he and STB got divorced. I wish he'd share the reasons with my dad. I'll ask him for a top-ten list if we ever meet.

My father parks in front of Happy Palace, the neighborhood Chinese restaurant, to pick up takeout. "Honey, will you ask for chopsticks for me?" STB the show-off asks as he gets ready to run in. As soon as he's gone (okay, it was a few minutes later, but still, she's so rude), STB whirls around. "Miri, how are your fingers? Have you stopped biting?"

Miri sits on her hands.

"Do we have to put the Band-Aids back on? And I won't have you giving me attitude like last time. Your mother might let you get away with that type of behavior, but it won't be happening at my house."

Miri's face turns redder than a stop sign. I'm hoping she turns STB into a frog, but nothing happens. She must be exercising her self-control. It's one of the things they learn in Tae Kwon Do. She'd be amazing on a diet.

"And Rachel, I'd appreciate it if you could try to keep your room tidy this weekend. I'm not a maid."

"Mommy doesn't like messes," Prissy adds.

STB laughs. "No, I don't. And sometimes your room looks like it was taken over by animals."

I wish Miri were sitting next to me so I could squeeze her hand. Hard.

My father returns with the food. "That was quick, honey," STB says, smiling sweetly, all traces of evil gone from her voice. He hands her the food and kisses her on the cheek. How does he not see through her sickeningly sweet facade?

"Lemon chicken, General Tso's shrimp, Szechuan beef, and crispy noodles with tofu for Miri," he says while backing the car into the street.

"Did you get me chopsticks?" STB asks.

He slams his hand against his forehead. "Oops."

"That's all right. Next time."

When we reach our driveway, I help my dad with the bags. Miri approaches our target. "You have dirt on your cheek."

STB wipes her face with the back of her glove. "I do? Where?"

"I'll get it," Miri says, and before STB can reply, Miri dips her gloved finger into the vial behind her back and rubs a drop of the concoction on STB's cheek.

"Thanks," STB says.

Miri smiles. "Oh, you're very welcome."

Score! I refrain from giving Miri a thumbs-up and lift my suitcase out of the trunk. Hah. I'll show her an animal. She's about to look like one.

The next morning, at some unearthly hour, we're awakened by a piercing scream.

Miri and I spring from our beds. A second later, we hear another, even more piercing scream.

"I guess it worked," I whisper.

We open our door and poke our heads into the hallway. STB shrieks yet a third time.

We slowly walk to my father's room and knock. "Hello?" I ask. "Is everything all right?" Then I whisper in my sister's ear, "Be subtle."

My father opens the door, looking half-asleep. "Girls, did either of you pack any pimple cream? Jennifer broke out."

I don't think benzoyl peroxide is going to do the trick this time, Dad.

"Can we see?" my not-so-subtle sister asks.

"What Miri means," I say, elbowing her in the stomach, "is that as teenagers, we're often afflicted with various unfortunate skin conditions. So perhaps we can help. Or at least empathize."

This seems to make sense to my dad, as he nods and says, "Jennifer, come show the girls."

"I'm not a freak show," she cries from their private bathroom. "I must have had an allergic reaction. No more General Tso, I can promise you that."

"Maybe the girls can help," my dad says.

The bathroom door opens slowly. I see an arm, and then . . . a face covered in clusters of good old-fashioned zits.

That's it? Where are the boils? The rash? Are pimples

the worst face condition a witch can come up with? There's hardly a day that goes by when I don't have a pimple. I'm finding this highly insulting.

"Any suggestions, girls?" STB asks.

"No," we say in unison. I'm trying not to laugh. "I'm sure they'll go away soon."

"Exactly," my father says. He pulls his precious fi-ancée into a hug. "They're kind of cute. Makes me imagine what you looked like as a teenager."

STB giggles and pats his bald spot.

I try not to gag.

Miri and I desert the lovefest and retreat to our room. "Acne?" I whisper angrily. "That's the best you could come up with?"

She shivers. "I hate pimples."

At twelve, she has yet to experience one and therefore sees them as the world's worst potential affliction. "Well, they're not going to be enough to propel our father out of love with her! He didn't stop loving me when I had that massive zit on my nose last Christmas, did he?"

She shivers again. That zit (which I referred to as Santa's Gift—we joked that I must have been really bad last year) had freaked her so much that she'd started stuttering in its presence. I don't know how she's going to manage high school. "Maybe if he's not so mesmerized by her beauty," she reminds me, "he'll see her true self."

I'm not convinced. "Hey, did you ever find out what *Taraxacum officinale* was?"

"Of course. It's in the spell. It's a fancy name for a dandelion."

137

"I'm going to the drugstore," my father says through our closed door. "I have to pick up some pimple medicine and some vitamin A. That'll be good for Jennifer's skin."

I climb back into bed. What would be even better for her skin is packing up and moving out. Can we give her that in a pill?

A few hours later, at a normal waking time, I pass my father on the stairs. My stomach is growling from hunger, and my dad is getting ready to go to the office.

I can't believe he's working again on the weekend. Which means Miri and I get to spend the day with the Pimple Queen.

And then I notice it. The nasty fist-sized red zit on his chin. I stop him in mid-step. "Dad, you're breaking out too." I've never seen my father with a pimple. Fathers aren't supposed to have them. They're also not supposed to cry or show signs of weakness. Or leave you alone with a wicked STB.

"I am?" He touches his chin. "I was wondering what that bump was."

I race back to our room and close the door. Miri is reading the spell book shielded by her science textbook. "He's breaking out too," I whisper breathlessly.

"What?"

"Dad has a pimple on his chin. Is it possible it's a co-incidence?"

She stares at me. And continues staring at me. Then with a trembling hand she points at my nose. "It's b-b-back," she stammers.

No. No, no, no. No way. "Don't tell me that."

She drops her book and covers her face with her hands. "I screwed up."

I can't break out now! Santa's Gift lasted for two weeks! Raf or Mick will never ask me to Spring Fling if I have a massive boulder on my nose! I push Miri away and peer into the nearest mirror. "No!" I cry, horrified. It *is* back. Bigger and badder than before. I thought sequels always paled when compared to their originals. And what's that on my forehead? "How did this happen?" I shriek, spinning toward Miri. "Did you put the spell on me, too?"

Miri gnaws on her thumb. "I don't know. Maybe it can spread. Maybe Dad touched STB with the potion and it spread to him and then you when he kissed you goodnight." Her hand flies to her cheek. "What if I get it too?"

She starts scribbling in her spell observation notebook.

I'm going to cry. What if it spreads all over? Onto my hands, my neck, my stomach? Who knows what this spell is capable of? My entire body could become one big erupting pimple. I grab her shoulders. "You need to fix this. Now."

Her eyes fill with tears. "I don't know how."

"Figure it out!" I storm out of the room and knock on my dad's door. I expect to find him and STB in a state of hysterics, but instead they're lying on the bed, cuddling and, worse, *giggling*.

"I have it too," I say, which for some inexplicable reason just makes them laugh louder.

139

"Let's see," my dad says.

I stand over them and point to my nose. STB's face has worsened. Her forehead is covered in pus. My father's acne has spread to his bald spot.

"The pimple cream is in the medicine cabinet," my dad offers.

As if that would work.

"We should call Harry," STB says. Harry is my father's friend who also happens to be a doctor. "In case it's shingles or the chicken pox. Or measles."

"I think those spread to your whole body and not just your face," my father says. "But I guess I should call him."

STB points to his blistering forehead and cracks up. They both start rolling on the bed, they're laughing so hard. Why isn't he repulsed and realizing how horrible she is? Apparently, like pimples, laughter is contagious. I back out of the room before I catch the latter, too, and run back to our room. We need a cure. Pronto.

I open the door to find Miri having a minor panic attack. A zit has appeared under her left eyebrow. I grab a paper bag from the kitchen and tell her to breathe into it so she won't pass out.

Then I start reading the book. Fixing this is obviously up to me.

"Aha," I say an hour later, when Miri's cheeks have regained color. "There are two potential solutions. Spell reversal, or a new spell for clear skin."

"Spell reversal," she says, pacing the length of the room. "No need to throw another unknown into the mix. We could end up translucent." She trips over the pants I wore yesterday and gives me a withering look. Then she hangs them up.

"The only problem with spell reversal is that it's a five-broomer. If you can't even handle an easy spell, how would you handle this one?"

Her face brightens. "I could call Mom."

"Are you crazy? She'd freak!" She'd be furious about our plan to make STB ugly, and she'd demand to know what other spells Miri has concocted. I'd lose my rhythm for sure. "Keep Mom out of this."

"Then I'll do the clear-skin spell." She lies on her bed, sticks her feet up against the wall. "Let me see the book."

I pass it, lie down beside her, and cross my big foot over her tiny one. She sighs. "I don't know about these ingredients. We need a teaspoon of salt from the sea, two-fourths of a cup of lemon juice, and five-fifteenths of a cup of milk. What is that?"

"A third of a cup," I say smoothly.

Miri slams her hand against the book in exasperation. "Why can't these ancient sorcerers just say what they mean?"

"Maybe it got screwed up in the translation." Or maybe it's the book's master plan to get me to help my sister.

"But where are we going to find salt from the sea? Do you think Dad will take us to the beach?"

Brainstorm! "Remember before school started when I used STB's mud mask and I got all pissed because it took off my tan?"

141

She nods.

"That was a Dead Sea mud mask. STB has a whole collection of beauty products from the Dead Sea, including salts. They're in the back of the bathroom cupboard behind Dad's Vi—" There's probably no reason to share the Viagra finding with Miri. It freaked me out enough for the two of us. "Behind Dad's vitamins. I'll get the salts. And there are lemons in the white pottery bowl in the kitchen."

Miri shakes her head and starts biting the skin on her pinky. "Rachel, those are fake. Haven't you noticed they've been there for a year? And that they don't smell?"

"Why would someone showcase fake lemons?"

142

"Why are there drawers in the kitchen that don't open? Who knows? They have lemonade in the fridge. I guess that will have to do. And they must have milk."

The skin on her pinky is bleeding. "They do, but since STB is lactose intolerant, it's all Lactaid milk. Do you think that makes a difference?" I take a breath, then frown. "Can you please stop mutilating your fingers? It's grossing me out."

She looks at her hand. "I didn't even realize I was doing it."

I throw her a tissue. "You're lucky STB's been too preoccupied to make you wear Band-Aids. Okay, let's get Operation Clear Skin in motion."

The doorbell rings, and we join the rest of the family downstairs.

"It's not measles or shingles," Harry says, scanning

our faces. "It looks like acne. But I have no idea why all of you have it."

STB swats Prissy's hand away from her face, which is now covered as well. "Stop scratching, honey. You're making it worse."

Prissy looks the most ridiculous with her acne, but seems to mind the least. "They're fun," she says, poking her pimples. "I can play connect the dots. In school we sometimes play connect the dots. . . ."

I tune her out and watch Harry write us a prescription for a new medicine called Xonerate. "It should alleviate your symptoms by midweek."

Midweek? This problem had better be history *tomorrow*. I can't go to school like this.

Thirty-five minutes later, while my father and STB go to the pharmacy to fill the prescription (STB is wearing a baseball hat and large sunglasses as a disguise—I couldn't believe she even went with my dad but she's probably wanting to get out of spending any extra time with the two of us), Miri cleans the beaker with boiling water, as the spell book directs. Then, in the bathroom—Miri by the sink, me on the rim of the tub—she mixes the lemonade with the lactose-free milk and the Dead Sea salts.

Prissy knocks on the door. "Can I come in?"

"We're busy!" Miri yells. "Come back later." Sometimes she talks to Prissy the way I talk to her. Or the way Jewel talks to me, as if I'm a groupie.

I wonder what Jewel did today. I called her yesterday, but hung up when I got her machine, and called Tammy instead.

"Why not now?" Prissy whines.

Because then you'll tell your mother we're casting evil spells on her, and she'll make us see a shrink? "We'll be out in a second," I say through the door. "I hope she doesn't set the house on fire while we're in here," I tell Miri. We're the worst babysitters ever.

"It's done," Miri says. "Now be quiet."

**Skin so smooth,
Feels like silk,
Face like an angel,
White as milk.**

I shiver from the cold and then snort. "Honestly, I could write this stuff. What if the witch is African American? Or Hispanic? If it adjusts to the twenty-first century, shouldn't it be politically correct?"

She shakes the potion and then dabs it on her face. "Did it work?"

"It's been a second and a half, so no," I say, applying it.

She stares at her reflection in the mirror. "I need it to work now."

"You're certainly not the fairest of them all," I tell her.

Prissy slams her foot into the door. "Let me in! Please?"

I unlock the door and Prissy falls through. Oh, no. She's taken the connect-the-dots idea to a new level, having drawn black lines all over her face.

144

"What did you do?" I ask incredulously.

"I used Mommy's makeup."

"I'm washing that off. Now." I gingerly wipe her face with a washcloth, trying not to gag. Then I medicate her. Touching someone else's pimples is not a pleasant activity. I'd rank it up there with changing a baby's diaper or cleaning up someone else's vomit.

"Thank you," she says softly, and blinks her big blue-green eyes at me. She has the same beautiful ones as STB.

My repulsion thaws. She's not so bad. Kind of sweet, actually. I hope she doesn't have the mean gene like her mother.

I rinse the cloth and when I face her again, her little finger goes up her nose. I can't help laughing. She laughs too, and wipes her hand on my wrist.

I laugh even harder.

"We should put the conconction into the Xonerate cream," Miri suggests, tidying up. "I don't care that STB looks like a pin cushion, but Dad shouldn't have to suffer."

When my dad and STB come home, Miri claims she needs to use the medicine first, grabs it, and sneaks it into the bathroom to replace it with her concoction.

By Sunday morning, all five of our faces are clear.

"I'm definitely investing in Xonerate," my father says over breakfast. "It's a miracle drug. And I'm sure the vitamin A didn't hurt either."

"You know," I tell Miri on the train home, "we could make a fortune if we sold your clear-skin potion at school."

145

"No. And we need a new plan."

"Why no? Try to see the big picture. We could be millionaires." I'd make a great businesswoman. I can easily imagine myself walking down Fifth Avenue, screaming into my cell phone, high heels *click-clack*ing against the pavement, hair flowing in the wind as I climb into my private helicopter on the roof of my office.

Miri taps me on the head. "Can you stop daydreaming and focus?"

"What new plan?"

"The new plan on how to get our father to cancel the wedding. Our first plan backfired. Dad didn't even notice how ugly she was."

I laugh. "She did look pretty ugly."

Miri bites her thumb and I slap her hand away. "I know," she says. "But he didn't care. In fact, he seemed to love her even more. How is that possible?"

"Well, he wasn't looking his best either." I think for a moment. "It's not enough to make her appearance ugly. We have to help him see her real personality, how awful she is. She's sweet in front of him, but as soon as he's out of the room, she morphs."

Miri nods. "So what do we do? Tape her with a hidden recorder and then play it for Dad?"

"Come on. You're a witch. You can do better than that. Otherwise, start thinking bridesmaid. As in dresses. As in putrid, puffy, and pink."

CRAZY, COOL, OR JUST PLAIN GOOD

12

Can't look. Must look. Can't.

It's first period, and I'm standing in front of the events bulletin board. I excused myself from homeroom as soon as I saw London walk past the door. I knew she was posting the results. I asked to go to the bathroom and then bolted to the board that holds my future in its thumbtack grasp. I'm too terrified to open my eyes.

If I got in, wouldn't Jewel have called to tell me? I so didn't get in. Maybe she wasn't allowed to tell me.

Maybe London threatened her. Told her she'd get booted out if she spilled the beans about the fashion show.

Maybe I did get in! My feet start tapping to an

imaginary salsa beat. I picture myself as the star of *Dirty Dancing III: Manhattan Nights*.

Or maybe not. Maybe they chose Wendy. Maybe Jewel blackballed me. Maybe she's not too busy for me; she just doesn't like me anymore.

Can't look. Must look. I'll open just one eye so if I don't get in, both my pupils won't be scarred.

First I see the words *freshman fashion show replacement dancer*. And then I see—

rachel weinstein.

I open both eyes to make sure it still says my name, then proceed to jump up and down. Abracarific! I'm about to moonwalk down the hall when I see the sadistic Mr. Earls. I skip back to class before he has a chance to give me another detention.

Not that detention is such a bad thing.

Detention + eavesdropping = fashion show.

Did I mention that I love math?

By the time we get to our lockers, the whole school knows.

On the way to my next class, Doree throws her arms around me. "Congrats!" she squeals. "I'm so excited to have someone in class to talk to about the show! This is so awesome!"

"Congratulations, Rachel," William Kosravi says.

The president of our high school just talked to me.

To me. He knows who I am. Now I can call him just Will too! Suddenly, everyone knows who I am. People I've never even seen are congratulating me.

This is so much more effective than a math tournament.

Or even bowling.

"Je suis très excitée de te voir danser!" Madame Diamon says as she passes me in the hallway.

"Enchantée," I murmur, sashaying past.

Tammy can't stop smiling. "I'm so happy for you." She gives me a thumbs-up. "Want to celebrate after school? We can go for pizza."

"Yeah, great," I say. We turn into the second-floor stairwell, and before I know it, I'm being suffocated by arms.

"Congratulations!" London and Mercedes scream. Two of the most popular girls in school are hugging me. Unbelievable.

"Practice starts today after school," London says, ignoring Tammy. Today she's in navy blue. Jeans, sweater, Yankees hat, boots, and eyeliner. "Plan on working your butt off. You have a ton of catching up to do. We expect you to be at practice every day after school except Wednesday for the next month."

Like that's a bad thing? I can't think of a better way to spend my afternoons than with Jewel and Raf.

"What are we practicing today?" I ask, trying not to appear eager.

London whips out her clipboard. "Jewel volunteered to teach you the opening during lunch. It's extremely vital that you know what you're doing because the freshman girls start off the dance, which sets the tone for the entire show. All lunch practices are in the drama room."

She offered to teach me? That's so sweet. She is such a great friend. See? She still likes me! "After school, the cast is meeting in the caf to review the first dance," London continues. "It's a medley of music from *Chicago*."

I knew there was a reason I bought Mom the DVD for her birthday. Besides her birthday, I mean.

"And tomorrow after school is the freshman and sophomore *Moulin Rouge* rehearsal. Raf Kosravi is your partner."

I know! Hooray! Abracazam! He'll fall in love with me and invite me to Spring Fling!

"And the girls will all be wearing Izzy Simpson."

Yes! Yes! Yes! "Oh. Cool," I say, shrugging.

"You have Wednesday off. Mercedes and I have Pilates. Thursday is the practice for the all-girl freshman and sophomore dance. It's to Will Smith's 'Miami' and I'm choreographing and it's going to be incredible. You'll be wearing Juicy. On Friday Mercedes will work with everyone on the closing, which is also the entire cast. It's to a dance version of Frank Sinatra's 'New York, New York.' Everyone will wear black Theory clothes." She snaps the clipboard under her arm. "Those are all the numbers you're in."

Can you say overwhelming? That sounds like a lot of work. Not that I'm going to complain. London seems to take this show *very* seriously.

"Oh wait—there's also the all-freshman Vegas

dance. Melissa put together a stripper theme that was fantastic, but the administration heard about it and said it was inappropriate. So you didn't miss anything because she's redoing it. Later," she concludes without ceremony, and they slink off.

Why is Melissa choreographing? And somehow I missed what label we'll be wearing, but who cares? I'd wear something by Judy if I had to.

Well, maybe.

"Wow," Tammy says. "Guess we're not going for pizza after school today."

"Guess not," I say, vowing to do it as soon as the show is over.

Tammy and I start walking. "But how amazing is it that designers let you model their clothes?" she says.

"So amazing," I say. "I guess they do it for the publicity. And rumor has it we get our hair and makeup done for free the day of the show," I add, half guilty.

"Lucky," she murmurs. All right, three-quarters guilty.

When we get to math, Jewel waves from the back. "I'll see you later," I say to Tammy.

"Hi, hon," Jewel says. "I'm so excited for you!"

I can't stop smiling.

"I was dying to call you this weekend. *Dying*. But London told me I had to keep it under lock and key." She makes a zipping motion to her mouth. She should be making a locking motion, but I don't want to call her on it. "Aren't you thrilled?"

"Thrilled," I repeat. "So how long do the practices last?"

"Not long. And then we go out for food."

Is it possible I'll be privy to the after-school hang-out? The bell rings, signifying the beginning of class. Ms. Hayward slams the door and starts to set up her books.

"So you have to tell me," Jewel says, leaning over her desk toward me. "When did you learn to dance like that?"

"I must have picked it up." Or bathed in it. Whatever.

"But how? I couldn't get over you. No one could. You were all anyone could talk about at Mick's."

"At Mick's?" Mick isn't in the show. He definitely wasn't at the tryouts.

"At his party on Friday. Honestly, we were all totally bowled over. Mercedes said she was glad that Laura Jenkins dropped out, because you're ten times better than she is. She couldn't understand why you didn't try out in October." Jewel shakes her ringlets. "Me either."

Ms. Hayward bangs her ruler against the desk. "Rachel, do you think you and Juliana can stop talking long enough so that I can teach my class?"

I open my textbook, the smile still on my face. Even Hayward can't ruin this perfect day.

※

"That foot spin at the end took me two weeks to learn, and you got it in two secs," Jewel tells me at fashion show rehearsal. I'm at *fashion show rehearsal!* Raf and Jewel and London and thirty other A-listers are wandering around and I'm not dreaming. At least I think I'm not. I'd pinch myself but that would look weird. The entire cast is in the cafeteria and we just did a run-through of the opening number that Jewel taught me at lunch.

"Thanks," I say demurely.

"It's true," says Stephanie Collins—Stephy to those in the know. She's standing on the other side of me and must be the only girl in school shorter than I am. She's under five feet and has long silky blond hair that she wears in two low pigtails. Her nose, eyes, and lips are so small, they look like miniatures. "I don't want to stand next to you. You're going to make me look bad."

153

Whoever said cool girls were mean is crazy. I've gotten nothing but compliments since I got here.

"Are you two going to Snack Shoppe after practice?" Stephy asks us.

Jewel winks at me. "Is that where everyone is?"

Stephy double-checks the text message on her pink cell phone. "Uh-huh."

"Rachel, you want to go?" Jewel asks.

"Sure." If I'm dreaming, I never want to wake up.

※

I feel like Cinderella. And Raf is my prince. My spell had better not run out at midnight.

I follow Jewel and Melissa to a booth at the back of Snack Shoppe. A booth where Sean Washington and Mick are seated. Yes, Mick. I've forgotten about Mick since being paired with Raf, but he's still extremely hot and has excellent boyfriend potential. I sit down across from him and try not to stare. He looks as if he belongs in an Abercrombie & Fitch catalog, but with more clothes. Sean is another super-hot guy. He has dark skin, a buzz cut, and the brightest, whitest smile I've ever seen. He's in the fashion show, too, and dancing with Jewel in the formal.

"Hey, dancing ladies," Mick says, and shoves a fry into his mouth.

"Hey," Jewel and Stephy say.

My mouth is too dry to speak. It feels as if someone attached a Dustbuster to my tongue.

154

Jewel orders an iced tea from the waitress. Then Melissa orders an iced tea. Then I order an iced tea. As if I need the caffeine. What I could use is water. Like this second. My mouth is a desert and I'm afraid it'll crack if I open it.

"What's going on?" Jewel asks Mick.

"Just hanging out. Crazy party on Friday, huh?"

"Totally wild," Melissa says.

"This weekend is going to be even crazier," Mick says. "Nat's in town."

"Excellent," Jewel says.

I have no idea who Nat is (girl? boy? cat?), but I nod as if I do.

"Rachel, you going to come this week? Show off the moves everyone's been talking about?"

He's talking to me. He knows my name. He invited me to his party.

He's talking to me. He knows my name. He invited me to his party.

He's talking to me. He knows my name. He invited me to his party.

Omigod.

"Hello? Rachel?" he says.

Super. We're on speaking terms for four seconds and I've already screwed it up. Way to go.

"She doesn't talk," Melissa says. "Just dances."

Well, *that* was pretty rude. "Sounds cool," I say. Is *cool* still a cool word to say? Does saying it take away from its cool nature? Should I have used *crazy* like he did? Or *awesome*? Or what about plain, reliable *good*?

Mick smiles and gobbles up another fry. He has beautiful plump lips. They remind me of ripe, juicy grapes.

Maybe he'll let me fan him and feed him a few?

The waitress brings our drinks and I take a big gulp. I need to be seriously cooled down. Seriously crazied down?

I feel a strong squeeze on my shoulder and spin around.

Omigod.

It's Raf. Touching me. Squeezing me. Mick is across from me, talking to me with his beautiful plump lips while Raf, with his electric hands and deep-sea dark eyes, is touching me. Did I already say that this is the best day ever?

155

This is the best day ever.

"Hey, partner," he says.

"Hi," I squeak.

He pulls up a chair from the table next to us and joins our group. "Ready for tomorrow?"

Am I ever. "Definitely. I hope I can keep up."

"Don't worry, you'll be fine. Why don't we meet at lunch and I'll go over some of the moves?"

"Great!" I agreed a little too quickly. But who cares? I have a lunch date. A lunch date! Yes! Isn't dancing kind of like cuddling standing up?

"Where do you want to meet? I'll get the music from Mercedes."

"Your locker?" I say.

"Sure. It's—"

"Right by Mr. Silver's class." Did I just say that? What reason could I have for knowing where his locker is except for being a psycho stalker? "I think," I add. Everyone's staring at me. Mick's staring. Sean's staring. Melissa's staring. Jewel's staring.

"Yeah," Raf says. "It's down the hall from yours."

Excuse me? He knows where my locker is? Why does he know where my locker is? He's never said one word to me. Is it possible he's a psycho stalker? My psycho stalker? How cool would that be? How cool! Crazy! Awesome! Good!

Raf pushes back his chair. "See you tomorrow, Rachel." And then he pops over to a table in the back where some senior football players are sitting. He is so cool. He's comfortable talking to everyone.

I gulp down my iced tea. I'm concerned that if I don't

weight my body down with liquid, I might float to cloud nine.

Have I already mentioned that this is the best day ever?

*

I am in Raf's arms.

No, really. And I'm not dreaming. (This time I did pinch myself to make sure.) I am fully awake, at school, and in his arms.

It's lunchtime on Tuesday, and Raf and I are in the drama room, practicing for the formal. Basically the dance goes like this: ten boys strut down the T (the cat-walk), then ten girls follow, then we stand in front of our partners. They twirl us, they dip us, we do a few sexy moves, we all walk back down the T to the stage, and then each couple walks down the T for a thirty-second romantic duet. Afterward we return to the stage for an-other minute of dancing.

The show is going to take place in the school audito-rium, on the same catwalk that they put up every year. Unfortunately, we hardly ever get to practice in the audi-torium, except during the week before the show. The drama club gets priority. It's highly unfair. They have a *drama room* to rehearse in. They claim it doesn't give them enough space. It's all kind of a joke, because being in the school play is nowhere near as cool as being in the fashion show, but teachers think the play is more educa-tional, so, whatever.

157

At the moment, we're practicing our duet—basically Raf pretending to kiss my outstretched arm. Oh yeah, we're fake making out. I can't believe actors get to fake make out every day. Maybe I should become an actor. Not in high school, obviously (not cool), but later on in life. Maybe I should just ask Mercedes to choreograph a real kiss into the routine. Is there a suggestion box?

"That's the end of our duet," Raf says. "Now we walk back up the T, and it's Melissa and Gavin's turn."

"Got it," I say as he spins me out of the twirl. Gavin is in my English class. His clothes are all black. He spends class drawing cartoons in the margins of the novels we're studying and has always been too cool/awesome/crazy/good for me to approach. But not anymore!

Raf twirls me one more time and then we're done. "Do you feel comfortable with the moves, or do you want to try it again to make sure?"

Hmm. That's a tough one. "I guess one more time wouldn't hurt."

During the after-school practice, Raf whispers, "You going to Mick's this weekend?"

I sniff him before answering. He still smells so delicious. Like soap and boy. Yum. "Yes. You?" Please say you're going, please say you're going!

"Yeah. Mick's is a fun night." We walk off the pretend T (Mercedes made it with masking tape) and take our position on the fake stage. His arms are wrapped around my shoulders.

Sniff. Yum.

Maybe he'll ask me to go with him. I know I'm invited on my own, but what do I do, just show up? What time? No one's mentioned a time. I can ask Jewel, but I don't want to remind her that I don't know.

Sniff. Yum.

"Do you have a cold?" Raf asks.

"No, why?"

"You keep sniffling."

Super. Now he's worried I'm going to get him sick. Just what every guy dreams about. An infectious partner.

"Allergies," I respond. Must stop sniffing and concentrate on his other attributes. Like his gorgeous dark liquid eyes, his wide muscled shoulders, his clear smooth skin . . .

"Rachel?" Raf says, nudging me and snapping me out of my reverie. "We're supposed to walk offstage now."

Right. I might have to beg Miri for an anti-love spell. I'm never going to be able to concentrate on the show.

159

ALWAYS LOCK THE DOOR

13

When I stretch my arms up to pull on my top, my entire body aches. Dancing is a killer workout. Who knew? All that aside, with my new buff bod, I'm ready for my big night. Yes, ladies and gentlemen, the day has come. After only one week of schmoozing with the important people, I, Rachel Weinstein, am going to an A-list party.

I spent most of the week panicking—what time am I supposed to be there? Should I ask Tammy so I won't have to walk in by myself?—but then today during math, Jewel turned to me and said, "Hey, can we go to the party tonight together?"

"Sure," I said, as if it were no big deal. "When do you want to meet?"

"Nine?" she said, rolling one of her curls around her finger. "At our spot?"

Our spot was at the corner of Ninth and Fifth, right outside the neighborhood ice cream parlor. We've clocked up many hours, and even more calories, at that corner.

Thank goodness I didn't ask Tammy. I was hoping all week I wouldn't have to. In fact, I mastered the art of changing the subject every time she brought up the weekend. For example, on Wednesday I interjected with an "Omigod, did I tell you about what happened at practice yesterday?" and then dove right into some random anecdote about London, like when she was practicing a jeté and accidentally kicked Doree in the butt.

I know I'm not being nice. But I can't tell her about it and then not invite her, can I? And I can't tell her to come along, because this is the first time I've been invited and how do I know what Mick's guest policy is? He didn't say *Come to my party and please bring a friend.* What if there's a head count? What if Mick is only allowed to invite thirty people and Tammy would make thirty-one? This isn't like Stromboli's Pizzeria; this is a *private gathering.* If he wanted Tammy to come, wouldn't he invite her himself? He knows her. He brought her a napkin when she got tomato sauce on her shirt!

The thing is, if Tammy tags along, I'll be tied to her the entire night. I need to be able to roam unattached.

I pretend Miri's room is a catwalk and sashay inside. "What do you think of this outfit?" I'm wearing jeans and

161

a tight red top, carrying my black slinky blouse as a backup.

She's lying on her bed, feet up, immersed in A^2. "Just as good as the last seven."

"Don't exaggerate. I've only tried on six outfits."

"Whatever. They all look the same."

"Exactly. They all look the same because the shirt I wanted to wear tonight, my tight white V-neck, smells like BO because *someone* wore it after Tae Kwon Do without asking if she could borrow it."

She grimaces. "Sorry."

"It's okay. I know how you can make it up to me. You see, the other reason these shirts all look the same is because I'm flat-chested." I examine myself in the mirror above her dresser. "I'm not asking for much. Maybe half a cup size. Or a full one. Two if you want to get crazy." Truth is, two might be a little obvious. If you're an A-cup Friday in world civ, you can't be a C-cup Friday night. People might notice.

"No boob spells, but I'll wash your shirt."

"You're no fun."

"I'm trying to find a truth serum," Miri says, frowning.

"I don't think that'll help me. No guy should hear the truth. If I tell Raf or Mick how hot they are, they'd get massive egos."

"Not for you, you freak," she says. "For STB."

I perch myself on the edge of her bed. "That's our new plan?"

"*Our* new plan? You mean *my* new plan. You've been too busy with your dancing to help me."

I've been at rehearsals practically every day. I guess I have been neglecting my sister. "Sorry, Mir. I'll spend tomorrow helping you."

"Yeah? That would be great. I want to stock up on some ingredients. Can you take me to get them?"

"Tomorrow's perfect. I don't have rehearsal until Sunday." See? I'm a good sister. "So explain *your* new plan to me." I hold the black top over the red and look in the mirror.

Hmm. Maybe I should change.

"Okay." She spins around and leans her back against the wall. "He has no idea what she's really like. So if we give her a truth serum, guess what happens."

The red. No, the black. Which complements my complexion? I think I should go with the red. Miri is staring at me expectantly. "I don't know, Miri. Unlike you, I'm not psychic."

"I'm not asking you to be. I'm just asking you to pay attention to me for two seconds!"

Oops. Maybe I *am* the worst sister ever. I pat her knee. "Let's not get cranky. Tell me your plan."

She sighs. "Once I give her the truth serum, she'll say what she really thinks in front of Dad. He'll see the horrible person she really is and then break up with her. See?"

For someone so young, she certainly is clever. "Ingenious. And tomorrow we'll buy the ingredients. But tonight I must look gorgeous. So what do you think? Red or black?"

163

I choose red. And then black and then red again, and then Miri throws a black marker at me, which she doesn't realize is open. It leaves a huge blob in the middle of my shirt. So I choose black. Then I try to line the inside rims of my eyes the way London does, and I almost poke my pupils out. Then I apply blush to the apples of my cheeks, like the beauty experts recommend. One stroke, two strokes. Uh-oh. I look like a clown. I wash my face and try again. One stroke, two strokes. Still clown-ish. And now the wet eyeliner has streaked down my face. I wash it thoroughly and reapply my eyeliner. It's in my best interest to go blushless.

"Going to the party!" I scream to my mom and Miri. I'm meeting Jewel at nine, and I have only two minutes to spare.

It's so cold that I can see my breath. When we were younger, Jewel and I used to wear matching earmuffs.

Over the past five months, every time I've remi-nisced about Jewel (like about the time we wrote a play and had her father video it, or the way we used to make ice pops with orange juice in the summer), it's made me sad. But not today. Today she's meeting me. Today we're hanging out. Life is good.

When I reach the corner of Ninth and Fifth, I glance at my watch. Nine o'clock. I'm right on time. Ten min-utes pass. She's always late. Like twenty to thirty minutes late. I used to give her a fake time of twenty to thirty minutes earlier so I wouldn't have to wait. Like telling her the movie started at ten after nine when it really started at nine thirty. But this time I forgot. And now I've been standing here like a moron for eleven minutes. The little hairs on my upper lip that I've contemplated waxing have frozen into needles. Maybe I can just snap them off now. Good thing I don't have a boyfriend who wants a kiss hello.

If only it weren't too cold for ice cream.

Twenty minutes later, I spot Jewel's curls bouncing down the street. "Hi, Bee-Bee!" she says, taking my hand.

It's just like the old days.

165

I love brownstones. My father's mother, my bubbe, used to live in one before my dad moved her into a retirement home on Long Island. She shared the building with three other tenants and lived on the top floor.

Mick's family has two, and I'm not talking about tenants. They own two full brownstones. They broke down the dividing wall and now occupy the largest mansion I've ever seen.

When Jewel pushes open the unlocked door, I try to keep my mouth from hitting the floor. "Crazy place, huh?" she says. We both start giggling. "Coats go in there." She points her chin at the walk-in closet.

The house smells like beer and pizza. The lights are dim and a low bass is blasting through the floor and ceilings. I recognize some sophomores and juniors sprawled on a beige leather couch. And . . . is that a senior? There are seniors here! And not the loser kind who don't have friends their own age. Some even look older than seniors. How cool is Mick?

"Do you know all these people?" I whisper to Jewel. I'm looking for Raf, but I don't see him. I can't believe I'm here.

"Some of them," she whispers back. "They're friends of Nat's."

Ah. The infamous Nat. Why does everyone assume I know who Nat is? Jewel must notice the confusion on my face, because she adds, "Mick's sister. She's at Penn but comes back some weekends."

We hang up our coats, and then I follow Jewel to the second of four floors. Jewel looks as if she's stepped right out of a music video. She's wearing jeans so low that her thong peeks out. How is wearing dental floss up her behind comfortable? Jewel is also wearing a tube top that exposes her . . . "Jewel, when did you get a belly button ring?"

She peeks down at her navel. "Over Christmas. You like?"

Two months ago? I can't believe I didn't know that. When Sean pats her behind as we walk into the living room, I wonder what else I need to catch up on.

A crowd of people is sitting on an L-shaped red leather couch. Music blares from speakers perched on every wall, and it sounds as if the band is in the room with us instead of on the wall-sized flat-screen TV. Who knows, maybe they are. From what I can gather, Mick's family has enough money to fly a group in.

Mick jumps from his seat. "Hey, gorgeous," he says to Jewel, wrapping her in a bear hug and lifting her off the ground. He puts her down, then turns to me. "Hey, gorgeous," he says, and picks me up. Hey, gorgeous? I love him!

Maybe Miri secretly put a love spell on him as a surprise favor. Or maybe, I think as I inhale the scent of booze breath, he's dipped into his daddy's liquor cabinet.

He eventually puts me down and takes off for greener pastures. When I look around the room, I realize that Jewel has taken his seat, and I now have no idea what to do with myself.

Maybe Jewel will introduce me to the blond girl she's talking to, and the three of us can engage in stimulating conversation. Nope, she doesn't seem to be in any great hurry to include me. Jewel? Um, Jewel? Hello?

There are bags of spilled chips on the marble coffee table, and I pick up what I think is a plain one and pop it into my mouth. Ew. Vinegar. Should I sit on the floor? I'm the only one standing. The shaggy red and white carpet looks pretty comfy. I think I'll take another chip.

Yup, I'm very busy here eating. Who needs people to talk to or a place to sit? I can eat. I eye a can of soda.

Ooh, I can drink, too. I pop it open and take a long sip. And then another. And again.

"There you are!" squeals a high-pitched voice, and I look up to see Melissa waltzing into the room. "Scoot that sexy ass over," she says to Jewel, and squeezes herself a spot. "Who did you come with?"

Why didn't I think of that? I could have just squashed myself in.

"Rachel," Jewel says, twirling a curl.

"Who?" Melissa asks, a blank look on her face.

Oh, come on. She knows who I am. Hello? I'm standing right here.

Jewel peers around the room as though trying to remember where she put me. "You know. Rachel. There you are," she says, finding me.

Melissa fixes her beady eyes on me. "Oh, right. Her. How are you, superstar?"

"Fine." I'd be better if I were in your seat. Melissa's eyes burn into me and I take another long sip.

"How sad were those tryouts?" Melissa says, rolling her eyes. "I don't know why all those pathetics bothered showing up. They couldn't dance the first time. I don't know why they thought they'd get in the second time."

Jewel laughs. She stands up and waves her arms like a chicken. "Who am I?"

"Janice Cooper," I say, and then instantly feel ashamed. I take another soda.

Melissa cracks up.

"Good call," Jewel says, then scoots over. Apparently, there's more space on the couch than she let on. "Why don't you sit with us?"

I'm in. Physically and metaphorically.

Thirty minutes later my bladder feels as if it might explode. I'm terrified that my seat will be gone by the time I return, or that Melissa and Jewel will disappear and I'll have to search the entire house, pretending to be busy until I find them. "Save my seat," I say, trying not to appear anxious. Notice how I suavely don't mention where I'm going. Above all, I resolve, I must maintain an aura of mystique and sophistication. I head off in search of the can.

I find it on the deserted third floor. Only one problem: the lock doesn't work. Super. What do I do now? Go back and find Jewel and ask her to watch the door? There's no time for that. My bladder won't make it.

I'll just be quick. The door is on my right, so I can hold it closed with my hand.

Obviously, as soon as I pull down my jeans, someone turns the door handle. I slam my arm against the door to stop it from flying open and scream, "I'm in here!"

The door closes. Oh, man. I really hope that was a girl.

"Sorry," says a low, boy's voice.

A familiar-sounding voice. Raf's voice.

I am never coming out.

Raf is waiting outside the bathroom door. How am I supposed to pee with Raf less than a foot away? I can't.

Not with a guy I like within earshot. I can barely pee when my dad is on the same floor.

Maybe if I take a while, he'll go away. Or he'll think I'm . . . you know. Having female issues. Or worse, stomach problems. Oh, gross. I'd better hurry up. Don't want him thinking *that*. Must pee. Now. Come on. Nothing comes. Where is the tinkling sound? How is this possible? I was bursting a second ago. The only sound I hear is the ticking of my watch. No, it's my heart pounding. I'm panicking. I shouldn't panic. I have to stop panicking.

Breathe in, out. In, out.

I know. I should turn on the water. The sound will mask the tinkling sound. The only problem is that the sink isn't within grasping distance, so I'll have to get up to turn the water on. Which will be fine, as long as Raf doesn't try to open the door when I'm in mid-grab. Not that he would. A horrifying thought occurs to me. What if in this excruciating silence he worries that I've drowned and bangs down the door to save me?

I'm going for it. Three, two, one. I hurl myself toward the sink, throw the water on, and fly back to the toilet.

Ah. I hope this is quick. Of course it isn't. It's the longest pee ever. He's probably long gone. I've been in here at least an hour.

Finally, I'm done. I flush and wash my hands, then open the door.

Oh, no. Oh, whoa.

Raf is leaning casually against the wall, looking hot in his low baggy jeans and a worn, soft-looking green

T-shirt. Out-of-control hot. Hotter than the sun. Hotter than the sun on fire. Hotter than the sun drenched in gasoline, then set on fire. Hotter than—

"What's happening?" he asks, patting me on the shoulder. "I was wondering where you've been hiding."

He was? And now he's found me. In the bathroom. Super. "I've been here. I mean, downstairs. You know." I could use that invisibility cloak right about *now*.

"I just want to use the bathroom," he says. Of course he does. I've been hogging it for hours. "And then, maybe you and I can catch up or something?"

"Sure," I say, admiring the ease he displays regarding his bodily functions. I mean, you have to be pretty confident to come right out and say, "I need to use the bathroom."

He smiles and disappears inside. He wants to catch up! Yes! Not sure what we're catching up on, since we've only known each other for a week. Any chance that *catch up* is a euphemism for *hook up*? Is he going to kiss me? Am I finally going to have my first kiss? Am I supposed to wait? I don't want him to think I'm stalking the bathroom. What should I be doing right now? For the first time I understand Miri's strange relationship with her nails. This would be a good time for me to start biting. If anything, it would give me something to do.

Luckily, being a guy, Raf is done two seconds later.

"Let's find somewhere to sit," he says as we head downstairs. He smiles at me, and my heart does flip-flops. He has such a nice smile. Why didn't I notice his nice

171

smile before? His teeth are so white and straight. I know I've noticed his wide shoulders and yummy smell and beautiful eyes.

I follow him into the living room and look around. Melissa and Jewel are gone. Thanks for waiting for me, girls. In fact, except for a passed-out sophomore, the room is empty. I hear group laughter from downstairs, which is fine by me. Alone time with Raf.

He hands me a soda and lounges on the couch. "So what do you think of the show so far?"

My knee is only two inches away from his. "It's fun."

"Yeah? How come you didn't try out in October?"

"How do you know I didn't?"

"You would have gotten in if you had."

Was that a come-on? I've never heard one before, but from what I've garnered from the movies, it might classify. "I wasn't sure I'd have time for everything."

A huge smile overwhelms his face, crinkling his eyes into half-moons. "Too busy winning competitions?"

Does he know about the math competition? Is there a hole for nerds where I can bury myself? "What are you talking about?"

"I spotted the trophy by the office with your name on it." He nods. "Pretty impressive."

I'm not sure if I should be dying of embarrassment or puffing out my chest. On the one hand, winning shows I'm smart.

On the other hand, it's math.

Maybe he didn't read the trophy carefully. Maybe he thinks I won a cheerleading competition. Rah-rah.

"Quick, what's the square root of two hundred and eighty-nine?"

So much for that theory. "Seventeen," I answer automatically.

He takes another sip of his drink. "Five hundred and fifty?"

"It's not even, but it's around twenty-three point four . . ." I laugh.

He looks at the ceiling and pretends to calculate. "I'll take your word for it. Smart and talented. Impressive."

Yes! He's impressed! I've impressed the hottest male specimen on the planet! "Not really. Just in math. I can't conjugate a French verb to save my life. Madame Diamon wants to kill me. Who do you have?"

"Monsieur Parouche."

"Who else do you have?"

"Henderson, Wolf."

Wow. All accelerated classes. Why does there have to be more than one accelerated class for each subject? Why couldn't he be in mine? "What's your elective?"

His cheeks turn pink. "Creative writing."

He'd be turning bright red if he knew that I'm currently picturing him serenading me. I'll be at my window, and he'll be on the street, standing beside the monthly parking garage, reading his poems. Bet he's a better rhymer than A^2. "Don't be embarrassed. That sounds fun."

"I guess you're right. It's far less geeky than winning a math competition." A wide grin stretches across his face. "Kidding."

Just then a group of seniors passes by, and Will jumps on Raf. "Are you flirting with a girl?"

How cute! Brothers wrestling.

"I was until you sat on me," Raf answers from beneath his brother, sounding annoyed, but pleased that his big brother is paying attention to him.

Will puts him in a headlock, messes up his hair, and then faces me. "So you're his new partner, huh?"

"Yup." I'm on the couch with Raf, the love of my life, and Will, the president of the student council. This must be heaven.

"His new girlfriend, too?"

Raf turns the color of the couch. I'm pretty sure I match. You'd think the class president could be a little more mature. Not that I mind. Say it again! Say it again!

"Will, I'm going to kick your ass later," Raf mumbles from beneath his brother.

Will laughs, messes up his hair again, and takes off.

"Brothers," Raf says, shaking his head. "I have two. Mitch is in his third year at NYU. They're both pains. What about you?"

"One sister." Hopefully Prissy will never make it to that level. And I don't want him to know anything about any potential wedding. No way. My schedule is wide open. Or so it will be once Miri's spell works.

"What's she like?"

"She's . . ." Magical? Focused? A brown belt? "Full of surprises."

We talk for the rest of the night. Or at least I think

we're talking. It's hard to tell what's going on from cloud nine. The conversation seems to revolve around school, friends, and television. Turns out he hates reality TV as much as I do. (See? We are *so* made for each other.) Around midnight, Raf glances at his watch. "I've gotta head out soon. I'm playing hockey at seven a.m. How are you getting home?"

He's a genius, a poet, gorgeous, a fantastic dancer, and athletic? Is it possible? "I'll get a cab with Jewel." I should be going home soon too. I have no curfew, but it's understood that I'll be home before twelve thirty.

He fidgets with his fingers. "Um . . . I was wondering . . . what are you doing for the rest of the weekend? Do you want to come to a concert tomorrow night? My dad got me some comp tickets, and I have an extra one. Do you like Robert Crowne?"

Omigod. Omigod. He's asking me out on a date. I seriously think my heart just exploded. Oh, wait. I just forgot to breathe. Must focus. In, out. Out, in. Oh, no, I'm screwing the order up. "O-Okay," I stammer, before I pass out from lack of oxygen.

He smiles that adorable smile. "Why don't I call you around one tomorrow and we'll make a plan?"

I nod, too happy to risk speaking. I write down my number for him while trying to catch my breath, and we go downstairs to find Jewel.

I can't stop the smile from spreading across my face. Having a date feels amazing. Like my back is being tickled, I'm biting into a brownie, and I'm floating all at the same time.

175

I bet this feels even better than having magical powers. I spot Mick picking some girl up off her feet and it doesn't even bother me. From now on all of my energy will be focused on Raf. Sorry, Mick.

I have a date.

MY FIRST EVER QUASI DATE

14

Raf has obviously changed his mind and decided to take someone else to see Robert Crowne.

It's one thirty. He has not called.

"Can we go now?" Miri whines. She's already in her coat and boots, waiting by the door.

"Ten minutes," I say.

"You said that ten minutes ago."

I ignore her and continue wandering around the kitchen, pretending to be busy.

"I know you're pretending to be busy."

I sit down on the tiled kitchen floor. "He said he'd call at one."

Ring!

I leap to pick up the receiver, but all I hear is a dial tone. "Hello?" Weird.

Miri is bent over and howling. "Sorry, I couldn't resist."

"Huh? You did that?"

"Yeah," she says between giggles.

My hopeful expression morphs into an annoyed scowl. "How?"

"I'm not sure. I kind of suggested that you hear the phone ring. Isn't that funny? It didn't even ring."

I wag my finger at her. "Not funny. Don't do that. Why isn't he calling?"

"He's a boy. He's late."

"What do you know about boys?"

"More than you, if you're expecting him to call on time. He'd better hurry up. I'm overheating."

Just then the phone rings. I eye her with suspicion. "Is that you?"

"No, I swear, it isn't."

"Are you forcing him to call?"

"Don't be crazy. What's the big deal, anyway? You said it wasn't even a date. That he got free tickets and has no one else to take."

I grab the phone. Then I drop it and grab it again. "Hello?" I did say that. If he got the tickets for free, then is it more of a friend thing than a date?

"Hi, is Rachel there, please?" It's him! It's him! It's him!

"Speaking."

"Hey, Rachel, it's Raf."

I try to infuse my voice with surprise. "Oh, hi, Raf. How are you?"

"Good. Just making sure we're still on for tonight."

"Definitely." Yes! He doesn't want to cancel!

"Great. It's at eight. Where do you live?"

I tell him my address.

"Hey, you're right on my way. I'll come by and pick you up?"

That is such a date thing to do. A friend doesn't pick a friend up. A friend meets a friend. Like how I met Jewel. "Sure. If you want." I say good-bye and hang up the phone. "I have a date! Kind of. Do you think it's a date?"

"If he's meeting Mom, it's a date."

"He's only meeting Mom because she's on the way," I clarify. Obviously, I don't want him to meet my mom. It will not improve my chances of future kind-of dates.

Miri pushes me out the door. "We can discuss this en route. We have a lot of shopping to do. Did you bring your Hanukkah money?"

"Loooooooong gone. I've bought shoes, jeans, makeup. . . . But I have twenty bucks on me from left-over allowance."

Miri blinks at me. "I have two hundred saved up from my birthday and the holidays."

How did she save two hundred? Oh, right. She borrows my stuff instead of purchasing her own.

As soon as I lock the door behind me, I ask, "So where are we going? Some mystical secret market? Is there a Diagon Alley in New York like in Harry Potter? Will we have to ride the four and a half subway line?"

"You're being crazy again," Miri says. "We're going to the supermarket. And we'd better hurry, because Mom said she'd only be running errands for a few hours."

"The supermarket?" That is so uninspired.

We enter the Food Emporium and push our cart down the aisle. "We should stock up," Miri says, thinking out loud. "So I don't have to keep stealing ingredients from Mom's kitchen."

"What's on your list?"

"Almonds, apples, basil, butter, chamomile, cherries, chile peppers, garlic, ginger, honey, horseradish, lemon, mint, mustard, onions, salt, tomatoes, and yogurt."

Any more food and we'd have a buffet.

"And maybe some mozzarella."

"Why? What spell is that for? Are you going to make us taller?" I start laughing. "Get it? Because it stretches?" Maybe I should be a comedienne.

"Ha-ha." She leans against the wall and almost knocks over a display of cereal that's placed under a giant cardboard strawberry. What is it these days with the dried fruit in cereal? Are we astronauts? Too lazy to cut up our own fruit? "No," Miri says after she catches her balance. "I'm in the mood for pizza. And Mom might be suspicious about why we went to the grocery store. If we make dinner, she won't grill us. Following?"

"Like our offering to make dinner won't be suspicious?"

She casts me an accusatory look. "*You* offering to make dinner would be suspicious, not me."

"You are so very clever," I say, and throw a candy bar into the cart. Yum.

"Don't get that," Miri says. "The manufacturer makes South American children work in sweatshops."

I almost take it out. But really, would one little candy bar make a difference? Bet Mir got that from some conspiracy theory Web site anyway.

"Let's get some bath salts for Mom," Miri says. "Maybe she'll like them. And maybe we'll need them."

I pick up the honey and the almonds. "So tell me, what do these things do? Honey makes you sweet? Almonds make you nuts?"

"All these herbs and foods and, um . . . condiments have magical properties. They send vibrations into the cosmos when combined with my raw will and the spell."

"I have no idea what you just said."

"You know how a smell will make you feel a certain way?"

Like Raf's smell. Yum. "Yeah."

"It's the same thing. The spell, the ingredients, and my power all work together to make what I wish for happen."

"Cool." I push the cart down the frozen food aisle. "But why does it get cold whenever you do magic?"

"I'm not sure. Maybe the energy in the room is being sucked into the spell?"

"Can everyone feel the temperature change? Or maybe just other witches?" I ask hopefully.

181

"Everyone. That's why Mom says it's especially dangerous to do spells in public."

"Oh." We head toward the meat and poultry section. Wait a sec. "You said the spell works with the ingredients and your powers. But you made the lobster move without a single word."

"But I didn't have any control over what I did. These spells allow me to be in control of what I wish for."

I hurry her toward the baking aisle, *away* from the dead animals, just in case. "So what do spices do?"

"Well, chamomile is a calmer. Salt is a cleanser. Garlic is a protector."

"What are we using for the truth spell?"

"It's easy. All we need for that are water, almonds, and a little mint to give it some kick. And there aren't even any crazy fractions to confuse me."

"Kick?"

"Yeah. Mint is an activator."

In the vegetable aisle I peruse the onions. Cipollini, Mayan, red, red pearl, white pearl, yellow, Maui. "Is there a specific type you had in mind?"

She looks mildly afraid. "I don't know. Can't we just get a regular one?"

"What's a regular one?"

She points at a beige one. "That looks like the kind Mom uses."

I toss it into the cart as though it's a basketball. Score! "Hey, any ingredients we can add to make me irresistible tonight?"

She shakes her head over the shopping cart. "Don't

you want him to like you for you, and not because of a spell?"

"You're the one who made him call me."

"No, I did *not*. I would never do that. It wouldn't be right."

Wouldn't be right unless I agreed to set the table for a whole year, I think, but refrain from saying. I wouldn't want her to get mortally insulted and accidentally-on-purpose sabotage my date tonight.

"Besides, you're already irresistible," she adds, making me smile. "I'm just a beginner at all this hocus-pocus, remember? Why risk what you already have?" She pushes the cart toward the condiments.

I plop a container of yogurt into the cart. "I already know Raf likes me for me. He asked me out, didn't he?"

183

Although, before I got into the fashion show, he'd never even talked to me. If Miri hadn't cast that dancing spell, I'd be watching TV tonight with Tammy.

So what? Maybe sometimes love needs to be kick-started. You know, laced with a little mint.

*

"I can't believe you girls made dinner!" my mother exclaims, swallowing another mouthful of pizza. While we were at the grocery store, we also picked up pizza crust, lettuce, and a loaf of French bread. Are we not the best daughters ever? "I might put you two girls in charge of cooking once a week. Who knew? How much did all this cost?"

"Only fifteen dollars," Miri says. The pizza stuff alone came to fourteen. The rest of the bill came closer to fifty. The nonperishables are hidden in Miri's closet, and the fruits are buried behind larger items in the fridge.

"Well, dinner shouldn't be coming out of your allowance." She reaches into her wallet. "Here's a twenty."

Maybe that's how Miri still has so much money. Our mother is lining her pockets. I have to give my sister credit. It was a pretty good idea and the pizza is tasty. Except for the sunflower seeds she for some reason thought would make a good topping. I keep piling them onto my napkin.

"Rachel, Tammy called."

"Oh, yeah?" I'm dying to tell her about my date. She's going to freak. But spilling the boy beans means I have to come clean about Mick's party, and how can I do that without looking like the World's Worst Friend?

I'll deal with it on Monday. I'll call Jewel instead.

"Girls, I'll do the dishes. Rachel, you go get ready for your date." She does a big freakish wink. It's weird; when she winks, her open eye doesn't move at all. Most people's eyes widen, but not my mom's. Creepy. She's pretty excited about this milestone occasion. Ever since I told her, she's been winking and patting my head. Could be worse. She could have said that I couldn't go, or that I was too young to date or something lame like that. I wouldn't have put it past her.

"It's not a date, Mom." Even though he's picking me up and not meeting me somewhere, he never used the word *date*. So my mom can't either.

"Sorry, your quasi date." She gives me another one of her freakish winks. "Do I get to meet this quasi date?"

"Not if I can help it. I know this is my first quasi date, but let's try to keep it low key."

"Does that mean no pictures?" Miri asks, exposing the pizza in her mouth.

"Ha-ha. Video camera only." And then, just in case either of them takes me seriously, I clarify, "No camera."

"Is he paying for the tickets?" Mom asks.

"What difference does it make?"

She scrapes a piece of cheese off her plate with her fork and deposits it in her mouth. "If he's paying, then it's a real date."

"What are you from, the nineteen fifties? Guys don't pay for dates anymore."

"Yes, they do," she says stubbornly.

"I'd hardly qualify you as a dating expert, Mom. Anyway, the tickets are comps, meaning he didn't pay for them. What are you two doing tonight?" I ask, hoping to change the subject. I'm nervous enough without the inquisition.

"Continuing with Miri's training," Mom says, scratching another piece of cheese with her fork. "We're almost done with the history of magic."

Miri's eyes light up like two candles. "So, we're going to start practical magic now?"

Mom quickly shakes her head. "No. Not yet. Next we're learning about consequences and ethics. Don't worry. You'll get to use real magic eventually."

Miri almost chokes on a piece of pizza. If Mom only knew.

"I'm going to get ready," I say, and push back my chair.

My mom makes smooching noises. "Do you think he'll kiss you at the end of this quasi date?"

"Wouldn't you like to know," I say, and run off to shower before they see how red my cheeks are. If I had one wish, it would be for him to kiss me. No, I take that back. If I had one wish, I'd wish for him to ask me to Spring Fling.

I turn on the hot water and step under it. It feels amazing. You get so much more pleasure from a shower when you do it at night rather than first thing in the morning, when you're half-asleep and would rather be in bed. Today I think I'll even shampoo twice, just like the bottle suggests.

I know my evening plans are causing *mucho* excitement around here, but that's because no one has gone on a date in two years. After the divorce Mom went out with a slew of men who she met through work (not that I met any of them—she only dated on the weekends when we were at my dad's, but I saw their names on caller ID), but she didn't like any of them. Eventually, they stopped calling.

The truth is, I think she still has a thing for my dad.

She kept his shirt. It was his comfy sweatshirt, the gray one with the soft worn-in neck and blue pen stain on the sleeve. The one he'd wear when we all hung out and watched TV. That was before he made partner and worked all the time.

I asked my mom if she'd seen it, but she said no. And then, a year later, when I woke up at seven one morning and couldn't fall back asleep, I sneaked into my mother's room to borrow a romance novel and saw her sleeping with it cuddled in her arms. Not wearing it. Just . . . holding it.

I went back to my bed and cried myself to sleep. Being in love with someone, marrying him, having two kids with him, and then being abandoned by him has to be the most tragic thing ever. He started dating STB only six months after he left, before the divorce was even final, but sometimes I wonder if maybe she was in the picture a wee bit earlier than he likes to admit. Like maybe while he was still living here. Maybe that's why he "didn't feel the same." Who knows?

I would have thought my mom would hate him, but she never says one bad word about him. Ever. She just cuddles with his sweatshirt. I'm hoping she's washing it occasionally for hygienic reasons, but it's really none of my business.

By 7:20, I'm all dolled up. I'm wearing my second-best pair of jeans (sucks that I wore my best pair last night) and a green shirt that hopefully accentuates my eyes.

At 7:25, Raf buzzes up.

"Your quasi date is here!" my mother yells from the living room.

"Can you please stop saying that?" I yell back.

Two seconds later he rings the doorbell, and I run to greet him before my mother can. Unfortunately, both my mom and sister instantly appear behind me in the hall. How did they get here so fast? Did they beam themselves over? I'll have to keep a closer eye on those two.

I open the door. Raf smiles. He looks so cute. He's wearing jeans, the same jeans as yesterday, I think—wish I could go put on my yesterday's pair—and his black wool coat.

I love him.

I wish my mother did have her camera with her. I'd blow up the picture and hang it on my wall.

"Hi, Rachel," he says. "Hello, Mrs. Weinstein."

188   I almost laugh at the sound of Mrs. *Weinstein*. No one calls her that.

"Please call me Carol," Mom says. "It's nice to meet you."

"And this is my sister, Miri," I say, motioning to her.

"Nice to meet you," he says.

Super. We're all happy to meet each other. Now, with the boring pleasantries out of the way, maybe I can go on my quasi date. "Be home twelve-ish," I say, and before anyone else can speak, I wave good-bye and close the door behind me. I catch my mom winking at me, and I think Raf does too.

I'm trying telepathically to tell him to hold my hand, but it's not working. His A-list friends Ron, Justin (he's one of the sophomores in the band Illuminated), and Doree (what's she doing here?) are waiting for us outside Irving Plaza.

"Hey, Rachel!" Doree sings, linking her arm through mine. "Isn't this awesome? Justin and I just started going out on Wednesday," she whispers. "I'm so happy Raf asked you. Now we can double." I hope Doree doesn't raise her hand during the concert.

Raf takes out our tickets and hands them to the bouncer, who proceeds to brand us with green we're-underage-so-don't-sell-us-booze bracelets.

We push through the crowd and squeeze as close as possible to the front. Doree's influence, obviously. By the time the band members appear, we're only a few feet back from the stage.

The lights turn off and Robert Crowne's voice yells, "Hello, New York!"

The lights flick on and there he is, Robert Crowne, only a few feet in front of me. Omigod. I can't believe I'm here. At a sold-out concert for Robert Crowne. There's no way I'm dreaming this time—it's way too loud.

The lights are low and a rainbow of primary colors washes over the room. Raf starts singing with the music. Justin plays his imaginary guitar, and Doree, shocker, waves her hands in the air to the music.

I can't help myself. I start to dance. The music, the crowd, the company . . . the gorgeous dark-haired

Robert Crowne on stage. He's wearing black leather pants and a long-sleeve silver shirt (I bet he's boiling) and is moving all over the stage. He looks just as sexy as he does on TV. Everything feels perfect. Who knew having rhythm could be so much fun? I spend the next two songs letting my body connect with the music. And then I remember Raf, and I look up, and he's watching me, and suddenly we're dancing together. No twirls or dips or anything like that, but just moving and flirting and having a blast.

"You're an amazing dancer!" he yells over the sound of the electric guitar.

"Thank you!" I yell back.

"Listen, I was thinking . . . Do you want to go to Spring Fling with me?"

Bull's-eye! "I'd love to," I say, and smile at him. He smiles back at me.

Now, that's a date. And not a quasi date. A 100 percent pure-date date.

GETTING 'TUDE FROM TAMMY

15

"Weren't you at your dad's last weekend?" Tammy asks.

"Uh-huh," I say, pretending to be preoccupied with the contents of my locker.

"So what happened to you this weekend? I called you a gazillion times." She looks genuinely confused. The fact that she doesn't even consider I blew her off makes me feel like a piece of gum on my shoe. (Can someone explain why there are so many pieces of gum on the ground? What reason could one possibly have for spitting his gum onto the sidewalk? Are people so lazy that they can't wait till they reach a garbage can?)

"Sorry. It was just one of those weekends," I say,

desperately racking my brain for something to distract her. Maybe I should pretend slip? Or dump my pencil case onto the floor? Brainstorm! "I have awesome news!"

She leans against her locker and gives me an OK sign. "Yeah? What?"

Operation Distract Tammy successful! Hmm. Now, how do I tell her the good news without mentioning my weekend? I don't want to get into a discussion about Friday since I probably should have invited her, so I'm going to dive right into the awesome part. I motion to her to follow me into the girls' bathroom. I don't want to hyperventilate in front of everyone. When the door swings closed behind us, I gush, "Raf asked me to Spring Fling!"

Since Tammy is well aware of my Raf/Mick obsession, I expect her to jump up and down in delight. Or at least smile.

Instead she shakes her head and looks at me as if I've just told her my mother is a Martian (which truthfully wouldn't be so far off since she's a witch, but whatever). "Are you crazy?" she asks. "You can't go to Spring Fling."

"Why?" What's her problem? I turn the water on, wet my fingers, then run them through my hair.

"Hello? Your dad's wedding is on the same night."

Oops. I forgot about that tiny snag. But still, that doesn't mean Tammy has to thunderstorm all over my parade. Maybe she's jealous that I have a date and she doesn't.

I see her concerned face in the mirror, eyes wide, slight overbite piercing into lower lip, and I realize what an idiot I am. Tammy isn't jealous. She's just stating the obvious. She got an invitation to the wedding, after all.

She doesn't know about Miri's new talent or our secret plan, so of course she thinks I have to go to the wedding. "I guess I was so excited that he asked me, I forgot it was on the same night," I offer as explanation.

"I'm really sorry." She pats me on the shoulder. "Don't be disappointed. I'm sure he'll ask you to the next dance." Her face brightens. "I have an idea. Why don't you ask your dad if you can bring a date?"

Poor clueless Tammy. First of all, there is no way I would make Raf suffer through the wedding, aka the horror show. It's one thing for Tammy to be there as a friend, but a boy I'm trying to get to like me? No chance. And second, and more important, there is *no way whatsoever* that I would allow Raf to see me in that hideous pink-flamingo monstrosity. "Yeah, that's a good idea," I say. As if. The bell rings, and I add, "We should get to homeroom."

We're heading upstairs when I spot Raf charging through the hallway, his coat still on. He perks up when he sees me, and motions for me to hold on. After shoving his stuff into his locker and taking out his books, he walks over to us. "Hey, girls."

"Hey." Sometimes my lack of creativity kills me. Why do I sound like such a robot around boys like Raf?

"Hi, Raf," Tammy says, grinning.

He smiles, and I notice he has a dimple in his left cheek. How adorable! How amazing that I notice some-

193

thing new and spectacular every time I see him. "Hurrying off to win another math competition?" he asks me.

He's teasing me! How adorable is that? "I'm not giving up till I come in first," I say.

He laughs and drums his pen against his notebook. "You tell me who the loser who beat you is, and I'll take care of him." The second bell rings. "Got to get to class. See you later, Rachel."

I exhale. I watch him disappear down the hall (what an adorable butt! It's barely even there!), and then Tammy and I hike the stairs two at a time.

"You two are so cute together," Tammy gushes. "So what's the story? Are you, like, a thing now?"

"I don't think so. We've only been out once." Kind of. And he didn't even kiss me. After the concert, he walked me home (Because it was a date? Because he didn't want me getting kidnapped/followed? Because he was dying to spend those few more precious moments alone with me? Who can say?), and when we reached my front door, I thought, This is it, he's going to kiss me, he's just going to dive into it and why oh why did I not pop the piece of spearmint gum that was sitting in my pocket the whole night into my mouth? Is it supposed to do its job from inside my jacket? And he leaned in . . . and patted me on the shoulder. On the shoulder. Is there something wrong with my lips? I knew they were too small—he keeps missing them entirely. Maybe Spring Fling will be the big night. I'm definitely investing in new lip liner. Anyway, I think it's time to fill Tammy in on Saturday night, which is when he popped the question.

I'll just have to leave out the details that led up to it. "I have so much to fill you in on."

"Seems like it. Do you want to do something after school today?"

What day is today? Oh, yeah. Monday. Since my amazing quasi date with Raf, my mind's been in a haze. "Can't. Sorry. I have rehearsal."

"Oh. Right," she says, and looks down at her shoes.

I feel like a jerk for continuously ditching her. She's never been anything but a good friend. "Why don't we do something on Wednesday?"

She half smiles. "Yeah? No rehearsal?"

"Nope. We have Wednesdays off. London has Pilates. It'll be great. You'll come over. We'll watch a movie. Maybe convince my mom to order Chinese."

"Sounds great," she says, and gives me the okay sign. We find two seats by the left wall in homeroom, and I tell her about my quasi date.

"Did you see what Janice Cooper was wearing today?" Stephy asks after school at practice.

Doree bursts out laughing. "Yeah, stirrups. From, like, the eighties. How funny is that? She's in one of my classes. I swear, just seeing what she'll show up in every day keeps me from falling asleep."

The rest of the girls in the cast laugh. We're sitting on benches in the cafeteria, taking a ten-minute break.

195

We've been working on our all-girls dance for the last hour. My bum muscles are killing me from all the shaking. Jewel and I have an awesome duet where we strut down the catwalk together and then both do the body wave. I love the body wave. I become the body wave.

"Her hair is from the eighties too," Melissa says. "I think she might actually crimp it."

I know they're sounding horrible, but I don't think they mean to. Gossiping is their way of letting off steam. In any case, I'm in too good a mood to let anything upset me. I'm going to Spring Fling! I'm going to Spring Fling!

Kind of. I still have to deal with the annoying little issue of my father's wedding, as Tammy so generously pointed out.

I dig inside my schoolbag to find the candy bar I bought at the supermarket. As my dance-mates continue cutting into every girl who isn't here, I tear open the wrapper. "Anyone want some?" I ask, and take a bite.

They all stare at me, eyes wide, jaws dropped, apparently completely dumbfounded.

Should I have offered them some before I took a bite? It's not a big deal. I can break off a piece from the other end.

"You're going to eat that?" Melissa asks.

Oh, come on, not her, too. "Why? Because of the South American thing?"

They all continue to stare at me. "In less than a month you have to dance in front of the entire school," Melissa says. "Do you know how many calories are in that?"

"Two hundred and seventy-two," Doree pipes up. Suck-up.

"Eleven grams of fat," Melissa adds.

Stephy scoots closer to us. "Thirty grams of carbs."

I'm about to wrap it up and hide it in my bag when Jewel says, "Who cares? If she's hungry, let her eat it."

Thank you, Jewel! I take a second (and a mite smaller) bite.

"Easy for you to say, Jewel," Melissa argues. "Not everyone is born with your body and your metabolism." She eyes my thighs.

I think I've lost my appetite. I stuff the candy bar back into my bag.

London strides into the room and we all scurry off the benches and back to our assigned spots, five freshmen on the right, five sophomores on the left. Today she's wearing green. Why is she entitled to make a fashion statement, but Janice just gets laughed at? Personally, I think Janice looked cool in a retro sort of way, but London reminds me of an M&M. (Or maybe my brain is stuck on chocolate.)

"Ready to finish up, girls?" London asks, and we all nod. Not that we have a choice. London's questions are always orders incognito. "Excellent," she says. "We're almost done. We'll wrap it up on Saturday. Then, on Sunday, I want to hold a full-cast rehearsal. So why don't we meet this Saturday afternoon at two? Just for an hour."

Uh-oh. I raise my hand.

"You don't have to raise your hand, Rachel. This isn't class. I won't give you a detention."

Melissa snickers, and my cheeks heat up. Is it possible they found out about my detention? Is it loserish to get a detention? I thought it would give me a rebel edge. Or maybe they don't even know and I'm making a crisis out of a spelling mistake.

I lower my hand and feel mildly ridiculous. "I can't make practice this weekend. I'll be at my dad's on Long Island."

"That's so cute," London says. "You still do the weekend at your dad's thing?"

Still? I didn't realize it was something you grew out of. "I kind of have to go."

London sighs. "Rachel, the show is in three weeks. And you've only been with us for one. When we accepted you at this late date, I warned you that you would have to devote all your time to the cause, and now you're backing out of your end of the deal. Is that fair, Rachel?"

Why is she talking to me as if I'm seven? All eyes are on me. I have a sinking feeling that maybe Laura Jenkins didn't drop out of the show, that maybe she was booted out. Please tell me that London's not going to freak out. I think I might cry if she freaks out.

"I-I-" W-why am I st-st-stuttering? "I have to be on Long Island."

There's no way Miri will cast the truth spell on STB without me. If I miss this weekend at my dad's, we'll have to wait two more weeks. That'll leave just one week before the wedding. What if the spell doesn't work? Would we have time to concoct something else?

"What if, instead of meeting on Saturday, we meet

on Sunday before the big rehearsal?" I offer. "I'll take a morning train back into the city. That way we all have our Saturday free."

Jewel and some of the sophomores nod.

"I'd prefer to meet on Saturday," Melissa quips.

I'd prefer she shut up.

London considers my proposal. "All right. Maybe I'll spend Saturday talking to the designers. Anyone want to tag along?"

Doree, of course, raises her hand.

Wednesday morning I'm running into school, late as usual, still in my coat, when an all-in-brown London blocks my path. "Today," she barks. "After school. Emergency opening practice."

I seem to remember having some sort of plan for after school. Pizza? Chinese? What was it? "I might have plans today. . . . Isn't it our day off?"

London wrinkles her nose, as if she's tasting something vile, such as mac and cheese with ketchup (Miri does this. Is that really necessary? Does ketchup need to go on everything?), then plants her hands on her hips. "I will not have my opening be a mess. My opening is going to be perfect. Do you understand? Perfect. And Pilates is canceled. You'd think the instructor could have waited until after the fashion show to give birth, wouldn't you?"

Tammy! I have plans with Tammy. "But—"

"No buts, Rachel. If you're going to bail on every practice, then you're not going to be in my show."

Bail on every practice? I'm leaving my dad's early so I can be at practice. Doesn't that count for something? "Okay. Fine."

She nods. "Three o'clock, sharp."

As soon as she slinks away, I run to my locker. Tammy is closing hers. "Hey, Tammy," I say, out of breath, "save me a seat in class, will ya? I'll be there in two secs."

"Don't worry. I'll wait for you." She leans against the locker. "Guess what I rented yesterday? The widescreen edition DVD of *Star Wars*. Fun, huh? And I brought the microwave popcorn that you love. The kind with extra extra extra butter."

My mouth waters. Then I think of that candy bar, and that makes me think of the show. "Tammy, I'm so sorry but London is forcing me to go to rehearsal after school."

Her smile withers like a plant that's been shoved into a closet. "Again?"

I pile the books I need onto the floor and snap my lock closed. "Yeah."

"Can't you not go?"

"Trust me, I tried."

"Whatever," she says, and storms off.

What just happened? I can't believe she did that. This is so not my fault. What am I supposed to do? I can't not go to rehearsal. Why does Tammy have to be such a drama queen?

I pick up my books and hurry to homeroom.

Tammy is sitting by the door, next to Annie, with no saved seat for me.

Humph. I'm about to take a seat by my lonesome when Doree gestures to me from the front row. Well, thank you, Doree. I'd rather sit with her anyway. At least she won't lay on the guilt.

"Hey, sexy," she says. She's tearing out pictures of hairstyles from a magazine. "So is it true? Raf asked you to Spring Fling?"

This is more like it. Fun, girly conversation. "Yup. How'd you know?"

"Justin told me last night on the phone! I can't believe you didn't tell me earlier. Do you guys want to go together? We could rent a limo. Did you buy an outfit yet? I'm trying to decide what to do with my hair. How are you doing your makeup?"

Definitely more like it. "I don't know. You?"

I feel Tammy's eyes on me, but I don't turn around. She can share her extra-extra-extra-buttered popcorn with Annie instead.

STB UNWITTINGLY SWEARS TO TELL THE TRUTH, THE WHOLE TRUTH, AND NOTHING BUT THE TRUTH

16

"So you're leaving Sunday morning?" Miri asks. It's Friday night, and we're lying like two sardines in our shared room on Long Island. Miri wants to talk, but I'm exhausted after a hell week of rehearsals. I had practice every day at lunch and after school. The only number I'm in that still needs work is the freshman dance. Even though Melissa is choreographing it, I'm looking forward to it, because I'll get to dance with Raf again.

I do feel a teensy bit guilty for leaving my dad's early on Sunday, but really, it's my only option. If I don't, I'll get kicked out of the show. I'm already annoyed that I'm missing a huge party at Sean Washington's apartment tonight. *Everyone* is going to be there. Everyone except me. At least this time my absence isn't because I wasn't invited. "Why don't you leave early with me?" I offer.

"Nah," she says, raising her recently Band-Aided fingers to the ceiling so she can stare at them with disgust. "I want to monitor the spell and make sure this is it. I mean *really* it."

Today's pickup from the train was identical to the last one. Once again, STB pulled a Jekyll and Hyde. When Dad jovially took us to the car, STB was syrupy sweet. I told them I had to leave early on Sunday, and she said it was nice that I was involved in school activities. But the second he shut the car door to pick up the Chinese food (after her show-offy "Honey, don't forget my chopsticks!"), she whipped her head around and glared at me. "Did you forget about our fitting appointment on Sunday?"

I withered into my seat.

"Now I'll have to reschedule. Oh well. And Miri, how are your fingers? Any better?"

Miri crossed her arms and shoved her fists under her armpits. Not her most attractive position.

"The wedding is in three weeks," STB reminded us, as if we needed reminding. "Here comes your father. Bet he forgot my chopsticks."

What I don't understand is why she doesn't just buy chopsticks. Then again, there's not much about her that I do understand. I mean, why does she even want to marry my father? She obviously doesn't like his kids.

203

Dad got into the car, deposited the food in STB's lap, and started driving.

"Did you remember my chopsticks?" she asked.

He slammed his hand against his forehead. "Oops. Should I turn around and go back?"

"Oh, don't worry, sweetie. It's not worth it."

What is up with STB's two faces? She's like Frosted Mini-Wheats. Sweet on one side, crusty on the other. "I can't wait to hit her with the truth spell," I say to Miri, who is now making shadow puppets with her bandaged fingers. I close my eyes and flip onto my stomach. "He'll soon see what a horrible woman she is, and that'll be the end of those fake *oh, sweetie*'s! So when do we put our plan into action?"

"In about an hour."

Ping. My eyes spring open. "What? I'm asleep here."

"You're not asleep. You're talking."

"I'm almost asleep."

"The spell needs to be done at midnight," she says. Her eyes are glowing in the dark.

"That abraca-sucks."

"That's what the book says. We have to do it then, or it won't work tomorrow when we give it to STB."

I pull the covers over my head. "Do you really need my help? Didn't you say this one has no complicated fractions?"

Something heavy hits my feet. I think she just threw her pillow at me. "I still need you!" she says. "You're the Cosmic Witness."

Whatever. "I'm taking an hour's nap," I say in my

most annoyed voice, and let my heavy eyelids close. "Wake me when it's time."

The next thing I feel is her shaking me. "It's time."

Groan. "There's no way that was an hour." I watch her open the blinds and move the glass of water she poured earlier to the windowsill.

She pulls the borrowed beaker, a handful of mint leaves, and two almonds from her knapsack, then proceeds to crush the nuts on a paper towel with a spoon. That done, she puts all these ingredients into the beaker, then goes back to the window. "At least it's not cloudy outside. The spell won't work if we can't see the moon." She clears her throat and whispers:

Honesty is clear at the midnight hour.
Let STB—

She slaps her hand against her forehead. "I meant Jennifer. I don't know if I can use an acronym. I'll have to start over."

Double groan.

She scratches her head as though in thought. "But since we call her STB, maybe I should refer to her that way in the spell." One of the Band-Aids comes off in her hair and dangles there, as if a spring has come loose from her brain. "But what if the spell gets confused because we don't call her Jennifer? Why don't I say She Who Drinks the Spell instead?"

"Sounds good," I mumble. Who cares? I want to go back to sleep.

Miri clears her throat again.

"It's clear already!"

She scrunches up her face and purses her lips in con-
centration.

**Honesty is clear at the midnight hour.
Let She Who Drinks the Spell show her
true colors.
This I command as I stand in the
moonlight,
Let her words ring right and true.**

Despite being under the covers, I feel the rush of
cold. She shakes the beaker, plugs it with its stopper, and
lays it on the floor beside her bed.

Was that the spell? That couldn't have been the
spell. "That didn't even rhyme," I say.

"Not all spells have to rhyme."

"I kind of like them better when they do. And that
would have been so easy to rhyme, too. Whoever wrote it
was just being lazy. All you had to do was switch *right* and
true." Raf's poetry skills must be rubbing off on me.

"Yeah, what about *hour* and *colors*?"

I rack my brains for a rhyme, but come up empty.
"Hey, I can't do all the thinking around here."

She gets back into her bed and pushes her hair out of
her face. "Send your comments to the complaint department."

"There's a complaint department? Where is it? In a
cave somewhere?"

"I'm kidding," she says.

"Well, duh," I snap. It ticks me off that she gets to do the fun part while all I get to do is be the Cosmic Witness. Where's the cosmic justice in that?

"*Girls, wake up!*"

What is that noise? Why is there a screaming in my head?

I open my eyes slowly to see STB looming over me. "I've scheduled an emergency fitting for your bridesmaid dresses at eight o'clock."

Eight o'clock? That means it's—I lift my head only high enough to see the bright red numbers on the clock—7:05. 7:05 on a Saturday?

She has got to go.

"It's too early" I hear from Miri's bed. She must be hiding, because all I can see of her is a mass of wavy brown hair.

STB's hair is perfectly straight and slinky, and her makeup is flawless. She probably goes to bed fully made up. "It's the only time Judy could fit us in," she explains. "So be thankful. Now get up. The bus leaves at seven thirty." By *bus* she means her Lexus purchased with my father's money. Maybe Miri should turn her into a real bus driver. As if working for her money would ever occur to her. I can just imagine her in a fluorescent yellow driver's vest.

"And I would appreciate it, Rachel, if you would tidy your side of the room before the departure," she says as she storms out the door.

She wants us to get up, eat breakfast, *and* clean? In twenty-five minutes? "You need to take care of her now," I hiss at Miri. "Just rub it all over her."

Miri sticks her bare feet into her slippers and shakes her head. "She needs to drink it, remember? Don't you pay attention? The spell was for She Who Drinks the Spell."

"Then we need to get it into her coffee," I say.

"When we stop at Starbucks, you'll run in and dump the potion into her cup."

"Why can't you do it?"

"Because I do everything else."

True. "Sounds fair. But why am I offering to get her coffee? She always gets it."

She fingers the Band-Aid on her pinky. "Tell her you want a cup of coffee too. Tell her you've started drinking it."

I take the fastest shower recorded—how many drops can fall in three seconds? And by the time I come out, both my and Miri's beds are perfectly made. I don't know if she did it manually or magically, but either way, I approve. Two pieces of toast and twenty minutes later, we're set to go. As soon as we pile into the car, STB says, "We're making a quick stop at Starbucks." When I tell her I want some too, and offer to run in for her, she looks surprised. She shrugs and hands me a twenty. She's paying for her own downfall! I love it; it's so sneaky. "I want an iced caramel Macchiato with soy milk and half an artificial sweetener," she says.

"Me too!" Prissy hollers from the backseat. "Can I have one too?"

"No, dear," STB says. "Coffee stunts your growth."

I look at my chest. All kinds of growth? I can't really afford to take chances.

I order two of the coffees that STB asked for from a supershort woman with a skunklike white stripe in her black hair. Might as well go with what STB asked for, even though I have no idea what it is.

"What cup size?" Skunk Woman asks.

Tee-hee. She said "cup size." "Small." Unfortunately.

"A tall?"

Maybe she didn't hear me. "No," I say. "A smaaaaaaall."

"A tall is a small."

"That's the most ridiculous thing I've ever heard." Besides, if she knows that small is tall, why even ask?

She sighs. "Do you want coffee or not?"

"Yes, please." The world of coffee is more complicated than I thought.

I pay her, and she tells me to wait at the end of the counter. After I watch a gazillion other people order— "Skim caffe latte!" "Cappuccino!" "Frappuccino!"— mine are finally ready. I gingerly remove the beaker from my purse and pour a smidgen of the potion into STB's cup, then return the rest to my purse. Then I add artificial sweetener to both.

Back in the car, as I'm about to hand her a cup, I'm

paralyzed by my own carelessness. Our two coffees look exactly alike. Which one did I put the potion in?

Miri watches my hesitation and drops her head into her hands in despair. Me blabbing the truth all over town could pose a problem. Must think. I try to remember which hand is holding which coffee. . . .

Hers is the left one. Definitely. I hand her the left one. Uh-oh. I think I made a mistake.

She immediately takes a sip. "They seem to have added mint."

Score! I gave her the right one! When we pull into the dressmaker's parking lot, I mouth to Miri, "How long does it take to work?"

She shrugs.

I continue mouthing. "And how do we turn it off?"

She shrugs again. Then she smiles. "I brought everything we could possibly need to make the antidote in case of a problem," she whispers.

Problem? Us having problems? You don't say.

※

"Thanks for seeing us on such short notice," STB says to Judy. "Rachel apologizes. Miri, you go first. You're always the most difficult."

I hate her. To keep my mouth too busy to tell her off, I take another sip of my yummy drink.

Miri sulks as she goes into the changing room. Maybe I should accidentally spill the coffee on our butt-ugly dresses so we won't have to wear them.

Prissy is on her knees, playing with slivers of past dresses on the floor with one hand and picking her nose with the other.

STB is staring weirdly at the ceiling. Soon Miri, clad in her now completed pink doily, stomps back into the main room. "Wow, Miri," STB says. "You look gorgeous. Like a princess."

I almost drop my coffee. Miri looks up in shock.

"When I was your age," STB says, blinking rapidly, "I always wanted a dress like this. You guys are going to look terrific in the pictures." She sighs. "Rachel, I don't know how you could have forgotten about the fitting. Weren't you looking forward to it? I was. I enjoy the time we get to spend just us girls."

What is she talking about?

Judy looks up. "Are you all right, Ms. Abramson?"

STB nods slowly. "I'm just happy. I'm lucky, you know? To have found love a second time."

"You're lucky, Mommy," Prissy sings. "And I'm going to be a princess!"

We must have given her the wrong spell. The sappy cheeseball spell.

Miri and I nervously eye each other in the mirror, waiting for her to speak again. She doesn't open her mouth until five minutes later, when I have my dress on.

"You look so beautiful too," she says, and sighs.

She's lost it. I do not look beautiful. But I do look a bit like Glinda the Good Witch. I squeeze my eyes tight and silently chant, "Let STB spill her coffee on this dress, let STB spill her coffee on this dress. . . ."

211

Maybe looking like a witch will help me kick-start my powers. Maybe I'll trick the fates into thinking I should be a witch because I'm dressed like one!

STB tosses her now-empty cup into the garbage pail. Guess that didn't work.

While STB helps Prissy change into her dress, I whisper to Miri, "I think you screwed up and made her hallucinate."

Miri looks terrified. "I know. Something's weird. What do we do?"

As they emerge from the dressing room, STB is playing with Prissy's hair. "I love you so much, honey. Do you know how much? More than the stars in the sky. More than a trillion billion stars!"

212

Baby talk? There's definitely been a screwup somewhere. "Maybe we gave her a nice potion?" I mouth to Miri.

Yes, must have been a nice potion. At least that's what I believe until STB calls my dad from her cell when we're finished and back in the car. "We're on our way home from the dressmaker. . . . You're where? At the office? . . . No, I'm not happy with you being at the office. Your children are visiting you and they want to see you. Rachel has to go back early on Sunday, which is another reason why you should be home today. You can go to the office on Monday. And it would be great if you could start preparing brunch." And then she hangs up.

What was that? Miri kicks the back of my seat. I can't believe STB just told my father off. I have never heard her tell my father off. Ever. I turn around and Miri and I share a look. Is it possible the spell just kicked in? My father is finally going to see what a horrible woman she is?

We arrive home to find my father in the kitchen, leaning over a frying pan on the stove. He's never made a meal in his life. I didn't even think he knew what a frying pan looked like, never mind where it was.

"How are my favorite girls?" he asks.

"Fine," we all say simultaneously.

Prissy dances around the kitchen floor in her socks. "I look like a princess in my dress, don't I, Mommy? For the wedding I'm going to wear lipstick and green eye shadow and—"

"What are you making?" I interrupt, putting my arm around my dad's waist.

He flips an egg. "Eggs with smoked salmon."

STB kisses him on the cheek. "And for Miri?"

And for Miri? What? Miri and I both freeze in our tracks beside the kitchen table.

"She can eat this," my father says. "It's not meat."

STB sighs. "Honey, can you please be considerate of other people's needs? You know she doesn't eat fish. Sometimes you can be so selfish. You tend to focus only on what you want, not on what makes others happy. Like yesterday, when I asked you to get me chopsticks and you didn't even bother to remember. We would all be a lot happier if you considered other people's feelings. And dietary preferences."

Um . . . have I been transported to an alternative

universe? Has STB's body been poached by an alien soul?

I'm in shock. My dad, Miri, and even Prissy are in shock. If our jaws had dropped any lower, they would have crashed against the perfectly polished floor. I don't think anyone has ever called my father selfish before. In the entire time he was married to my mother, I don't recall her ever telling him off.

His face contorts into a configuration I have never seen. His mouth gets all squiggly and crooked. He's going to blow a fuse. He's going to freak. There's going to be a screaming match louder than the most deafening rock concert of all time.

He opens his mouth. He closes his mouth. He opens his mouth again. Time has stopped, like in those sci-fi movies with the cool special effects.

"Sorry," he says. "I didn't realize I was being selfish. I'll try harder to be more considerate." He divvies up the eggs and slides them onto plates. "Miri, what can I make you? How about some pancakes?"

Omigod.

Miri looks at me and then at my dad. "Thanks," she responds slowly.

Our spell must be kicking in. STB is saying what she really feels. Any second now, she's going to start ripping into us.

Except for my dad, who's still cooking, we're all sitting at the kitchen table.

This would be a good time, Monster Dearest. Go ahead, do your stuff. Start berating us.

214

She smiles at me.

Time to take this into our own hands. Literally. I kick Miri under the table, and I motion for her to bite her nails.

She nods. Then she picks off the Band-Aids one by one from her fingers and goes to town, as if she hasn't eaten in weeks. She's nibbling, she's chomping, she's picking, she's ripping. It's a virtual nail feast.

STB pats her on the head. "Miri, I can see I'm fighting a losing battle with your fingers, so I'm going to stop bugging you. But I want you to know I'm only trying to get you to stop because I know how tough a habit it is to break. I used to bite too, and I seriously damaged my teeth and nail beds. I also got sick all the time, because the germs on my fingers ended up in my system. The Band-Aids trick worked for me, and I was hoping it would for you. But I guess not."

215

Miri stops picking and looks at me for help.

But I'm as confused as she is. Why isn't STB being mean? Why isn't she hurling insults across the salt and pepper like a volleyball over a net? We need to try something else. What else would she be mean about?

I peruse the room and settle on my dad's striped yellow shirt as he cooks the pancakes. He hasn't changed since returning from the office, and he's wearing one of his most hideous items of clothing.

"Great shirt, Dad," I say. "Don't you like it, Miri?"

"Oh, I love it," she says.

Here it comes. I point to the yellow atrocity. "Jennifer, what do you think?"

"I don't love it," she admits.

Yes!

My dad looks down at his shirt in surprise.

She shrugs. "It makes you look like a banana."

Prissy giggles. "A banana! You look like a banana!"

I try to wipe away a smile with the back of my hand. Too much. What's he going to say to that? He's not just going to stand there and be insulted, is he?

The room is so silent I can hear the sizzling of the pancakes. "Really?" he says finally. "But you've never said anything before. Speaking of bananas, Miri, do you want some in your pancakes?"

"Um . . . sure," she says.

Prissy jiggles in her seat. "Can I have bananas in my eggs?"

"No, honey, bananas don't go with eggs," STB says, and then turns back to my dad. "I know, and I should have. Sometimes you don't have the best taste in clothes."

He's going to blow up. He's going to put down the banana he's cutting for Miri and explode. He shakes his head and . . . laughs. "I thought you liked it. That's why I keep wearing it."

Why is he laughing? She just insulted his wardrobe! He should be freaking out.

She adds some salt to her eggs. "Well, I don't. Sorry."

He turns off the stove. "Are there other articles of clothing of mine you don't like?"

"Definitely." She chews slowly, seemingly taking a mental inventory of his wardrobe. "Your green fluorescent sweater? I wouldn't wear that in public if I were you."

"I wish you would tell me these things. I rely on you to be my mirror for the outside world."

"We'll go through your closet after brunch. Put together all the clothes I don't think suit you and give them to a shelter."

"Thanks, Jen. I appreciate it." And then he leans over the table and kisses her. Yes, kisses her. This is *not* the plan.

When he finally pulls away, STB says, "Why don't we have a fashion show with your stuff, just like Rachel's fashion show? Rachel, you can show your dad how to do the walk!"

Abort plan! Abort plan! Why are they planning horrendously embarrassing family activities instead of yelling and screaming?

"When is the show, Rachel?" my dad asks. "I'm sorry. I forgot the date."

"The Friday night before Spring—before your wedding." Oops. Caught myself just in time there.

"Honey," STB says. "You knew that. That's why we scheduled the rehearsal dinner for Thursday night. I'm very excited to see you in the show, Rachel," she continues. Her eyes are blinking furiously and she fingers her earlobe, as if even she can't believe what she's hearing. "And I'm really proud of you."

Miri drops a forkful of banana pancake.

"And I'm proud of you, too, Miri. Really. The fact that you've dedicated yourself to Tae Kwon Do training shows excellent focus and drive. You're a wonderful role model for Priscilla. You both are. Except for Rachel's slobbiness. I know you girls think I'm tough on you two," she continues, "but it's only because I care about you and want you to learn to be the best people you can."

My father's eyes start to tear, he's so happy.

I'm about to spit out my eggs. "Er . . . thanks. Um, Miri, can I talk to you for a sec?"

She jumps from her chair. "Yeah. I'm done anyway."

I drag her up the stairs by her elbow and close our door. "What did you do? This isn't an honesty spell; it's a nauseating spell!"

"I swear I followed the instructions properly," she says, shaking her head in dismay. "I don't know what's happening."

"It must be the wrong spell. This isn't her being honest. She doesn't think we're role models. She hates us." I narrow my eyes. "And we hate her. It's making Dad like her even more! You have to make an antidote! You have to reverse the spell!"

"I can't reverse it if I don't know what kind of spell it is." Her face clouds over. "There's only one way to find out. One of us has to take it," she says slowly.

"Don't look at me. I'm not taking another potion. What if it counteracts the dancing spell? I have to be in a social situation tomorrow. You take it."

She nods, bites her thumb in contemplation, then pulls it away. "All right. I'll take it." I pull the beaker out of my purse and she downs the rest of the potion. "I think I'm going to puke," she says. "That tasted like garbage."

218

I hear laughter coming from my father and STB's room. "That sweater is so ugly!" STB shrieks. "It's so ugly we couldn't even give it away. We'll have to burn it. Rachel, Miri, come and join us!" she calls. "This would be more fun if you were here!"

What is wrong with her? "In a minute!" I shout back. Apparently, the post-brunch fashion show activity has begun. I lie on my bed, kick my heels up against the wall, and focus on Miri. She's sitting in the center of the room, blinking repeatedly. "Is it working?" I ask.

"I don't know."

"I should start asking you things. Like a lie detector test. Is your name Miri?"

She rolls her eyes. "Yes."

"How are you feeling today?"

"I'm mad at you because you're leaving early tomorrow." As soon as the words are through her lips, she clamps her hand over her mouth. "Oops."

What? "You're mad at me?"

She nods. "I can't believe I just said that."

"You can't be mad at me."

"Why not? You're deserting me to be with your friends. This is our time together. And I think you're being selfish. Yesterday I had to play solitaire in bed so I could stay up until midnight." Her face looks so sad. "Why couldn't you have waited up with me? And then you made me feel guilty for waking you."

My cheeks feel hot. "Mir, I was exhausted. I'm sorry."

"It's not just that. I know you're jealous about this whole witch thing, and I'm sorry about that. I don't

219

know why I have it and you don't, but it's not my fault. And I'm scared. I'm really scared. I'm afraid I'm going to accidentally cause someone to get hit by a car, or maybe start a war. And I don't like doing spells by myself. I made up that thing about needing a Cosmic Witness." She starts to blink repeatedly. "I'm just really scared of this power."

Miri—scared? I do a backward somersault off the bed and lay my head in her lap, resting my ear against her knee. "I'll try to be more supportive, okay? But I have to leave early tomorrow. I don't have a choice. If I'm not at practice, I'll get kicked off. You don't want that to happen, do you?"

She shakes her head and waves her hands in the air, as if she's trying to get someone's attention. "The whole idea of the show is stupid. I know it's how the seniors raise money for prom, but I think it's just an excuse for obnoxious elitism." She clamps her hand over her mouth again, stifling a gasp. "Sorry!"

"I guess the spell is working, huh?"

She nods, mouth still held closed.

"Girls?" STB calls from the hallway. "Are you going to join us?"

I cover the spell book with my feet, and Miri wipes her eyes.

STB opens the door without knocking. "I wish you girls would want to spend time with me. I know you think I'm mean, but I only get mad at you when I think you're doing something wrong. I wish you liked me. Because we're going to be a family. I'm going to be your mother and—"

"We already have a mother," Miri interrupts.

Uh-oh. Two truth-tellers cannot possibly lead to anything good.

STB nods. "I know. Your poor mother. I feel terrible for her." She licks her lips, as though all this honesty is drying them out. "Sometimes I worry that your father will stop loving me, and leave me. He's so wonderful. Smart and generous and loving and full of energy. I'm so crazy about him it terrifies me. Maybe I'm also tough on you two because I want to keep my emotional distance in case he does leave me—"

This is too much. I do not want to hear about STB's deepest fears and insecurities. Especially since I'm trying to make them come true.

Miri nods. "We're hoping that's what's going to—"

"Never happen." I tackle her before she gets us grounded for life.

STB backs out of the room. "Well, come join us when you're finished."

"Are you crazy?" I whisper to Miri.

"I couldn't stop myself. Next I was going to stand up and scream that I'm a witch." She gives me a sheepish smile. "I guess the spell really does work."

"Well, you downed a huge amount."

What does that mean, then? STB likes us? Does she really think we're role models? Did she realize she was acting out of character? Is she looking forward to us being a family? I don't buy it. And I don't care. She's still not good enough for my father.

But something she said is bugging me, like a tag left in the back of my underwear, scratching at my lower back. About being afraid that my dad will stop loving her. Is that why I never get mad at him? Or tell him when his clothes are ugly? Am I afraid that he'll stop loving me too? Like he did Mom? My head hurts from all this truth-telling.

"Antidote," I say. "For both of you. Now."

She starts mixing.

PLAN C

17

"Hi, Bee-Bee," Jewel says, pinching my waist. "How was your weekend?"

"Fine. Yours?" My weekend was not fine at all. What am I going to do? My father is never going to break it off with STB if our plans keep backfiring.

"Crazy. We went to Sean's on Friday."

Groan. "Was it fun?" Perhaps a pipe burst and the apartment had to be evacuated?

"It was the best," Melissa interrupts. "Too bad you couldn't make it. Hope coming today wasn't too much of an inconvenience." She's lying on her back on a cafeteria table, her chin pointed up at the ceiling as though she's tanning.

Excuse me? What is with the attitude?

London shows up twenty minutes late, clad in cherry red. Red sweatpants, red tank top, red running shoes. She looks as if she's bleeding.

We spend the next two hours practicing. And I have to say, I'm pretty good.

"I just can't get that move," Jewel complains, hands on her hips.

"The spin at the end?" I ask, shuffling over to her. "Let me show you."

Melissa butts between us. "I can show her," she says, grinding her teeth.

Why does she look as if she wants to bite my head off? Jewel was my friend first. Really, this chick has some nerve. "What's your problem?"

She points a finger at my face. "You're my problem."

Uh-oh. This is getting a wee bit heavy for me. She's not going to want to fight me, is she? I have no idea how to fight; that's Miri's department. And she's way taller than I am, so I'm pretty sure I'd lose.

The other dancers are staring.

"Liss, you've got to chill," Jewel warns.

Melissa looks as if she's about to yell at all of us, but instead she storms out of the cafeteria.

Jewel shrugs, as if this happens all the time. "I'll go get her." She chases her out of the room.

What was that? "Did I miss something?" I ask the other girls.

Doree shakes her head. "She's such a prima donna. Just ignore her."

"But what did I do?"

"She asked Raf to Spring Fling and was *not* pleased when she heard he'd already asked you."

"Melissa likes Raf?" I ask. That's news to me.

"Yeah," Stephy says. She's sitting on the floor, stretching. "I didn't know until Friday. When she freaked out. She actually puked in the bathroom."

"I heard she might be bulimic," Doree says.

"She's so pathetic," London adds, then waves us closer. "When Laura dropped out, Melissa begged Mercedes to let her be Raf's partner for the formal wear number. She can't stand Gavin. She claims he's a goth freak who steps on her feet." She lowers her voice. "But Mercedes can't stand her and said no." She looks around the room. "Why don't we break for lunch? Everyone's coming in thirty minutes anyway."

Stephy, Doree, and I head back to our lockers. "So that's why Melissa is so rude to me, huh?" I say. "Because of Raf."

"My hair must look like crap," Stephy says, reparting her hair into new pigtails. "What were you saying? Oh right. Liss. I'm sure it doesn't help that Jewel's your new best friend. They used to be inseparable."

My new best friend? Jewel and I were best buds for *ten years* before we even knew Melissa existed. But to these girls I didn't exist before the show. They probably think I transferred to JFK in February. Something occurs to me. "If Mercedes and London don't like Melissa, why is she choreographing the freshman dance?"

"Because of her mom. London thought that if she was nice to her, she'd get to be in a video."

"It ain't going to happen with those thighs," Stephy comments.

"What thighs?" London has no thighs. Are these girls insane?

"They're massive," Doree agrees. "A junior who saw them in the flesh in the Hamptons last summer said they're all cottage cheesy."

"Just because Melissa was the best dancer doesn't mean she knows how to string together a routine," Stephy declares. She snaps an elastic on her pigtail. "So, what do you girls want for lunch? Mixed or low-fat Caesar?"

I'd suggest burgers, but they'd probably faint if I so much as mouthed the word. Calories! Carbs! Grams of fat! But before I can even think about lunch, I need to have something cleared up. "What do you mean, 'was the best dancer'? As in past tense. What happened?"

Stephy snorts. "You did."

I'm known as the best dancer in the cast? Imagine if that goes on my yearbook caption! Best dancer. Awesome. Much, much cooler than math genius. Although together they make me look pretty well-rounded. Perfect for college applications.

I'm starting to feel sorry for Liss. After all, I've stolen her boyfriend, best friend, title, and potential Ivy League position.

My sympathy subsides after lunch when I sense her sending virtual poisonous darts at my head. If Melissa were a witch, I'd be a cat for sure. Not even. Catnip.

The glowering gets worse when the rest of the cast, specifically Raf, shows up. "Hey," he says after giving me a quick kiss on the cheek. "I missed you at Sean's."

He kissed me! He missed me! "I was at my dad's."

He tosses his coat onto a table and unravels his gray wool scarf from around his neck. "You go every second weekend?"

"Yeah."

"Good thing the dance falls on an odd weekend, huh?"

"Yup," I say quickly. Nothing else important happening on that weekend. Nope, nothing at all. Especially not my dad's wedding. Sigh.

I have got to take care of that.

227

When I finally arrive home at seven that night, I discover that the elevator is broken. Again. I trudge up the stairs, and even though I'm exhausted, I am far less out of breath than I was a few weeks ago.

I open the door to find my mother, hands on her hips, glaring at me. "Freeze, young lady."

Uh-oh. The apartment reeks of smoke, so I know I'm in trouble. We must have been found out. Outed from the broom closet. She must have been tidying Miri's room and come across Miri's lists of spells.

"I-I-I think b-before you say anything, you should know—"

"Rachel, I was expecting you hours ago. You have to

let me know where you are." Her cigarette ashes fall onto the floor. Very classy. "I pictured you lying on some subway platform, hurt. I even called Tammy, looking for you."

Yes! We have not been outed. Shows how psychic I am. "Sorry, Mom. I'll try to remember to call." Tammy must have been surprised. We've barely spoken since I had to cancel our after-school get-together. We're not ignoring each other—we say hello and good-bye—but we've been sitting with other people in class.

Mom crouches down to wipe up the spilled ash, then wags her finger at me. "No, you *will* call, or you won't be in the show."

I swallow hard. Too much is riding on the show to not be allowed to be in it now. "If you bought me a cell phone, then you'd be able to call me."

"There is no reason for a fourteen-year-old to have a cell phone. But if you want one so badly, save up."

"There is a reason, if you don't know where I am," I say, and slip off my coat. "I bet Dad would buy me one."

She turns around and marches into the kitchen. "So ask him. Let's talk about something else."

"Maybe I will," I say, following her.

She gives the bubbling pot on the stove a stir. "Miri mentioned that you're taking her to the peace rally this Saturday. That's nice of you. Can you pass me the olive oil?"

Peace rally? Oh, right. I lift myself onto the white counter so I can reach into the cupboard. I hand my mom the bottle. Then I stay seated where I am and swing my feet. I forgot about my sister's bargain.

And to think Miri was giving me grief about ditching her today, when I already generously agreed to take her to this peace rally. Outside. In the cold. That's a pretty sisterly thing to do. Unless I happen to have fashion show practice at that time. Uh-oh. "What time am I going to this peace rally with Miri?" I ask, slightly panicked.

My mom shrugs. "Sometime in the afternoon. I'm going to the office while you're there. We're swamped with summer honeymoon planning. I'm sorry I've been at work so late, but the good news is, we've done some great business. Did I tell you I was nominated as one of *New York Magazine*'s best travel agents?"

"That's cool, Mom," I say, a little distracted. Saturday morning is rehearsal for the freshman dance, the one Melissa is choreographing. And Saturday evening is the all-girl rehearsal. Which means no problem for the peace rally, but no possible time for a date with Raf. I'm hoping he'll be at Mick's on Friday. Apparently Mick's parents are going out of town. Again. And I should see plenty of Raf in the next three weeks, since we have dance rehearsals scheduled every day after school and every lunch period. As well as Saturdays and Sundays. There's no way I'll be able to go to Long Island in two weeks. Miri's going to freak.

Next week we have our designer fittings! I am so excited for my Izzy Simpson dress! And to get my hair and makeup done at Bella Salon in Soho. I guess they're hoping all JFK's wannabe girls will book them for prom. The JFK administration lets us take a half day to prepare for the show. I've never had my makeup done. Maybe I won't wash my face before Spring Fling. Speaking of which, what am I wearing to Spring Fling? And how am I going to pay for it? I can't ask my mother to buy me something when she doesn't know I'm going. Maybe I can borrow the Izzy Simpson dress. I can't wait to wear it onstage in front of the entire school!

"Hello? Rachel?" my mother asks while stirring the pasta. "I seemed to have lost you over there. Everything okay?"

"What?"

She reaches for the strainer and then carries the pot to the sink. "Excited for the big day?"

Am I ever. My fifteen minutes of fame. "I think it'll be a lot of fun. You're coming, right?" I forgot to ask her if she wants any extra tickets. Everyone in the show gets six reserved seats right up front. I promised three to my dad (although I'm hoping STB and Prissy will be history by then), and there will be one for my mom, one for Miri, and I guess one for Tammy if we ever make up.

My mom drops the strainer, and the pasta spills all over the sink. "Am I coming? To your father's wedding? No, honey, I think I'll sit that one out." She picks up the noodles. Her fingers are shaking.

My cheeks feel hot, and it's not from the stove. "I thought you meant the fashion show."

She presses her fists against her stomach and laughs.

Her eyes squint into slivers. "Oh, of course I'm coming to your show. How much are tickets?"

"Ten bucks apiece," I say, staring at my hands. They're my dad's hands. Long fingers, barely-there cuticles, fat thumbs. "All money goes to the senior prom. But you're guaranteed good seats."

Weird how she won't be at the wedding. If there is a wedding, I mean. How do you live with a man for fifteen years, have his children, and then not be invited to the most important day in his life? The second most important day, if you count the day he married you.

"We'll be there," my mom says, shoulders relaxed now that we're no longer talking about the wedding. I'm not dying to discuss it with her either, but if my ex-husband were getting married, I would want to know all the gory details.

Unless the gory details hurt.

I remember when my dad broke the news. It was a Friday night in August. Jewel and I had spent the afternoon in Central Park, working on our tans for the fast-approaching first day of high school (the same tan that I later accidentally exfoliated off with the Dead Sea mud mask). Miri and I took the six o'clock train to Port Washington, and when they picked us up, we went straight to Al Dente, a fancy Italian restaurant.

I didn't notice the rock until halfway through my Caesar salad. STB (we christened her later that night) was wearing a glittering diamond the size of an apple. I nearly choked on an anchovy. I'm not a fan of them on a good day.

I stared in horror. "Is that . . . ?"

My dad squeezed STB's bare shoulder (she was wearing a white silk strapless top with her black pants) and announced, "Jennifer and I have decided to get married."

I almost barfed the croutons across the linen table-cloth.

Miri's eyes filled with tears. My father assumed they were tears of happiness and said, "Look how excited the girls are!" And then his glass of red wine spilled all over STB's top, which thankfully killed the Hallmark moment for them.

Hmm. In retrospect, the wine mishap must have been Miri's subconscious at work, since no one touched his glass. My dad blamed the table's uneven legs. Way to go, Miri!

When we arrived home on Sunday, we found my mother washing her weekend dishes. As Miri opened her mouth, I tried telepathically to tell her, "Don't say anything! Don't tell!" but it didn't work. She said, "Daddy's getting married," and the happy-to-see-us expression vanished from Mom's face. Her cheeks puffed up as if she were blowing a bubble, and she put down the plate she was holding and slowly crumpled onto the kitchen floor. The water in the sink continued running.

"I'm sorry," Miri whispered, shocked at the effect of her words. Then my sister started to cry. I didn't know if it was because of the pain she felt or the pain she had just caused. And then I started to cry. I sat down next to my mom and buried my head in her lap.

232

I felt her fingers running through my hair. I didn't want to look up, didn't want to know if she was crying too. I couldn't bear it. How could he do that? How could he leave us and marry someone else? How could she let that happen?

Then my sister sat down on the floor and told me that everything would be okay. And the two of them braided my hair until I felt calm.

Except for mentioning a few mandatory details ("Sorry, Mom, I won't be spending that weekend with you. It's the you-know-what"), I wasn't planning on ever talking about the wedding.

"Can you get two plates down?" she asks now.

Another wedding conversation safely avoided. Now all we have to do is avoid the wedding.

233

I spend the entire next day at school trying to come up with Plan C. When I get home, after an exhausting day of classes and both lunch and after-school fashion show rehearsals, my mom is reading a romance novel and Miri is grunting and counting in Korean behind her closed door. "*Hana!*" Grunt. "*Tul!*" Grunt. "*Set—*"

I burst in to find her barefoot and snap kicking at her reflection in the mirror. "We have less than three weeks left." I'm panicked. Practically hyperventilating. "Why are you wasting time with anything besides the plan?"

"I have other responsibilities, besides the wedding,"

she says. "Like Tae Kwon Do? Schoolwork? *Net!*" She snap kicks and grunts one last time before sitting down at her desk. "Don't you?"

Who has time for responsibilities during a crisis like this? Although now that I think about it, I have a math midterm on Wednesday. And I'm supposed to finish *Huckleberry Finn* for next Wednesday. Which shouldn't be a problem, because I can normally read a book in a week. I'll start with fifty pages tonight. And I have a French midterm next Thursday and . . . Stop! Must keep my priorities straight! "What are we going to do?"

"We've run out of options," Miri says. And that's when I notice what I never, ever thought I'd see in a billion years. "What is that?" I shriek.

"What?"

"That!" I point to her fingers, which are wrapped in Band-Aids. Willingly. "Have you lost your mind?"

She turns bright red and looks down at her notebook. "I don't want to ruin my nail beds."

I *know* that's not the only reason. Too bad she took the truth-spell antidote and is no longer being honest. "Are you getting soft on me? On her? We have not run out of options. Magic is unlimited!"

"Well, I don't know what else to do," she says, blinking her long eyelashes repeatedly.

That's because she's not even trying. Where is A^2? I spot it beside her bed, on the floor underneath a sleeping Tigger. On the floor! Is this how you treat an authentic spell book? I tilt it sideways so that the fur ball slides off, and I heave it onto her desk. "Look at the book. It's right in front of you." Must think. Wait a sec . . . right in front of you. My heart rate speeds up. "We're missing the obvious."

She flips open the book. "What's the obvious?"

"We need him to stop loving her."

"We already tried that," she says slowly, as if I'm in preschool and she's teaching me the alphabet. "Everything we do makes him like her more."

"Not everything," I say, suddenly giddy and light-headed, as if I'm floating in a sea of helium. "What if he falls in love with someone else?"

Miri flicks through the pages. "With whom? He doesn't know anyone else."

"Yes, he does." I raise my eyebrows, and give her my best *hello?* look.

"Our mother?" Miri says, finally understanding.

"Yes, our mother. We make him fall in love with Mom." We're both silent, savoring the sweetness of the possibility like melting chocolate ice cream in our mouths.

After a few moments, she looks up at me, excitement creeping into her cheeks. "I . . . but . . . emotion spells aren't permanent," she says, her voice creaking. "Especially love spells."

"It doesn't matter," I whisper. "By then, the wedding will be canceled."

Miri shakes her head slowly. "What about Mom? She'll be hurt all over again."

"Don't you see? It won't wear off. If he fell in love

235

with her once, he can do it again. He just needs a shove in the right direction. A push to help him realize that he made the biggest mistake in his life by leaving. This is perfect! Not only will we be saving Dad from marrying STB, we'll be getting him back with Mom. We'll be killing two birds with one stone."

"Dad and Mom back together," Miri says wistfully.

"She's still in love with him," I say. My heart is thumping fast and hard, as if I just ran up a hundred flights of stairs.

Miri nods. "I know. She still has that sweatshirt. You know the ratty gray one? The one he—"

"The sweatshirt," I say. "Perfect! We can use that for the spell! Let's go get it."

"She's reading," Miri says, jumping from her chair and pacing the room. "Here's what we're going to do. I'll distract her when she's making dinner. I'll ask her about the witch trials. She loves talking about that. Do you know that we can trace our roots to Salem? Isn't that cool? Mom says we still have relatives there, and I can't wait to meet them. I didn't even know we had family in Massachusetts. I asked her if that's where Aunt Sasha lives, but she still wouldn't talk about—"

I tap the side of my head. "Focus, Miri, focus. We can take a road trip next year. Right now let's work on Operation Steal Back Dad's Sweatshirt."

She jumps from foot to foot. "Sorry. Okay. You sneak into her room and find the sweatshirt. Then, after dinner, I'll put together the spell—let's hope we have the ingredients in the house—and then we'll slip it under Mom's pillow before she goes to sleep."

"She's going to sleep on the entire sweatshirt? Don't you think she'll notice?"

"Maybe we'll cut off the arm and just use that." She flips through the book until she finds the appropriate love spell. "Let me get a head start on the other ingredients."

At eight, my mom finally gets off her bed and heads to the kitchen, deciding it's time to make us dinner. Maybe I should put on appropriate spy clothes. Just what do spies wear these days, anyway? Maybe I should stop worrying about my clothes and go find the stupid sweatshirt before she's finished in the kitchen.

Her bedroom door is open, and I slither in. Hmm. Now, if I were a sweatshirt that was being hidden by an ex-wife, where would I be? Under the bed? I drop to my knees and lift the bed skirt. No, but she could certainly sweep under there.

Maybe she keeps it with her other sweatshirts. Camouflage. So we won't notice. I open her dresser and search through the drawers. One shelf. Nope. Two. Nope. Three. Nope.

Where is it?

I check in the closet. No Dad's sweatshirt, but plenty of purses, shoes, and old concert T-shirts. Would it kill her to buy some new clothes?

The microwave dings. Uh-oh. Time's running out. Where is it? I rifle through her bra and underwear drawer. She could use an update here. All her lingerie is beige. No wonder she doesn't have a boyfriend. She'll need to invest in some new stuff now that Dad has been exposed to STB's unmentionables, because I've seen them drying around the house, and they're all pink and frilly. At least now I know what to get Mom for her birthday. Is it creepy to get your mother lingerie?

I've checked everywhere and it's gone. Impossible. I search the dresser again. And then the closet. It must be under one of these purses. Why does she have so many purses? And wedge sandals. Does anyone even wear wedges anymore? Where is the stupid sweatshirt?

"Rachel?"

Busted. Mom. Standing at her door. Wondering why I'm in her closet. Why am I in her closet? I try to appear nonchalant by twisting my ponytail around my wrist. "Yes, Mom?"

"What are you doing?"

"I-I-I . . ." Must think fast. Why can I never think fast when I tell myself to think fast? "Looking for shoes. Yeah. I need a lot of shoes for the fashion show. You know, a different pair for every number. So I thought you might have something I could borrow." I hope I didn't already tell her the designers are lending us heels.

She looks confused. "But you wear a six and I'm a seven."

Right-e-o. "I know, but some of these shoes are so old I thought you might have bought them when you were a smaller size."

She shrugs. "All right. But dinner's ready."

That was close. Close, but no cigar. Or sweatshirt.

A few minutes into our plates of revolting peanut tofu, my mom throws down her fork. "What's wrong with you?" she demands. "Stop making faces; it's not that bad. It's a new recipe and it's healthy."

First of all, it is that bad. The lumps of tofu are jiggling on my plate like Jell-O, but that isn't why I'm making faces. I'm attempting to illustrate to Miri that we're having serious sweatshirt-locating issues.

"I wasn't making faces about the food. I was thinking that I *couldn't find* the shoes I wanted. I don't know *where* they are. I'm thinking you must have *thrown it out*." Oops. "I mean, thrown them out," I correct.

"What shoes?" my mom asks.

"Um . . . you know. The silver ones."

"What silver ones?"

Distraction needed! "Mom, um . . . this recipe is delicious."

She beams with pleasure. "See? You have to give new tastes a chance. I'll definitely make it again."

Fantastic-e-o.

When we're finally finished, Miri and I clear together (it's technically her turn again, *finally*, but she set the table for me while I was rummaging in the closet) and my mom goes to her room.

"I can't find it anywhere," I whisper. "I even checked the wash, despite my skepticism that she ever cleaned it."

Miri's head wobbles from side to side. "That's so sad."

"I know. But that's why we're doing this. He's going

to fall madly in love with her again, and she'll be happy."
I dump the leftover tofu into the garbage. Good rid-
dance.

"Right. Except what do we do if the spell wears off?"

"I told you, once he's out of STB's grasp, he'll stay in
love with Mom." Miri's brown eyes widen with doubt,
so I decide to tell her what I've always suspected
but never wanted to admit. Even to myself. "The
Step-Monster was probably responsible for them
breaking up."

"What are you talking about?" Miri asks, rinsing off
a dish.

"Come on, think about it. He claims to have met her
six months after he left Mom. Isn't it possible he met
her . . . um . . . before?"

Miri pales. "You mean he cheated on Mom?" We
both stand still, listening to the sound of the water. And
then Miri rips off each of her Band-Aids. "She has got to
go. If we can't find the sweatshirt, we have to find something else that belongs to him. It can't be a gift he gave.
It has to be something that was his personally. Do you
have anything?"

"His math trophy?"

"I think she'd notice a metal statue under her pillow," Miri says.

If she didn't look so forlorn—probably because of
what I told her about Dad's quasi or otherwise affair—I
might laugh. "So what do we do?" I ask, filling the
baking tray with soap to let it soak. "Wait until next
weekend?"

She sighs. "I guess so. Although that only leaves one week for him to call off the wedding. What do you think?"

I blow a soap bubble over her head. "We have no choice."

So much for unlimited options.

WHY GAMBLING DOES NOT PAY

18

"One more time!" London screams at us.

It's Tuesday and I'm sweating through an all-cast after-school practice for the opening. Since the freshman girls are up first, London has already made us repeat our part twenty times.

The music starts again and we go through the motions. It's really not that hard. All five of us will be spread across the stage, and when the *Chicago* medley starts, five spotlights will shine on us as if we're nightclub singers. Then we do a twenty-second choreographed dance, and the rest of the cast rushes on.

"You're not in sync!" London shrieks. She starts the

music again. I feel as if I'm a scratched CD that keeps playing the same line.

After we finally get it right, Jewel and I go to Soho to scout for my Spring Fling outfit, and I find the perfect dark green dress.

"You look hot," Jewel says, circling me in the changing room. "You should wear your hair up."

Jewel has always liked my hair up. For our middle school Valentine's dance she helped me put it into a French twist. And one Halloween she spent an hour making me two perfect Princess Leia buns, or cinnamon buns, as Prissy called them.

"Let me see what it would look like," she says, untangling the chopsticks from her hair. Her curls spring over her shoulders, and without even thinking, I pull one so it uncoils and then bounces back, and she laughs.

243

She twirls my hair until it perfectly tops my head, and strategically places two long strands onto my forehead. "We'll style those with my curling iron."

We smile at each other in the full-length mirror. "Thanks, Jewel."

I'm going to look perfect. Thank God Miri lent me her last eighty dollars to buy a dress, which I promised, promised, promised to pay back out of my allowance. Eventually.

After shopping, Jewel and I go back to her place to study for math. "Rachel, honey, what a surprise!" Mrs. Sanchez says when Jewel asks her if I can stay for dinner. "We missed you," she adds, and I almost hug her. I missed her too.

✳

It's lunchtime on Wednesday, and I rush to the drama room, where the freshman dancers are meeting. I open the door to find Raf by his sexy self, lying across the carpet, a textbook under his head.

"Hi," I say, and sprawl down beside him. Yes! Alone time with Raf! Maybe he'll take this opportunity to kiss me! Or to ask me out for Saturday night. Our quasi date was *two weeks* ago. Doesn't he want to go out again before Spring Fling? Does he like me or not? Did he just ask me to Spring Fling because I'm a good dancer? This whole dating/quasi-dating thing is turning me into a chronic question-asker.

Omigod, I'm turning into Prissy!

"Hi," he says. "What's up?" He runs his fingers through his dark hair and I wonder what it feels like. Smooth? Soft? Silky? Maybe like cashmere? Not that I've ever worn cashmere. Or know what it feels like. Would I even be able to feel the difference between it and cotton in a Pepsi/Coke–style test? I imagine myself blindfolded, hands out, palms caressing the different materials.

"My parents want me to go to New Orleans with them during spring break," Raf announces, shattering my daydream.

Oh, no. He's backing out of Spring Fling! He's going to leave early, and then my dad's wedding will be canceled, and after all the scheming, I'll be at home on April 3 watching *Star Wars*. Again. "Oh?"

"My brothers don't want to go, but I told my parents I'm game as long as they fly down on Sunday after the dance."

How sweet is he? Not only does he still want to go to the Fling with me, but he's a good son. He's like chocolate mixed with cotton candy mixed with Kool-Aid. If I weren't so in love, I would get a cavity.

Jewel walks into the room, smiling when she sees us together. "Hey, lovebirds. Bee-Bee, how'd you do on the math test?"

"Okay," I say, trying to sound nonchalant. I definitely aced it. I finished in twenty minutes and spent the rest of class studying for next week's French test and writing in my notebook *Je m'ennuie.* "You?"

"Pretty good," she says, still smiling. "Thanks for helping me study."

I figured she had done okay. During the test, she was scribbling furiously, wrapping her curls around her thumb like she always does when she's thinking hard. She wasn't eating the back of her eraser, which is what she does when she's upset.

I wonder how Tammy did. I'd ask her. If we were talking.

The rest of the freshmen trickle in. Finally Melissa storms into the room, carrying two plastic chairs. "Everyone up. The moronic JFK administration wouldn't approve my stripper choreography, but they said I could do a gambling theme. So we'll be using chairs in the dance to give the number an edge."

Chairs? What is she talking about? I don't want to dance with furniture.

"Eight of us," she continues, dropping our plastic dancing partners into the center of the room, "Jewel, Sean, Raf, Doree, Stephy, Jon, Nick, and I will be the main dancers. We'll be gamblers at a poker table on the catwalk. Rachel and Gavin, you two will be dressed as casino dealers and will remain at the sides of the stage and *off* the catwalk."

Quelle surprise. At least she didn't relegate us to behind the curtain.

Free lunch! Free lunch!

It's Friday and this is the first lunch all week that I don't have dance practice during! It's my first real chance to sit at the A-list table. I search for Jewel in the caf. Where is she? I don't see Doree, either. Or Stephy. Where are they? I don't see Raf, but he normally leaves for lunch. Come to think of it, I haven't seen him all day.

Did everyone go out for lunch without me? I feel sick to my stomach, and I haven't even eaten yet, so I know it's not food poisoning. Maybe they don't like me after all. I buy a grilled cheese and fries from the lunch ladies and then look for someone, anyone, to sit with. I spot Tammy at my old table, fourth from the back, eating with Janice, Annie, and Sherry. Oh, well.

I carry my tray to their table and sit next to Tammy. "Hi, girls." I take a bite of my sandwich to make sitting here feel less weird.

Tammy squints at me. "Excuse me? Do I know you?"

"Do you want me to sit somewhere else?" I spit out, along with small crust remnants.

She stares at me for a long second and then pushes her hands down, her scuba way of telling me to relax. "I'm kidding. It's just that I never see you anymore. Of course you can sit with us."

Oops. I kind of overreacted there.

Sherry is giving me a strange wide-eyed smile from across the table. She pulls a sopping wet strand of hair from her mouth. "Hi, Rachel. Love-ee your sweater."

My sweater? I'm wearing the green one I bought at Macy's and have worn a million times. Is she kidding?

Annie is also smiling at me weirdly, and I squirm in my seat. What's wrong with everyone?

Janice stares at me, her face all serious. "How is the fashion show?" she asks. She's wearing faded jean overalls. "We're looking forward to cheering for you."

Ah. The fashion show. I'm a celebrity returning to her hometown. I give the group my most benevolent smile. "Hard work," I say.

"What's London Zeal like?" Annie asks, leaning toward me, squishing her supersized breasts together and giving the boys at the next table an eyeful.

"She's a riot," I say with a wave of my hand.

"Is it true you're going to Spring Fling with Raf?" Sherry asks.

"Yup," I say, then notice the confusion on Tammy's face. "I think so. I had another event that night, but it's off now."

Tammy's eyes bulge. "What? The wedding is off?"

I give her my best this-is-hard-for-me-can-we-talk-about-it-later? look. She nods, eyes still bulging. When the bell rings and my groupies disperse, Tammy pats me on the back. "What happened?"

"I'm not supposed to discuss it," I say softly, lifting my legs onto the bench and hugging them into my chest. Probably bad luck to talk about the canceled wedding before it's actually canceled, huh? Kind of like letting the groom see the wedding dress before the ceremony. In a twisted sort of way.

"I honestly understand. Nobody knows family politics better than I do. But if you need to talk, I'm a hundred percent here for you. I remember how screwed up I felt when my mother married my stepmother."

My heart melts. Tammy is so nice. I've treated her horribly since I got into the fashion show. I should have Miri whip her up a happiness potion.

She smiles shyly. "So does that mean I can tell Aaron I can go to the dance with him? I told him I couldn't because of the wedding."

Omigod! "What? He asked you to Spring Fling?"

She pulls the elastic from her hair, fluffs the light brown strands, and lets them sit on her shoulders. I like when she wears her hair down. It makes her face look softer. "Yup, he finally asked me."

"Why didn't you tell me?"

"He asked me last week and we weren't exactly talking." Her dark eyes cloud over. "Look, I'm sorry for not being more understanding about your work schedule. I know it's tough, and I should be more supportive about something that's so important to you."

She is so cool. If there were an award for the world's greatest friend, she would so win. She's apologizing for my not making enough time for her. And she said no to Aaron even though she's dying to go to the dance as much as I am. She would rather hang out with me at my dad's lame-o wedding. She honestly deserves a medal. Maybe I'll have Miri whip up one of those, too.

"Thanks, Tammy," I say, overflowing with gratitude. Then I add, "And I should make more time for my friends." With that, we link arms and head to our lockers.

On the stairs we run smack into an all-in-white London. She shakes her fist at me and screams, "Where were you?" at the top of her lungs.

Whoa. I slide backward in fear. "Where was I when?"

"Hello? At lunch? We had a meeting today. I took off class so I could meet with all the freshmen and soph-omores to see the formal."

What is she talking about? "I thought we were sup-posed to practice the formal dance on Sunday."

"I changed my mind last night. I phoned Melissa and she said she would call the rest of you. She told me she spoke to you."

What a witch. And I mean that in a positively neg-ative way. Melissa purposefully didn't tell me about the rehearsal so I'd look bad. Or maybe she didn't want me dancing with Raf. She makes me want to puke. Maybe her bulimia is contagious. "I'm sorry," I say. "But Melissa never told me."

"Whatever. It's too late now. But you'd better not miss any more rehearsals or you're out of the show. I don't care how good you are," she growls before stomping off.

I lean against the wall, shell-shocked.

"Don't worry about it," Tammy says, patting me on the back. "They can't kick you out now. The show's in two weeks. And you're too good." She tries to make me feel better all the way to our lockers, but I'm too busy steaming to pay attention. I hate Melissa. If only I were the witch instead of Miri. I'd put a hex on her for sure. Turn her into a mouse. No, too cute. A rat. Or a frog. Or a tuna fish that I can mash up and feed to Tigger.

"What are you doing tonight?" Tammy asks as she spins her lock combination.

Should I invite Tammy to come with me to Mick's? He's having another party. I probably should. But then I'll have to hang out with her, and I would rather spend the evening flirting with Raf than, sorry, babysitting Tammy. I open my locker and pull out my books. "I don't know. I'm usually really tired after rehearsal. I'll probably just crash."

"I understand. Call me if you want to hang out. I could just come by. We don't have to do anything crazy."

"Why don't we see how the day goes? Oh hey, wait a sec." I hand her one of the fashion show tickets. "I don't know if you want to sit with my family, but I got six awesome seats."

"Thank you!" she says, and gives me the okay sign.

I charged my family for the tickets, I had to—London was very clear that we were responsible for the cost. I'm not made of money. But I owe Tammy.

After school, I head to the cafeteria for the all-girls dance rehearsal and make a beeline for Melissa. She's in her pretend tanning position. But this time she's wearing sunglasses.

We're inside. There's no sun.

I loom over her, so that if there *were* sun, I'd be blocking it. "Thanks a lot for telling me about the lunch practice."

She lifts her shades and bats her eyelashes. "Didn't I?"

Of course her eyes are blue. Why aren't my eyes blue? It's so unfair. She gets red hair and blue eyes. "No, you didn't. I missed it and got told off by London."

"That's too bad." She flicks her sunglasses back down.

Loathing overwhelms me like nausea. Maybe this intense emotion is enough to spark my long-overdue powers. I close my eyes, purse my lips, and focus.

> Next time this chick
> Is on her way back from class,
> Give her a push . . . no . . . a
> kick, yeah, a kick,
> And make her fall on her—

Jewel pinches my waist before I can finish the thought. Hey, that was pretty good. If this witch thing doesn't work out, I can always become a poet.

※

I'm sitting with Jewel, Melissa, Doree, and Stephy on the living room couch at Mick's, and Melissa is making fun of all the people who were not lucky enough to be invited.

"Oh, shut up," Jewel says, and rolls her eyes. "Not everyone can be as fabulous as you, Melissa."

"As fabulous as us," Stephy says, giggling.

That's me. Fabulous. Part of the fabulous group. Fabulous and miserable. Miserable because Raf isn't here. I'm wearing my good jeans and a great silver V-neck top I borrowed from Jewel. And I spent twenty minutes doing my eyeliner.

And then I got here and ran straight into Will, who told me that Raf is sick at home with a fever.

I should bring him chicken soup. Does it count if it's instant?

Melissa kicks the marble coffee table. "Did you guys see what Janice Cooper was wearing today?"

Stephy cracks up. "Yes! Overalls. What, is she a farmer?"

And that's when the worst thing in the world happens.

Before I left the apartment, I gave Miri two

instructions. One, if Raf calls, tell him I'll be at Mick's and I'll see him there. Two, if Tammy calls, tell her I was really tired and went to sleep.

So here I am, cross-legged next to Jewel on the couch, when Jeffrey Stars walks into the living room. Followed by Aaron Jacobs. Followed by . . . Tammy.

What is she doing here?

Her mouth drops open when she sees me. And then she just stares.

"Hi," I choke out. I want to sink into the couch pillows. I want to disappear. I really wish I had that invisibility cloak. Maybe she didn't call my house. Maybe I can tell her I called her, and her moms told me she was here.

"I just spoke to your sister," she says. Her top teeth grind into her bottom teeth. "I guess you woke up."

"Yeah," I say, and slump deeper into the couch. I played Russian roulette and lost.

She turns to Aaron. "I want to go home." Aaron puts his arm around her, and without looking back, the two of them leave.

I should chase her. But what would I say? I didn't want to babysit you? I wanted to hang out with Raf? With Jewel?

The girls beside me immediately crack up. "What was that?" Melissa shrieks.

"Are they a couple?" Doree asks.

"Shnoz and Acne?" Melissa says, then laughs.

My mouth drops open. "Why do you call them that?" I ask.

Doree giggles. "Because yesterday he had the biggest zit ever. And she has the biggest shnoz. But I shouldn't say that," she tells the others. "Rachel used to be friends with her."

Doree, Melissa, and Stephy laugh even louder.

I stare at the carpet. *Used to be friends with her.* But now I've traded her in. For the *fabulous* company beside me.

Jewel pats me on the back and gives me a quarter smile.

I wonder if just a few months ago Doree said something demeaning about me and then added, "But I shouldn't say that. Jewel used to be friends with her."

And Jewel just sat there, staring at the carpet.

I'm eating a quick breakfast before Saturday's rehearsal when Miri runs into the kitchen, wearing a T-shirt and underpants. "You'll be back at one, right?"

"Yes, Mir, I'll be back at one. For the rally. I haven't forgotten."

Her smile lights up her face. "Awesome! I'm so excited. I'm going to spend the rest of the day training with mom and then practicing my high roundhouse kick." She squats and lifts her fists to her hips, in the ready position. "I can't seem to nail it. It's much weaker than my snap kick. It's probably because—"

"Do you have everything you need for Dad's love

spell next weekend?" If I wanted a Tae Kwon Do lesson, I'd sign up. And I'm beginning to wonder what exactly takes place during these mysterious training sessions. If I didn't have, oh, ten million things occupying my thoughts, I'd ask.

"Almost," she says, and whips out a list from her shirt pocket. "I need to pick up some yogurt. The one we bought last time is past its expiration date. Oh, did I tell you that Tammy called last night? I told her you were sleeping, like you said. She left you a message."

I swallow my cereal along with the lump in my throat. "What did she say?"

"That Jeffrey invited Aaron to a party, and Aaron invited her. They wanted you to go with them. And if you woke up, to call her cell."

Tammy definitely gets the greatest-friend award. And I get a kick in the butt.

255

The day gets worse. Melissa is in charge at rehearsal, which makes it particularly painful, and Raf is home sick.

At least I have Jewel.

"Melissa, how much longer are we going to be?" I ask.

She stops the music and positions her hands on her hips. "Why? Do you have something else to do that's more important? I'm sure London would love to know what it is."

I can't believe she's threatening me. We were only supposed to be here until noon, and it's already half past. "Whatever." I'm out of here in ten minutes, no matter what.

"You sure? I don't mind if you go. London told me to tell her if you gave me any attitude."

Why does she even need me here? I don't have to do anything but stand and look interested. I'm about to tell her where to get off when Raf hunches through the doorway.

Melissa gestures to all of us to stay put. "How are you feeling?" she gushes.

"Okay," he says. "I'm still tired, so I'm just going to watch instead of dance." He looks pale, as if someone rubbed chalk on his cheeks.

An *aw!* goes through the room. Melissa massages his back. No way am I leaving now, when she's trying to fondle my quasi boyfriend.

"I'll be right back," I mutter. Not that anyone can hear me from my exile in the corner of the room. I call my sister from the pay phone by the bathroom.

"Where are you? I want to go already," she squeals into the phone. "I am so excited. I'm wearing tights under my jeans so I can stay warm."

I take a deep breath. "Mir, I'm really sorry, but there's no way I'm getting out of here anytime soon."

"Oh." Silence. "But you promised."

"I know I promised, but I can't leave. Melissa is being horrible and the show's in two weeks."

"But the peace rally is today."

256

"Miri, I can't. Ask Mom to take you."

The next thing I hear is a dial tone. Did she . . . Did my little sister hang up on me? I don't believe it. She's never hung up on me. She's never hung up on anyone.

I slip back into my spot in Siberia.

"So nice of you to join us again," Melissa yells over the music, then returns her hand to Raf's forehead. "You don't feel too warm," she coos.

What a miserable week. My sister and Tammy hate me, and my rival is flirting with my quasi boyfriend. Can't something good happen?

My body starts to tingle. I look up. Raf is watching me. I give him my best aren't-I-cute smile, and he winks. My skin feels warm, as if I'm being kissed by the sun.

This will all pay off in two weeks. When I'm at Spring Fling with Raf. When I won't need the sun to feel like I'm being kissed.

It's all worth it.

Isn't it?

THE ENCHANTED PARENT TRAP

19

The next week passes in a blur of rehearsals, midterms, and assignments.

Monday: Rehearse at lunch, rehearse after school. Go to Soho and get fitted for Izzy Simpson dress. Woohoo! Come home, still getting silent treatment from Miri about missing peace rally. Trail her around apartment, tail between my legs, until she finally breaks down and forgives me. Realize I've forgotten all about Huck Finn. Plan on reading a hundred pages. Fall asleep after five.

Tuesday: Rehearse at lunch, rehearse after class. Go back to Soho for second designer fitting. On way home from practice, realize impossibility of reading an entire book in one night. Do something always promised self would never, ever do. Stop at bookstore and buy Cliff's Notes.

Wednesday: Rehearse at lunch. English class. Oddly, instead of getting nailed by Ms. Martel for reading Cliff's Notes instead of real book, know all answers and come across as Huck Finn genius. Apparently, Ms. Martel gets questions from teaching guide at back of Cliff's Notes. Would call her lazy, but that would be like pot calling kettle black. (No idea what that means. Why would a pot call a kettle black? Who has a black kettle? Have never seen black kettle.) Rehearse again after school. Return to Soho for third designer fitting. Feet begin to ache.

Thursday: Mortified by Hayward when she holds up perfect score in front of whole class. Jewel gets A-, which she's pretty excited about. No idea what Tammy gets, since we're no longer friends. Rehearse at lunch. Write French midterm. Rehearse after school. Back to Soho. Feet begin to swell.

Friday: Rehearse at lunch. Rehearse after school. Back to Soho for final fitting. Feet now feel as if they've been set on fire whenever pressure is applied. Get home in time to argue with sister about reasons for not accompanying her to Long Island. Reminded by sister that STB will be mental case with wedding so close, and that twenty-nine wedding updates have been sent to guests in past week. (In-boxes have twice been clogged with massive JPEGs.) More begging follows. Notice sister's pursed lips and sudden waft of cold air, and warn sibling that if she jinxes the show in any way, she will find herself in serious hot water! Lips unpurse and room warms up. Review plan to steal father's belongings, and send sibling on way. Will miss father this weekend, but happy ending is in store.

Saturday: All-day rehearsal. Feet in severe pain. Might have to amputate.

✴

By the time I stumble home from *another* all-day rehearsal on Sunday, I feel like a cavewoman, barely able to stand upright.

"Did you get something of Dad's?" I ask, poking my head into Miri's room. She'd better have. The wedding is in six days.

Six days!

She's writing at her desk and doesn't look up. "Yup."

"What did you take?"

"A sock," she says, still not looking up. I know she's mad at me because I deserted her this weekend, but there was nothing I could do. It's now eight thirty Sunday night, and she arrived home even earlier than I did.

Why is she being so annoying? Hello, Miri, look up! I plop myself onto her bed and lean my feet against the wall. "A dirty sock or a clean sock?"

"Clean."

"Good. Because I've smelled Dad's dirty socks, and I doubt Mom would be able to sleep on one." At least that's one trait from my parents I didn't inherit. Smelly feet. I think. I bend my leg toward my nose. Smells fine. "What other ingredients do you need?"

She keeps writing. "Don't worry, I took care of it."

"You took care of all the ingredients?"

"Yeah. All done. And the spell. And the fractions. The sock is already under Mom's pillow."

Oh. Well. "All righty then. You're very efficient."

She continues writing, fully ignoring me. How long can a person hold a grudge?

Monday night we're in the middle of yet another revolting vegetarian dinner (sloppy joes made with spinach, mushrooms, cabbage, and some unidentifiable beige vegetable) when someone buzzes from downstairs.

"Are you expecting anyone?" Mom asks, putting down her fork.

We both shake our heads. Raf coming to proclaim his love? I skip over to the intercom. "Who is it?"

"It's Dad!" Dad? Omigod. Dad! It worked! He's here! "Come on up!" I scream into the intercom. I know screaming is annoying for the person listening, but I'm too excited to think clearly.

My mom takes a long sip of her water. "Is that your father?"

"Why, yes," I say, trying to act all cool and casual,

261

which is mighty difficult. Miri jumps up from the table and starts tidying the kitchen.

"Why is he here?" my mom asks, then flattens down her hair. Bet now she wishes she paid more attention to those roots, huh? "Did you girls get into any kind of trouble? Something happen I should know about?"

"No," Miri and I say simultaneously.

Knock, knock. I leap toward the door. "Hi, Dad!" I sing, and then try not to gasp at the sight of him.

His shirt isn't tucked in, the few hairs he has left on his head are standing up and pointing in different directions, and he has thick bags under his eyes. "Hi, Rachel. I...uh...found a book Miri left at the house. I thought she might need it." He thrusts the book at me. "Can I come in?"

"Sure." I step aside to let him pass.

My mom, still fidgeting with her hair, joins us in the hallway. "Hi, Daniel. Nice to see you. Everything all right?"

His eyes light up like two headlights when he sees her. "Hi," he says softly. I don't believe it. He's looking at her as if he's Romeo and she's Juliet. He's in love with her again! Hallelujah! Cupid's arrow has landed!

"Miri forgot a book and I thought she might need it," he rushes to explain.

"Yes, she did. Look!" I hold up the hardcover like a trophy. It's my science textbook from last year, but who's counting? "So, Dad, would you like some tea? Mom was just going to make a pot."

My mother stares at me as if I've lost it. "I was?"

She'd better not blow this. "Why don't you two sit down and catch up, and I'll boil the water," I say. I fill up and plug in our white kettle.

My father accepts the invite and sits down next to Miri at his old chair at the table. My mom has that baffled, I-just-woke-up look on her face, but sits across from him anyway. I wipe off the glob of sloppy joe that's smeared across the Formica counter and clear the dinner plates.

"Look how helpful they are," Dad says to Mom. "What's gotten into them?"

She twirls her hair between her fingers. "Miri has always been helpful, but Rachel is a whole new girl these days. She's even in great shape. That fashion show is doing wonders for her. She actually took the stairs yesterday without complaining."

That's not true. I complained, just not out loud.

My father snorts. "This is the same girl I had to carry on my shoulders in the Diabetes Walkathon?"

They both laugh. Normally, I would get mad at him for bringing it up (I got tired and bored ten minutes into the walk and forced him to carry me the rest of the way), but not this time. The kettle whistles and I place their teas in front of them, saying, "I have a lot of homework to do, so I'll be in my room if needed."

"Me too," Miri adds, and we both burst out of the kitchen, high-fiving all the way to our rooms.

By eleven, I'm in bed, and I can still hear their voices. Hers, girlish and giggling; his, happy and relaxed. Miri opens my door and tiptoes inside. "He's still here," she

263

whispers, beaming. The laughter from the kitchen wafts through the walls.

"I know. I just said good-night." Seeing them together, sitting at the kitchen table like they used to do in the old days, gave me a surge of warm happiness. Like it's cold outside, but I'm sitting on a cozy couch, wrapped in a woolly blanket, facing a roaring fire.

The next morning, my mom is sipping her coffee, a half smile on her face.

"What time did Dad leave?" Miri asks, chomping her oatmeal as if she's been fasting for weeks. I pour myself some Cheerios.

"Around one," she says. "It was nice. And weird. We haven't talked—you know, *talked*—in a long time. But I don't understand what's going on with him. Has he been fighting with Jennifer?"

Miri and I get very interested in our cereals.

My mom goes back to sipping her coffee.

STB must have freaked if he came home at two in the morning. Maybe he didn't go home. Maybe the wedding's already been called off. "What did he say?" I ask. That he's in love with you? That he has dumped/is about to dump STB and is moving back home?

"We just talked. About you two. About life. And how it . . . creeps up on you."

Yes! Awesome! Woo-hoo to the power of a billion!

Abracadabra fantastica! Welcome back, Dad! And Spring Fling, here I come!

＊

Good things happen in threes.

First, with the help of my new best friend, A^2, I've managed to reach the Holy Grail of divorced kids and get my parents back together.

Second, Raf has been a sweetheart all day. He dropped by my locker to say hello not once but *twice* and sat next to me during lunch rehearsal.

"Justin wants to know if we want to split a limo so we can all go to the dance together on Saturday," he says.

Is showing up to the dance in a chariot with my prince charming okay? Duh, yeah.

Third, after school we picked up our designer outfits. At the Izzy Simpson boutique, I was handed a gorgeous red embroidered silk tea-length dress and adorable wooden three-inch heels with red bows, which I seem to have no problem dancing in. Jewel's outfit is similar, but her dress is green and flows all the way to the floor. It's a little long for my taste (I like my calves), but she's happy.

I'm going to look so glam! I wonder who will bring me flowers. After the closing number, we all stay onstage and the MC (Will Kosravi) calls all our names in alphabetical order, and we walk down the catwalk to accept our bouquets. I'll have to remind my mom to make sure to buy me one.

The only damper on my great day was Tammy. She fully ignored me. She didn't acknowledge me when I walked late into class, or even when I passed by her locker.

I tried to apologize. "Tammy," I said, blocking her in the hallway. "Can we talk?"

"No," she muttered, and walked away. And the hand gesture she gave me is just too rude to even discuss. Unbelievable. She'd better not be planning on using that fashion show ticket. With attitude like that, she can cough up the ten bucks and sit in the back.

I get home from rehearsal, expecting to hear news of the canceled wedding.

"No news," Miri says. She's lying on her bed, legs up, reading.

But Spring Fling is in four days! I plop down beside her. "Maybe I should call him."

"Don't, Rachel," Miri warns, shaking her head. "He's probably confused right now, but he'll do the right thing. He won't marry one woman when he's in love with another, especially when the object of his affection is the mother of his children. He'll call us by tomorrow for sure."

"He'd better. It must take at least a few days to cancel a wedding properly. They have a hundred guests. Someone has to call them and tell them not to come."

"Maybe she'll e-mail them. It'll be the perfect closure for the annoying wedding updates. Or maybe they'll make the announcement at the wedding rehearsal dinner and then call everyone else."

Groan. I do not want to trek all the way to Long Island on Thursday for a soon-to-be-defunct-wedding rehearsal. The final fashion show dress practice is after class until six, which means I'll have to run from school to the train to make it to Long Island by seven thirty.

No. My dad would not do that to us. Tomorrow he'll call us with the cancelation news. It's the right thing to do.

By the time I get home at eight at night on Wednesday, I'm soaking wet from rain and extremely nervous.

The entire cast has been outfitted for all our numbers, the dances are perfect, the stage crew has finished the sets, and the limo for Spring Fling has been reserved. The entire kickoff weekend for spring break has been perfectly arranged except for one slight issue: the stupid wedding hasn't been called off yet.

I ignore Miri's advice and dial my dad's number.

STB answers on the first ring, her voice wobbling. "Hello?"

"Hi, ST—Jennifer, is my dad there?"

"Rachel? No, he isn't. He went for a walk."

"In the pouring rain?"

She laughs, but it sounds strained. "He took an umbrella. I don't know why he went, honestly. He's been acting strange all week."

Yes! Strange! An I-have-to-reevaluate-my-life walk! "All righty. I just wanted to say hi."

"So you'll be here by seven thirty tomorrow?"

"Yup."

"And everything's ready for the show on Friday?"

"Yup."

"After the show, do you and Miri want to come back here? That way we can get ready for the big day together."

"Uh, why don't we wait and see on that one?"

"Whatever you want. I'll tell your dad to call when he gets back." She hesitates. "If it's not too late."

He calls. But not until twelve thirty. (Must have been a marathon of a walk—yes!) I'm already halfway into Spring Fling dreamworld when I hear the phone ring.

My mom picks up. "Daniel, hi," I hear her say. "Are you okay? You don't sound okay. Are you on your cell?" Her voice drops to an infuriatingly low pitch, so I'm forced to climb out of bed, sneak into the hallway, and shove my ear against her door.

"I can't help make that decision for you. . . . You made your bed and now you have to lie in it. . . . It's been so long. . . . My feelings have changed. . . ."

Oh no oh no oh no!

And then: "Of course I still care about you. . . ."

Oh yes oh yes oh yes!

268

I fall asleep, with the door as my pillow, a satisfied smile on my face.

✳

I can't believe I still have to go to the sham of a rehearsal dinner. Between the fashion show and the wedding, I'm all rehearsed out.

The fashion show dress rehearsal goes perfectly. The sets are gorgeous. The designers managed to put the Eiffel Tower back together for the formal, they've imported real sand for the all-girls "Miami" number, and they've painted massive slot machines for the Vegas freshman dance. Their most impressive accomplishment is their virtual Manhattan skyline for the closing, which features a mini Empire State Building that changes color every thirty seconds. The auditorium is lined with rows and rows of chairs, and the twenty-foot-long catwalk has been resurrected from storage.

The rehearsal begins with us, the five freshman girls, onstage. We run straight through the ten numbers, right to the final bows. I'm pretending to receive my flowers when London Zeal's name is called. After she does her fake wave to the audience, the entire cast cheers and applauds. Clad all in black (okay, I'll be fair here: we're all in black for the New York number), she's smiling from ear to ear. "In my four years of being in JFK fashion shows," she says, "this one is by far the best show. Ever."

We cheer even louder. I have to admit, despite all

269

the hard work, this was definitely an amazing experience. I'd probably be enjoying the payoff more thoroughly if the whole wedding fiasco hadn't turned me into a wreck.

"Now get some beauty sleep," she concludes, "and I'll see the girls at one tomorrow at Bella Salon!"

We head to the gym locker rooms, which are squashed between the auditorium and the cafeteria, and are where we'll be changing our outfits between numbers tomorrow. I'm about to dash to the train when Raf waves me over. "Hi," I say, too nervous to look him in the eye.

"Where are you off to?" he asks, buttoning up his jacket.

"Oh, um . . . I have to talk to my dad about something."

"Cool. See you tomorrow. It'll be chaos, so if we don't have a chance to talk, I'll pick you up at eight thirty on Saturday."

I feel queasy. What am I going to do if my dad's a big wuss and doesn't call off the wedding? It's in two days! What am I going to tell Raf? Oh, sorry, my dad's getting married tonight, did I forget to mention it? Can the limo make a pit stop in Port Washington so I can run down the aisle and then jump back into the car?

What to do, what to do, what to do? Skip my dad's wedding and be grounded for the rest of my life? Can a parent who's not living with you do that? Tell Raf I'm sick and I'm stuck in bed and miss the best night of my life?

"We're going to party on that dance floor," he says, then salutes me as he strolls off.

Is that all I am to him? A dancing partner? Or will he finally kiss me? How will I ever graduate from quasi girl-friend to girlfriend if I have to be on Long Island?

Here I am. At the private room at Al Dente. I'm hav-ing the same Caesar salad I almost vomited when STB and my dad first announced they were getting married, and I'm about to puke again. This time I should have asked them to hold the anchovies.

And this isn't even the end of it. After we all finish stuffing our faces, we have to head to the hotel banquet hall, The Garden, and practice walking down the aisle. Come on. Don't they think we can figure it out? We all know how to walk.

Miri has gnawed away most of the skin on her fingers and is trailing blood on the white tablecloth. Ew. If I weren't so nervous myself, I would let her know how vile she's being.

It's over. No, not the wedding. My life.

There are twenty people here, including my father's law partners; my uncle Tommy and his second wife, Re-becca; my cousins; Jennifer's sister and brother and their spouses and kids (thankfully Prissy is off chatting gibber-ish with them); Jennifer's parents; and my bubbe.

She's the only person who seems even more pissed off than me and Miri about being here. She's sitting in the corner, scowling, constantly asking the maitre d' if

271

the heat is still on. She's not the best-tempered of women.

Except for my grandmother, everyone of age is highly tipsy. Especially my father. Everyone else has been polishing off bottles of chardonnay, but my dad has opted for vodka on the rocks. Many, many of them. This is the first time I've ever seen him drink anything besides wine with dinner.

"I guess we lost," Miri whispers. "He's not going to break it off. Maybe he doesn't want to hurt her feelings. Maybe he'll turn himself into an alcoholic for the next month, trying to drown his pain, and then the spell will wear off and he'll love STB again and that'll be that. She's horrible and now she'll be related to us and we'll have to get used to it."

I sigh and take another bite of my salad. I can't believe it. What's the point in having a sister who's a witch if you can't even get rid of one lousy step-monster? "Maybe we should put a spell on Mom and have her interrupt the wedding. You know, when they ask if anyone cares to object, she'll jump up."

Miri snorts. "Why don't I cast spells on everyone at the wedding? Have all the guests simultaneously object for various reasons."

I giggle. "Now that's funny."

"So that's it? We give up?" she asks.

My heart sinks like the *Titanic*. It's over? My potential happiness was so close, and now it's swamped at the bottom of the sea. Is there no way to hoist it back to the surface? There has to be a rock left unturned . . . something I haven't thought of. . . .

Nothing. I've got nada. Do you know what two positives multiplied by zero is?

[Brilliant plan + brilliant plan] X zilch = a big, fat zero.

"I give up. I'll have to tell Raf I'm sick." I practice coughing. Maybe I'll tell him that I have meningitis. Or that I'm dying of a broken heart. That one certainly feels true. Or maybe I'll tell him I caught whatever he was sick with last week so he feels guilty, too guilty to ask Melissa to replace me in the limo—or in his arms. Sigh.

STB taps her glass to get everyone's attention.

"Thank you all for coming," she says, standing up. "I want to take this opportunity to say how much I love you all. How blessed I am to have met Daniel and to have fallen in love with him. He's kind and generous and loving and sweet and brilliant, and I'm honored that he has chosen me to be his wife."

The guests politely applaud. My father rises. "I love you too, Carol."

Everyone freezes.

Carol?

Did he just say Carol? Not Jennifer, but Carol?

Yes! Yes! Yes! Yes to the power of a trillion!

STB's face drains of color. Like an orange shirt washed in the laundry with bleach.

The awareness of what he has just said pops into my dad's eyes. "I mean . . . I meant . . . I think . . ." He sits down. Omigod. Are those tears in his eyes? "I'm sorry, Jen," he whimpers. "I'm still in love with Carol. I can't marry you."

Total chaos ensues. My dad is crying, Prissy is crying, Mrs. Abramson is crying, and even my grandmother is crying (which is strange, considering she never liked STB either). And STB looks as if she just swallowed a lobster—whole. Mr. Abramson jumps up and tries to punch my father in the nose, but hits a waiter instead when my dad ducks. A plate of someone's penne arrabbiata splatters onto Mrs. Abramson's yellow suit.

Miri and I stay perfectly still, squeezing each other's hands under the table. The wedding is off. I should be screaming for joy, but I'm too afraid to move.

And I can't help watching as a fat tear spills from STB's eye and splashes onto the tablecloth.

If this is what I want, why do I feel so nauseous? I push away my plate.

Must be those anchovies.

274

THIS IS NO APRIL FOOLS' JOKE

20

It's baaaaaack!

It's only six thirty in the morning, but I'm wide-awake, rehashing the disaster of last night. The silent train ride home with Miri. The queasiness in my stomach. My mother asking us how the dinner went, our evasive shrugs indicating that it went well. (Yeah, right.)

"No more spells," Miri said before we disappeared into our separate rooms.

I tossed and turned all night, wondering why my dad hadn't come straight over, if he had called his guests to tell them the wedding was off, if STB had blown a cork—while worrying that all this wondering would make my eyes puffy from lack of sleep.

If only puffy eyes were my one facial issue. The pimple I feel expanding on my nose is much, much worse than any under-eye circles. Circles can be concealed with makeup. A second nose cannot be masked. I fly (well, not fly exactly; I'm not the one with powers) out of bed to the mirror. My nose is one big red zit. Santa's Gift has returned! Too bad none of the numbers tonight is set in the North Pole. I can't believe that today, of all days, my nose is the color of a fire hydrant. The one day I'm going to be onstage in front of the entire school, in front of a thousand people. What am I going to do? I can't have this pimple on my face during the fashion show! No one will be able to pay attention to the routines—they'll be too distracted by my huge pimple. No, I take that back. No one will be able to see the routines because my pimple will block their view.

Eureka! An idea!

I knock twice on Miri's door and then open it and tiptoe to her bed. Her mouth is open and her hair is fanned out over her pillow and she looks really young and sweet. I almost can't bring myself to disturb her. Almost.

I tap her on the shoulder. Repeatedly.

She opens her right eye. "What?"

"Look," I say, full of desperation.

She opens the other eye and grimaces. "How could you wake me with that horrific thing?"

"Don't joke. I need you to make the clear-skin spell."

She flips onto her stomach. "I don't want to do any more magic."

"I know you said that yesterday, but please? Puh-lease?" Don't tell me she's going to draw the line now. With this red lightbulb on my nose.

"It's too early," she whines.

"Don't make me rub it on you."

She shrieks and pulls the covers over her head.

"My face is loaded and I'm not afraid to use it," I threaten.

"Okay, just don't touch me. Step away from the bed."

I take five steps back, and she pulls the covers down to her shoulders, revealing a grin. Then she glances at the clock radio and moans, "It's only six thirty!"

"I know. But it's a big day."

She rubs her eyes. "Let me find my notebook. Good thing we bought lemon juice and those salts for Mom."

It's two thirty and I'm gorgeous. Pimpleless and gorgeous.

Maybe gorgeous is a slight exaggeration, but I look good. Really good. Better than I've ever looked in my entire life.

Sophie (a very tall, broad-shouldered hairdresser with bright fake-red hair and a face full of makeup, who might have been a man before he/she became a stylist) spent thirty minutes putting my hair in curlers. Then I sat under a heating lamp for another twenty minutes, giggling with Doree, who's having her hair put into a tight bun. Melissa's having her long red hair braided. Jewel is straightening hers. Stephy chopped her locks and now has a short bob to her chin and looks a bit like Tinker Bell.

And just when I began to worry that my earlobes were melting, Sophie let me out and used a dozen curling irons and other unnamed contraptions to turn each strand of my hair into a perfect curled tendril. I am no longer an ocean head. I am more of a . . . mermaid enchantress.

Then Natalie (who looks as if she could be Sophie's twin sister/brother) tweezed my eyebrows, then spent forty minutes applying my makeup. I have cheekbones (who knew?)! My skin is flawlessly smooth, my brown eyes look huge and Bambi-esque (he/she used so much mascara that my lashes are almost touching my nose), and my lips look luscious, red and kissable. Like a delicious plum. Raf may not be able to wait for Spring Fling—he may spring and fling himself on my mouth during the Moulin Rouge formal for a taste.

I can't stop staring at myself in the many mirrors. Of course, when I stand too close to my reflection, I can see the four inches of foundation, which is a bit clownish. But from far? Gorgeous.

"You girls look so hot," London says, parading through the room in a white cotton bathrobe and white cardboard flip-flops. She and Mercedes are getting full-body treatments, including manicures, pedicures, and massages, courtesy of the salon.

We're done by six, two hours before the fashion

show doors open, and the five of us hail a cab. The driver doesn't want to squeeze us all in, but we beg and plead and try to look our cutest, and he tells us to hurry. Jewel climbs in first, then me, then Doree, and Stephy squishes onto our laps. Pouting, and bearing a striking resemblance to Pippi Longstocking, Melissa mopes as she gets into the front seat. "JFK High School," she orders. "And drive carefully because we just had our hair done."

"It's going to be awesome," Doree says. "*We're* going to be awesome."

"I can't believe the show is today!" Stephy squeals. I expect her to start tossing pixie dust around.

I can't believe I'm here. In the cab with these four A-list girls, looking the best I have ever looked.

"I'm so nervous," Jewel shrieks. "I think I'm going to vomit." The cabbie slams on his brakes to avoid hitting a pedestrian, and Jewel groans. "And this drive isn't helping."

"Come on, everyone," Doree screams. "Get excited. It's going to be the best night of the year. Rachel, you gotta smile. They sold one thousand tickets. One thousand people are going to be watching us!"

I give her a half smile. I should be feeling euphoric. This is everything I ever wanted. Isn't it?

The cabbie slams on his brakes and my knees slam into the divider. This time it's not to avoid an accident. My stomach cartwheels into my throat. The moment has arrived.

"We're here! This is it!" Doree shouts, and we pile

out. We enter the school through the auditorium door and find the rest of the cast lounging around the caf.

Raf is sitting with Sean Washington and Will, eating pizza. He whistles when he sees me. That should cheer me up. He should cheer me up. He's cool and smart and sexy and sweet, and he likes me. Maybe.

I feel a nagging in the pit of my stomach. What's wrong with me? This is supposed to be one of the best days of my life. Why am I being so gloomy and cynical?

"Hey, Raf," Will says, tousling his brother's hair as I approach them. "Your Spring Fling date is smoking hot."

"Get your greasy pepperoni hands out of my hair," Raf says, swatting him away. "Or I'm going to get Mom to throw tomatoes at you while you're MC-ing. She's in the front row, thanks to you."

Who'll be in my reserved seats? My guess is that STB isn't coming tonight. Or Prissy. After the rehearsal from hell, my dad might not make it either. I don't even know where he is. Or where he spent last night. Maybe he moved back into Putter's Place. I'm assuming Tammy isn't going to use the seat I gave her either. Super. I'll have four empty seats in my section. At least Mom and Miri will be here to cheer me on.

I follow the other girls into the locker room to change. I can already hear the rustling of people in the auditorium, parents arriving early, chatty friends excited to see their classmates. One of London's friends is standing guard at the auditorium's back door, making sure that no one sneaks out into the hallway and to the locker rooms to see us before the show.

Despite the designer clothes and freshly washed and sprayed hair, the locker room still smells like feet.

"This is it," Jewel says, stepping into her metallic pink strapless dress. I'm wearing an identical dress, but in metallic red. I zip up the back of her dress and tell her how awesome she looks. The dresses make us look more like we're at a rave than singing at a 1920s jazz club, but whatever. The fact that the five of us are opening the entire show is cool.

I pull up my skin-colored tights, then step into matching red metallic shoes and ask Jewel to zip me up. "Thanks," I say, and spin around. "How do I look?"

She starts at my feet and slowly looks up. "Amazing." But then her gaze rests on my face, and she grimaces. "Uh-oh," she says.

"Uh-oh? What's uh-oh?"

"I think you need some more concealer. Or you might be having an allergic reaction to the makeup."

"Are you kidding?"

"I have some concealer," Doree offers, already in her metallic yellow outfit.

I run into the connected bathroom to look in the mirror at what they're all yammering about.

Oh, no. It's baaaaaaack.

How is it possible that Santa's Gift is making a comeback when I just used the clear spell on it this morning?

"Excuse me," I hear from outside. "You can't go in there. You're not one of the dancers."

"I have to talk to my sister," pleads a voice. Miri? What is she doing back here? She's not supposed to come backstage.

The next thing I know, she's inside the bathroom, gaping beside me in the mirror. Her face is pale, her lower lip trembling. "I have to talk to you," she says. "I have to talk to you *now*."

"Apparently so." I point at the hideousness on my nose. "What's going on?"

She looks around furtively, and despite us being alone by the sink, she gestures for me to follow her into a stall.

I lock the door behind us. "What's going on?" I ask over the toilet bowl. She's starting to freak me out. "Did you hear from Dad?"

She gnaws on her thumb. "Don't get mad at me. It's not my fault."

The roof of my mouth gets desert dry and I feel dizzy, but I have no desire to sit on the toilet seat while wearing my metallic red gown. "What are you talking about?"

She chomps her thumb. After spitting a crumb of nail into the toilet bowl, she pours out the whole story. "Dad showed up when we were getting ready to come to the show. He said he wanted to go as a *family*. And then he started begging Mom to get back together with him. Claiming that he was so in love with her that he couldn't see straight. Saying that he called off the wedding and that he wants to move back in. I was in my room getting changed and I heard the whole thing. And then Mom said she needed to think and she had a headache, and she went into the bathroom to get an aspirin. And here's the thing. I think I kind of made a mess under the bathroom cupboard this morning with the sea salts, and I think she must have figured out that something was up." Miri winces. "Um, I don't think it helped that I left my spell observation notebook on the floor."

"Miri!" I scream. "I'm going to kill you!"

"I know, I know, but I was tired and in a rush." Tears spill down her cheeks. "First she saw the clear-skin spell. And then she must have seen the love spell, because she barged into my room. She motioned to the kitchen and demanded, 'Did you do this?' I had to tell her the truth, don't you see? And not because of any truth spell, because I just had to! She ripped a piece of paper out of the notebook, licked it, and ripped it into a million shreds, then opened the window and tossed them outside, reciting some spell. Afterward she turned to me and said, 'I've overruled every spell you have ever done.' And then she yelled at me and told me I was irresponsible and asked me if you had been in on this too. I had to tell her. Then we went back to the kitchen. Dad was all pale and confused-looking and was pacing back and forth. And now we're all here. In our seats. And Mom is all pissed off and Dad looks miserable and it's really uncomfortable out there."

283

I feel sick. "So does this mean what I think it means?"

She points to my nose. "None of the spells I cast work anymore. Not the clear-skin spell, not the Dad-in-love-with-Mom spell, not the high roundhouse kick spell, and not the—"

"What high roundhouse kick?"

"Oh, never mind that. But I'm really sorry. What are you going to do?"

Wait one sec. Did she say *none of the spells?* "What about the dancing spell?" I yell.

"Gone," she says sadly.

Omigod. I can't breathe. Did this stall just shrink? I think I'm hyperventilating. I look at my watch. Ten of eight. "I have to find London," I mumble. I unlock the door and run back to the locker room. "Has anyone seen London?" I squeak.

No one pays any attention to me. They're all too busy squealing and practicing last-minute moves. I can't go on. London will have to understand. I hurry into the hallway.

She's standing at the door to the auditorium, reviewing her clipboard. "Ready?" she asks when she sees me.

"I'm sorry, London, but I can't do it. I'm sick. So very sorry. You'll have to work around me."

Her eyes narrow, and she shakes her fist at me. "I don't care if you're *dying*, Rachel. Dying! You're going up there." She looks at her watch. "Now."

No way. "I can't."

"You have to." She digs her nails into my arm and drags me back to the locker room. "All freshman girls, on the stage, let's go, the curtain opens with you."

"But, but—"

"Shut up, Rachel. You are not going to screw this up for me, do you understand? You have stage fright. I had it my first year too. You'll get over it as soon as the lights go on. You'll be fine. You know the moves."

I take a deep breath. It's true. I *do* know the moves. I've learned how to dance. I can remember how to do it.

I look down at my red shoes. Maybe it's like *The Wizard of Oz*. Maybe the magic has been in me all along. I just had to realize it for myself. Yes! I can do this! The magic is in me!

Heart hammering, I follow London and the other girls backstage. The five of us get into our positions on the pitch-black *Chicago* set. I hear the roar of the crowd, a thousand people in their seats.

I can do this.

"Good luck, guys!" Doree whispers.

And then the medley starts. The crowd screams again, the curtain pulls up, the spotlight shines.

Showtime.

I'M SO GOING TO NEED TO BE HOME-SCHOOLED

21

The music begins.

"Go, girls!"

"Looking good!"

"Yeeeaaaaaaaaaaaaaaaaaaaaaaaaaaaaah!"

The spotlight is beaming into my eyes, and I can't see farther than the end of the stage.

I can do this. I can so do this. I remember the moves. I lift my arm the way I'm supposed to, the way all the girls are doing, and I'm fine. Yes! I'm fine.

Sort of. They're about a half second ahead of me. Oh, no. I'm off a beat. Why can't I catch up? It's like I'm the girl in the choir who's singing just a little louder and squeakier than everyone else.

But as soon as I'm about to start panicking, our five-second segment is over, and the rest of the cast comes in and it doesn't matter anymore.

Phew. No one seems to have noticed my off-key rhythm. At least, I don't think so, since no one comments.

So far so good.

The next dance I'm in is the freshman Vegas number, the one Melissa choreographed. After I change into my pink skirt suit, I move into my Siberia position and say a little prayer to Melissa, thanking her for sticking me in the back—way, *way* in the back, away from everyone else. I don't have any complicated moves; all I have to do is pretend to deal cards, which I manage without looking like an idiot.

So instead of worrying, I take a moment to peer into the audience. Even in the dim lighting, my reserved section isn't hard to find, since it's way up front, and more significant, it's the only row with three empty chairs. The occupied seats are occupied by three of the most uncomfortable people I have ever seen. My mother is at one end, a ferociously livid expression on her face, her arms angrily crossed in front of her chest. On the other side is my dad, who can't stop fidgeting and looks as if he's counting the seconds to making a fast escape. Slumped between them, like droopy, week-old meat in a sandwich, is Miri.

I try telepathically to tell my sister not to worry. *I'll be fine. I'm Dorothy, and the magic is within me.* Yeah, right, as if that's going to work.

287

I change into my all-girls "Miami" outfit—designer velour sweat shorts, flip-flops, and a tank top. (I wasn't one of the girls asked to sport a bikini top—thank goodness.) When Will introduces the freshman and sophomore all-girls dance, it's full steam ahead! I can do this!

The ten of us get into position. Go, Dorothy, go!

The music starts.

Five, six, seven, eight, left arm up, right arm up, twirl, groove, bend, kick ball . . . kick ball . . . kick ball what?

Oh. Kick ball change. I forgot to change.

Oh no oh no oh no. I'm on the wrong leg. Everyone's kicking her right leg and I'm kicking my left. What do I do? I'm severely out of sync.

Time for the Harlem shake. I know the Harlem shake. So why can't my shoulders listen to my brain? Stop wobbling, shoulders! Time for a butt groove. . . . My butt is not grooving.

I'm pretty sure I look as if I'm being electrocuted.

Beaming colored lights are swirling around me, and now I don't even remember what I'm supposed to be doing. I'm spinning and kicking the wrong way, and people in the audience are starting to snicker. Yes, snicker. How rude. At me. Because of how bad I suck. Jewel's eyes widen when she realizes I'm on the wrong side of the stage and not strutting down the catwalk with her like I'm supposed to.

She points her chin toward the T, trying to clue me in. Oh, no. I don't want to go down the catwalk. While I'm doing the body wave, everyone's gaze will be on little ol' me. No pressure here. Argh. There is no way I should be doing the body wave in this condition, but I follow Jewel down the plank anyway. Do I have a choice? And then, there we are, each of us standing on the edge of the cat-walk, doing the body wave. Except—I can't do it. My body is just not waving. It's spasming. Someone in the front row is wincing at the sight of me. With my luck it's probably Raf's mother. I won't be invited for dinner any-time soon.

"What's wrong with you?" London says through her teeth when, finally, the torture is over and we're back-stage.

"I told you I wasn't feeling well," I snarl back.

"Take a Pepto and get over it! Now go change for the formal!"

I avoid the other girls' gazes as I put on my gorgeous Izzy dress. It can't get much worse. Anyway, the formal is slow, and slow dancing is all about the sway. Anyone can sway, right?

Uh-oh. I realize there is another problem as soon as I step into the hallway. These wooden heels are high. Now that my rhythm isn't quite perfect, I shudder when I think about what these stilettos will do to my balance.

I'm just about to fall flat on my face when I feel a strong arm around my waist. Raf. "You look amazing," he says, beaming. Obviously, he *wasn't* watching the all-girls dance. He was probably backstage changing and has yet to hear about my disastrous performance.

Oh, no. I forgot about the pimple. *He's looking right at the pimple.* I am a hideous, catastrophic freak.

"Ready to knock their socks off?" he says.

I'm more concerned about knocking him off the catwalk. "Yup," I say, shielding my nose with my hand.

I wobble backstage. I can do this. It's slow. Slow and romantic. I can do this. As long as I don't trip over my own feet, I can do this.

When the *Moulin Rouge* song starts, the twenty of us are in proper position. Then the ten boys strut down the catwalk, and we follow. I wobble, but make it to my spot in front of Raf. Woo-hoo! I made it! He twirls me, and then we do our sexy moves. Well, he does the sexy moves, and I try to look sexy, but I guarantee I am coming across as wooden and therefore unsexy. This is confirmed when Raf whispers, "Relax," during our dip. His lips are only an inch from my face. And then he asks, "Are you okay?"

This is not the romantic moment I've been waiting for my entire life.

I nod and try very hard to remain focused. Once that part of the dance is done, I breathe a huge sigh of relief. Yes! Now all I have to do is make it off the catwalk and back to the stage.

Couple by couple, we walk to the stage in two lines. We're the last ones in line, Jewel and Sean right in front of us.

And that's when it happens.

I step on the back of Jewel's dress. I told her the dress was too long.

She goes down fast. And then, like dominoes, so do Melissa, Doree, Stephy, and the entire line of girls in front. One of the sophomores lands in the Eiffel Tower and beheads it.

The set designers scream from offstage.

The entire audience gasps.

Dazed, Stephy looks around, rubbing her elbow. Doree's bun is undone and a mess. Melissa rubs the back of her head.

Omigod. Omigod. Omigod.

I send Miri a desperate look, silently begging her to make the stage swallow me up, but her head is in her hands.

Omigod. Omigod. Omigod.

The music continues playing, but no one moves. They're all glaring at me. Eventually, the music stops and we shuffle silently offstage. Raf won't even look at me. He'll obviously never talk to me again. I destroyed the entire show.

As soon as we're offstage, Melissa, Jewel, Doree, and Stephy circle me like sharks. I can hear Will making MC cracks about bringing France to its knees.

"What the hell were you doing out there?" Melissa yells. "You ruined everything."

There's a golf ball in my throat. "I'm sorry."

Jewel just shakes her head.

"I'll skip the closing," I say. "So I won't do any more damage."

"No way," Doree says, waving both her hands. "We need you in the closing. The freshman segment is only twenty seconds, and it'll look stupid without all of us. But wear your sneakers instead of the stilettos so you don't ruin that number too."

"Idiot," Melissa snorts. "Loser."

Unfortunately, along with my talent, my designer sneakers have disappeared. So against my better judgment, I change into my all-black outfit and beaten-up black boots.

✳

I'm sitting on the toilet seat, silently bawling my eyes out in the same bathroom stall Miri and I visited earlier. I am never coming out. Ever. Well, at least not until everyone has left the building.

Melissa was right when she called me an idiot. How much worse can it get? I thought. How could anything beat decapitating the tower and everyone laughing at me?

It got worse.

After I changed into my black pants and tank top, I got into position. But when the entire cast was supposed to be in sync, I sashayed the wrong way. I swerved at the wrong time. I turned at the wrong time. I was a total mess. But wait. That part wasn't the horrible part.

Since the bows were right after the closing number, I had to wait onstage (while all the freshmen and sophomores gave me poisonous looks) as Will called each person's name in alphabetical order. He called out the entire cast, and of course, the audience cheered and screamed and rushed the stage to give their loved ones bouquets. And then he announced, "Rachel Weinstein!"

No one cheered. Or maybe someone did, but I couldn't hear because of all the laughter. I walked to the front of the catwalk like I was supposed to, only to find that no one, *nadie*, was waiting to hand me flowers. Not even my parents, although I could hardly blame them. They likely had other issues on their minds.

And then, before I could run off the stage in humiliation, Will called, "London Zeal!" the final name in the show, and she strutted down the catwalk, waving at the audience like a queen and grabbing her bouquets.

That's when I tripped on my own two feet, fell into London, and knocked myself, her, and all her flowers off the stage.

And heard the sickening *crack*.

"My leg! You walking *disaster*!"

That was her screaming, not me.

She shrieked again and then hit me on the head with a rose. I apologized profusely before bailing out of there like a convict on the lam.

I've been in this bathroom stall for forty minutes and through the door have had to endure the worst kind of berating, since no one knew I was here and they ripped into me freely. Not that I expected any mercy, after what I did. Melissa called me a loser, Doree said she would never talk to me again, and when I heard Stephy say that London was carted off in an ambulance, I fully lost it. I had to flush repeatedly so no one would hear me crying. No one's come into the bathroom in the past ten minutes, but I'm still not ready to come out.

I'm going to have to transfer to another high school

293

immediately. Unless the news of this disaster has spread to every school in the tristate area, in which case I might have to be home-schooled or convince my mother to move with me to Iowa. Although now she probably hates me too, so she'll most likely ship me off to boarding school.

Needless to say, I am not looking forward to going home. If only there were somewhere else I could go. I can't even escape to my dad's, since I've just ruined his life. STB's life, too. Prissy will have to be in therapy for the rest of hers. Tammy hates me. There is no way Raf will ever talk to me again, never mind take me to Spring Fling.

I will never again be A-list. I've been permanently demoted to the L-list. As in *Loser*.

Someone enters the bathroom and takes the stall next to mine. I try to stop crying. I recognize the pointy-toe shoes under the stall. Jewel's shoes.

"Jewel," I murmur. Jewel was my best friend for so long. She'll know what I should do. She won't dump me now in my time of need.

"Rachel?" She flushes and opens her door.

"Is anyone else out there?" I whisper.

"Just me."

I venture out and, again, burst into tears. I'm like a broken water fountain.

She's fingering her still-straight hair, which is starting to frizz at the tips. "Um . . . don't cry. Everything will be okay." I want her to pat me on the back or something, but she keeps fidgeting with her hair.

Then I get an idea. I don't have to go home. When I used to get into fights with my mom, I would just go sleep at Jewel's. "Do you think I could sleep over tonight? This has been, like, the worst day ever."

She takes a step back. "Tonight? Actually, I'm going to Mercedes' tonight. For a cast party? Maybe another time."

I look her in the eye. "But I need you now."

She backs out of the bathroom. "I can't," she says, a little sadly. The door swings closed behind her.

And just like that, she dumps me. Again. I don't know what to do with myself, so I walk to the mirror and stare at my reflection. A cast party. Nice.

I've stopped crying, but my makeup is a mess, my pimple is screaming, and my hair is all over the place. The ocean has been through a nasty storm. I've gone from superstar to social leper in less than four hours. I've lost my best friend, again, as well as my almost-boyfriend.

I take a deep breath and leave my refuge. My mother and sister are waiting for me, leaning against the wall in the hallway. I try to read the expression on my mom's face. It ain't looking happy. Super. Just what I need. To get yelled at.

She puts her arm around my shoulder and hugs me.

I start crying all over again.

295

When we get home, all I want to do is crawl under my covers and never come out, but my mom says, somewhat ominously, "Come to the kitchen. I want to talk to both of you."

Miri and I sit and stay silent while my mom makes and then pours herself a cup of tea. She sits at the table and shakes her head. "What you two did was cruel. Cruel to your father, cruel to Jennifer—"

"But she isn't good enough for him," I interrupt.

She silences me with her hand. "I know you two don't like her, but who your father marries is not for you to decide. But not only were you cruel to them, you were cruel to me. Do you have any idea of the hurt you caused?"

"We were trying to help you," Miri says, sniffing.

"Help me? You thought making me think that your father was in love with me again would help me?" She shakes her head and takes a sip of tea from her I♥NY mug. "It took me two years to get over him. When he left, I was a mess. I cried myself to sleep every single night."

"I didn't know that," Miri says softly, her eyes filling with tears. Mine do the same.

"I was trying to be strong for you girls. I was so crazy about him, and then suddenly he announced that he didn't feel the same. I didn't even try to get him to change his mind. I figured what was the point? You can't make someone feel something he doesn't want to feel. So I did my best to make a life for myself. To care about my career and to raise you two without him. And soon I found that I was able to fall asleep at night without crying. Slowly, I got over him. Gave away the hope I'd been clinging to."

Gave away the sweatshirt, I realize.

She smiles sadly. "I began to see what the marriage

had really been like. The way he used to work late every
night and not be there for me—or for you. The way he
always put himself first. My unhappiness led to anger, but
in time that faded too. I realized that he wasn't solely to
blame. When we were married, I never told him how I
felt. I used to be so quiet and meek. Maybe if I'd been
stronger . . . if I'd spoken up . . ." She shakes her head.
"Would have, could have, should have," she intones, as if
casting a spell. "I've moved on, and so has he. I've grown
stronger, become more confident. And he's changed too.
He's not so self-absorbed."

Miri rolls her eyes, and my mom laughs. "Okay, so
maybe he has farther to go than I do, but you have to admit, he's trying." Her face turns solemn. "Part of me will
always love him—but not in that way. That's gone." She
points an accusatory finger at us. "But you two! Just as I
was starting to feel happy again, really happy, he reap-
pears in my life, claiming to love me again. And then I
find out that it's all fake. . . . All the pain came back, and
it hurt."

"We thought you wanted him to love you," I say
through a constricted throat.

"If I valued a relationship based on love that was
fake, love that was an illusion, don't you think I would
have cast a love spell myself?"

Oh. Miri and I both slump in our chairs.

"I'm a witch, remember?" she continues. "When your
father left me, I could have cast a spell to make him stay.
But I didn't. Because that's not the kind of love I want."
And then she stands up and puts her mug in the sink.

My cheeks burn with shame. After the way I made a

297

fool of myself onstage, you'd think I'd be used to the feeling by now, but I'm not. *Self-absorbed*. That's me, all right. Miri got Mom's witchcraft, and I got Dad's self-absorption. If there's an S-list, sign me up.

Stupid list.

Shame list.

I've used everyone—Mom, Dad, Miri, and even STB—to get what I thought I wanted. Only, what I thought I wanted is worthless. Fake friends. Fake love. Because love that's not voluntary isn't love at all.

For the first time ever, even though her nails are gross and her roots are a mess, and even though she doesn't date, I wish I could be more like my mother. Wise. Powerful.

"I'm sorry, Mom. I'm sorry, Miri." My eyes fill with tears. Again. "How am I going to fix this?"

Miri shrugs. "Dad went home to apologize to STB, but I doubt she'll take him back. I don't know how to fix it either."

I put my head in my hands, and my mother runs her fingers through my disheveled hair. "I don't know if this is something you *can* fix," she says.

And I know she's not talking about my hair.

298

SHAKE THAT BOOTY

22

Instead of sleeping, I plan. And drink instant coffee. Lots of instant coffee. It's no iced caramel macchiato, but it does the trick.

I wake Miri up at seven. "Here's what we're doing. I am going on the 8:22 train to Port Washington to convince STB to take Dad back. Until then I'm calling the one hundred and eight friends and family members on that e-mail list to tell them that the wedding is back on. Assuming that they're mostly couples, that's fifty-four phone calls at forty seconds each. Should take me thirty-six minutes. Meanwhile, you'll shower and call the hired help beginning at nine. I've allotted you three minutes a call to speak to and plead with the sixteen essential service people. Altogether it should take you forty-eight minutes. Tell them that the wedding is still on. If any of them give you a hard time, call me at Dad's at ten and I'll start banging on doors. Got it?"

She jumps out of bed, looking relieved and amazed. "Wow. Your brain is like a magical calculator. So you'll fix it?"

"I'll try," I say, even though I have no idea how. Hmm. Maybe math is my superpower. Maybe I'll quiz STB on various equations until she breaks down and forgives him. Nah. I'd be better off threatening to start biting my fingernails. Of course, I still have to find my dad, and no one seems to have a clue where he is. Maybe this isn't such a good idea.

"Rachel," my mom says, poking her head through the doorway. She's wearing her usual charm of an outfit that's sure to pick up the men: T-shirt, green-striped sleep shorts, and white sweat socks. "Can I talk to you girls for a second?"

We nod, and she sits on Miri's desk. "You know I don't believe we should use magic to play with people's emotions. I believe that everyone should be allowed to feel real emotions."

Yes, Mom, we know, we know. I glance at my watch.

"But I think that ST—" She clears her throat. "I mean, Jennifer, is probably suffering from some emotional trauma right now, and I feel partly to blame. After all, the powers did come from me. And Miri, I should have realized that despite your maturity, you're just a child, and that of course you would want to explore and play with your powers." She hands me a spray bottle. "That said, I want you to use this on your future step-mother."

Huh? "You want me to clean her?"

She shakes her head. "Last night I made a spell for you . . . and worked a little magic on the wedding band, caterer, and all the nonguest cancellations that took place."

Miri claps. "My job just got loads easier!"

"Yes, but this doesn't mean I condone the use of magic for any future problems," my mom goes on, wagging her finger at Miri. "In fact I hope this experience has taught you that every spell has a consequence." She closes her eyes for a second, looking pained. I wonder what she's thinking about. "In this case," she continues, opening her eyes, "we can make an exception. After all, magic got us into this mess."

"And this will get us out?" I ask, pointing at the bottle.

"It's not complicated," my mom explains. "All you have to do is spray it at Jennifer's chest. It's a heart-reversal potion."

Yes! Miri and I throw our arms around her frail shoulders. "You're the best!" I tell her.

"I know," she says, smiling.

301

Fifty-four phone calls, lots of hasty explaining, and one train ride later, I arrive at the house on Long Island. I ring the doorbell and get into firing position. It's freezing. Why is it so cold today? It's already April!

I hear footsteps, the door opens, I'm ready to spray . . .

My father and STB are holding hands.

Oh. Well. "Hi," I say, for lack of anything better.

"Hi, honey," my dad says. "We made up."

So I see. STB, still in her low-cut bathrobe, is smiling broadly. I follow them into the living room and close the door behind me. "When did you get here?" I ask my dad.

"After the show. I spent all night pleading and begging Jennifer to forgive me for my cold feet."

I spot what appear to be at least ten dozen long-stem red roses in vases on the dining room table. I'm sure those didn't hurt my father's cause either.

STB pats my dad's bald spot. "The ranting at the rehearsal dinner was a case of temporary insanity."

"I should have had a bachelor party to get the craziness out of my system," he jokes.

She casts a warning glance at my father. "Don't get any ideas, Daniel. Your bachelor days are over. You'd better be on your best behavior for the rest of your life because you're on permanent probation." He kisses her on the cheek and she blushes. Then she turns back to me. "Rachel, don't tell me you've dragged slush in from outside. Has no one ever taught you to take off your shoes before entering someone's house?"

Hmm. If I spray this potion all over her exposed cleavage, will her heart get reversed again?

Be good, I remind myself, resisting the urge to shoot.

STB sighs. "We'll have to reschedule the wedding. On Thursday night, I called everyone to cancel."

"No!" I say, banging the spray bottle against the table. "You don't. Miri is calling everyone as we speak to tell them it's still on. I um . . . I knew you two would get back together . . . yeah. I just knew . . . and um . . . I think I'll go . . . um . . ." I hold up my spray bottle. ". . . dust."

STB looks at my dad and beams. I'm hoping it's because of the wedding, and not the cleaning.

The next thing I know, the two of them are making out. It's kind of gross, actually. I can see tongue. So I back out of the kitchen and call home to make sure everything is working out as planned. Miri assures me that everyone is back on schedule for tonight.

Of course they are. My mom is an awesome spell-maker.

To be nice, I start running a bath for Prissy (we've got to get a move on, here!), and while the tub is filling, I take a deep breath and make a phone call.

Tammy's answering machine picks up on the first ring.

"Hi, it's me," I say. "I know you probably hate me for everything I did. And you have every reason to. I've been a crappy friend, and I want to say that I'm sorry. Sorry for what happened at Mick's, for blowing you off

303

for Jewel, for everything. You've been a terrific friend from day one, a real friend, and I didn't properly appreciate you until now. Anyway, the wedding is back on, and I'm at my dad's. You don't have to call me back or anything. I know you're busy getting ready for the dance tonight. I hope you and Aaron have a blast." I hang up and hope that one day she'll forgive me.

Time to get Prissy ready. ("I love baths because they're warm and soft and I have a bath pillow and it smells good and do you like baths, Rachel?")

It's the least I can do.

Miri gets to my dad's two hours later ("You were right! The phone calls took me exactly sixteen minutes! Why can't I have a cool superpower like math?"), and then we change into the putrid pink outfits, which are unfortunately ready and waiting for us in our closets.

"Can you girls help me?" STB calls from their room. Prissy and Miri jump onto her bed. My dad's in the bathroom, shaving.

STB is facing the mirror, her back to us. The zipper on the back of her elegant A-line strapless beaded beige dress is undone. Her blond hair sits in a perfect bun at the nape of her neck. "I'm sorry I didn't make it to your show yesterday, Rachel," she says. "I was really looking forward to it. But I couldn't . . ." Her voice trails off. In the mirror, her cheeks glow and her lips shimmer.

"I understand," I say, and zip up her dress. And I realize I'm finally ready. Ready to let STB become Jennifer.

The ceremony is simple and beautiful. Except for Prissy picking her nose, Miri going to town on her fingers, and me still looking like Rudolph, the entire service is picture-perfect.

After marching back up the aisle, I bolt to the bathroom. Too much instant coffee. When I swing open the doors, I see familiar hair and a familiar nose.

Tammy, in a long blue satin dress, is washing her hands.

My throat tightens and I can't speak. I run to the sink and throw my arms around her. "I . . . can't believe you're here," I whisper.

She hugs me back. "Of course I'm here. It's your dad's wedding."

"But I was so horrible."

"Yeah, I know. But I remember when my mom was getting married. It's hard. I acted like a nut-job too. I cut all my hair off and hid in the closet." She shrugs. "Anyway, I remember how it feels."

"You're awesome." I will never blow off Tammy again. She's a true friend. Wait a sec. "What about Spring Fling? You were so excited that Aaron asked you." I can't believe she'd miss the dance for me!

"Actually," she says, blushing, "he's here. I figured that maybe Jewel wouldn't be here, and I know you were allowed to invite two friends, so I asked him." She

305

grimaces. "Uh-oh. Should I not have done that? Did you ask Raf instead?"

I laugh, even though hearing his name pinches my heart. "No, after last night's disaster, trust me, Raf doesn't want anything to do with me. Especially be seen dancing with me." Or take me to a dance.

At least I'm not at home watching *Star Wars* again.

"You're sure it's all right that Aaron's here?"

I give her the scuba OK, and arms linked, we walk back into the reception hall, where the band is playing some cheeseball wedding celebration song.

Miri and Prissy are dancing in the middle of the room, along with most of the guests. "Come here!" they both shout when they see me.

Are they crazy? I'm never dancing again.

"Let's boogie," Tammy says, and waves Aaron over. He looks really cute in his gray suit.

"I don't think that's a good idea," I mumble.

And then my dad and Jennifer join the crowd, and suddenly everyone's shaking and grooving and I don't really have a choice, do I?

So without even a trace of rhythm, and looking as if I'm undergoing shock treatment, I join my friends and family on the dance floor. And have a blast.

NOT A GLASS SLIPPER BUT CLOSE ENOUGH 23

"Hello?" we call into the apartment.

It's Sunday morning, and we're back home. My dad and Jennifer dropped us off at the train and then caught a plane to Hawaii for their honeymoon. Prissy went home with her grandparents. I hope they can take it. . . . All that chattering can be a bit much for old people.

"Hi, girls," my mom says from the kitchen. "I'm in here making that peanut butter tofu you love so much."

She arranges the grossness in a casserole dish as we slide into our chairs. "So?" she asks, raising an eyebrow. "How was it?"

"Nice," Miri says.

"Yeah," I add. "Really nice."

She smiles. "Good." Then she scratches the back of her neck and grimaces. "Rachel, you had a very unhappy visitor last night."

What? "I did? Who?"

"Raf. He was wearing a suit and claimed he was here to pick you up for a dance. When I said I didn't know what he was talking about, Tigger tried to attack him. I told him you were at your father's wedding."

I don't believe it. Not for a single millisecond did I expect him to show up. To want to be seen with me in public. "What . . . happened?" I croak.

"What do you think happened? He left. I wasn't going to the dance with him."

I leap from my seat and run to the phone in my room. I dial his number (which I know by heart, even though I've never had the nerve to call him). It rings once, twice. Three times. Answer the phone, Raf!

"Hello?" a deep voice says.

"Raf? I am so sorry. I feel like such an idiot."

There's nothing but heavy silence on the other end.

Oh, no. Oh, no. "I didn't think you'd want to go with me to the dance after—"

"Rachel? Is that you? It's not Raf. It's Will."

The humiliations just keep on coming. "Sorry," I mumble. Stupid, stupid, stupid. "Um . . . is Raf there?"

"No," Will says. "He's in New Orleans with my parents."

"Oh, yeah." I forgot. I stretch the phone cord out and wonder if it will fit around my neck.

"Why did you tell my brother you'd go out with him when you knew your father's wedding was the same night? Not cool. He was looking forward to going to the dance with you. He really liked you."

His choice of tense is not lost on me. "I am so sorry," I repeat.

Again, silence. Guess there's not much else for us to chat about. "Bye," I say.

"Later."

I can't believe how badly I blew it. Even after I made a complete fool of myself, he still liked me, and I ruined everything. Stuck a pin directly into the balloon of my potential happiness. Not a pin—I attacked the poor balloon with a chain saw. I flop onto my bed and groan into my pillow.

My mom knocks against the open door. "Yes?" I say through the pillow. I am never coming up for air. I don't care if I suffocate.

"Did you two make up?" she asks. La, la, la. How simple she thinks my life is.

"Not yet."

"Okay. When you do, give him back his glove. It must have fallen out of his pocket when Tigger attacked him. Dinner will be ready in ten minutes." Humming to herself, she returns to the kitchen.

Glove?

I pop into a sitting position.

A gray wool glove is resting on my comforter. A gray wool glove that belongs to Raf.

I stare at the glove. The glove stares back at me.

309

Okay, I know we agreed that love spells are off-limits. But come on! This glove isn't just a normal glove. It's a sign.

Why else would Tigger have attacked him and made him drop it?

One little spell can't really hurt anyone.

What was it Mom said? When magic gets us into a mess, we can make exceptions? Right?

"Hey, Miri . . ."

frogs & french kisses

For Laura Dail, my awesome agent.
Because she loves Rachel as much as I do.

acknowledgments

Thanks to the power of a trillion to:
Wendy Loggia, my extraordinary editor, as well as the rest of the
Delacorte Press Random House Children's Books team: Beverly
Horowitz, Chip Gibson, Isabel Warren-Lynch, Tamar Schwartz, Gayley
Carillo, Kenny Holcomb, Adrienne Waintraub, and Jennifer Black. Special
thanks to Christine Labov for her tireless (and always cheerful) publicity
skills. The superb group on the other side of the pond: Ruth Alltimes, Sarah
Davies, Lisa Grindon, Laura Burr, and everyone else at Macmillan. Artist
extraordinaire Robin Zingone for creating the original gorgeous cover art.
The people working like mad to make the movie: Lisa Callamaro, Claire
Lockhart, Helen Wan, and everyone at Fox 2000 and Storefront
Pictures. Shannon Browne for her fabulous assistance. Gail Brussel, my
superb publicist.

My trio of longtime readers, whom I would be helpless without: my
mom, Elissa Ambrose (who always knows just what I'm *trying* to say);
Lynda Curnyn (my partner in crime); Jess Braun (who's never afraid to
tell me when something sucks). And my newest and youngest reader
and test audience, Avery Carmichael. You guys rock.

Dad, Louisa, Robert, Vickie, John, Jen, Bonnie, Robin, Ronit, and Jess
D., for their love and support. Aviva, my sister and inspiration for Miri.
(No, Squirt, I promise you weren't, um, that geeky.) Gary and Darren,
the Swidler brothers, who were kind enough to teach me how to give a
mooshie. Special thanks to Todd(ie), the littlest brother, my own personal
superhero (and husband), who not only knows *everything* but is kind
enough to let me steal his best lines.

My Love Life Is Up in the Air (and So Am I) **1**

I'm perched on a floating broom, my arms squeezing the life out of my little sister's waist.

"You girls all right?" my mom calls down. She's watching us from behind the second-story cottage window. "You're not airsick? Maybe I shouldn't have let you talk me into this."

"I'm fine," Miri chirps.

"Me too," I lie as the two of us wobble up and down like we're on a haunted seesaw. We're straddling a plastic broom four feet above the dewy ground. In what deranged world would I be fine? My eyes are cemented closed, I'm biting my lip, and every one of my muscles is clenched in fear.

"I don't want you girls gone for more than an hour," my mom warns. "So be back here at eleven p.m. sharp. I'll leave the window open so you can fly straight back in. If you think anyone has spotted you, return here immediately. And, Rachel, don't you dare take off that helmet!"

How does she know my secret plan? "But it's itchy!"

"She won't." Miri pats my knee. "You ready? Here we go!"

Nausea and dizziness wash over me. Maybe this isn't such a brilliant idea. My legs are dangling like a rag doll's, and the broom is starting to chafe.

"Don't go too fast," I plead in a super-high-pitched voice, like I just inhaled a balloon full of helium. "And don't go too high. We don't want to smash into an airplane. And don't—"

The broom jerks forward, I swallow a scream, and suddenly we're flying through upstate New York.

"Be careful!" my mom hollers in the background.

I'm flying. I'm flying! I'm flying!!!!!!!!!!!!!!!!!

I may be dreading going back to school, but at least I'm flying high during spring break. Literally.

I gingerly open my right eye as we shoot past the gate to our rented cottage and zoom over the dirt road. The wind caresses my cheeks, my arms, my hair. . . . I think the wind just blew a leaf up my nose. But who cares? How cool is this?

Don't look down, don't look down!

I look down.

My shoelaces are hanging over the sides of my new pink sneakers like floppy dog ears. I really should have double knotted. These are the new pink sneakers that my mom bought to cheer me up. To make a long, heartbreaking story short, I spent the first few days of vacation moping because Raf Kosravi, the love of my life, hates me because I (unintentionally) stood him up for Spring Fling to go to my father's wedding.

Buying the shoes was really thoughtful of my mom. She's definitely trying to be more understanding. On the same night she surprised me with the cheer-up present, she dropped her slice of pepperofu (vile, flavorless, pepperoni-shaped slabs of tofu) pizza and announced, "Miri, banning you from using witchcraft isn't working. If you're going to do it anyway, as you've been doing for the last two months, I want to teach you to use magic responsibly. The three of us are going on a trip. Start packing."

My jaw fell open in midchew. Mom was finally seeing the light! See, I've only just recently discovered that my mom's a witch. My sister, too. Everyone's a witch except me. Well, not my dad or any of my friends. But everyone I live with. And my mom had a very strict rule: absolutely no magic until Miri finishes her training. My mom is antimagic herself, preferring to be a nonpracticing witch. So this change of heart was a major coup.

"Yes!" I cheered while debating what to pack. Going-out clothes or won't-be-seeing-anyone-worth-impressing sweats? I didn't mind leaving the city, mostly because my best and now only friend (since I embarrassed myself phenomenally at the school fashion show), Tammy, is spending spring break in the Gulf of Mexico with her mom and stepmom (yes, her mom is married to a woman). "Magic for everyone! Can we put a love spell on Raf?"

"Don't push your luck" was my mom's response. "Love spells are *not* what I consider responsible."

What is the point of having a witch for a mom if she won't perform one measly love spell on the boy of my dreams? If only she were more like a friend and less like a mother.

Anyway, the next morning we left extra food for Tigger, our cat, and Goldie, our goldfish, rented a car, and drove from our cozy downtown Manhattan apartment to a rented

3

cottage in the middle of nowhere, where Mom claimed we'd have no nosy neighbors to witness our shenanigans.

We arrived on Wednesday night, two entire days ago. Forty-eight hours in a two-bedroom cottage that smells like a mixture of mothballs and apples. Forty-eight hours of no cable. No DVDs. No Internet. I've had nothing to do except watch while my mom trains Miri, which surprisingly isn't that much fun. Fine, it's semifun. At least my mom is finally letting Miri perform practical magic instead of just making her recite the history of witchcraft. But watching Miri attempt to levitate inanimate objects gets old *fast*.

The peach-colored coffee mug's hovering three inches above the kitchen table is unbelievable. Four inches is awesome. Five is funky. Six . . . yawn. After two days, rising kitchen dishware gets a wee bit repetitive. Actually, downright sleep inducing. It wasn't until this afternoon, while my mom was showing Miri how to float a paper towel, that it occurred to me that if Miri could make a towel fly, why couldn't she make *us* fly?

I found the broom in the hallway closet. It was old and scraggly, and some of the bristles were bent at odd ninety-degree angles, but it would do the trick. "Is there any truth to the witches-flying-on-brooms legend?" I asked, yanking it out, causing a dustbin to fall on my head.

"Well . . ." My mom hesitated. "No."

I didn't buy it. If a paper towel could levitate, why couldn't a broom? I walked over to her and looked deep into her green eyes. "Do you swear?"

Instead of answering, she ran her bitten fingernails through her shoulder-length bottle-blond hair and shrugged.

4

"What?" Miri cried, jumping out of her chair and causing the paper towel to float back down to the table. Good thing she'd raised glasses the day before. "You told me flying brooms were a myth!"

"I know." My mom took a moment to bite her thumbnail. She and my sister share this disgusting habit. "But I was worried about you. I didn't want you flying around Manhattan, bumping into the Empire State Building."

I clapped with gleeful excitement. From now on I'd travel in style. Sweaty overcrowded subways? Never again. Running late to school? I don't think so. The only road I'm taking is Highway Broom. "Teach me how!" I shrieked.

"You mean teach *me*," Miri said snidely.

"If I'd known I was going to teach you to fly, I would have brought cigarettes," my mom said.

"You promised to quit!" I muttered.

"I know, I know. I quit, all right? It's just that letting you fly is going to be stressful." She bit her thumbnail again. "I'll teach you, but you have to promise—"

Be careful, go slow, stay low, whatever, yes, yes, yes!

"—to wear your bike helmets."

Groan. Only my mom could make something as cool as flying look geeky.

The ferocious wind blows a lock of my shoulder-length brown hair into my mouth. But it's worth it. I'm flying! Yes, the loser helmets are fastened and itching, but I'm still feeling pretty lucky. Come on, how many fourteen-year-olds get to fly outside the pressurized cabin of an airplane? No peanuts, no exit doors, no flight attendants. No crying babies. No stranger hogging the armrest. No fidgety traveler climbing over you every two seconds to go to the bathroom. This is far more civilized.

Plus my mom showed Miri how to add a cool night-vision visor to the front of each helmet, so Miri and I can see in the dark.

Whoosh! Whee! Cool! Cold.

Even though it's already April, it feels like we're smack in the middle of winter. Despite the tights I'm wearing under my jeans, as well as the sweater under my jacket, my body is covered in goose bumps. I'm convinced that if I let go of Miri with even one hand, I'll be sent plummeting to an early death. Yet I really want to scratch under my helmet.

"Where do we want to go?" Miri shouts from the front.

"Who cares? Just fly!"

I'm a bird soaring through the night. A kite coasting along the beach. We pass over the tops of budding trees, and in spite of my head problems, I can't stop smiling. "Higher!" I shout.

She lifts the nose of the broom, and though I have to cling tightly to her so I don't slip off the rear as we sail upward, I want more. "Do a three-sixty!"

"I can barely go straight!" she says. "And quit talking; I'm trying to concentrate!" Even though she and Mom enchanted the broom, flying still requires Miri to manually (and magically) steer it.

We pass another dark road. The town is completely

empty, which is why Mom is letting us fly. We won't be spotted. It's a bird, it's a plane, it's two girls on a broom!

"Look!" I squeal, pointing with the toe of my new shoe to a farm below. At least fifty cows are grazing and watching us as we pass overhead. I get a whiff of manure and wish I didn't need my hands to cling to Miri, so that I could hold my nose. Ew. "What's over there?" I shoe-point to a gleam of colored lights in the distance.

She redirects the broom and we head toward the flashing blues, reds, and yellows, which as we get closer start to look like a giant woman's face.

"It's a drive-in!" I cheer. Only one car is there, which can't be good for business. But it does mean fewer potential spotters. Miri hovers behind a tall tree so that the driver and his date won't see us. I have always wanted to go to a drive-in movie. I didn't think they existed anymore. What a blast from the past. The ground is paved with cobblestones instead of concrete. Leading up to the massive screen are two rows of lanterns casting a tender glow through the night. How romantic. Sigh.

If I were a witch, my one wish would be for Raf to like me again. I don't even care that I have just one friend left. Nope, my only request would be Raf.

Okay, and maybe that my head would stop itching. But it's a far second on the list.

I close my eyes and swallow the lump in my throat. Mustn't think about Raf. Mustn't think about what could have been. Must keep moving. "Can we get out of here?" I ask. Miri kick-starts the broom and we reverse back onto the

7

neighboring road. "Be careful," I warn her. "There's a car driving toward us."

She jerks the front of the broom up so the small white Toyota Tercel won't see us. "I think it's parked," she says.

Fantabulous. Probably two people making out, just to rub my face in it. Everyone has a boyfriend except for me. I've never even had a first kiss. Not a real one. And I probably never will. Unless Raf forgives me. . . . Three days till R-day. Raf day. Rekindled Romance day. At the moment, he's in New Orleans for spring break. If I knew which hotel he was staying at, Miri and I could fly the broom down there and serenade him with songs of sorrow.

No way. Too stalkerish. (As if walking by his locker forty times a day wasn't.)

Wait a sec. That's not a couple in the car. It's a woman. By herself. Banging her head against the steering wheel. And now she's opening the car door. She's walking around to the back and opening her trunk.

Omigod. Maybe there's a dead body in there! Maybe we're about to witness the tail end of a murder. But we won't be able to tell the police how we know, so we'll have to make an anonymous phone call from a random pay phone and use one of those voice modifiers that will make us sound like men—

She pulls out flares. Oh well.

Itch. Itch, itch. It's not like my mom would know if I took it off for half a second.

Miri's about to make a U-ie out of there when I tell her to hold on.

"What?" she asks, annoyed. "We can't let her see us.

What if she has a cell camera and e-mails a picture of us to the tabloids? And then we're institutionalized in a top-secret government facility like Area Fifty-one?"

"Just stop!" I order. Besides, I'm not the one who'll be put in the rubber room with electrical wires rammed into her head. I'd definitely visit her, though.

She grinds the broom to a halt, and we resume hovering, bobbing up and down over the road. "She can't start her car," I say.

"So?" Miri asks, turning her head to face me. "What are you, a mechanic?"

So dense, this little one. "Don't you think we could help her with some of our other skills?" Hint, hint. Her forehead wrinkles in confusion. "You're a witch!" I remind her. How are her powers not on the top of her mind? They're *always* on the top of mine.

Still wrinkled. "You think I should start her engine?"

"No, I think you should make her car fly. We can drag race." I kick the toe of my shoe into her calf. "Of course, start her engine!"

She elbows me in the arm and I almost go sailing off the broom. "Are you trying to kill me?" I yell.

She turns back toward the lone woman and rubs the spots on her helmet where her temples would be. "Shush. Let me concentrate."

We drop two feet toward the ground. "Careful!" I scream through clenched teeth.

"Oops. Sorry." The broom wobbles. "I'm trying to help her, but it's not so easy to concentrate on two things at once."

"Just do it quickly."

Miri's entire body tenses, and then with a burst of cold and a whoosh the Tercel roars to life, and the woman jumps at least a foot in the air, not knowing what just happened.

"Yes!" I say, and pat Miri's back with the forehead of my helmet.

"I did it!" she squeals, lifting her arms in a V. And that's when the broom starts making circles.

"What are you doing?" I ask nervously.

"I-I d-don't know," she stammers.

"Just stop it, please!" Getting dizzy again. Super dizzy. Flashbacks to the hora dance at my dad's wedding. "Slow down!" I scream—not that she listens. My jaw is clenched, my teeth are grinding into each other, my feet are dangling, and I may have just lost one of my new cheer-me-up sneakers. Hair spilling in all directions. Think I just swallowed a bird. Now would be a superb time for my own powers to kick in.

Or now.

We're making wide circles. Ten feet in radius, twenty feet. Thirty feet. We're both clasping the broom and screaming, and I don't know which way is up and which way is down and why am I smelling manure again?

Blur of speckled white and black. Oh my. Oh, no. I think we're circling the farm. We're *descending* onto the farm. We're about to *plunge* into the farm.

"Hold on tight!" Miri yells as we—

Oh, no. Please no. It's too gross! It's—

—crash.

10

Got Milk?

2

Moooooooooooooooooooooooooooooo.

You've got to be kidding me.

"I think I broke my head," Miri says.

I'm lying on my stomach, my legs splayed froglike, my eyes clamped shut. "If you broke your head, you wouldn't be talking," I tell her, secretly thankful for the wisdom of moms and their helmet nagging. Despite my sister's being a brown belt in Tae Kwon Do, she's only twelve years old, four and a half feet tall, weighs only seventy-five pounds, and is quite fragile.

I feel warm breath on my face. I really hope that's Miri. I open my eyes. A cow's mouth is inches away.

I shut my eyes again. "A cow is about to eat me. Mir? Seriously, are you in one piece?" The breathing stops, and I look up again to see the cow already bored and moving on. Ouch. My leg is burning. I sit up to find my left knee bleeding right through a rip in my jeans *and* tights. Ow, ow, ow. And my chin hurts too. I think I broke my face. It chlorine-in-my-eyes stings.

"Yes," she grumbles.

At least fifty black-and-white speckled cows of all sizes are surrounding us. I roll to my feet gently, careful not to disturb the livestock. I'm pretty sure cows don't eat humans, but I don't want to provoke them. Are they attracted to blood? I eye my scraped knee nervously. I *think* that's sharks. I hope.

Once on my feet, I help Miri up. "Ouch," she says. "You cut your chin. Does it hurt?"

"Not too much. But I'm sure it's gorgeous. My leg hurts more. Are you okay?"

"Fine. But the broom has seen better days." She points to what's left of it. It's cracked down the middle and now lies in shreds on the muddy (I hope it's mud) ground.

I hoist off my helmet and scratch my head like crazy. Ah. I point at one of the animals. "Any chance we can fly one of these things home?"

Moooooooooooooooooooooooo.

I leap back. "Maybe not."

Miri sneaks toward the cow and gingerly pats him (her? I'm not checking) on a black patch on his/her side. "Come see," she says. "He's not scary up close. He's kind of cute." (She's obviously decided on its gender.) She pats him, like he's a dog.

Moooooooooooooooooooooooo.

Only my sister would think a nine-hundred-pound cow is cute. "He's useless unless he's sprouting wings and taking us home," I say. "We have to get out of here. Ideas?" Happily, I didn't lose a shoe after all. But they're definitely not looking their pinkest. I step up on tiptoe and scan the area for an

12

exit. Ow, ow, ow. Knee hurts. About twenty feet away there's a fence.

Moooooooooooooooooooooooo.

"What do you think *Moo* means?" Miri wonders out loud.

"No idea." And at the moment I don't really care. "Any clue how far we are from home?"

"I bet it means he's happy. Like when Tigger purrs."

"Miri! Focus! Home—how far are we?" Our cat hardly ever purrs. Not when I'm around, anyway. He prefers my mom and Miri. Must be the witch thing.

She stops caressing the cow and glares at me. "We only flew for ten minutes, we can't be too far away. Let's go if you want. Good-bye, sweet cow! Moo!"

We hurry toward the fence—Miri skips, I limp—and try to find a gate. Even with the night-vision visor, I'm having problems seeing.

"And you're sure you can't cast a spell on the cow?" I ask. "So we can fly it home?"

She shakes her head. "What if someone sees us?"

"Come on, what's the difference? Someone could have seen us on the broom."

"Maybe another witch. And then we could hang out," my sister says, pining for a witch peer. Apparently I am not enough for her.

"As if there's another witch in upstate New York. Bet they all live somewhere cool like Transylvania, or Salem. Now come on, Miri. Make the cow fly!" My leg is really starting to burn.

13

"I'm not making an animal fly. A broom is one thing, but I won't treat a cow like an object!"

"We're not doing circus acts," I say, exasperated. "We just want to ride him. People ride horses, don't they?" I can see I'm not getting anywhere. "So how are we going to get home?"

She points to my shoes. Now she's talking! "Perfect," I say. "I'll click them together three times and we'll be zapped back to the cottage?"

She rolls her eyes. "Nooooo."

"Hot-air balloon?" I ask hopefully.

"Your shoes are made for walking."

Groan. "Here's the gate," I say, spotting the hinge.

"What do you think this place is, anyway?" Miri asks.

An instant milk bar? "A dairy farm, dummy."

Once we're back on the road, we notice a sign on the door. "It's called Sammy's," I say, rubbing my still-burning knee.

"Good-bye, cute cows!" Miri sings, waving.

And then we walk all the way home, the broom sadly dragging behind us.

Forty-five minutes later, we're back at the cottage. My mom is sprawled on the mossy green couch in the living room, reading a romance novel. "Why didn't you use the window?" she inquires. Her gaze falls on my ripped jeans. When Miri tells her about the broken broom, she has a full-blown panic attack. "That's it," she asserts as she examines my chin. "No more flying. And why, oh, why did I quit smoking?"

The next day is full of disasters. First, I wake up to see that my small facial scrape has ballooned into a massive red blob on my chin. The second happens when we're at the grocery store that afternoon, picking up dinner. My mom is considering brands of veggie burgers, Miri is squeezing tomatoes, and I've just thrown a box of matzo into the cart because I feel I should have some since it's Passover this week—not that anyone would know that from all the bread we've been eating. My mom is so not religious. My dad isn't religious either, but he usually keeps Passover, which means no pasta, no pizza, no bread of any kind in the house. And he always has a Seder on the first night. No Seder this year, though; he and my new stepmom are on their honeymoon in Hawaii. I kind of miss the Seder. Last year my stepsister, Prissy, asked the traditional four questions, we sang that song about the goat ("Then came a cat and ate the goat, that my father bought for two *zuzim*. One little goat, one little goat." I have no idea what a *zuzim* is or why a cat is eating the poor goat, but we all sang along at the top of our lungs), and we hid the matzo. My dad eventually gave us twenty bucks each to give back the matzo, as is the custom. I wonder what I spent my money on? I could really use that twenty bucks now.

Anyway, after taking the box of matzo, I look longingly at the beef filets, knowing that there's a better chance of Mom getting us all makeovers than making us steaks. Zilch for both. And that's when I see it. The sign over the luscious, juicy meat reads SAMMY'S GRADE-A BEEF.

Sammy's? Oh, no. Step away from the aisle. *Step away from the aisle*. Sammy's is no dairy farm. It's a slaughterhouse! I take a quick step back and almost trip over a spice rack. Then I step on a small sneaker. Miri. Maybe she didn't see?

15

She shakes out her foot. "Be careful, clumsy. What's wrong with you?"

"N-nothing," I stutter. I oh-so-casually turn so that my back is to the meat section and stretch out my shoulders so that I'm blocking the sign.

"What are you doing?" she asks, and tries to peer over my left shoulder. I lean farther to the left. She tries to look over my right. I shift. Left, right, left, right.

I need a distraction. "Did you see the tomatoes? Yum."

"Are you hiding something?"

"The inner workings of my soul?"

She takes a bite of her thumbnail and the accompanying skin. "I know they sell meat here, Rachel. I'm not an idiot."

You'd think a vegetarian wouldn't bite her own body parts, but no. I wrap my arm around her thin shoulder and usher her toward the cereal aisle. She wiggles out of my grasp and turns back toward the meat fridge, her eyes filled with disgust as she inspects the beef chunks. Maybe she won't notice. Maybe someone will scream *fire*. Maybe—

Her face pales. Her jaw drops. Her eyes tear. I think she noticed.

"Oh, no," she moans.

"Miri, don't get upset."

"But all those cute cows are going to die!" Her lip is quivering and her shoulders start shaking and she looks a bit like she's trying to do a body wave. "They're going to be someone's dinner!"

I nod. "Unfortunately not mine."

Which doesn't help, because it causes Miri to fully cry right in the middle of the grocery store.

Where is our mother? I peer through the aisles and spot her tangled in those impossibly frustrating plastic vegetable bags. No need to bother her. I can handle this.

I hate watching my sister cry. I know she's being psychodramatic here, as well as taking this cow thing too personally, but only a soulless person can watch her sister be this upset and not feel pain. It's like having a clump of hair ripped from my head. Or a lung from my chest. Or a kidney from my . . . Hmm, I don't know where kidneys are. I should definitely pay more attention in bio. I got a B on my last assignment. But this month I'm going to focus and study and do my homework when it's assigned, just like Miri, and maybe I'll be able to save my final grade. . . .

What I really need to save is my love life.

What Miri really needs, I gather from her expression, is a tranquilizer. But back to saving . . . Eureka! "Miri," I say, tapping my temple. "If it makes you so upset, why don't you save them?"

She stops crying, and I see, beyond her ridiculously long, glistening lashes, the hope in her eyes. "How?" she asks.

Must I think of everything? "Use your powers, silly. You can't save all the cows in the world, but you can probably come up with a plan to save the ones at Sammy's."

She fingers a package of beef and then wipes her hand on her jeans. "You think I can?"

"Of course. We'll look through A^2." Otherwise known as *The Authorized and Absolute Reference Handbook to Astonishing Spells, Astounding Potions, and History of Witchcraft Since the Beginning of Time.* My sister prefers using spells to cast her magic, rather than just zapping something with her raw will, since mixing the ingredients and chanting gives the witch more control. After last night's impromptu car-starter spell and subsequent nosedive into the cow field, I wholeheartedly agree with the strategy. "And we'll need to buy a new broom," I add.

"You think Mom will let us fly again?" she asks dubiously.

"Of course. When I fell off my bike, didn't she insist I get right back on?"

"I guess." Miri doesn't look convinced.

"Leave the permission stuff to me. You focus on finding the right spell." Maybe we can make the cows indestructible. Maybe Miri can put a spell like that on us, too.

"I flipped past a safety spell a while back," Miri says. "That might work."

"Or you can find an immortality spell." Nothing could hurt us! We'd look a little worse for wear when our hair started to fall out in a few centuries but we'd be as indestructible as vampires, without having to drink blood, but getting to wear the sexy red leather outfits and high-heeled shoes.

The safety spell wins. It seems Miri believes she has more of a say in this magic stuff than I do. I can't imagine *why*. On the plus side, I manage to convince Mom that Miri will be scarred for life if she doesn't get back on the broom immediately. So Mom takes her on a test run around the neighborhood before letting us go out alone again. We opt not to tell her about the Protect the Cows plan. She's in bed, reading, and there doesn't seem to be a point in worrying her over nothing. After all, she said Miri was allowed to use magic, right? And saving cows shows a social conscience (for the cows), so that makes it definitely responsible.

"Can you stop bumping into me?" Miri whines as my knees once again (unintentionally) smack the backs of her calves.

Okay fine, that last one was intentional. "If you stop zigzagging, I'll stop bumping into you," I say, negotiating.

She jerks the front of the broom up and I slide backward, nearly falling off the back end. Excellent. Maybe being in a body cast will help my social status. Not. My redesigned chin sure won't do me any favors.

My stomach is somersaulting and I don't think it's because we're suspended twenty feet in the air. Although I'm sure that's not helping. Now that school is less than forty-eight hours away, I can no longer be in denial about the trauma I'll be forced to endure.

19

See, a few months ago I convinced Miri to cast a dancing spell on me so I could be in the JFK High fashion show and finally be on the A-list. But when my mom freaked out and reversed the spell, my dancing ability sank to zero and I made a complete fool of myself. And I don't mean that in the annoying I-look-so-fat-says-the-ninety-pound-model sort of way. I knocked over castmates like they were bowling pins. I smashed up the sets. And then I (sob) stood up Raf, because I thought he'd never want to be seen with me. I'm officially socially ruined.

Maybe Miri will sprinkle some of the safety spell on me. I need to be protected from London Zeal, the senior who headed the show, whose leg I broke when I accidentally knocked her off the stage.

Although I might need the spell more to protect myself from Melissa Davis, I realize as we pass over Sammy's fence. I know it's wrong to hate, but she's evil. She's a mini London Zeal, a fellow freshman who tortures anyone not A-list, flirts with my quasi-used-to-be-almost-boyfriend, Raf, and stole my ex–best friend, Jewel. Although Jewel might be slightly evil these days too, since the fashion show corrupted her. Like it did me, temporarily. But at least I'm reformed. I realize that there are more important aspects to life than the A-list. I'm practically a do-gooder. I'm saving cows!

"Ready?" I ask as Miri steadies the new broom. I tried to convince her to buy the one with the hot pink bristles, but she thought we should get traditional straw to blend in. And so potential witnesses don't think they're seeing a fuchsia comet.

20

"Yup."

We spent the day finding a spell, finding the ingredients, and mixing, and now all we have to do is sprinkle the concoction over the cows. I keep one arm around Miri and use the other to open the fanny pack around my waist and pull out the Ziploc bag. The pack is my mom's, obviously. I would never own anything this obscenely orange and tacky. Or anything referred to by the word *fanny*. In the bag is a potpourri of garlic, mint, salt, and rice. It looks more like laundry detergent than magic ingredients if you ask me, but what do I know?

Miri takes a deep breath and recites:

"From a danger direct,
I vow this day forward,
To cherish and protect."

Who writes this stuff? I cringe at the bad poem. The spell sucks up the energy and warmth around us, causing the air to become instantly freezing. All right, I admit I can't really tell the difference between the magic and the cool April wind.

Meanwhile, Miri sprinkles the substance onto the live-stock, reminding me of throwing rice at a wedding. Con-gratulations! Mazel tov! The concoction lands on the cows, sticking to them like snowflakes on a playground, or dan-druff on a black sweater. It's all very scenic.

And then the cows disappear. Yes, vanish. Evaporate. Like a stain being washed out of a shirt. Or like Raf's feelings for me.

I can feel the (super-small, practically nonexistent) hairs on the back of my neck standing at attention. "Um, Miri?"

"They must be moving somewhere safe," she says, specu-lating as she continues sprinkling.

Eventually, all that's left is an empty field. The spots where the animals were grazing are bare. The night is sud-denly quiet. Not a moo anywhere. Kind of creepy. "They're not . . . dead, are they?"

"No way. That would kind of defeat the purpose of a safety spell," she says, handing back the Ziploc. "We saved the cows."

"At least they've escaped their cheeseburger destiny, right?" I say, trying not to slip off the broom as I zip up the fanny pack. Why would my mom even own something so ugly? She's a witch! She could zap up the hippest purse in the world! Louis Vuittons on Monday mornings; Izzy Simpson bags for the afternoon. She doesn't even have to carry a purse at all. She could just zap up money, credit cards, keys, lipstick (not that she wears lipstick) whenever she needed them. She doesn't even need credit cards. She could zap up whatever she needed into the living room, direct from the Home Shopping Network or the Internet.

"Let's get out of here before the butcher spots us," Miri says. "I was thinking we'd fly back to the drive-in and see if anything good is playing. We deserve to reward ourselves. We'll tell Mom we had a really long practice session."

"You're the best, Miri." I'd give her a hug, but I don't want to mess up our balance. My sister snaps her sneakers together, and we jet off toward the drive-in. As we approach, I see the latest Spider-Man movie blasting on the screen. Fun! Some entertainment, finally.

Miri hovers over a tree.

"Why don't we get off and sit on the branches?" I suggest. "That way we'll have a good view."

I gingerly climb down first and find a makeshift ledge in a fat V-branch. Miri parks the broom and then squeezes in beside me. I'm watching a drive-in movie! There are no branches directly above me, and I can see straight up to the twinkling stars. I am the luckiest girl in the world.

Fine, if I were the luckiest girl in the world, I'd be here with Raf in a Mercedes and not with my little sister up in a tree, but whatever. And the branch is hurting my bum. I try to make myself comfy as Spider-Man swings from telephone line to building. "You know," I whisper over a budding leaf, "in a way, you're kind of like Spider-Man."

22

Miri turns to face me and her eyes glow in the moonlight. "How so?"

"You have powers, and you can use them to help the world. Like you did tonight by saving the cows."

She bites her pinky nail and asks, "But what else can I do?"

"You can do anything you want," I answer, suddenly excited by the idea of being a superhero's mentor. "Stop wars, find homes for orphans—"

"Save the whales!" she squeals.

"Exactly. And you could wear a silver cape, a pink leotard, and some kind of sexy eye mask. With sparkles! Of course, I'd wear something similar as your sidekick." We're like Batman and Robin!

She reaches for the thin branches above her and pulls herself up. "Let's go home and make a list," she says excitedly.

I was wrong. My mom is clearly not the only person who can make magic geeky.

23

The Wheels on the
Bus Go . . . Kazam!
3

"Girls," my mom says as she swerves into the right lane, totally cutting off an unsuspecting driver, "I have a confession to make."

I've ridden with my mother three times in my entire life, which is three times too many. She. Is. The Worst. Driver. Ever. She's caused at least six almost-accidents in the last twenty minutes. I cling to my seat belt for safety. "Let me guess," I say. "You don't have a driver's license?"

My mom giggles. "Hilarious. Actually, smarty-pants, I'd like to discuss something important. Something serious . . ."

Maybe she'll finally tell us why she gave up witchcraft! About what caused the rift between her and Aunt Sasha, the aunt we never see.

"I want to talk about dating."

Oh, no. A sex talk from Mom. Can anything be more embarrassing? To add vinegar to the wound, I'm trapped in a car driving back to the city, so I can't even feign doing homework. My only option is to fake sleep. I roll my head so that it leans against the passenger's side window, close my eyes, and exhale a thunderous fake snore.

"Rachel," she says, "relax. Not about you dating. About me dating."

I pop my eyes open. That I can handle. "You dating?" This should be fun. My mom dated a bit after the divorce, only on weekends when we were at my dad's (she didn't want to be the type who brought home lots of "uncles"), but then she gave up. She hasn't so much as grabbed a cup of mocha joe with a man since then. "Anyone special? Someone at work? Do you have a crush?" Cuteness! Mom with a crush! Mom with a secret boyfriend? Has she snuck out of the apartment to see him at night?

"There's no one in mind. But I'd like to start again. Seeing your father remarry has made me think that it's time for me to move on. And I wanted to know how you two felt about it."

A new boyfriend! Fun! Someone who will explain the inner workings of the male mind to me. Or—someone who has a hot son. Now we're talking. They'll get married and I'll have a sizzling stepbrother. Too bad Raf's parents are still together. What a horrible thing to think. Wishing him years of divorce anxiety just so my mom can marry his dad. And anyway, then he'd be my brother, which would make it *mucho* creepy if we got married. Or worse: what if my mom and his dad then got divorced? Raf and I would be forbidden to see each other. Just like Romeo and Juliet. How romantic.

"You should definitely start dating again," I say. "It's time." At the very least, we would have a man around to change lightbulbs. My mom is so lazy about that. The one in my bedroom ceiling lamp blew out just the other day. And

25

what was my mom's response to my claim that she should change it? That I should do it myself. Come on. What if I got hurt? That's such a stepdad's job. So is taking out the garbage. And setting the table. And taking my mom on trips so I can have wild parties.

"Miri?" my mom asks. "What do you think?"

"I . . . I don't know," Miri mumbles.

"Come on, Sis, be supportive!" I twist my body sideways to glare at her. Doesn't that girl ever watch Oprah? A "Go, Mom, go!" or at the very least a "Go, girl!" seems situation appropriate.

My mom sighs. "I asked for *her* opinion."

Miri wraps a frizzy strand of her brown hair around her thumb, making the tip turn red. "It's just that I'm not ready to wear another pukey pink bridesmaid dress so soon."

My mom laughs. "I said dating, honey, not marriage."

I roll my eyes. "Yeah, Mir. Way to get ahead of yourself."

"Whatever makes you happy, Mom," Miri says.

Anyway, there's no chance we'd wear pukey pink dresses to Mom's nuptials. I'm thinking long, sexy black. Maybe we should get out of the country and do a location wedding. Like in the Caribbean. Fun, no? Then we can get married on the beach—I mean, she can get married on the beach—and we can tan at the same time.

"So do you have anyone lined up?" I ask, excited. She should ask out Fireman Dave from the second floor. He's *hot*.

"No," she says. "Truth is I don't even know how to go about meeting quality men these days. The last time I had a real boyfriend was seventeen years ago!"

Ping! "I've got it!"

"No, you are not signing me up for one of those dating Web sites again, Rachel. They're so humiliating."

"That's not what I was going to suggest, big shot," I say haughtily. I was actually thinking she could apply to the reality show *Who Wants to Marry My Mom?* Even though I hate watching reality TV, at least I'd get to star on it. But if potential for humiliation is her litmus test, I'd better think of something else. "It's best you realize now that it won't be so easy to meet good men in Manhattan. Don't you watch TV? Aren't the chances of remarrying in your forties like one in a hundred? Aren't most men in your age group married, dead, gay, or jerks?"

"First of all, I'm thirty-nine." She veers into the path of an oncoming car but just before impact swerves back to her lane. "Maybe you're right. My single friends haven't found it so easy. Where am I going to meet men?"

I wish that my mom has more luck than I have. If I haven't been able to find a guy in my age group and none of them are married, dead, or out of the closet yet, the odds are not in my mom's favor.

She raises her hands as if in question and veers to the left, cutting off a bus diagonally behind us. She really is the worst driver. As the bus passes us, I peer into the windows and almost faint in shock.

One hot man. Two hot men. Three . . . omigod. It's a bus *full* of hot men.

I don't believe it. My heart pounds against my rib cage. Did I . . . did I just make that happen? Maybe I'm

27

finally a witch! I attempt telekinetically to roll down the car window.

Nada.

A coincidence. But still. How lucky is that? "Chase that bus!" I scream, pointing.

My mom gapes at me like I left my brain at the cottage. "Excuse me?"

"It's a bus full of men! Talk about a dating pool. Go get it!" I'm bobbing up and down in my seat like a yo-yo.

"I am *not* chasing a bus," she says, shaking her head. "I don't want a speeding ticket."

"Do you see a cop?" I do an exaggerated look out the window. "I don't see a cop. Go get 'em!"

"You're crazy."

"Use magic!" I cry.

"I don't use magic! I'm a nonpracticing witch!"

"Mom! It's a new chapter in your life. Make some changes!"

The gulf between us and the bus is widening. "I don't know," she says. "That's not what I meant. . . ."

"Now is the time. Give the bus a flat tire! Empty its gas tank!" The bus is now almost a football field away. Two football fields! Three! They're getting away! "Follow that cab!" I scream.

"It's not a cab," Miri snarls from the backseat.

Why must she be so literal? Anyway, I know, but I've always wanted to say that. It sounds glam.

"Rachel, give it a rest," my mom says, but as her mouth forms the words, her eyes tell a different story, lusting longingly for the Hunks-on-Wheels. And that's when a gust of cold air bursts through the car.

I'm wondering why the air conditioner just kicked on when *boom!*

The bus is tilted to its right. Oh my. Oh yes! My mom just gave the bus a flat tire! It grinds to a halt and pulls to the side of the road.

I'm bursting with pride, like I just watched my child take her first steps. "You did it!"

"I—I—I," my mom stammers.

"Quick, pull over beside it," I instruct.

She listens and parks the car on the shoulder of the road, right behind the bus.

"Well, what do we do now?" Miri asks, kicking the back of my seat. Big baby.

"We offer our assistance," I say. "I know I'm not the best wingman at the moment because of the scrape on my face, but it's better than it was yesterday and Miri looks pretty cute in her overalls—"

"What if they're dangerous?" my scaredy-cat sister complains. "They could be serial killers."

"Yes, a bus full of serial killers, that's realistic." Come on, Miri, get with the program. "Let's go!" I sing, and unlock my door.

I glance over at my mom. She looks completely shell-shocked, blinking repeatedly as if specks of dirt just flew into her eyes.

"Come on! Now or never!"

She ogles the bus, looks at me, and then, just when I

think she's going to reverse right out of there, flips open the overhead mirror and gives herself the once-over. "All right, let's do it."

Wahoo! I wish she wasn't wearing her nerd-o jeans pulled up right to her waist. Although they do make her butt look all J-Lo.

I flip open my mirror for a quick peek. Besides the chin absurdity, everything looks normal. Complexion = clear, nose = small, eyes = brown, teeth = straight.

"This is so stupid," Miri says, sulking. "What are you going to do? Help change the tire?"

"We're not going over to help them. We're going so Mom can meet men. Now, put on a pretty please-date-my-mother smile and let's go."

"Forget it. I'd rather stay here and edit my Save the World list. And leave me the cell phone in case you two get accosted, so I can call the police for backup."

Such a drama queen.

"Keep the doors locked," my mom says insistently, and then jumps out of the car. She cautiously checks for oncoming traffic, hesitates, and then, holding my hand, leads me toward the bus.

Before we can get to the front, the door swings open and a tall, skinny man wearing a brown suede hat (in an obvious attempt to cover his thinning gray hair) steps outside. He's wearing a thick green Patagonia sweatshirt, and a badge that says *Baseball Hall of Fame, Tour Leader* dangles from his wrinkled neck. A baseball tour! Excellent. The tour guide stretches his arms over his head and then scratches his burly gray eyebrows, looking startled to see us approaching. His gaze sways from Mom to me, then back to Mom, and then he smiles. "Hello."

My mom stands up straighter. Go, girl! "Hi," she says, sounding almost . . . coy?

"Hi," he says. Excellent to the power of two! We've made contact.

I elbow my mom in the side.

"Anything we can help you with?" she asks, feeling my not-so-subtle cue. "Give you a ride?"

Old Man Tour Guide shakes his head. "Nah. Thanks, though. Much appreciated. Very sweet of you to offer." He (oh yes) tips the front of his hat as if he's some sort of cowboy. Maybe he was a cowboy. In the 1940s. "The driver just called Triple A, but it will take them at least thirty minutes to get here."

"Great," my mom says, eyes still on him. Old Man Tour Guide doesn't look away.

Yikes. Old Man Tour Guide is flirting with my mother! He's a hundred years old! Fine, he's at least fifty.

OMTG sticks out his pale hairy hand. "My name is—"

"How's it going, Lex?" says a booming voice. As the owner of the voice steps off the bus, my heart literally swoons. Like if I were a cartoon, it would pop out of my shirt and jiggle. He's *gorgeous*. About half OMTG's age, at least six feet tall, thick light brown hair, and topped off with deliciously chiseled cheekbones. He's wearing faded jeans and a Yankees jersey. I wonder if he's a ballplayer.

"I think the boys are getting restless," he says, and cracks his knuckles. "Hello, ladies," he adds as he notices us.

Ten more men follow him off the bus. Ten more *hot* men.

As each man steps off, he smiles at my mom. This is the dating pool jackpot.

"So what kind of tour is this?" my mom asks Lex, who hasn't yet realized he should get out of the way. I mean, come on. My mom should not be spending precious time with him when there are more appropriately aged stepfathers available. Lex could be my stepgrandfather. I could fix him up with my *bubbe*.

"I lead a day-trip tour to the National Baseball Hall of Fame in Cooperstown every Sunday from April to October. Have you been?"

"Nope," she says. And bats her eyelashes. Oh, no, what's she doing? She's wasting her flirting! I raise my eyebrow as a suggestive cue to move on.

"I'd be happy to take you one day, Mrs. . . ."

My mom blushes a deep fuchsia. "Ms., actually. But please call me Carol."

"I'm Lex," he says, and sticks out his pale hairy hand again. Mom takes it, apparently oblivious to my eyebrow signals. Abort plan!

"And this is my daughter Rachel."

I shake his hand reluctantly. And then I turn to the crowd of younger, hotter men and extend my hand to the specimen closest to me. "And what's your name?" I ask.

"Jimmy," the guy says. He's cute. Red hair, jean jacket, nice teeth.

I tug my mom away from Lex. No need to date the frog when we're surrounded by princes. "Mom, meet Jimmy."

She giggles. "Hi, Jimmy. I'm Carol."

"Nice to meet you," he says, sounding gruff yet sexy. "You live in New York?"

"Yes, I do," she answers in a chirpy Mouseketeer's voice I didn't know she had. Impressive. Somewhat nauseating. The old broad has some tricks up her sleeve. "You?"

Go, girl!

"Nah," he says, shaking his head. "Florida. I came up to visit my wife's brother and . . ."

I should have looked at his ring finger before getting excited. Oh, no. What if these men are all married? Or if they all live in Florida?

I can handle Florida. I'm not opposed. New school, perma-tan, Disney World . . . But my mom's being a high-priced mistress? Not so much. Too much drama. I'd see the other woman's kids at school and would have to pretend I didn't know where their father was spending his nights. What if I fell in love with his seventeen-year-old son? Would it be my ethical duty to tell him, even if it would tear his soul apart?

I snap back to attention just as my mom is being introduced to Adam, the hot guy in the Yankees jersey, Florida Man's single brother-in-law (no ring). Much better. "I live in Jersey City," he's saying. Oh well, no tan for me, but being nearby will make their courtship easier. Fewer flights.

"I'm a travel agent," she's saying.

"One of the best in the city!" I pitch.

The apples of her cheeks redden.

"Isn't she cute when she blushes?" I add, and she inserts

33

her thumbnail into her mouth and is about to take a nibble when I gently yank her hand away. Must she gross them out?

"Very cute," Lex says, startling me. Enough, old man! Stop stalking my mom!

"I was thinking of planning a trip down to visit Jimmy, my sister, and the kids," Adam says, sidling up closer to her. "Do you think you could give me advice?"

"Actually," she says as she picks at her fingers behind her back, thinking I won't notice, "I specialize in honeymoons. . . ."

I quickly step on her foot. Is she that clueless? "Mo-ther, I'm sure you could help him out. Why don't you give him your *business* card. And then he could *call* you." I try to use my nonexistent telepathy to help her get it. Card . . . phone call . . . date . . .

She nods and then stops picking long enough to reach into her purse and pull out a card.

Adam smiles as he reads it. "Thanks."

"I need to book some trips too," pipes up Lex. "Is there one for me?"

Sigh. How transparent can you get, old man? I thought cowboys were supposed to be suave.

Smiling, my mom starts handing cards out like candy canes at a mall in December.

"Where do you recommend this time of year?" Lex asks, once again hogging the conversation.

"France is beautiful in the spring. . . ."

Where you should go, Lex, so you can leave my mother alone! Just as I'm about to interrupt, a new hottie, a blond

34

hottie with big green eyes, butts in for me. "Are you a travel agent? I could use some help with my miles. . . ."

Wink, wink. Sure he can.

Twenty minutes later, we're back in the car and Operation HM³ (Help Mom Meet Men) was a smashing success. What can I say? I'm brilliant.

"I can't believe that worked," Mom says giddily. "I gave out eleven business cards!"

"You took forever," Miri moans. "It's freezing in here. Can you start the car already and turn on the heat? I'm going to catch a cold."

I turn on the heat and then the radio and do a little seat groove to the beat. Maybe I'll become a matchmaker. I'm like a puppeteer, commandeering the emotions of unsuspecting innocents. Who needs magic? All I need are clever strategies. Fine, we needed the magic to stop the bus, but otherwise it was all me. I can do anything I set my mind to, just like my mother always told me! Well, not anything. There's nothing I can do about school tomorrow. If only I could conjure up a cancel-school spell. Or at least a freak snowstorm.

I *cannot* face going to school tomorrow. Is it possible the JFK kids have forgotten about the fashion show fiasco? It's been an entire week.

Yeah, right.

Even if the masses have forgotten, there's no way the fashion show horribles have. London has probably spent the entire week preparing ways to torture me. After all, I did knock her off the stage and thus break her leg. Oh God. I

35

need to go into hiding. Maybe my bruised chin will act as a disguise? No, I'm pretty sure it will be gone by tomorrow. The red has already started to fade.

But Miri had the right idea. If I catch a cold, I can stay in bed the entire day.

I turn off the heat.

"Are you crazy?" Miri asks. "It's freezing in here. Do you want to get sick?"

"Yup." I roll down the window and inhale.

Not Quite Gone, Not Quite Forgotten 4

Beep! Beep! Beep! Beep!

Nononononononononooooo. It's seven a.m. Monday morning and my throat doesn't hurt at all. How is that possible? I inhaled bitterly cold air. I showered last night and walked around the block—without blow-drying! I purposely didn't take a vitamin before bed! (Don't tell my dad; he's obsessed with vitamins.) Also I didn't have my evening glass of fresh orange juice. And I love my evening glass of juice. The rush of vitamin C gives me sweet dreams.

Maybe I have a fever. I *am* feeling pretty headachy. I could have at least 101, maybe 102. My throat isn't sore but I'm burning up. Might have to be hospitalized. Maybe the kids at school will feel guilty about bad-mouthing someone who's sick and send me flowers and one of those life-size cards that everyone signs in different colors. In fact, they'll probably realize that my horrendous fashion show performance was a result of this sickness, and I'll be forgiven, because you can't be mad at someone who's sick. A-list, here I come! Plus I'll have a superhot doctor nursing me to health. Yes!

I hurry to the bathroom, park myself on the edge of the bathtub, and shove the thermometer under my tongue.

"Oh, give it up. You're perfectly healthy," Miri says, barging in and flipping on the faucet.

" 'et ot!" I mumble, which translates to "get out" in non-thermometer-speak. "I'm thick. Pwobably contaios."

She applies toothpaste to her brush. "Suck it up and go to school. You'll be fine."

I will not be fine. I catch a glimpse of myself in the mirror and gasp. My chin has completely crusted over and seems worse than ever. It looks like a beard. Isn't this all Miri's fault to begin with? Losing my dancing skills, bruising my chin . . . I'm about to tell her where to get off but decide to try to calm myself down instead. I shouldn't be getting so emotional when I'm deathly ill.

38

The thermometer beeps and reads . . . 98.2?

What? That's impossible. How could I not have a fever? I'm perfectly healthy. How can this be? Hmm, isn't normal body temperature 98.6? Perhaps there's a dangerous medical condition that causes your temperature to drop. Maybe by noon it'll be down to ninety, by this afternoon eighty, and by this evening I'll be a frozen Popsicle, unable to move without my fingers snapping off like ice-capped branches.

Miri grabs the traitorous thermometer from my hands. "You're fine. Go get dressed."

Speaking of ice, maybe it's snowing outside. Then the school will call a snow day and I'll get to stay home. I sprint back to my room and hurl open the window blinds.

Sunny. A beautiful sunny day. Shouldn't the weather know that it's supposed to reflect my mood?

"Mom!" I holler. "Can I stay home today? Pleeeeeease?"

"No!" she yells back through the walls.

I flop onto my unmade bed and pull the covers over my head. "But I'm going to be a social outcast! And I have a beard!"

"I told you, if you're mature enough to use magic, you should be mature enough to face the consequences. Besides, you can't hide away forever."

Not forever. Just until my classmates graduate. So I'll be a few years older than the others when I finally go back. At least my body will have caught up to them. Hopefully. Even my own little sister has me beat in that department, with her B-cup breasts. How unfair is that? "But I look like a man!"

I can hear her laughing. Ha-ha. "It's not that bad, Rachel. Get ready for school."

Get ready for social mortification is more like it.

39

If I make my steps really small, I'll be late. Because I don't have a note, I'll get expelled. And then I'll never have to go to school again! Although then I won't get into college. I'll never get a good job and the only place that will hire me will be McDonald's and all I'll eat will be Big Macs and fries and one day my neighbor will find a five-hundred-pound me unable to squeeze through the front door of my cat-infested apartment.

I make my steps *slightly* bigger. And tighten my puffy black coat. The bright sun deceptively makes the weather look warm when it's actually even colder than yesterday.

As I approach the last few blocks before school,

something seems off. Like a silent Times Square. A crowd of
students have gathered outside the building. Jeez. Are they
all waiting for me so they can mock me? Am I so famous?

"This rules, man," a passing senior says. "I'm going back
to bed."

I'd like to go back to bed. I'd like to go back to middle
school. I sprint toward the mob and try to eavesdrop on a
cluster of sophomores to hear what's going on.

". . . cows in there. How funny is that? It was so the
senior prank," one of them says.

Cows?

"Best prank ever," someone else comments. "How did
they do it? Get fifty cows into the school gym without anyone seeing?"

Fifty cows?

40   The words and noise around me swirl, like I'm on a
merry-go-round.

". . . doubt any of the seniors were smart enough to pull
this off . . ."

". . . probably those jerks at Brentwood High . . ."

". . . classes are going to be canceled . . ."

". . . major property damage . . ."

". . . health officials have to decontaminate . . ."

I feel instantly light-headed, like I just gave blood. They
couldn't be Miri's cows. The Sammy's cows? No. Maybe. Did
Miri wish them into the school gym? Why would she wish
them into *my* gym? She doesn't even go to this school. She's
still in middle school.

Am I partly responsible for the destruction of school

property? I feel sick. On the other hand—no school! How sweet and sour. And then I spot Raf.

My cheeks heat up despite the cold.

Even though he's not facing me, I can tell it's him by his camel leather jacket. It's his fall/spring jacket, the one he wore when I first spotted him back in September and thought he was cute. For the rest of my life I will think of Raf whenever I see a boy in a camel jacket. Or anything camel colored. Like caramel sauce. Which is just as delicious.

Raf is not wearing his gloves. He dropped one of them at my apartment the night he came to pick me up (unsuccessfully) for Spring Fling. Since a piece of clothing is the key ingredient in a love spell, of course I asked Miri to whip one up for me. Unfortunately, she's still scarred from the mess caused by the love spell we put on Dad and isn't quite eager to get back in the fake-affection saddle just yet. (Small disaster involving us trying to break up my dad and his fiancée's wedding. Obviously we sorted it out, since they're currently honeymooning in Hawaii. Long story, but let's just say our stepmother turned out to be not as bad as we first feared.)

I hope his hands aren't cold. I guess, since it's April, there isn't much point in buying a new pair. Although he could probably find a fantastic sale.

Did he see me? Does he hate me? Should I duck or apologize again? You've got to make things happen, I remind myself. If I can fly on a broomstick with no seat belt, I can talk to a guy who used to like me.

First I need to hide my chin. I unroll my turtleneck so that

41

it covers the lower half of my face. Much better. Okay, now I'm going over. In ten. I tap my feet against the ground and count.

Nine, ten.

Ten more seconds.

He's leaving. My knight-in-camel is disappearing into the horizon like a setting sun. I know I should run after him, but my new shoes are stuck to the ground like lumps of pink clay. I wallow in my own pool of sadness until I'm snapped out of it by the sound of snickering.

I look to my right and see Jewel Sanchez, Melissa Davis, and Stephy Collins standing in a semicircle, all smirking at me. With their brown, red, and blond hair, they remind me of evil Charlie's Angels. They are all wearing brand-new trendy back-to-school outfits: tight jeans, designer spring coats, sunglasses perched on freshly highlighted hair. Even though I know that Melissa is the same height as Jewel, five foot six, she seems to tower over Jewel. The ego must add inches the way the camera adds pounds. Jewel's mahogany curls are clipped to her head in a style that tries to look like she just threw it back, even though from our years of Bee-Bee (Best Buds) status I know it took her at least an hour. Stephy's long blond pigtails are gone, and her short Tinker Bell do, along with her petite frame, makes her look like she's seven years old. A malicious seven-year-old, the kind who steals your candy. The three of them and Doree Matson were lucky enough to be London's chosen freshman four in the fashion show. They are therefore super A-list. Unfortunately, if their three pairs of eyes were laser beams, I would have disintegrated by now. I instantly look down at my shoes. I'll just walk away before they can attack me. Slowly, controlled. One step, two, three. Run, run, run!

Flump.

Controlled means not tripping over a bike rack and falling on my elbows, doesn't it?

I see a flash of light and I hope I've fallen unconscious. I'll wake up in the hospital, finally living the pitiable loads-of-flowers/life-size-card/hot-doctor scenario. But no such luck. I can hear the trinity of freshman evil cackling. I can't believe that Jewel, my ex–best friend, is actually laughing at me. Ignoring me is one thing, but laughing? From my spot on the ground, I see my surroundings blurring, mostly because of the prickling at the backs of my eyes.

Until a familiar hand reaches to help me up.

"Hi!" says Tammy. "There you are!"

I've never been happier to see my new best friend's face. "Thank God," I say, scrambling to my feet and brushing dirt from my coat. "I missed you! When did you get back?"

"Last night at eleven." She wrinkles her nose and gently touches my chin. "That looks like it hurts."

"It's fine, and you look amazing," I cry, and give her a bear hug. Unlike me, she's tanned and relaxed looking. "How was it?"

She drops her backpack to the pavement. "Fantastic. I went shark diving!"

"Excuse me?"

"I was in a cage underwater surrounded by great hammerheads! It was so cool."

"Is that safe? Why would you want to do that?"

"The cage totally protects you. And what do you mean, 'why'? Where else could I see sharks?"

I motion to Jewel, Melissa, and Stephy with my chin and then roll the turtleneck back up. Those girls are sharks in the sea of high school. "Maybe I should bring a cage to class."

Tammy laughs and then steps on tiptoe and scans the yard. "Have you seen Aaron?"

"No. Have you spoken to him since you've been back?"

"No. And he hasn't e-mailed me since I left on Sunday. Why? Do you think something is wrong? I know he was going to Mick Lloyd's party on the night I left for the Gulf of Mexico. I'll die if he hooked up with someone. You haven't heard anything, have you?" She immediately rubs the tip of her nose, like she always does when she's feeling insecure. It's a little on the large side, and she's convinced that its size is the reason she never had a boyfriend before Aaron.

"From who? You're the only person still speaking to me." Not getting an e-mail from your boyfriend for eight days doesn't sound promising. Not that I'd tell her that. There are certain things a best friend must never say. One is "I don't think he likes you." Two is "Yes, your nose is big." But the truth is her nose isn't why she's never had a boyfriend. She's never had a boyfriend because boys are morons. I mean, I've never had a real boyfriend, and nothing's wrong with me, right? Well, except for my extreme slobbiness and weirdo family. And my beard, but that's new. But in any case, I think it's bad news he hasn't been in touch over the break. Especially since after my dad's wedding they kissed for

44

three hours on her couch, and that was barely eight days ago. "I'm sure he's just busy," I say.

She scowls disbelievingly and then yawns, covering her mouth. "I'm tired."

"Probably because of the time zone difference."

"It's only an hour," she says, and laughs.

"Students! Hello? Students?" Mrs. Konch, the principal, is shouting into a loudspeaker. She's short and plump and reminds me of a dinner roll. "Everyone, please vacate the premises! Check your school e-mail tonight for an update!"

"Insane," Tammy murmurs. "Do you think the cow rumor is true? Seems unbelievable." She shrugs and yawns simultaneously.

"Um . . . yeah. Unbelievable." I know I should be more worried about the cows, but at the moment I'm more concerned by the laser beam of a glare coming at me from London Zeal. She's a few feet away, surrounded by her über-glam and shiny fashion show friends. The girls are all made up with their heavy lipstick, short denim skirts, and black knee-high boots, and the guys are wearing their coolio black leather jackets and crumpled jeans. London is all white: white jacket, white leather skirt, and a white two-inch heel on her unbroken foot to match the all-white full-leg cast. She wouldn't want to break her one-color-per-outfit rule.

I shouldn't make fun; the cast on her leg is all my fault, and I feel awful. I timidly approach the crowd. "London, I am so sorry," I say sincerely. Even though she's evil, she does not deserve to have a broken leg.

The group snickers. London shuffles toward me. "Sorry?" she hisses. "You'll be sorry. Very sorry when I'm done with

45

you." She jabs her french-manicured nail into my chest and then hobbles back to her friends.

Having the freshman A-list hating me is one thing. But the senior A-list too?

I'm doomed.

"Let's get out of here," Tammy says.

"Let's. Wanna come over?"

Tammy does a final scan around the yard, seemingly searching for Aaron. Then she gives me an okay sign with her right hand. In scuba diving, this can mean anything from are-you-OK to do-your-ears-hurt to yes-I'm-OK to I'm-terrific. So sometimes I'm not entirely sure what she means, but at the moment I think she's saying "Sounds like a plan."

"Please vacate the premises!" Principal Konch says again, sounding frantic and angry, as though it's our fault the cows have invaded our gym.

As though.

* * *

"The cows are in the gym?" Miri shrieks at six that night, stamping her foot on my carpet.

"Keep your voice down," I say. "Mom is watching the news in her room."

"How is that possible? Are you sure we did it?"

"No, but it makes sense. You zap them to safety, they disappear, and this morning there are fifty cows in the school gym. A coincidence? I don't think so." She kicks her chair and it teeters on its side. "Careful," I warn her. Miri's kicks are like mini weapons. "The spell was more of a moving spell than a safety spell," I add, nodding. "Although maybe your raw will stupidly thought that the cows were safer in the gym. Who knows?"

She waves her hands, clearly exasperated. "But . . . but . . . what's going to happen to them now?"

"How should I know? You tell me; you're the one who moved them!"

She tries to bite her fingers, but I hit her hand away. "They must be our cows," she says. "But how did they end up at your school? Do you think I was subconsciously trying to get you out of going to class?"

Aw. "Miri, that's so sweet! But listen, as much as I appreciate the thought, I think you should just do a spell reversal."

"No way," she says, shaking her head. "First of all, the spell reversal is a five-broomer, and I don't want to screw this up any more." Next to every spell in the book are broom icons. One broom means the spell is light and easy; five mean extremely intricate and difficult to cast. "And second, I'm not sending the cows back there. There must be another way. We'll have to move them somewhere else."

47

"And how are we going to do that?"

"We'll go over and zap them." She nibbles on her finger, then swallows.

"Did you just eat your skin? That is so vile." I shake my head in disgust. "And no, we can't just hop over to the school. I heard police sirens when I was leaving. It's hardcore there now. Someone will see us."

She looks panicked. "Do they know it was us?"

"Yes, Miri, when they spotted cows in the gym they assumed one of their student's little sisters had cast a magic spell."

She throws her hands over her eyes. "Oh, no!"

"I was being sarcastic. Of course they don't know! They think it was a senior prank."

She takes a deep breath. "Well, what's going to happen?"

"I just got an e-mail. School is closed tomorrow and Wednesday but reopening on Thursday. So the good news is I get two more days off. Thanks for your help!"

The phone rings and I grab it.

"He has mono!" Tammy says happily. "That's why he didn't e-mail! He was too tired to even make it to the computer. Isn't that great?"

"Hold on," I say, and lead Miri out of my room.

"Can you call her back, please?" Miri cries. "Hello? Important?"

"Give me two secs. This is a private conversation," I say, and push my door closed. "Tam, I'm happy that he wasn't breaking up with you, but aren't you worried you're going to get sick?" And then she'll have to miss school. Some people have all the luck.

Pause. "I feel fine."

I whisper into the phone since Miri's a little young to hear this. "But it's the kissing disease. You know? Passed from saliva? And you guys . . . made out."

"I'm healthy. And anyway"—now her voice drops to a whisper—"my mom would kill me." You'd think that having two moms would make Tammy's household super-liberal, but Tammy doesn't tell them a thing. "But isn't that great news?"

"You fell asleep on my couch today. Watching *Casablanca*. You love that movie," I say, more to myself than to her. Sleepiness is one of the signs of mononucleosis.

"I was tired, Rachel. Diving is exhausting. Especially with sharks."

Miri is banging on the door. And Tammy so has mono and is going to desert me at school. "Terrific. I gotta go. Wanna come over again tomorrow and watch *Titanic*?" She likes anything that won an Oscar. And maybe we can share toothbrushes and I'll catch mono from her. Awesome.

We hang up and I let my sister back in. "What are we going to do about the cows? Should we tell Mom?" she asks helplessly.

"Rachel!" my mom, apparently psychic, screams from her room. "Your school is on TV!"

Miri and I run to my mom's bedroom and there, on TV, are the cows.

A reporter is standing in front of them. "Today, at JFK High School, a school prank has been taken to a new level. Someone has moooooooooved"—I groan—"fifty cows into a high school gym. In related news, this explains the mysterious Saturday disappearance of the cattle at Sammy's, a slaughterhouse in upstate New York."

The scenery changes to Sammy's. "Hey!" my mom says from under her purple duvet. "Isn't that near . . ."

La, la, la. Miri starts biting her nails. I twirl my hair. An elderly man is on TV. "It was the strangest thing," he says,

49

looking utterly mystified. "The animals were here grazing at seven p.m. but gone by four a.m. We didn't hear a thing. It's almost supernatural. If we didn't know better, we'd think it was the work of aliens. . . ."

"Girls," my mom says, her eyes bearing into us, "something you want to tell me?"

Squirm.

"Rachel," she begins. "This is your plan to get school canceled?"

She thinks I did this? Hello? I'm the kid who was left behind. The child to whom nature forgot to hand down the witch gene. "Mom, I swear, I did *not* know this was going to happen."

She thumps the still-tucked-in spot beside her. "Why don't you two sit down and explain."

Miri's face squishes up like a raisin. Here come the waterworks. "It's my fault!" she wails, tears spilling. "I was trying to save the cows!" Sob. "I didn't mean to put them in the school gym, I swear, and now someone innocent is going to get blamed. And it can't be me because then people will know, but I don't want it to be someone else because that would be so unfair." Miri then climbs into the spot next to our mom, and I plop down on the corner of the bed.

My mom pats Miri's hair. "So you were trying to save the cows," she says.

We nod frantically. "Yes!"

"I see."

Okay, now that she knows, everything will be fine. Mom will tell us how to fix the situation, and all will be taken care of. Problem solved!

"So how are you going to fix it?" Mom asks.

What? "Um, us?" I say.

"I said you're allowed to use magic. But I also said that you have to face the consequences. And that means not expecting me to clean up your messes." She shakes her index finger at us. "You two are on your own."

Miri sinks into the mattress. "Do you have any advice?" she squeaks.

"Yes. Next time you cast a spell, think about what you're doing. Where did you think the cows were going to go?"

"Somewhere safe?" my sister answers.

"Yes, but where?"

"I don't know."

"Now you do," Mom says sternly. "So you'd better be more careful next time." And then she . . . smiles?

Where did that come from? "Are you okay, Mom?"

"Sorry," she says, still smiling. "Just thinking about something else."

Something else? What could possibly be distracting her from our moving cows across the state? "What's up with you?"

She aims the remote at the TV and clicks it off. "Lex called today."

"Lex?" Miri looks confused. "Luther?"

"Yes, Superman's nemesis called Mom," I say, and lie across Miri's legs. "What planet were you hatched on? Lex is the old guy from the bus." I can't believe he called already. It's only been a day since we got back. He's obviously desperate. "What did he want?"

"To take me out to dinner," she says, her smile widening.

Miri pulls the covers over her head. "I don't want you to date again! You're going to forget all about us!"

"Never ever," Mom says reassuringly.

"Well, I'm not worried," I say. "I want you to date again. Just not him. You're not going to go, are you?"

"Of course I am," she says. "Why wouldn't I? Didn't you think he seemed nice?"

"Nice and old," I say. "He probably eats dinner at five o'clock and orders the early bird special." Miri giggles from under the covers and I add, "You should be dating younger guys." I join Miri under the covers and then sit up so it feels like we're in a tent.

My mom sighs. "Don't be mean, Rachel. And it's not like any other guys are knocking down my door."

"When are you going out with him? Saturday night?" At least someone in this place has a date. I lift the comforter and pull my mom underneath with me.

"No," she says, sitting up beside me. "I told him I'd be happy to go out with him on the weekend of the eighth."

Apparently Mom plays hard to get. No last-minute plans for her. Someone's been reading her dating books. "That's in three and a half weeks!"

"It's not that long," she says. "And it's the next time you girls are at your dad's."

"We're not babies, Mom," I huff. "You're allowed to have a life when we're here. Dad has a life. You should too." I can make out her shrugging shoulders in the dark. "So what did you agree to?" I ask. "A Saturday-night dinner?"

"I didn't. I told him to call back closer to the date."

"That's good," Miri says casually. "Since he's so old, by then he might have kicked the bucket."

My mom snorts, and then the three of us laugh, and our tent feels warm and cozy like a cocoon. "I should start dinner," Mom says, and reaches to dismantle our hideaway.

"Don't," I beg. I don't want her breaking this bubble. I don't want to return to reality just yet. I don't want to worry about cows or going back to school or Raf or London or any of that.

"It'll be fine," she says, patting my knee.

Maybe she's right. The cow problem will eventually go away. And how bad can London's revenge be?

www.ineedtobehomeschooled.com

5

Kick. Kick.

Thank goodness for Tammy. If she weren't sitting next to me, I would definitely have to transfer.

The last two days went by too quickly. Why do good things disappear so fast? Vacation. Money. Ice cream.

The two of us are sitting on the right side of the auditorium, in the fifth row. I warned Tammy that her proximity to me would contaminate her social status, but she was convinced that, after a week and a half, the fashion show clique would have forgotten all about me. Teen years are like dog years. Thirteen days translates into thirteen months.

As always, there's good news and bad news. The bad news is they have not forgotten. London Zeal is kicking my chair. Yes, London and her posse of slick A-list seniors followed me to my seat so they could sit behind me and harass my back with their pointy-toed boots. Very mature, no? I'm pretending to ignore them. The other bad news is that the entire school has a lingering smell of cow excrement.

The good news is that my beard is gone. Since I

very cleverly hid it under my turtleneck on Monday, no one ever knew it was there, and now it's as if it never happened.

Kick. Kick. If the auditorium didn't have built-in seats, my chair would have been jolted across the room by now.

Kick, kick. She's making me wish I had broken both her legs.

Tammy yawns.

"You sound tired," I say. "You're not, right?"

"Nope."

"And your throat doesn't hurt?" Swollen glands are another sign of mono.

"Nope. Poor Aaron has mono. Not me."

We're both in denial. Tammy fell asleep on my couch again yesterday. But I cannot bear to be at school without her.

Kick. Kick, kick.

Enough! I spin to face my nemesis. "Yes, London?"

Her good leg is raised in midkick. "If it isn't Rochelle Weiner," she says.

"It's Rachel Weinstein," I say. "Can I help you?" What does she want from me? One of my good legs? I already told her I was sorry.

"I'm surprised to see you."

"I *do* go to school here."

"Yes, but it won't be a pleasant few months for you, I can promise you that. You may want to transfer. Unless you're enjoying all the coverage." The fashion show lackeys beside her giggle.

What is she talking about? What does she mean by

55

coverage? I look at Tammy for an explanation but she's sound asleep. I have no retort, so I spin back to the front. How did I manage to get the most popular girl in the school to hate me?

Onstage, Mrs. Konch, Vice-Principal Earls, and Will Kosravi, Raf's brother and the student council president, are huddled together. Then Mr. Earls clears his throat into the microphone. London kicks my chair again.

I nudge Tammy with my elbow. "You okay?"

Her eyes pop open. "I'm not tired."

Mrs. Konch takes the microphone. "I wish we could welcome you back under happier circumstances, but unfortunately, the school was a victim of a terrible prank." She glowers at the rows and rows of students. "We are currently investigating who is to blame. If anyone has any information, there will be a reward. And for those of you responsible, punishment will be less stringent if you turn yourselves in."

I slither in my seat. Kick.

"The animals," she says, frowning as snickers wave through the rows, "have caused severe damage to the gym floor—"

They have?

"—as well as damage to the ten classrooms neighboring the gym, the changing rooms—"

Those, too?

"—and the cafeteria."

Stupid, hyperactive cows.

"We will have to undergo a few changes," she continues. "First, all gym classes will now be held outside, so please dress appropriately. Second, until the classrooms are repaired, some freshman classes will be doubled up. Check the revised class schedules on the activities board. Finally, the library will be open for lunch."

Would you like some fries with that Shakespeare? Maybe Raf will be in some of my classes.

Kick.

Snore.

Groan.

Just my luck. Instead of getting doubled up with Raf's homeroom, I get Melissa and Jewel's.

I pull a groggy Tammy into the back row. As I'm about to sit down, Melissa slides into my seat. I lunge for the desk in front of her.

"Saved for Doree," Melissa says.

I point to the empty desk beside her. "And that?"

Jewel slides into the chair with a shrug. My stomach sinks. Not that I expect her to help me out.

At this late stage in the game, only one empty seat remains. It's by the window, so I sit Tammy in it—perhaps the fresh air will keep her awake—and crouch down beside her on the cold, hard linoleum. By the time I look up, Tammy's cheek is already flat on her desk. Which leaves me with no one to talk to.

Doree Matson, by far the most annoying of all the A-list freshman girls, mostly because she thinks she's smart and never stops talking in class, sashays into the room. "Hello, darling!" she sings to Melissa as she sits in the saved chair.

Janice Cooper, a friend of Tammy's, sits on the floor beside me. "I am so sorry," she says in a very serious voice. "How are you dealing?"

"Sorry about what?" I ask cluelessly.

She stares at me. "That you were added."

What is she talking about? "To what?"

Instead of looking at me, she fidgets with the gold barrette in her long brown hair. "You haven't seen?"

"Seen what?" Panic is taking hold like a straitjacket.

"Oh, you know. Never mind." She flushes and looks down at her book.

This is bad news. Cockroach-in-the-bathroom bad. I stretch upward and shake Tammy's arm and try to keep my voice down. "What's going on?"

Tammy opens her eyes. "Not tired."

"What have I not seen?" I whisper.

She reddens and snaps to attention. "Oh, Rachel, I'm trying to find someone to take it down. . . ."

Has something been written about me on the bathroom walls? My bra been hung up on the flagpole? "Take what down?"

"Your picture on the freaks Web site."

"What?" I shriek. I didn't even know there was a freaks Web site.

Tammy leans down toward me and whispers, "Rachel, I'm so sorry. I didn't see any point in telling you since I knew it would just freak you—I mean, upset you. It's a stupid thing started by some of the senior girls. Aaron told me about it, and I've already spoken to Mrs. Konch, demanding that the site be taken down, but I guess the administration is too busy with the cow stuff to do anything right now."

I think I might hyperventilate. "What does this Web site say?" I whisper.

"You don't want to know. But don't worry. We'll get it deleted."

I'd like to get myself deleted.

The day goes from very bad to very worse. Our math class isn't doubled because we're advanced, but Hayward gives us a pop quiz, which I completely fail because I can't concentrate. And I've never failed a math test in my life. Math is my thing. I swear I'm not being conceited, but some people have even called me a math genius. During the quiz, though, I can barely remember what a polynomial is because all I can think about is getting online.

And then Jewel, Melissa, and Doree are also in my bio class, something I would have loved a month ago, but now I just want to knock them over the head with my beaker.

I spot Raf as he's about to leave for lunch. His dark hair is curling over his eye. He slips his arm into his leather jacket. I need an icebreaker, something that can lead to real conversation. So how about those Mets? Sunny out, isn't it? Come here often? I could tell him that he dropped a glove at my apartment. But then I'd have to give it back. And then what would I sniff when I miss him?

I'll just apologize. I take a deep breath, as if I'm about to dive underwater, and then I walk straight over to him and say, "Hi."

59

He zips up his jacket without making eye contact. "Hey."

"How was New Orleans?"

"Fine."

"Did you have shrimp? I heard the seafood there is supposed to be . . . um . . . amazing. Was it? Is it Mardi Gras this time of year? No wait, it's in February. Or March. I just read something about it in *Cosmo*. Did you read it? Probably not. . . ." My babbling trails off. "Raf, I am so, so sorry that I stood you up for the Spring Fling."

He closes his locker. "Whatever."

He smells so good. Why was I so stupid? I should have told him that I had my dad's wedding that night. I should have known that he wouldn't care that I screwed up the show. I should have trusted him. I lean against the neighboring locker. "No, really. I thought that you would never want to be seen in public with me after what happened at the fashion show."

"Why would I care about what happened at the show?"

"Because I made a fool of myself." I keep my eyes on the floor.

"So?"

I was kind of hoping for a no-you-didn't. I look up and realize he's looking right at me. I meet his dark brown eyes. "So, I thought you'd cancel."

There is green in his eyes too, emerald speckles I never noticed before. "Listen," he says. "I couldn't care less about a stupid show. But it's too bad you think I'm so superficial that I care about what other people say. Plus," he continues, "the whole wedding thing was weird. Why did you say yes to being my date? You must have known your dad's wedding was on the same night."

"Well, I . . . I didn't think the wedding . . ." My voice trails off. Explaining that I was trying to cancel my dad's wedding will make me look even more psycho. "I'm sorry" is all I can manage.

"Whatever," he says again. "See ya." And with a shrug he takes off down the hallway.

Ouch. It's so unfair. Doesn't he know that I would have given my molars as well as my eyeteeth to go to Spring Fling with him? I've missed three of JFK's dances: Fall Ball, Winter Mixer, and now Spring Fling. Since prom is exclusively for seniors and their dates, I will officially be the only person in the entire school not to go to one single dance in a given year. Not that I know how to dance, but that doesn't mean I don't really, really want to go.

Tammy slides up beside me and puts her arm around my shoulders. "Wanna go out for lunch?"

I nod without saying a word.

I finally get online during seventh period, when we have computers. Since we pick our own stations, I arrive extra early to get the window seat way in the back. At least this class isn't doubled up.

Tammy sits next to me. "I don't think you should look," she says, resting her head on her hand. "I don't want to see it again."

"Well, you don't have to sit next to me if you don't want to. In fact, you shouldn't get this close to anyone, since you

61

have mono. And I have social leprosy. Now, what's the name of the Web site?"

She types it in for me.

Maybe it isn't about me. Maybe it's about a girl who looks just like me . . . my doppelganger. In Russia.

And that's when a close-up image of me and my beard fills the screen.

Okay, it's not just me. There are other people on the screen too, about ten or so additional students unfortunate enough to have made it onto this site. There is also the heading: The Freaks of JFK High. But I can't breathe. My beard is on the Web, and here I thought I concealed it so well. There's also a picture of my tripping over the bike rack. I guess that light I saw was a flash.

"Don't look up," Tammy says. So of course I do. London is standing at the door. All in white. Smirking.

*

I thought, It can't get worse than Thursday! How could it ever get worse than Thursday?

It gets worse on Friday.

"I'm sick," Tammy says via the traitorous telephone receiver.

"I'm going to pretend you didn't say that."

"I have a doctor's appointment this morning. My throat is burning."

"No. No. No! You're not sick! Mind over matter!"

"I'm so sorry."

I can't believe she's making me go to school by myself. When I'm the star of the freak Web site.

And it gets worse. I sit on the floor in almost all my classes. Even though I didn't fail my math quiz, like I thought I did, Ms. Hayward is very concerned by my A- and makes me stay after class. When I'm done, there is a picture of me and my beard glued to my locker.

It starts to rain. I have gym outside. JFK's obnoxious gym teacher makes you participate no matter what. Rain? Cramps? Broken leg? Doesn't matter—yesterday I even saw London in her gym clothes. We play softball, since April is softball month. I drop the ball repeatedly and get very wet.

Since I have no one to go out to lunch with, I eat alone in the library.

I don't see Raf all day.

I spend Friday night alone, definitely not at one of Mick Lloyd's legendary A-list-only parties. (I'm so far off the A-list I'm practically Z-list.) On Saturday, I wake up with a miserable cold with no fever, which means, unfortunately, I don't even get to have mono. Since I have no friends, I do nothing but work on assignments and stare at my picture on the freak Web site. I change the screen whenever my mom or Miri is around. Letting them see what a loser I am is just too humiliating. And Miri is in too good a mood for me to upset her. Because of some chemical in our gym floor, the cows cannot be used for beef production. So Miri called SALA, the Saving Animals' Lives Association, and they raised money to have the cows moved to a refuge in Alabama. Guess they were safer in the gym after all. They will now be able to live long and happy lives. Yay, them. I wish I were a cow.

On Monday, the lock on my locker doesn't work.

Someone had my lock clipped and put on a new one. I have to get the janitor to snap it open.

No matter how hard I look, I don't see Raf all day.

On Tuesday, I find a caricature of me and my beard in the first-, second-, and third-floor bathrooms, drawn right onto the backs of the stall doors, alongside the graffiti. And I'm not saying this because I'm oversensitive, but it so looks more like a caricature of a caveman than one of me. If it weren't accompanied by the slogan "Rachel Weinstein is a man," I wouldn't even have known it was supposed to be me. I attempt to wipe one off with the cheapo school soap, but it won't budge. The janitor, my new best friend, promises to take care of them over the weekend.

I see Raf only once, in the distance, but he doesn't see me.

On Wednesday, my clothes are stolen. Since we no longer have access to the gym lockers, I leave my jeans, sweater, and shoes in a bag by the bleachers while I'm playing third base. Unfortunately, by the end of the period, the bag, along with my clothes and my (sob) new shoes, is gone. So I have to wear my smelly gym shoes, a long green T-shirt, and my green gym sweatpants for the rest of the day. And the pants are giving me a wedgie, which I constantly have to stealthily adjust. Okay, fine, pick. Of course, once I'm in my gym clothes, I see Raf every four seconds. In the hall, on the stairs, at the water fountain. I can feel him watching me too, staring. Once, he opens his mouth as if to say something, but I quickly duck out of view. I don't need him making fun of me too.

On Thursday, as I walk through the senior hallway on

my way to second period, I hear hysterical laughter. And I see a large crowd of students circling London, who is dressed in another all-white outfit. Her arms are shuddering above her head. Her hips are bumping from side to side. Her one good leg is quaking. What's wrong with her?

"You look just like her," one of her lackeys shrieks. "You're nailing it!"

London's nasal voice pierces my eardrums. "I call it the Electric Rachel."

Oh, no. Ah, jeez. I knew it looked like I was being electrocuted when I danced. I knew it! Miri always told me I wasn't *that* bad, but this proves it. Keep your head down, and speed up, I tell myself.

"There she is!" one of the other lackeys cries as I pass them.

Don't look up, don't look—

"Rochelle! Why don't you show us how it's done?" London cackles.

Ignore them. Just ignore them. Pretend they don't exist.

"Rochelle!" I hear her hollering as I turn the corner, away from them.

By the end of the day, patches of kids all over school are doing the "Electric Rachel." In the hallways. In the classrooms. In the library. It's become more popular than the Macarena was.

By last period, I can't take it anymore, and I hide in the bathroom. Tears spill over my cheeks as I stare at my bearded self. Okay, I know I deserve some karmic punishment for all the awful things I did last month . . . but come on. I have no friends except an absentee best friend (mono

65

now confirmed), the love of my life hates me, and now the entire school is mimicking me? This is too much.

And if London can name a dance after me, how come she can never remember my name? Huh? Huh?

When I get home, I am beyond depressed. Mom is working late, so I am free to wallow. I lie facedown across my floor, letting the pink carpet absorb my frustrated tears. Tigger chooses this moment to sit on my back.

The phone rings and rings and rings, and I know it's Tammy calling to check on me, but I can't bear to get up.

When Miri gets home from Tae Kwon Do, she picks up Tigger and sits beside me.

"Howdy," she says. "Why are you lying on the floor?"

"I . . . they . . ." Though I promised myself I wouldn't, I break down and tell her the whole story, except for the freak Web site. That was *too* humiliating. "And I wouldn't even care so much, but the fact that Raf doesn't like me anymore is the worst part."

My sister looks horrified. Like Tigger just got run over. "What a you-know-what. I hate her. What can I do to make you feel better?"

I turn over and face the ceiling. "Zap them into cats." Although they'd probably circle me and scratch me to death. "Don't bother. What's the point? There's no point to anything."

"I know what will cheer you up!" Miri says, eyes brightening. "Let's do something from the Save the World list we made on vacation."

"Why not?" At least I'll have something to do. And I knew she would ask me to help her with the list eventually. Too bad I kind of fell asleep while she was making it.

She runs into her room and then returns, waving an article from the *New York Times*. "I've done some research on number one, helping the homeless. This article is all about the malnutrition of the people living on the streets in Manhattan. I was thinking we could zap up some food to hand out."

"All right," I say lifelessly. They can have my dinner. I'm not even hungry. I didn't have lunch today. The library was packed, so I hid in the bathroom and talked to my caricature.

Miri peers at me strangely. "Why don't you relax? Take a bath. Watch TV. You look stressed. We'll work on this over the weekend." She skips back to her room.

Instead of watching TV, I pull myself off the floor and turn on my computer. And it's just as I feared. There's a new picture of me right beside the beard one. I'm in my gym clothes, picking the wedgie in my butt. It's so pathetic looking that I start to laugh. I've officially hit rock bottom. And on the bottom I have a wedgie.

"What's so funny?" Miri asks, and before I can switch the screen, she sees it. A younger sister just shouldn't see her big sister looking so humiliated. It's like seeing your dad cry or your favorite actress without makeup. I expect her to start sobbing, but instead her face turns red, and her clenched fists pound against my desk. "London did that?"

"Don't worry. It's a joke."

"Don't say that! You're making me really mad!"

"I'm a loser, all right? Your big sister is a social failure!"

* * *

I cry through dinner. I cry while I take a bath. By the time I climb into bed, my eyes are swollen and I look like a raccoon. Hope London brings a camera tomorrow. The shot should be a real winner.

I fall into a dreamless sleep. At about three in the morning, I wake to a shadow looming over me.

"What are you doing, Mir?"

"I'm not Miri; I'm the tooth fairy," the shadow says. "You're dreaming."

Weird dream, I think as I fall back asleep. When the alarm beeps me awake, I rub the crusted tears from my eyes. I'm not going back to school. I'll just hide. I pull the pillow out from under my head and cover my face with it. I lie on something scratchy. Something that smells . . . like a boy? Raf's gray wool glove? Why is his glove under my head? I don't remember taking it out of my T-shirt drawer to cuddle with. I squeeze it. And then I look up . . . and see Miri in the doorway.

"I came up with a few plans to make you feel better," she says sheepishly.

Sweet scratchy glove. I look back at Miri. Then back at the glove. Does this . . . does this mean what I think it means? "Tooth fairy my butt! Did you do the love spell?"

She gives me a shy smile. "I did."

Yes! Raf is going to *like* me again! And once he *likes* me again, he'll always like me—even when the spell wears off. At least, I hope so. "But I thought you were afraid of doing love spells."

"I was. But I couldn't stand seeing you so sad. So I got over it. Got to get back on the broom, right?"

How sweet is she? The cloud over my head dances away. Boogies away. Electric Rachels away. "I love you!" I say, and rub the glove against my cheek. Okay, it's itchy, but who cares? Raf is going to love me again! We could be frenching by lunchtime!

"Now, remember, emotion spells are temporary. And a love spell only lasts like three to four weeks. And it takes a day or two to kick in."

Drat. "Another lunch in the bathroom for me."

She smiles again and holds up what looks like a home-made tennis ball, except it's made of rubber bands, glue, and aluminum foil. "Not necessarily. But you have to bounce this against London Zeal."

"What?"

"Throw it at her, let it bounce, and I promise your day will get better."

I feel a flush of excitement. "What did you do?"

She tosses me the ball and winks. "You'll see."

69

Bounce, Baby, Bounce

6

I don't see Raf or London all morning. Unfortunately, I do see the drawings of me still on the stall doors.

I finally cross paths with Raf when I'm on my way outside for softball, in full gym attire. He hesitates but then gives me a half smile and walks away. *A half smile!* Wahoo! Does that mean the spell is working?

After gym, I spot London hobbling down the hall alone, looking like an icicle. White baggy pants, white hoodie, white fedora. She must have invested in an entirely new leg-cast-appropriate colorless wardrobe. "Nice outfit," she snarls at me. "It really suits you."

Now's my chance. I've been carrying the gluey ball around with me all day, gripping it in my hand, which didn't improve my note-taking or softball skills one bit. I throw it at her leg.

"What are you doing, you freak?" she demands as it hits her in the good ankle, bounces twice, and then rolls down the hall.

I lunge. Got it!

"You are such a weirdo," she says. Nothing happens. Too bad. I was kind of hoping she'd turn into a frog.

"Have a good day," I say, and run toward the stairs. It's not like she's going to run after me. She's not very mobile these days. I sprint to my locker (where I left my clothes for safekeeping) and try to remember my new combination. Doesn't work. Oh, no. Did she change my lock again?

The thing is . . . this lock looks a lot like my old lock. My original lock. I try the combination: 27, 12, 33 . . . It works! My old lock is back! How did that happen?

I open my locker and find my clothes. And not only the clothes I was wearing today but the clothes I was wearing on Wednesday. As well as my—gasp!—pink shoes. Abracatastic!

Miri's spell must have something to do with all this. I grab an outfit and run to a bathroom stall to change. And on the door where the beard drawing was? There's a picture of a girl inserting a wad of Kleenex into her bra. It's a rough drawing in black marker, but I know it's of London. How do I know this? Because on the picture are the words "London Zeal stuffs."

"You have to tell me what that fantastic spell was," I say, throwing myself onto Miri's bed. I haven't stopped smiling all day.

She swivels in her chair. "With this rubber and glue, your actions will bounce right back to you. It's temporary but still a goody."

I laugh. "It was awesome. You have no idea. When I got to computer class, everyone was on the freaks site, and it was

71

filled with weird pictures of London. London bleaching her mustache. London before her nose job. London drooling on her pillow. All of my photos were replaced with shots of her! She was furious and yelling at her entire posse, because apparently they're the only ones who know the password to get on the site. And then, when I walked down the hall, everyone was doing this weird dance-shuffle thing. And you know what they were calling it? The Hobbling London Limp! Ha! By the end of the day, she was practically Z-list!" Okay, fine, maybe just B-list, but still, she had undergone a definite demotion. Her own posse was avoiding her! "But do you want to know the best part of the day? Her clothes went missing! She had to wear her gym clothes all day." At least they're all green, so she didn't have to break her one-color rule.

Miri giggles. "And what happened with Raf?"

Sigh. "Not much."

"I thought so. I warned you it might take a while."

"I know, I know. I'm just so excited! It was the best day ever!"

"You know," she says coyly. "Being happy is really the best revenge. And one way to be happy is to help others. So will you help me with the feeding-the-homeless spell tomorrow?"

"Absolutely," I promise. "Your wish is my command. And I owe you big time."

I'm still hopping about at dinner.

"Girls," my mom says, dishing us mashed-potato-and-broccoli stew. Ew. "Remember Adam from the tour?"

"Um, yeah," I say. "The Yankees hottie."

My mom laughs, her arm jiggles, and the gravy she's holding splashes on her shirt. "Oops. Yeah, him. He left a message asking me out."

"Go, Mom, go!" I shriek. Score! "I knew my plan would work. See? I told you. Now do you promise to listen to me whenever I have suggestions?"

"Yes, Rachel, you were right. I promise to take your dating advice."

I pass her a napkin. "So when are you going?"

She scrapes the spill and shakes her head. "Going? I'm not. I already have a date with Lex."

I don't believe this. "Hello? Don't be crazy, Mom. You can date more than one man."

"Rachel, that's not fair to them," she says.

Snort. "Mom, until there's a ring on your finger, you can date a hundred men. A thousand." Although I don't know how she'd remember all their names. Sometimes she has difficulty remembering mine. I guess it comes with the territory when you're over thirty. Anyway, she'd definitely need some sort of dating filing system.

"I don't know, honey. I don't have that much free time."

"Mom, what are your plans for tonight? Read a romance novel? Tomorrow a murder mystery? You'll find the time."

She chews a piece of broccoli, looking thoughtful. "Maybe I'll see how it goes with Lex first and then set up a date with Adam."

I throw my spoon down in disgust. "Mom, Adam called today. You're not seeing Lex for two weeks. Adam is a hot

73

commodity. In two weeks he could be engaged." She obviously doesn't read *Cosmo*. "This is what you're going to do," I say authoritatively. "You are going to call Adam back. You are going to tell him that you *will* go out with him *this* weekend."

"But—"

"But nothing. I know Miri and I are in town. Big deal. We're practically grown-up. We don't need to be babysat."

She looks doubtful. "Are you sure?"

"Yes!" I scream, and kick Miri under the table. Backup?

"Yes," she adds reluctantly.

My mom takes a sip of her zucchini juice, sets down her glass, and then says, "Okay, I'll call him back."

"When?" I ask.

"Tomorrow?"

Zap! Wrong answer. "Call him now before you chicken out." I reach over and pick up the phone. "What's the number?"

She shakes her head. "I can't talk to him with you two watching."

"We'll go to the other room." I drag Miri out by her arm.

Once we're safely on the other side of the closed kitchen door, Miri smacks my hand away. "She's not ready."

"She's ready. And she's dialing, so let her do her thing."

"What do you know?" Miri grumbles. "You've been on, like, one date."

I shush her with a wave of my hand. "How did you know how to make a broom fly? Some things are innate."

"You're innate," she counters.

"That didn't even make sense. Can you shut up now?" I press my ear against the door.

"Hi, Adam?...Yes, it's Carol....Good, thanks, how are you?...Saturday night? That's tomorrow. Well... I..."

Normally I would never recommend that a woman accept a date *the day before*. But this is a special case. I push my way back into the kitchen and nod vigorously.

She shrugs at me and says, "Okay, sure. Why not?"

Wahoo to the power of two! My mom has a date!

"Does he have any sons?" I mouth to her, but she doesn't get it. Oh well. I need her to hurry up the call anyway, to keep the line free for Raf's declaration of love.

"I can't go," my mom cries, blond hair dripping down her shoulders, fluffy pink towel wrapped around her skinny body. "I have nothing to wear."

That's true. And trust me, I've attempted to raid her closet on many occasions. "Try on what I put on your bed," I say.

Luckily for her, while she was in the shower (for an entire hour, I might add; I hope she took the time to shave her legs for the special occasion), I set out the outfit I felt was her most date appropriate. Her sexy (sexiest, anyway; she seriously needs to do some shopping) black pants, a lime green low-cut sweater, her highest black heels, and her heart-shaped silver necklace that she bought years ago and never wears. I asked Miri if she agreed with my choices, but she wasn't the least bit interested. Not that she'd be any fashion help. She thinks polka dots and stripes match. Anyway, she's too busy finishing up her homework. Yes, English essays on a Saturday night. Real winner, huh? Not that I have anything wild and crazy on deck. No A-list parties to go to. No plans except helping Miri with her Save the World spells.

"How do I look?" my fully-dressed mom asks, pirouetting.

"Awesome." She looks feminine and classy. Her boobs are sagging a bit, but there's nothing she can do about *that*. I promise you, I'm never breast-feeding. What I should do is encourage her to buy a push-up bra. I might have to become her full-time stylist. Maybe that's what I'll do when I grow up. Seriously. I could work exclusively for stars. Designers will send me all their latest, desperate to dress my clients. Of course they'll send extra pieces for little old *moi*.

Although I'm not sure I really want a career in which I have to deal with people's fragile egos all day. I need to find a job that I can do on my own. Maybe I'll be a painter. Or a novelist. After all the pain I've been through lately, I'm sure I could come up with something really dark and terrifying, something that will really sell.

"What's your makeup strategy?" I ask my mom. Not that she isn't cute on her own, but adding color to her cheeks won't hurt. If we had some extra time, I would encourage a visit to the hair salon (i.e., make the appointment) so that she could get rid of her absurdly dark roots.

"I want to look natural," she says. "Some blusher?"

"All right, that'll work." I lead her to the bathroom mirror as though she's on a leash. "With a little mascara and lip gloss."

She sucks in her cheeks and applies the color. I didn't even know she had blush! I flip the compact over. Plum Fairy. I'm impressed. She seems to know what she's doing. Why doesn't she put on makeup more often?

When she's finished, she starts fidgeting with her outfit and biting her nails.

"What time is he coming?" I ask.

"Not till seven-thirty."

"It's only seven! You'd better relax or you're going to be too eager and he'll sense your desperation."

"I'm not desperate. I'm nervous. Why am I nervous?"

I take her quivering hand and pull her toward the kitchen. "Why don't you pour yourself a glass of wine, sit down, and read one of your books? Get in the mood for romance."

Nodding, she uncorks a bottle of Merlot. "Now just chill," I say, and hand her a book. For the next twenty minutes I don't hear a peep from her. Until . . .

"Oops."

A large blob of red wine has somehow landed on the left breast of my mom's pretty sweater. "What did you do?" I ask incredulously.

"Spilled."

The clock on the wall says she has five minutes. What am I going to do now? I've searched her wardrobe and there are no other choices. And that's when I notice her teeth.

77

Why do they look so . . . dirty? "Mom, have you brushed your teeth lately? They look brown."

She rests the wineglass on her book and runs to the mirror. "I think it's because of the red wine. They're stained."

"Well, brush them again! You can't go on a first date with stained teeth!" The clock now says four minutes.

"But what am I going to wear?" She's eating her fingers in distress.

"I don't know! I'll find something while you scrub your teeth." Who knew red wine did that? It should be illegal.

Three minutes.

I frantically grope through the clothes in her closet. Too frumpy, too ugly, too worky. Maybe something of mine? The cute V-neck . . . No, too young.

Two minutes.

"Is it coming off?" I scream.

"Almost," she says, and then I hear gurgling. Spit. "Did you find anything?"

"Yes. I found the lime sweater, but you ruined it." If only there was some way to get rid of the stain. Yeah, right. Even I know red wine doesn't come out so easily. If only we had some superstrength stain remover. If only . . .

If only my mom was a witch and could zap the stain away.

She's standing in front of me, clad only in her pants and beige bra. "So? What should I wear?"

I put my arms on her shoulders, look her straight in the eye, and say, "What you had on before."

"But it's stained," she says, bewildered.

"Zap it clean."

Her nostrils flare. "Rachel, you know I'm a nonpracticing witch."

"No, Mom, you used to be a nonpracticing witch. But
it's time to evolve. There will be no consequences to cleaning your shirt. Seriously, what can happen? All the dry
cleaners in the country will unexplainably burn down? I
know you didn't use magic when we were kids because you
wanted us to have normal childhoods, and that totally
worked. We experienced lots of lows, not to worry. But you
promised to take my advice. And I'm telling you to zap it.
Trust me. Just do it." She zapped the wheels of the bus, so
what's the big deal about zapping a stain? She should really
just zap herself a new wardrobe, but let's take this magic stuff
one baby step at a time.

She pushes past me into the closet. "Rachel, there must   79
be something else for me to wear." She holds up a boring
white button-down.

"Will your date be at the office?"

Then a black long-sleeved sweater.

"A funeral home?"

A striped turtleneck.

"Ski hill?"

The buzzer rings, interrupting our fascinating exchange.
Panic drains the Plum Fairy right off her cheeks. I hold up
her lime sweater and wave it like a flag. "Just zap it!"

"I . . . but . . ." She gnaws on her thumbnail. The downstairs buzzer rings again.

"Mom?" Miri calls out. "Do you want me to get that?"

"Zap it!" I holler.

"Fine!" Her lips purse, the temperature in the room drops, and the stain is . . . gone.

Whoa. That was cool. And freaky. How did she direct her energy right at the shirt? What if it's like radiation? Should I have worn one of those X-ray blankets like at the dentist? "Well done. Not so bad, was it?"

The buzzer goes off one more time.

"Miri, can you get it?" I scream, and toss the sweater to my bra-clad Mom. She slides it over her head and models in front of the mirror. "Perfect," I say. "Go get 'em! Oh, and Mom? Now that you're comfy using magic . . ."

"I won't need to use more magic," she says, tight-lipped.

"Yeah, yeah, I know, but if the date is boring, like if he starts droning on about sports or his job or something, zap your cell phone to ring, and pretend it's one of us with an emergency."

She rolls her eyes, which isn't her most appealing look. "Don't do that on your date," I advise.

By the time Adam gets to the front door, my mom and I are ready to greet him with smiles. I try gently to move Tigger out of the way with my foot, but he isn't budging. Miri is there too, and she's scowling.

Actually, I'd like to be the one Adam is taking out. He's hot. In his copper sweater (upgrade from the Yankees jersey, definitely) and with his modelesque cheekbones, he looks like a Greek god. I wonder if there's really such a thing as a Greek god? If witches are real, then maybe Adonis is too! Maybe he's Adam!

Would a Greek god live in Jersey?

"Hi, girls," he says. "Hi, Carol. Ready to go?"

Miri makes an I'm-constipated face and disappears into her room. Tigger hisses and follows at her feet.

"You two have fun!" I call down the hallway. "And make sure to have her home by midnight! Kidding!" Kind of. We don't want any hanky-panky just yet. At the moment, two witches in the family are plenty.

The Fountain of Juice

7

"Why do you think he hasn't called yet?" I wonder out loud a few minutes later. Miri and I are lying on the kitchen table, feet up against the apple-patterned wallpaper.

Miri shrugs. "I don't know. Maybe he's just not that into you?"

I gently kick her ankle so that she teeters to the side.

"Now can we focus on my stuff?" she asks. "You promised."

"Yes, let's save the world. What's your plan?"

"I told you, number one on the list. Feed the homeless."

"All of them?"

"Eventually, yes. But my current plan centers around the homeless in Washington Square Park. And I found a multiplying spell. So all we need to do is pick a food, multiply it, and then give it away for free. What do you think?"

"Good idea. When do we give out the food?"

"Tomorrow. If it works. We have to pick a food first."

"Brownies?"

"We want to feed them, not make them fat."

Time to put on the thinking cap. What a lame

expression. My dad uses it all the time. He called today from Hawaii; he and Jennifer were at a luau. Could not understand a thing he was saying over the ukulele music. All I could hear was him reminding me to take my vitamins. Hey . . . "The food should have lots of vitamins. Like spinach."

She pretends to gag. "They're homeless, not taste budless."

"Good enough for Popeye but not for them?"

"Rachel, we can't hand out plates of spinach. We need something that people like. And that's healthy. And that tastes good."

"Orange juice," I say, suddenly inspired. "Or oranges so we don't need cups."

Miri claps her feet together. "Perfect! You're a genius. Very easy. And vitamin C not only nourishes but improves people's moods!"

"We can even whip some extras up for Tammy. Maybe then she'll get better and drag her butt back to school."

Miri flips around so that she's sitting upright on the table and leans into A^2. "We need a teaspoon of mint, one-seventh of a cup of chocolate, ten grams of grape skin. And one example of what we want to replicate. So one orange. Okay, you check for the ingredients, and get the measuring spoons. I'll set up in my room."

A half hour later, we're all mixed and set. Miri's sitting cross-legged on her carpet, the orange in her hand, and I'm standing behind her. She uses a silver spoon to coat the fruit in the yummy-looking mixture and then lowers it to the carpet.

"That's so going to stain," I warn. "We should do it in my room—my carpet has seen better days." Once orange, it is now pink due to flea extermination chemicals (Tigger's fault).

"We would if your entire closet weren't on the ground." She takes a deep breath.

"Here is one
Placed on the floor,
I nod three times
And now there are more."

Suddenly, the room fills with cold and the strangest thing happens: the orange starts morphing.

It splits in two, like it's giving birth. And then both blobs begin to regrow to their adult size, giving me the shivers.

I don't think I've ever seen anything this creepy.

About twenty seconds pass, and the orange and its clone do it all over again—they each split in half and regrow. And then the four do the same. It's like we're watching a science fiction movie. The next thing I know, there are at least *fifty* oranges covering the floor and it's starting to smell like a grove in here. A hundred oranges. Two hundred. Wow. Coolest trick ever. I take a step back.

"Watch your feet!" Miri warns. Four hundred. The carpet is blanketed in at least two layers of oranges. Her room is flooding with fruit. She stands up and climbs onto her bed.

Eight hundred. "Um . . . Mir? How many are there going to be?" I step onto her desk chair as the pile of oranges doubles in height.

"I . . . um . . ."

84

Our eyes lock over the citrus explosion and we can't help laughing. But the amusement quickly turns to alarm. We could *drown* in here. "Can't you make it stop?" I ask, and leap over the fruit to stand beside her on the bed.

"I don't know." The oranges are touching the top edge of the mattress. If she didn't have a super-tall pillow-top mattress, we'd have gone under by now. She frantically flips through the spell book's pages.

"Miri, find a stop spell!"

"I'm trying!"

The oranges spill over onto her bedspread. "We're going to suffocate in here!" I say, and get ready to drag the two of us to noncitrus safety. But just as I'm about to leap, Miri mutters something and the multiplying jerks to a stop.

"That was close," Miri says, giving A^2 a grateful pat. She gently steps off the bed and tries to wade through the deluge. "I'm so sleeping in your room tonight."

85

* * *

"So tell us everything," I say as I stuff a forkful of poached egg into my mouth. We're sitting in a booth at our neighborhood diner, on Tenth and Broadway. It used to be our favorite brunch spot, but we haven't been here in ages. The fries are extra crispy. My mom always refuses to order any, then eats most of mine.

"It was *interesting*," my mom says from across the table, ripping open a sugar and dumping it into her coffee. Her short hair is tied back into a tight ponytail, which only helps to display her horrible brown roots. Apparently, she needs me to be her stylist 24/7.

By the time Mom got home last night, Miri and I were already asleep in my bed. Okay, fine, that's a lie; we were wide awake, but we didn't want to explain Operation Orange. We closed Miri's door, hoping Mom wouldn't look in. Mom always checks my room first anyway. I guess that's because she's been doing it longer, since I'm the older child. She crept into my room at eleven-thirty and tucked us in with an "Aw, sweet." Which it was, until Miri rolled herself in the duvet like it was a sari and I almost froze to death.

We are planning on telling her about the oranges. That's why we suggested brunch. We're definitely going to tell her . . . after we pepper her with date questions for as long as possible.

Miri dumps a bowlful of ketchup onto her fries and her tofu omelet. "How so?"

"We went to a place in Little Italy. First we ordered—"

"He didn't do anything stupid like order for you, did he?" Miri asks.

"No, why would he do that?" She steals one of my fries and dips it in Miri's ketchup.

Miri shrugs. "I heard that some men do that."

She's doing an excellent job with our peppering-Mom-with-questions plan.

"We were small-talking about silly things," Mom says, "like the weather, New York, you kids . . ."

"So we're silly?" I ask.

"You know what I mean. Anyway, when the appetizers came, the conversation just dried up. And we both focused intensely on our plates. The goat cheese salad was suddenly the most interesting piece of food I had ever seen. A minute dragged into two, and then three, and then four . . ."

Oh, no. That's the worst. I've pushed my mom into dating again before she's ready and now I've scarred her for life. She's going to give up dating and get another cat.

"And then I couldn't take it anymore. So I looked into his mind."

"You can do that?" I ask in amazement.

"I read his mind so I could know what to talk about. At first he was thinking that I seemed nice but we obviously had nothing in common. And he was wondering what the score on the Yankees game was."

"What a jerk!" I interject.

"So I blurted out, 'I wonder what the score on the Yankees game is.'"

"Way to go, Mom!" I can't believe it!

"You don't need to be a mind reader to come up with that one," Miri says. "Wasn't he the one wearing the Yankees jersey? On a baseball tour?"

I motion to her to shush. "Brilliant idea, Mom! What did he say?"

"His eyes lit up. And he said he was wondering the same thing!"

Miri shovels her eggs into her mouth. "I hate Yankees fans. He'd be far more interesting if he were a Mets fan."

"*You* don't have to date him," I tell her. I lean across the table. "So what happened next?"

My mom steals a handful of my fries. "We talked about baseball for a while."

"You don't know anything about baseball," Miri says, frowning.

"Right. So I had to do more mind reading. You'd be shocked how much sports trivia this man has in the front of his mind. It's amazing really. Scores, RBIs . . ."

"RBI what?" I ask. My mom can finally explain to me the secret language of boys!

"Who knows? That's all I got. Men think a lot about sports. And about other stuff," she says, and then blushes.

Ew. I want my mom to date, but I don't need the unnecessary details.

"Anyway, I basically kept talking about what he was thinking," she says.

"Mom," Miri says, shaking her head with disapproval, "what happened to wanting a guy to like you for you?"

"I know, I know. But it's not like I was in love with this man. I was really nervous, and I saw the night as an experiment. To find out what could happen."

"And what happened?" Miri and I both ask.

"Jinx," I say. "Buy me a Coke."

Mom smiles. "He begged me to see him again. Tonight."

I'm in awe. "Are you going to?"

"No. I told him maybe next weekend."

"Do you like him?" I can't believe this.

"He liked me. I believe his exact words were 'You might be my soul mate.' But I haven't decided how I feel about him. Seeing him tonight seems a bit excessive. But I have to admit, it's nice to feel wanted. Anyway, we'll see. What were you two up to last night?"

Abort topic! Switch gears! I want to avoid this subject

for as long as possible. "Um . . . what did you have for the main course?"

"Fettuccine Alfredo. Now back to you two."

"Wait!" Miri says. "What about dessert?"

My mom smiles. "Lemon sorbet. And what did you two eat? Oranges?"

So my mom saw the fruit. And she wasn't too angry. After Miri outlined her plan, Mom gave us her "just be careful" lecture (whatever, she's using magic to help her dating life; how careful is she being?) and then shocked us by offering to help distribute. "I'd rather be around if you're talking to strangers," she explained.

And that's where we are now. In Washington Square Park, handing out oranges to anyone who looks hungry. The three of us filled two shopping bags each with as many as we could carry. The sun is shining, and my first bag is almost empty.

89

"Would you like some fruit?" I ask an elderly woman in a sleeping bag on a bench.

She eyes me suspiciously, so I gently place it on the edge of her bed. She picks it up, squeezes it, and then nods. I hand her another one, and the three of us move on.

My hands are starting to chap from the cold, but my insides feel warm, like I just finished a cup of hot chocolate. I don't remember the last time the three of us had so much fun. Once our bags are done, we stop back at the apartment for a refill and then head over to the Lower East Side.

"Oranges! Who wants fruit?" Miri sings, looking happy

but determined. Her cheeks are flushed, her hair is wind-blown, and she hasn't stopped smiling all afternoon. Next to her, my mom has the same sun-kissed tousled look. And I bet I do too. I lock my arms through theirs, and we giggle as we skip down the sidewalk, smiling and reeking like a fruit stand.

My good mood lasts until the next morning, when Raf walks past my locker. I wave and our eyes lock and I think, This is it! But then . . . he gives me his half smile, waves back, and walks away. Hello? He's supposed to be under my spell. Why isn't it working? Is his hatred for me that intense?

I don't have time to dwell because we're rounded up for a second all-school meeting in the auditorium. I shuffle inside and find a chair in the front row. Alone. With an empty seat on each side of me. Apparently, my loser status is still intact.

Mrs. Konch, Mr. Earls, and Will Kosravi are back on-stage. "We have some unfortunate news," Mr. Earls says. "The damage to the gym, the cafeteria, the locker rooms, and the downstairs classrooms will cost approximately forty thousand dollars to repair."

The room collectively gasps.

"Even more unfortunate is that the insurance company does not cover acts of cows. Especially since they're sure that this is an act of vandalism, or as some might call it, the senior prank."

I sink lower in my seat. Insurance won't cover it?

Will takes the microphone. "Guys, I'm pleading with

you: if you know who's responsible, turn them in. Because the money has to come from somewhere. Please do the right thing." It's almost as if he's looking directly at me . . . right into my liable soul.

Guilt explodes in my stomach like a bad case of food poisoning. Maybe I should come clean. I'll go to Konch's office and admit it's my fault. My family's, anyway. Yeah, right. I could never turn Miri in. The government would go nuts, and she would be forced to live in a glass box where creepy scientists would study her every move. Poor Miri. I want to wrap her in a warm blanket and protect her, not turn her in. Anyway, she didn't mean any harm. She was trying to save the cows.

Mr. Earls is glaring at the seniors in the back row. It's not like anyone suspects me. I look up at Mrs. Konch. She's eyeing the last few rows with extra suspicion. And Will is . . . still staring at me. Right at me. Intensely at me. I quickly look away. Oh, no. He knows. Gulp. Impossible. He can't have a clue. He's probably not even looking at me. He's most likely admiring some hottie behind me. Why am I such a diva? I twist around, but the block of rows behind me is filled with sophomore boys. Hmm. Slowly, I lift my head back up. Oh, no. He's still staring! I know, he probably hates me because of Raf. That must be it. Of course he doesn't know about the cows. He hates me because I stood up his baby brother. Just as I want to protect Miri, Will wants to protect Raf.

91

I sit on Miri's spell book to get her attention. "We need to zap up some money."

"I have forty bucks," she says, pointing her chin toward her piggy bank.

"A little more than that." It still stinks like oranges in here even though we gave them all away.

She drops her pen. "How much?"

"Forty thousand."

"Are you crazy?"

"Unfortunately not. The cow damage is expensive to fix. And they don't know where to get the cash."

Her face drains of color. "What are we going to do?"

"Rob a bank?"

She jumps out of her chair and cracks open her piggy bank, which looks nothing like a pig, since it's a plastic slot machine. You press a cherry and it opens up. I know this not because she's shown me, but because I once had to borrow five bucks. Fine, ten bucks. All right, fifty, but I was desperate. She waves a twenty in the air. "Let's do a multiplying spell!"

"I don't know," I say, feeling squeamish. "I didn't mean we need to zap up money literally."

"Why not? It's perfect! We'll whip some up, and you'll mail it to the principal. Problem solved."

"I'm pretty sure that's mega-illegal."

She sits back down in her chair. "Why?"

As much as it pains me, I explain. "We'd be creating counterfeit bills. And each bill has a serial number. So the school would know. And if they didn't know, we could get them into a lot of trouble." When did I become the responsible one?

"I don't think anyone would notice," she says stubbornly.

"It's too risky. We've already caused enough trouble. And you have to think of the consequences. In this case, jail." I try to remember what we learned during first semester in economics. "Anyway, you can't just make up your own money. It would cause inflation."

"I don't get it."

"Me neither. But it doesn't matter. We need a new plan. We have to *earn* money."

She drags her spell book out from under me. "I told you my idea. If you don't like it, come up with something else. Anyway, I'm busy. I need to find a way to get oranges to Africa."

"Excuse me?"

"Helping African orphans is number two on my list. You'd know what I was talking about if you hadn't fallen asleep when we were making it. They need the vitamin C even more than New Yorkers do. We could take the broom there, but there must be a faster way."

"There are airplanes. Come up with a way to earn money and we can take a trip." I should really take a look at this list.

Miri snorts. "Airplanes. Please. Don't you get it? I have powers."

Better make it a first-class ticket for her big head.

※

It's Tuesday morning, and I still have no new moneymaking ideas. I'm stuffing my jacket into my locker, trying to be as inconspicuous as possible, when I spot Will standing like a statue, staring at me. Again, intensely, like he's burning up.

His black hair looks messy, and his big brown eyes are flashing. Come on, Will, it's time to move on. Raf and I are going to be back together as soon as the spell kicks in and then you're going to feel stupid for hounding me.

I pile my necessary books into my arms and march away from him. What a jerk. A sexy jerk, but still a jerk.

*

"Do not drink from that glass," Tammy tells me, wagging her finger at me in disapproval.

"Oops." I return it to her glass coffee table with a bang. "My mistake."

"That was your third try," she whispers. "I'm on to you."

Tammy has no voice because she's still sick. We're both sitting on the mauve suede couch in her living room, watching a classic-movie marathon. Our heads are at opposite ends, and our feet are scrunched into a ball in the middle. "Trust me, you don't want to get sick. Aaron and I are both miserable. We can't even leave the house! How can a relationship last when the couple doesn't even see each other?"

"If you want it to last, it will last," I say. "And trust me, being at home is better than being at school," I whine. "I can't handle another day. You don't know what it's like. No one will talk to me. Jewel won't look at me. Melissa hisses." At least London has been suspiciously absent. Guess she can't deal with her own revenge, huh? At least she's taken down the freaks Web site. "Raf ignores me. And now his brother hates me too! I told you, he's stalking me! And I had to eat lunch in the library again by myself. No one wants to talk to me!"

94

"Rachel, I spoke to Janice and she asked about you. She said she always looks for you at lunch."

"Oh. Right." Well. I forgot about Janice, Sherry, and Annie. "I guess I could do that." But they're Tammy's friends, not mine. And they're a little annoying, I'll be honest. "I could sit with them." Or . . .

I make another (unsuccessful) lunge for her water glass.

※

The final bell just rang, and I'm about to leave the building when I turn and notice Will behind me.

Why has my crush's brother become my stalker? And is he still a stalker if he's so cute? The eyes, the hair . . . just like Raf but with broader shoulders.

I hurry out the door. He follows. I sprint down the street. So does he. I turn onto Tenth Street. Ditto for him. I quicken my pace. He quickens his pace. I make a sharp left at a corner and duck into a magazine store. Seconds later, he walks past. I read *Teen People* and then, ten minutes later, when the coast is clear, head home.

※

"Mom, can you help me take out the recycling?" I ask. "There's a lot to carry."

We've finished dinner and are cleaning up. Something smells like burnt sardines. Must be coming from the recycling cupboard. I grab the pizza box, my mom gathers the empty cartons that have been piling up, and we carry the riches to the dump on the second floor. Now the hallway smells.

"So how's school?" my mom asks.

"Better." Slightly, anyway, since I spent lunch with Janice, Annie, and Sherry. But they're not a reason to get up in the morning.

Dave, aka the hunkalicious fireman, is locking up his apartment. He waves, heads to the stairs, pauses, then shuffles back to us.

"Do you ladies need help?" he asks, giving us his sexy, toothy smile.

"We're fine," my mom says. "But thanks."

"You smell amazing, Carol," Dave says, making me almost drop the glass bottle I'm holding.

What is he talking about? All I can sniff is the sardine thing. Yuck.

My mom blushes a deep red. "Thanks. That's so sweet."

"I was wondering, maybe you'd like to stop by sometime for a drink?"

Welcome, ladies and gentlemen. We've officially entered the Twilight Zone. We've been living in this building for a decade. True, my mom has been single for only a few years, but still, the fireman has never shown any interest in her. What is it about the recycling bin that has caused his change of heart?

"Perhaps," my mom says coyly, whisking a strand of her hair behind her ear. She waves good-bye, and we silently return to the apartment.

As soon as she closes the door, I say, "What was that about?"

Blush. "What?"

I can still smell the burnt sardines. Where is that coming from? I lift my nose in the air and inhale. To the right. Closer to Mom. Still closer to Mom. It *is* Mom. I sniff her neck. "Why are you wearing sardine juice as perfume?"

She steps back. "It's a new scent I'm trying."

My mother has not purchased an eau de anything since 1989. Something's fishy here, and it's not just the perfume. "Why would you buy something that smells disgusting?"

She hesitates. "I didn't buy it."

"Was it a sample?"

"Not exactly."

Abracazam! "It's a spell!" I shriek.

Mom turns bright red. "It's an . . . attraction perfume. I was looking through my old spell book, and it looked interesting, so I thought . . . well, I thought why not give it a try? To see. Anyway, judging by what just happened," she whispers, "I think it works."

"Um . . . hello? Can I have some of that?"

"It's too strong for a teen. When you're older. Maybe. If you can prove to me you'll use it responsibly and properly."

I could properly use it right now.

✳

Friday lunchtime! The week is almost over. I'm about to go inside from gym when I spot Will waiting for me outside the door.

I hide behind Janice and sneak into the bathroom. About ten minutes later, when most of my class has left for lunch and I assume senior classes have started, I tentatively

97

open the door. But there he is, pacing the hallway, waiting for me. "Rachel!" he says, looking relieved. "Hey, hang on. I've been trying to talk to you all week."

The jig is up. I have nowhere left to hide. I'll have to stand here and be told off. "Yes, I've noticed."

"There's something I have to say to you," he says, his voice rising.

I hope this doesn't take long. I'm starving. And Janice invited me to meet her and the girls at the Quiznos down the block. "I know. So just do it already."

He takes a step toward me. He really is handsome. I've never been yelled at by a stud before.

"I think I'm in love with you," he says, and before I die from shock, he steps closer, looks deep into my eyes, and kisses me.

Something Borrowed

8

If I had died from shock, by now Will Kosravi would have resuscitated me. Because he is kissing me. At first it's like I'm watching the scene from afar: I see Will's hand gently caressing my cheek as his lips press against mine. It's all very romance-novelesque. But then he opens his mouth, and my brain slams back into my body.

My tongue just touched someone else's tongue! And it's squishy!

Oh. My. God. I am kissing Will Kosravi. I am *french-kissing*. And this whole tongue thing makes kissing a real boy far more interesting than kissing, say, my pillow or the back of my hand. I can't believe that after all the many years of imagining what kissing is, and what it feels like, I'm doing it.

Because he's almost six feet tall, my face is tilted up at a ninety-degree angle, which doesn't hurt, because his hand is now very thoughtfully supporting my neck. He smells musky, like aftershave. Omigod, I'm kissing a boy old enough to shave!

I have to admit, this is very nice.

Am I supposed to be doing anything? Besides letting my mouth hang open while my tongue gets pushed around like a grocery cart? Perhaps I should do something with my lips? Jiggle them? What if I bite his tongue by mistake? Am I the worst kisser ever? If I knew he was going to kiss me, I would have spit out my gum. Where is my gum? It was definitely in there before this kissing commotion began. It might be hiding between my molars and gums like a frightened turtle. I don't want to send out a search tongue for it, because what if that's the one thing you're not supposed to do while kissing? Oh, I think I feel it at the back of my mouth. Maybe I should just gulp it. But what if I swallow his tongue instead? And then I choke?

The next thing I know, Will pulls away, signaling that the kiss is over. Now he's smiling at me, saying, "Cool."

"Uh, yeah." I'm mildly unclear as to what planet I'm on. Why did Raf's brother just kiss me?

"I was serious before. I think I . . . love you," he continues, his eyes getting all googly.

What, what, what? Love? How is it possible that the love of my life's brother loves me? When I love his brother? Will leans over to kiss me again, but this time I use my hand to stop him. "What about Raf?"

"I know you two used to be together, but I asked him if I could hang out with you and he said it was cool. Can we do something this weekend?"

"Okay," I say, partly out of shock and partly out of rejection. Raf doesn't care that his brother likes me? *Loves* me? How can that be? No way I'd let Miri date Raf. Unless I was completely and utterly over him.

My heart sinks. Raf must be completely and utterly over me. Not even Miri's love spell could overcome his distaste.

"Another kiss?" Will asks, raising his hand back to my cheek.

"Sure." Well, why not?

*

"It makes no sense," I say to Tammy via the phone in my bedroom. I'm lying on my bed, my feet up against the wall.

"I don't know what to tell you," she says, her voice still hoarse.

"Should I cancel the date?"

"Do you want to go out with him?"

"I want to go out with his brother! I just don't get it. I never had a clue he had any feelings for me at all!"

"Did he say when he started liking you?"

101

Good question. Did he like me while I was dating Raf? Or maybe he's liked me since the first day of school but didn't feel it was appropriate for a senior to date a freshman. He must have been out of his mind with jealousy when Raf asked me to Spring Fling.

I hear Miri's key jingling in the front door. "Rachel? You home?"

"In my room!"

"Guess what!" she screams at the top of her lungs while throwing open the door. "We're going to Africa! I found a transport spell!"

I hastily attempt to cover the receiver with my palm, but I think it's too late. "Are you crazy?" I mouth. I wave the phone at her.

Her eyes widen and her jaw drops.

I place the phone back against my ear, take a deep breath, and try to sound oh-so-nonchalant. "What was your question? When Will started liking me? I'm not sure. It could have been recently."

Silence. And then: "Did your sister just say that she found a transport spell? And that you're going to Africa?"

Terrific. I shake my fist at Miri. "What? Oh, no, you must have heard wrong." Think fast! "She said the train, um . . . smelled. Like . . . Africa."

Miri rolls up into a ball by my bed, and her lips are quivering with fear.

Another silence. Tammy's not going to buy it. Our cover is ruined. Miri has just ruined everything! I trust Tammy and all, but you never know; this is a big secret. What if she tells her Moms and they call the press, and then Miri and my mom are institutionalized? Oh, no. I'll be forced to live with my dad!

"What does Africa smell like?" Tammy asks.

I exhale. "Um . . . dry? Listen, Tammy, can I call you back? My sister is having some mental issues."

"Sure. Talk to you later."

Miri climbs onto the bed beside me. "Whoops."

"Try not to tell the entire world you're a witch, okay? And excuse me . . . ," I add as I recognize the seat of my favorite jeans hanging loosely over my sister's scrawny behind. "Did I give you permission to borrow my clothes?"

"What's the difference?" she mumbles, face pressed against my pillow. "You weren't wearing them."

And that's when the cold water of realization is dumped

over my head. Stupid, stupid, stupid. Will isn't *really* in love with me. "This is a disaster."

Miri turns her head sideways to look at me. "You're not really mad, are you?"

"Raf's glove," I spit out, "wasn't Raf's. He must have borrowed the gloves from Will."

"Huh?" She sinks her face back into the pillow. "Oh, no."

I start laughing. I can't help it. I recount to Miri the events of the day and finish with a flourishing "Doesn't that suck?"

She nods. "What should we do? Do you want to use the heart-reversal spray? We have one already made and ready to go. Or I can try making a spell reversal, but it's a tough one, a five-broomer. Maybe we should just use the heart reversal."

"I guess." I sigh. It's Raf I want to like me. It's Raf I like. Although Will is a good kisser. But I'm sure Raf is too. "I'll use it on the date tomorrow. He wants to take me out for dinner."

"You're going to reverse the spell at a restaurant? What if he freaks out?"

Good point. New plan needed. What if he deserts me at the table? "Best to get it over with as soon as he rings the doorbell. Like ripping off a Band-Aid," I say. Sigh.

"What's wrong?"

"It felt good to have a guy like Will say he loves me. Even if it seemed weird and over-the-top. Especially since lately everyone else has been treating me like a major loser."

"I can do another spell on Raf if you want."

"Let's focus on one love spell at a time," I say.

103

She shuffles next to me and leans her legs on the wall. "Did it feel good?" She turns bright red. "The kissing part."

"Yeah. It was cool."

"Gross?"

"No, not gross. Fun." But not Raf.

"Hi, guys!" my mom says, popping into the room. I didn't know she was home. "What are you doing?"

"Discussing a magic disaster," I admit. Why not? Maybe she'll have some advice. "We put a love spell on the wrong guy."

She perches on the corner of the bed. "Girls, I warned you to be careful."

We hang our heads.

She sighs. "Why don't you tell me all about it while I make you some pasta for dinner before my date." She retreats into the kitchen.

I'm concerned that an alien has taken over my mother's body.

"Another date?" Miri calls.

"Yes," Mom calls across the apartment. "It's a busy weekend. Dave invited me for a drink tonight. And tomorrow Adam is taking me to a play."

"Two dates in one weekend?" I shriek. Despite my new fake boyfriend, my mom is getting more action than I am. Pathetic.

"Three, actually," she says, and we hear the water turn on. "I'm meeting Jean-Paul for wine and cheese on Sunday."

Triply pathetic.

"Jean-Paul?" At this point I jump off the bed, go into the kitchen, and heave myself onto the counter.

"Who is Jean-Paul?" Miri asks, annoyed, arms crossed, in the doorway.

"Just someone I met this week. He's French."

Bet he *really* knows how to kiss. "Where did you meet a Frenchman?" Where can I meet a Frenchman? I've always wanted to be fed cheese fondue while being whispered to in the language of love.

She opens the cupboard and pulls out the noodles. "It was the craziest thing. I was walking down the street and he bumped right into me. He knocked my purse off my shoulder. At first I thought he was some sort of hustler, like he was going to take off with my money, but he helped me pick up my things, told me I was *magnifique*, and asked me out! Incredible, huh?"

"*Incroyable.*" Surely the eau de sardines didn't hurt.

She pulls a wooden spoon from the drawer and points to herself. "Any suggestions on what I should wear?"

"Why don't you whip yourself up some new clothes?" Miri suggests. Somewhat sarcastically, I might add.

Mom hesitates. "I'm trying to use magic sparingly."

Miri snorts. "Right. Well, I'll be in my room."

Mom looks like a wounded bird. "Homework?"

"No. Saving-the-world work. I'd tell you more about it, but you're far too busy." And with that, she stomps off.

"I'm only trying to be a happier person," my mom says sadly. "Maybe this is a bad idea."

"No, no, no, I'll talk to her," I promise. Mom's off to such a promising start; she can't quit now. I adjust her hair so it looks like she has bangs. "Oh, that looks great."

"You think? Time for a new do?"

"Yes. Definitely." I've only been saying that for two years.

"Longer? Or shorter?" She folds strands in half and hides them under her chin. "What do you think?"

I feel warm and girly. "Longer, definitely. You should grow it out. And do your roots!"

When dinner's ready, Miri and I eat while my mom showers.

As I'm doing the dishes, my mom sashays back into the kitchen. "I'll be downstairs if you need anything."

"Have fun," I say distractedly. And then I look up.

Oh. My. God. "Um, Mom?"

"What do you think?" she asks eagerly.

"Don't you think"—how do I put this?—"Dave might notice that your hair grew two feet overnight?"

And it did. Not overnight but in the last sixty minutes. Seems Mom took a trip to the beauty parlor of magic. It's long, and blond, and gorgeous. Roots? What roots? She looks like Barbie. Like Cinderella. Rapunzel.

She nibbles on her thumb. "Did I go overboard?"

"Well . . ." I probably shouldn't burst her bubble. She needs the confidence boost. "You look hot. Smoking."

She gives me one of her big freakish winks, with her open eye not moving at all. "He is a fireman."

Groan.

106

"Get on my back," Miri says the next morning, barging into my room, holding her knapsack close to her chest.

"Excuse me?"

"Come on. I want you to come with me to Tanzania so we can help the orphans."

There are so many parts to that statement I don't understand. I climb out of bed and stretch my arms above my head. "Explain slowly, pretty please?"

She rolls her eyes. "There are children in Tanzania—"

"Where?"

"Tanzania—it's in Africa, dummy—who don't have enough food, clothes, or books."

"And . . ."

"And we're going to make some for them!"

"How are we going to get there exactly? We are so not taking the broom. That'll take forever. Don't forget I have a date I need to dispose of tonight."

Miri stomps her foot. "Don't you listen? I found a transport spell. I can zap us anywhere we want to go. All I have to do is think of the place, hold two lithium batteries together, positive and negative charges facing each other, say the spell, and off we go."

Fun. "That is so cool. And Mom's letting us go to Africa?"

Miri is suddenly very interested in the zipper on her bag. "Kind of."

"Did you ask?"

"Is it my fault she's still half-asleep? I asked her if I could help the orphans, and she said, 'Bring your sister.' Good enough for me."

Sounds fair. I slip on a pair of sweatpants and a hoodie. "All right, let's go. What do I have to do?"

"I have to carry you on my back, because only me and what I'm holding will get transported."

"Can I pee first?"

She sighs. "Fine, but hurry up."

I use the bathroom quickly and then return to my room. Miri crouches. "Let's piggyback!"

Giggling, I hop on and wrap my arms around her neck. "I'm going to give you a hernia."

Miri groans and stands up. "This is the only way to do it. Grab my knapsack. Everything we need is in there."

"Malaria pills?"

"Ha-ha. We're only going for five minutes. Just try not to get bitten by a mosquito." She tilts her head to the left. "And I wouldn't drink the water either. Now be quiet while I say the spell."

This is a bad plan, I know it. "Miri—"

"Shush, I have to concentrate." She makes a tight fist around each of the batteries, twines her thumbs together, and clears her throat.

"Transport to the place inside my mind,
The power of my fists shall ye bind!"

My arms slip, and I'm about to tell her that I'm going to fall off when a jolt of electricity runs through my body. Ouch! I bet that's what getting struck by lightning feels like. Suddenly, my skin feels hot and dry. Instead of my bedroom, all I see are dots and swirls of blue, red, and yellow, as though I'm looking into a kaleidoscope. Even though I'm holding on to my sister, my body feels weightless, like we're swimming underwater. The next thing I know, the blur of colors in front of me is solidifying into a wood and stucco house. The hair-dryer wind turns off, and I can feel gravity again.

"We're here!" Miri cheers.

Dizzy, I slide off her back, and my feet touch the earthy ground. I look around but can't see much besides the one-level building because it's so dark. "Is it already night? The transport only felt like a second."

Miri shakes her head. "It's seven hours later here," she whispers. "Let's try not to attract any unwanted attention. There could be lions, you know."

My arms are covered with goose bumps from the idea of potential killer animals as well as from the cold. "Are you sure we're in Africa? Isn't it supposed to be hot?"

Miri reaches for her knapsack. "Don't you take geography? The seasons are reversed in the southern hemisphere."

This is too much. My head is pounding, although it could be from the supersonic travel and not from the info. I hate how I look when I get a headache. My eyes remain half open like some kind of demented puppet. Miri, however, looks fine. Another benefit to being a full-fledged witch is that they apparently don't need aspirin. "Can we get going?" I ask. "What's your plan, anyway?"

"Follow me," she says, and pulls out a flashlight. She approaches a building and finds the door handle, and it opens easily. The people around here must not be too worried about breaking and entering by a criminal lion.

I follow her inside to a small classroom, the floorboards creaking under our every step. The few chairs and tables all look worn out. On the wall is a small rectangular blackboard with numbers and letters scrawled across it. Miri unzips her

109

knapsack and pulls out an orange, her math textbook, and—is that my green shirt?

She lays each item on the dusty floor next to the teacher's desk. "These students are all orphans, and they need food, clothes, and books. So we're going to use the multiplying spell." Next she pulls out a plastic container of an already mixed concoction of mint, chocolate, and grape skin. "Ready?" she asks.

Even in the darkness, I can see that her eyes are shining. I feel a rush of pride. My sister is truly a superhero.

She takes a deep breath and begins:

"Here is one
Placed on the floor,
I nod three times
And now there are more!"

By the time we transport back to the U.S., I'm emotionally overwhelmed . . . and sleepy. Miri just about filled the school with oranges, books, and tops. In preparation for spritzing Will with the heart-reversal concoction, I shower, diffuse my hair, dress up, and apply lip gloss. The reason I've dolled myself up (including putting on my fave jeans and a sexy new red shirt) is that I cling to the hope that, after the reversal spell freezes his heart, Will might still think I'm cute and convince his brother to like me again. I'm well aware of the power of sibling suggestion.

My mom is equally entrenched in her primping process, and we're having a ball. The radio is blasting, the two of us are singing over the blow-dryer, we're sharing mascara.

Miri wanders into the bathroom as we're in midprimp. "Why don't you let me put some makeup on you?" I ask her. "It'll be fun!"

She rolls her eyes. "I have more important things to do with my time than paint myself. Like number three on my list: ridding the world of land mines."

Mom looks up from lining her eyes. "Have you already done your homework?"

Miri shakes her head. "I'll do it tonight."

"Good. And I made you tofu-and-broccoli potpie for dinner. All you have to do is heat it up in the toaster oven. You know how to do that, right?"

"Yes, Mom. Unlike your other daughter, I know how to use the kitchen appliances."

One little kitchen fire and I'm never going to hear the end of it. How was I supposed to know that marshmallows were flammable?

I don't get offended, because I know she's upset about my mom's new dating dossier and not at me. While waiting for the shirts and books and fruit to multiply, I tried to talk to her about her feelings, but she refused to discuss them. I told her that Mom needs to see other people. And that Miri has to learn to share. She threw an orange at my head.

The buzzer rings.

Yay! What can I say? Even though I know I won't be leaving the apartment, since he'll sprint to safety as soon as the spell hits him, I can't stop chills from running down my spine. I buzz him up. "Miri? You ready? Do you have the heart reversal?"

She joins me in the foyer and hands me the bottle.

111

"Okay. Ready?" I say. "You open; I'll squirt." I get into position. Knock, knock. I mouth to Miri, "Ready?"

She nods. Here goes everything.

My finger is on the trigger, and I'm about to spray when all I see is red.

Will has roses. Three dozen roses. Long stemmed. I can barely see his face because it's blocked by the forest of flowers. I have never gotten flowers from a boy before. (That's a lie. When I was five, on Valentine's Day, my dad brought home a teddy bear for Miri and two wrapped boxes, one for me and one for my mom. One was in silver paper and one was in Barbie wrapping. He told me to pick. I chose the silver, since it was shinier. He laughed and told me to pick the other one, but I refused. A deal was a deal. He agreed. My box had a dozen red roses in it. My mom got a Barbie convertible. We traded.)

112

"Hi, Rachel," Will says. "These are for you."

Gasp! Adorable! Pretty! Sweet! I drop the spray bottle on the carpet and hug the flowers. "Thank you! Let me put them in water." I retreat toward the kitchen. So sad. The first nonrelated boy/man to buy me roses and I can't even go out with him. If only I could, just for tonight . . . no. That would be a waste of time. I'm not going on a date with him just so I can spray him afterward. Ridiculous. Masochistic. For both of us. And he'd only be left wondering if he'd lost his mind. Taking a freshman to dinner. Insane! There are social norms that need to be upheld or high school society will crumble into ruins!

"How beautiful!" my mom says, intercepting. "Let me take care of those. You go ahead on your date, honey."

"It's a pleasure to meet you, Mrs. Weinstein." Will offers his hand. "I'm Will." He's so adorably grown-up.

My mom takes it. "Nice to meet you, too, Will. But I haven't been Weinstein for a while. It's Carol Graff, but please call me Carol." Is it weird that she's not freaking out that I'm going out with someone so tall? I'm a little freaked out myself. He looks like a man. Instead, she's batting her eyelashes. Is my mother flirting with my date? How embarrassing. "So where are you off to tonight?" she asks. Bat, bat.

"Well, my friend . . . ," he begins as I search for the bottle. I must put a stop to this snowball of a disaster immediately. I must spray. "London"—London?—"is having a party tonight. And I promised I'd stop by before dinner. If that's all right with you, Rachel."

Talk about sweet revenge!

Miri picks up the bottle from the floor and aims. She looks at me for approval.

"No!" I practically shout. "Hold on a sec." Heart pounding, I grab the spray bottle from her hands, stuff it into my purse, say, "Be back by twelve," and pull Will out the door.

113

<hr />

"What," London says, narrowing her eyes, "are you doing here?" Her cheeks are as rosy as her plunging red shirt, red jeans, red boots, red nail polish, and red cast. I have no idea how that last one is possible.

I have just exited the bathroom on the first floor. (Yes, London lives in an insane triplex. I take a minute to enjoy the image of her struggling up and down the stairs in her cast.) The evil one is waiting for me, fuming with anger.

All eyes in the room are on us. "Can you please get out of my apartment, Rochelle?" She stabs her finger at me like it's a sword. Why is she always pointing at me?

Snickers ripple through the room and I want to die. Or at least cry. It seems the party has worked and London has regained her perch at the top of the JFK social ladder. And I'm once again lower than a worm. I'm about to slither back out the front door when Will comes to my rescue. "She's with me. Why? Is there a problem?" How teen-movie sweet is that?

London's mouth opens, but at first no sound comes out. Finally, she growls, "Why would you hang around her? She's a freak!"

"Rachel's my new girlfriend," he replies.

The crowd goes wild. Senior girls whisper to their friends, and the juniors lucky enough to be invited send frenzied text messages to their posses. Oblivious, Will squeezes my shoulder. "Want to see what's happening up-stairs?"

I'm still reeling from the G-word. I am a girlfriend. *I am a girlfriend!* I'd love to plaster the slogan on a T-shirt: I, Rachel Weinstein, freshman nerd, am the (temporary) girl-friend of the student council president! Wow. Awesome.

I nod, and Will takes my hand—yes, takes my hand in front of everyone—and we pass a still-in-shock London on our way upstairs. I resist the urge to stick out my tongue at her. (Fine, I do it, but I stick it out only an inch and Will doesn't see.)

When we get to the second-floor living room, Bosh, a

senior, high-fives Will. "Hey, dude." Bosh is on the student council with Will. Even though he's the treasurer, he was definitely not voted in because of his math abilities. He's one of those straight-to-fraternity guys who live in sports jerseys and baseball caps, look like teddy bears, and are loved by everyone. You can almost imagine him growing up to be Norm from *Cheers*. I assume Bosh is his last name, but I'm not sure. That's all he goes by, like Madonna.

"Bosh, do you know Rachel?" As Will introduces us, his eyes stay firmly planted on my face. I'm like a potato chip. He just can't get enough of me.

Bosh high-fives me. "By name only, dude. Will hasn't stopped yammering about you all week."

"Would you like a piece of licorice?" Will asks, and pulls a small package out of his pocket.

"Sure," I say.

He rips off a piece and hands it to me. "I always have it on me. I'm a total sugar addict." He takes a bite off each end of his piece and blows through it like a straw.

He's so cute.

I'd be lying if I said I wasn't loving this. The news of our May-December relationship is spreading faster than the flu. People are knocking me over with their pointing.

"Hey, Rachel," says Mercedes Redding, senior and former cohead of the fashion show with London. "How are you?" Mercedes has not spoken to me since the disaster. But I'm now back on the radar, baby!

Wahoo to the power of two!

I happily meet the rest of Will's posse. (As if I didn't

115

already know who they are. Hah!) There are Jerome, Nelson, and Schumacher. One was in the fashion show, and two are on the basketball team. All three are A-list. Obviously.

As I prance around the room, I'm the queen on the arm of my king. No one will ever be mean to me again. How can they when I have been deemed dateable by Will? I'm finally out of the doghouse!

The tugging of my heavy purse on my shoulder reminds me that it's not for long, though. I'm supposed to spray him tonight and reverse his heart. And then I'll be the girl Will dumped after one day. It doesn't matter. It's Raf I like, anyway, not him. I stuff my mouth with licorice and analyze my dilemma. The sooner we end it, the better.

Speak of the devil. I nearly choke on the red candy. Raf is sitting on the couch with Melissa on his lap.

Are they dating? No, no, no! What on earth does he see in her? She laughs at something he says and throws her long, glossy red hair behind her shoulder. She's wearing a tight sky-colored off-the-shoulder top to reveal her lanky body, big boobs, and baby blues. Show-off.

How did she finagle her way in here, anyway? This is a *senior* A-list party, and she's only a meager freshman.

Will wraps his arm around my waist. Raf looks up. Our eyes lock.

I'm going to be sick. I quickly look away. How can he do that? He knows how awful Melissa was to me. What a jerk. I need to get out of here; I can't watch Raf and Melissa be all touchy-feely. The walls start to close in as images flash through my mind. Raf and Melissa holding hands in the hall. Raf smiling at Melissa the way he used to at me. I'll be watching from afar, alone again. Alone as usual. I wish someone would turn on a fan. The air in here is spongy and too thick to breathe.

"Wanna go eat now?" Will asks, reading my mind.

"Yes! I definitely do." I trail behind him like a depressed puppy as he says his good-byes. I'll spray him as soon as we're outside. No need to waste his time on dinner. What's the point? I might as well get it over with. My heart sinks as we close London's door behind us. I have nothing to look forward to. Raf is falling in love with Melissa, and London will make my life even more miserable when she finds out Will dumped me. It's a return ticket straight back to Loserville.

Will is holding my hand, silently helping me down the stairs. He's probably realized what a pathetic person I am and overthrown the spell all on his own. To add insult to injury, he's going to dump me even before I get to spray him. When we're on the street, I reach into my purse. Not that there's a point. He's already all pale and queasy looking.

He coughs twice. "I need to say something."

I don't believe it. My horribleness has actually broken the spell. I'll break up with him first. "I don't think it's—"

"Would you like to be my date for prom?"

Oh. My. God.

Prom? As in the senior prom? A freshman going to prom? That would so make up for all the dances I missed this year, since it's the *mother* of dances. The climax of all teen movies. Crinoline, limo, corsage . . .

I'm going to prom! If I don't spray. But then what about

117

Raf? Raf, prom, Raf, prom. As I weigh the two on my imaginary scale, my hand still gripping the spray bottle inside my purse, Will leans over and kisses me.

Yum. (Three kisses in one week! I'm on a roll.) He looks a lot like Raf. So cute. Only taller. And older. And he tastes like licorice. And Raf wants nothing to do with me. He's probably kissing Melissa at this very second. Maybe, I think, as Will's tongue does this cool semicircle thing, this new relationship will help me forget about my last love.

I drop the heart reversal back into my purse. Well, why not? Prom, kisses, getting off the loser list . . . What else could I ask for? I pull back and smile.

"I thought we could go to Spark's," he says. "Is that cool? Do you eat steak?"

Moo.

And the Oscar Goes to . . . 9

"Lookin' hot, Rache," says a random junior.

Bosh gives me a high five. "What up, dude?"

"Are we in an alternate reality?" Tammy asks.

I give a half wave to my subjects. I've been working on it all morning. Kind of like a Miss America wave with a touch more flutter in the fingers. "Weird, isn't it?"

It's not even nine a.m. on Monday, and word has gotten around *fast*. Once again, I have reached the pinnacle of high school society. All I have to do is date the king and everyone pretends they like me. It's faker than London's boobs. On the plus side, I'm going to prom! In other good news, classrooms are back to their non-doubled-up capacity. Construction guys have been working overtime—not sure (gulp) where the money is coming from.

But neither the adulation nor the solo desk is the best part of the day. Oh, no, the true prize is that Tammy is back. She surprised me at my locker this morning. I fully attacked her with hugs. Aaron, unfortunately, is still in bed. Seems his case is much, much worse. "I don't even remember what he looks like anymore," Tammy complains. "My moms haven't let me even visit him yet! They're afraid I'll have a relapse."

I feel bad and all . . . but this way I get Tammy all to myself!

Even though I warned her that Will and I are an item, she was not prepared for the sudden worship of our peers. It's like I've just won Best Director and now everyone wants to be in my movies. And this time, I've learned my lesson. I am not, I repeat *not,* ditching Tammy for the A-list. If they want to adore me, they'll have to adore Tammy, too.

Case in point: we walk into math, and Doree and Jewel are sitting in the back.

"Hi, Rachel!" Jewel says. "I saved you a seat."

Doree pats my chair like a throne. "Come sit with us."

I give them the half wave.

Tammy sighs. "Go sit with them if you want."

As if. "Are you kidding?" No way am I giving *those* girls a second chance. Or in Jewel's case, a third chance. "Let's sit here," I say, pointing to two empty seats in the front row.

Tammy gives me her scuba OK and smiles.

"Thinks she's too good for us, does she?" Doree huffs.

Yes. Much too good.

We're on our way out for lunch when two large sexy hands cover my eyes. "Guess who, gorgeous?"

Obviously the spell has made Will blind. Cute, yes. Pretty, maybe. But gorgeous? I wish.

I untangle his hands and kiss his cheek. "Hi, Will." My entire class is staring.

He leans against my locker. "What are you doing now?"

"Going for lunch."

"Want to come hang out with us instead?"

"Don't you have class?" Freshmen and sophomores have lunch from eleven to eleven forty-five; juniors and seniors have it the following period.

"Yeah, I want you to come to physics." He laughs. "No, Sock gets freshman/sophomore lunch period off in order to work."

I must look confused.

"Sock is student council."

"Why do you call it *sock*?"

"I don't know. I guess it's because you can't really pronounce S and C. So we added a vowel. And O is better than I or U. Anyway, we have an office downstairs. Coming?"

121

I guess it's *soc* and not *sock*. If I were them, I would have gone with *sac* or *sack*. Who wants to be associated with feet? *Sac* at least makes me think of a purse. And everyone likes purses. "I can't. Tammy and I are going for pizza."

His face falls. "Can't you both come? Please?"

Tammy pops up behind me. "He did say please."

"So let's hear your suggestions," Will says to us. "We need to come up with a theme. Prom is May twenty-seventh—in three and a half weeks."

What I need to come up with is a dress. A gorgeous princess, where-did-she-get-that stunner.

I'm lying on a pink sofa, my feet up on the school

president's legs. I'm not sure what's more amazing: my access to school couches or my access to a boy's legs.

The room is small but cozy, filled with couches, posters, and a stocked fridge. Who knew? It's like a college dorm room in the school basement.

"Vampires?" says the soc secretary, River Eugenicks, an über-cool senior. He's the only person ever to be able to get away with having four eyebrow rings yet wearing a bow tie to school every day. I mean, come on. Those two styles just don't go together. Unless, like River, you're A-list, super-smart, and an intern at MTV.

"Black attire only," he continues, munching on a piece of red licorice Will handed out at the beginning of the meeting. "And the lightbulbs in the gym would all be red. All we need is a smoke machine and we're golden."

122   At least no one has mentioned the possibility that the gym won't be cleaned up in time for prom. Because it has to be. Having the prom in the gym is a JFK tradition, just like the fashion show is traditionally a prom fund-raiser. The ten thousand dollars raised at the fashion show is to be used for decorations, food, and music.

"Shall we call it Night of the Dead?" Kat, the VP, says, laughing. Her full name is Katherine Postansky. Her beige capris and hoodie sweatshirt, pale face, and mop of straight black hair make her look like an ice cream cone. And she keeps a purple pen behind her ear, like a sprinkle. She's about my height, probably five foot one, and a size small. And she smiles a lot—for good reason. She's adorable and A-list. She was one of the few juniors invited to London's party on Saturday. Never mind she's the only girl in the soc (in soc? on the soc?), hanging out with these cool guys every day.

The only other people in the room are Tammy and Bosh, and they're sitting together on the third couch. I've been noticing that every few minutes Bosh inches his way a smidgen closer to Tammy. Maybe he's developing a crush! Imagine if Tammy found a new boyfriend in the soc. How cute would that be? I mean, I like Aaron—he seems harmless—but I can't exactly double with them. The president of the student council wouldn't want to be seen with a lowly freshman. Besides his girlfriend, of course. And his friend's girlfriend. And this way Tammy and I can go to the prom together. We'll go dress shopping, rent a limo, smile at each other as we're locked in our partners' embraces. I can't believe I was considering breaking up with him! Was I crazy? Blind to the possibilities?

Oh, I think I am blind. I just noticed that there is someone else in the room: Jeffrey Zeigster, who's sitting in the corner, doing his science homework. His brown hair looks painted on with gel, and his glasses are so thick that they look like bulletproof windowpanes. Hello, has he not heard of contacts? He's part of the soc but the only person not elected to it. He was appointed by Konch because of his high GPA. Apparently, he sees this meeting as more of a study hall than an opportunity to help improve the quality of student life at JFK.

"Let's just hope the gym is ready in time," Will says. "We've already scored some major donations from alumni for repairs. The administration put the money toward the classrooms first. But the gym and cafeteria have to be *completely* redone and are going to cost a ridiculous amount of money."

Oh yeah. I've been meaning to follow up with Miri about that. Unfortunately, I've been a little preoccupied with the whole Will love spell stuff.

Kat nods along with Will's every word, her head like a bouncing ball. "Until you hear anything, let's hope for the best."

"All right. Any other ideas? Costume party?" Will suggests. "Is that lame?"

"No," says River. "But I doubt London Zeal and her posse will want to dress up."

Most of the room laughs. I perk up. It seems not everyone is her biggest fan.

"Maybe she'll come as a witch," Kat says. "She wouldn't even have to put on a costume."

Funny as that is, witch jokes make me a wee bit uncomfortable.

"She's not that bad," Will says. "She's a friend of mine." Such a politician—he's friends with everyone.

"What would you be?" I ask Kat, anxious to change the subject. But I like Kat. She's funny, and her anti-London politics make her a potential mentor. I resist the geeky urge to beg her to be my friend.

She shrugs. "I don't get to go. I'm just a lowly junior."

"Let's keep brainstorming, people," Will says.

That is so sad. She comes up with the ideas and then doesn't get to go?

"What about Atlantis, dudes?" suggests Bosh. "You know? The lost underwater city. I took some great pictures when I was scuba diving last month."

Tammy's eyes light up. "You dive?"

124

Bosh straightens his posture. "Yeah, dude. Why, do you?"

"Of course! I live for it."

"High five!" he says, and they slap hands.

Did Tammy just blush? They are so going to fall in love, get married, and have scuba babies.

"I hate the water," River says, fingering an eyebrow piercing.

"Whatever you say, *River*." Kat laughs. "Let's think of something else."

Tammy clears her throat. "What about an Oscar night?"

Bosh gives her a scuba OK. "You could have a red carpet leading up to the gym."

"We could give out random mini Academy Awards," River says quickly. "You know, for best mustache."

Weird, but funny. As long as it's not for best beard.

The idea seems to be rolling around Will's brain. "I like it," he says. "We could project old black-and-white movies on the wall."

125

"The photographer could stand outside snapping photos like the paparazzi!" Kat suggests.

"All in favor," Will says. We all raise our hands. All except Mr. Studious in the corner. Will peers at him over the back of the couch. "Jeffrey? You in?"

Startled, Jeffrey drops his pencil. "In where?"

"Oscar theme for prom."

His eyes squint in mystification. "Prom?"

"End-of-year dance. Prom. Oscar theme."

"All right," he mumbles, and then goes back to his work.

"He's shy," Kat whispers to me.

"So we're done," says Will, and squeezes my knee.

Kat raises an eyebrow. "What about Amy?"

River snorts. "If she's too busy with her boyfriend to make it to meetings then she doesn't get to vote."

I forgot about Amy Koppela. She's in the soc too, supposedly in charge of prom. Very tall, very skinny, very blond, and very A-list. Apparently too cool to come to soc meetings. "Who's she dating?" I ask.

"Some NYU guy," Will answers. "She spends both first and second lunches in his dorm. We'll count her as pro-Oscar. So six votes say yes. Oscar theme it is. Thanks, Tammy."

I give Tammy a thumbs-up. I know in underwater language it means something besides good job, but she gets the idea.

126

Tammy and I head to English on cloud nine. If we were floating any higher, we would hit the ceiling. As soon as class starts, I slip a note into her copy of *A Midsummer Night's Dream*, the Shakespeare play about love spells gone amuck. How fitting. Should I be concerned about what's going to happen when I'm a sophomore and we study *Macbeth*?

My note: *Awesome ideas!*

She blushes happily as she reads my scribble and then tosses a note back to me: *I can't believe you get to go. So lucky.*

I write back: *You might get to go too. Bosh was drooling over you.*

And then I get: ☺

Me: *What does that mean??? Do you like him?*

Tammy: *I already have a boyfriend, remember? I can't go to the prom with Bosh! Does he even have a first name?*

Me: *No clue. But maybe they'll let you go since you came up with the idea.*

Tammy: *No way. They won't even let Kat go.*

Me: *Crazy, huh? I like her. She's so sweet for someone A-list. Did you like her?*

Tammy: *Yup. She was nice, considering . . .*

Me: *Considering what?*

Tammy: *Considering that she's in love with your new boyfriend!*

I stare at the note and sink into my chair. Two seconds later I lean over to Tammy and whisper, "Why do you think she likes Will?"

"She kept looking at him. And anytime he talked to her she blushed. I could just tell. Couldn't you?"

I shrug. I didn't notice a thing. My self-centeredness is extraordinary—almost a superpower.

"Don't worry," Tammy says. "He was *not* looking back. He only has eyes for you."

That's one thing I'm not worried about. At least not for another few weeks, before the spell wears off. I'll have to remind Miri to extend it to make sure I get to go to prom. I'll reverse it after that, though. Immediately after. Forcing someone to like you isn't the nicest thing to do. And Will is such a terrific guy, he deserves to be truly in love.

When the bell rings, we pile up our books and head out the door. And that's when I run smack into Raf. And I mean Smack. Into. Raf.

127

I guess I wasn't paying attention or something, because I swing around and my forehead collides with his shoulder, and my copy of A Midsummer Night's Dream and the accompanying notes soar through the air, the covers of my binder spread like a pigeon's wings. Meanwhile, I fly backward and somehow end up lying on my back, my hair all over the dirty floor, wishing I could zap myself to another country. Canada, maybe?

Raf is suddenly on his knees, by my side, hand on my shoulder. "Are you okay?" he asks, his forehead wrinkling into adorable little folds. I look deep into his speckled eyes and feel like I'm being submerged in a warm bubbly bath.

My heart sinks. And not because of my pounding forehead. Unrequited love hurts.

"Rachel?" his yummy lips say. They're red and plump and juicy and . . . "Rachel?" he asks again.

"Hi, Raf."

"Hi, Rachel. Did I hurt you?"

"Yes," I say. My heart has been torn into thousands of shards that will no longer fit together. "I mean, no, I'm fine. All good."

He places his hand under my elbow and gently helps me back to my feet. He then lets go of my arm, picks up my binder, and hands it to me. "I think this is yours," he says, and then, after giving my elbow and heart a final squeeze, he disappears out of my life and down the hallway.

❋

"The heart-reversal spell is broken," I tell Miri, pushing open her door.

"What?" She's at her desk reading A² and doesn't look up.

"I tried to use it. I feel sick to my stomach every time I see Raf. I can't deal. So I tried spraying myself but all it did was mess up my hair. Why didn't it work?"

"The spell is only a one-broomer. It's not advanced enough for selfsummie."

I know what a one-broomer is, but self-what? "I have no idea what you just said."

"Selfsummie is when you're trying to trick yourself with an emotion spell. And it won't work unless the spell is at least a four-broomer."

"So what can I do? Nothing?" The pain must end.

She hesitates. "We could try an anti-love spell. That's a five-broomer. Should achieve selfsummie."

Perfect. "Give it to me."

"You sound like a junkie."

I flop backward onto her bed. "I'm serious. Can you make me one?"

She puts down her pencil and tilts back her chair. "Do you—"

"Don't do that. You're making me nervous," I interrupt.

She tilts her chair back farther just to annoy me. "I'll give you a spell if you want. I know the perfect one."

Excellent. I'll no longer feel the pain. Raf who? "I need it now."

Her chair still diagonal, she flips through the pages. "Are you sure?"

"Of course. Why not?"

"Are you sure you want to wipe out your feelings?"

"I feel crappy, so yes."

"Don't you remember all the stuff Mom told us about experiencing the good and bad in life?"

"This is the same Mom who magically bleached her hair blond on Saturday?"

Miri makes a sour face. "She said it way before she dyed her hair, when she still had perspective. She said experiencing the bad makes you stronger."

I flex my bicep. "I'm plenty strong."

She tilts even closer to the floor. "Bad things make you a more interesting person. More profound."

"In that case I must be the most interesting person alive." But maybe she's right. Maybe zapping away my unrequited crush will make me bland and boring. Who cares? I'll be happy instead. "Let's do it!" I scream, and Miri's slanted chair suddenly sails backward and she crashes to the floor. She makes a surprised squeak.

"Told you. You okay?"

She nods and I lunge for the phone, which just started ringing. Maybe it's Raf calling to tell me he's still in love with me, and I won't need the anti-love spell at all.

"Aloha, Rachel!"

"Daddy! You're back!" My father has finally returned to the mainland. "How was it?"

"Rad. The *kaukau* was *ono*. That means the food was delicious. And the surfing was primo. The . . ." I space out a bit, thinking about Raf. I hear a muffle, and I realize a few seconds too late that he might have just said, "My babe new wife, Jennifer, wants to say aloha."

130

Groan. The truth is during the wedding process I realized that she wasn't as bad as I made her out to be. But does that mean we have to be phone pals now? And what's up with the Hawaiian-surfer-speak? They didn't actually surf, did they?

"Aloha!" she chirps.

"Hi, Jennifer. Did you go surfing?"

"Oh yeah. You had to see me rippin' it up." She continues to tell me about how they "scored some great rides" and really "hung loose." Eventually she offers to e-mail me her "bodacious" pictures and tells me she's "stoked" to see us this weekend, then asks to talk to Miri.

Miri scowls as I hand her the phone and then rolls her eyes, then rolls her eyes some more. Meanwhile, I wonder about the merits of subjecting myself to an anti-love spell. Or any spell, for that matter. Miri's track record hasn't been impeccable. There were cows in my gym.

131

Miri finally hangs up, groaning. "She's e-mailing us pictures! I just finished cleaning out my in-box from all their wedding crap."

"Let's talk about the ingredients," I say.

"You'll need to get a black candle, Dead Sea salts, sunflowers, and a lock of Raf's hair. And then any feelings you have left for Raf will be gone. At least temporarily."

Groan. How on earth will I get Raf's hair? But do I really want *all* my feelings for him zapped into la-la land? "What if I decide I want to grow up to be a writer? Or a painter? Will I still be able to draw on this pain?"

She sits back down in her chair. "What are you rambling about? I thought you wanted to be an astronaut."

Right. I did say that. Or a pilot on an astro-tourism jetliner, because according to *60 Minutes*, that's so going to be the next big thing. Astronaut. Painter, personal shopper. All sound demanding. Whatever doesn't kill us makes us stronger, right? I decide I really don't want anything unnatural tinkering with my feelings. I mean, let's be honest. My sister isn't all that experienced. What if the spell backfires, and instead of falling out of love, I fall into a well or something? "Forget the anti-love spell. I'll deal. Keeping it real, you know?" And anyway, I'm really way too lazy to try to locate all those ingredients.

She shrugs and flips the page. "If you say so. I bet the real reason is that you're too lazy to get the ingredients. Can I get back to saving the whales now?"

How did she know?

The rest of the week flies by in a surprising haze of happiness. Will drops by my locker after every class and always gives me a quick kiss on the lips. He slides I-Love-You notes into my textbooks. Afternoons are spent hanging out at the A-list in-spot. Lunches are spent with the soc in the lounge. On Tuesday, we order pizza, which is delivered right to our room! How fun is that? On Wednesday, I catch Bosh rubbing Tammy's shoulders. On Thursday, I notice the way Kat blushes whenever Will pays her any attention. But the weird thing is she's nice to me. And not super-over-the-top-nice-but-secretly-bitchy nice. She lends me her purple pen when mine runs out of ink. Laughs at my jokes. Genuinely nice. If I were her, I would hate me.

Even though London Zeal is back at the top of the

A-list, she seems to have forgotten her hatred of me, or at least, she is no longer exacting her revenge. Because of my new girlfriend-of-Will status, I have been forgiven and approved by the freshman, sophomore, junior, and senior A-lists, and therefore by the entire school. Everyone, that is, except Raf.

These days, when he passes me, I don't even get the half smile. Raf is not impressed.

What's his problem now? He doesn't like me, so no one else can like me either? Why are boys so annoying?

On Friday, Tammy and I are sitting in bio when someone knocks on the door. I see Will through the window and I feel warm all over. Special. Chosen. Strange. I used to feel that way only around Raf. Is it possible that I'm starting to like Will, too? To *really* like him? Is it possible to like two boys at once? Two brothers?

133

"Come in, Mr. Kosravi," Mr. Frederick says.

The cool thing is that no matter which one I marry, I'll be Mrs. Kosravi. If I change my name, which I don't think I'll do. I can't just give up my identity! I see Will's face and block the argument out of my mind. (I guess it isn't something I have to decide on immediately.) He whispers something to Mr. Frederick, who nods and then looks up. "Ms. Weinstein and Ms. Wise, please go with Mr. Kosravi. You're excused for the rest of class."

Wahoo! Tammy squeezes my hand as we excitedly follow Will out the door, passing Doree's envious, longing gaze. I'm sure nothing is really wrong. How awesome is Will? Pretending something's wrong just to get us out of bio!

"Thanks!" I say, kissing his cheek. He smells good.

"That was awesome," Tammy says. "It was soooo boring in there."

Will shakes his head. "Don't thank me. I need your help. We're having an emergency soc meeting. The prom is on the verge of being canceled."

How I Ruined the World

10

"Tell us what happened," Bosh says, shaking his head, his hand gently resting . . . on Tammy's knee? Whoa.

Tammy turns white and then bright red, and then she smiles, then frowns, then slowly shuffles out of Bosh's reach.

Meanwhile, Will paces the room, his arms waving over his head. "The gym won't be ready in time."

My stomach feels like I just swallowed a balloon filled with sand.

"Even once the repairs are complete," Will says, "the floors will be too fragile for the first month to have students dance on them. Same goes for the cafeteria. I'd like to kill the people who pulled that cow prank."

La, la, la.

River groans. "Can't we rent a place?"

Will shakes his head. "That's the second problem. Since Konch is convinced that the cows were a senior prank, she wants to cancel prom until someone confesses."

"What?" we all scream. I may throw up on the floor.

"I convinced her not to. So instead, she's making us fork

over the money the fashion show raised for the prom to help with repair costs."

"What?" Bosh screams. "Dude, how can we afford prom if we do that?"

Will continues. "She recommended we start by canceling the band and the photographer. And possibly the rented tables."

"But where does she expect us to eat?" River asks indignantly. "On the floor?"

"Oh, don't worry," Will says sarcastically. "She suggested canceling the dinner, too. But then she remembered that we already gave the caterer a deposit with the money from advance ticket sales. What are we going to do? The prom is supposed to be in three weeks. But at the moment all we have guaranteed is the meal. And not even the entire meal. The deposit was only seven grand, which means it will cover appetizers and maybe half of the stale chicken plates."

136

"That sucks, dude," Bosh says. "We can't party in the street. Let's just rent a space and listen to a CD or something."

"We need a band," River argues. "I can listen to CDs at home."

Will shakes his head in disgust. "Ah, man, I'm going to be the soc president responsible for the lamest prom ever."

"We should just cancel it," River says.

No way! Then Will will be the president responsible for canceling prom! "Hold on. What's the total cost of prom?" I ask.

Will sighs. "It's supposed to be twenty-seven thousand

five hundred dollars. Which covered everything. And it worked out perfectly before the cows, because we had almost ten grand from the fashion show, we had a free space, and the prom tickets were fifty dollars a person. And since we're expecting about three hundred and fifty ticket sales, it worked out to . . . well, it worked out."

"You absolutely cannot cancel prom," says Kat, tapping her purple pen. (How does she never lose that pen? I lose about one per day.) "We'll just have to come up with the money. Let's raise ticket prices."

"If you raise ticket prices too high," River says, "people might not want to spend the dough. If anything, you may have to give them a rebate if you don't even have a band. Or dessert."

"We can't raise ticket prices," Will says, shaking his head in dismay. "We've already sold some of them. The price is set." **137**

I do the calculations. "So you're expecting seventeen thousand five hundred dollars in ticket sales. Which means that if we need to reraise the ten thousand from fashion show funds to be able to keep prom as planned, as well as say a few thousand for a location, we're looking at trying to raise twelve to fifteen thousand dollars."

Will nods.

Kat continues tapping. "We can do it. Let's find a new location. Then we'll worry about paying for it. We won't book it unless we have a way to raise the money, but we'll come up with it. We have to."

Will hesitates. "Are you all sure? We only have three weeks. It's going to be tough. And exams are coming up—"

"We can do it, dude," Bosh says. The rest of us nod.

"All right." Will takes a deep breath. "Let's brainstorm. Jeffrey, can you pass me the licorice?"

In the corner near the cupboard, Jeffrey looks up from his notebook. He's like a ghost. Again, I didn't even notice him. He mutters something to himself, reaches into the stock cupboard, and tosses Will a package.

"What we need to do," Kat says, "is find out what clubs or hotels are available."

Will smiles gratefully at Kat. I feel a spark of guilt for causing him all this grief. And a tiny spark of jealousy. "Right," he says. "That makes sense. Let's make a list, and Rachel and I will check them out over the weekend."

Ha! Take that, Kat! Oh, drat. "Oh, um, I'm going to my dad's," I admit.

His face falls. Like, to the floor. "What? You are? I won't be able to see you all weekend?"

I shake my head. "It's only two days. I'll call you." Luckily, I already know his number by heart because of Raf. Not that I've ever called Raf.

He pouts for a few more seconds and turns to Kat. "Kat, would you mind coming with me?"

"Of course not. I'd be happy to."

I roll my eyes at Tammy. And I can't even be mad, because Kat's so . . . nice.

*

"We ruined the prom," I tell Miri on the train to Long Island. "I don't believe it."

"Uh-huh," she mumbles, slumped in her seat, reading A^2.

"I'm about to make freshman history by going to the prom with the soc president, and I can't even go. Can life be any more unfair?"

"Uh-huh," she repeats.

Hmm. "Is there a rhinoceros on this train?"

"Uh-huh."

"You're not paying attention to me!"

"Uh-huh."

I wave my hand in front of her face.

"What?" she asks, finally looking up.

"We ruined the prom with the cows. Do you get it?"

"Yes, I get it, but is that really such a big deal? It's just a dance. A stupid elitist dance. A dance that you wouldn't even be going to if not for the love spell," she says, whispering the last two words. "There are far more important issues you should be worrying about."

I know I'm normally a little selfish. But I'm pretty sure Miri should be taking some responsibility for this crisis. Not that I'm one to point fingers, but it was sort of her fault. "What are you doing, anyway?"

She whips out a notebook. "Worrying about things more important than prom. Like ridding the world of land mines, number three on my list, and of slave trafficking, number four. Fixing the ozone layer, number five. And there was an oil spill this morning off the coast of France. Do you know how many whales are going to die?" She makes an arrow in her notebook. "The oil just got bumped up to number three."

I squirm in my seat. "Okay, I'm sorry. Sounds serious."

She shakes her head and I notice the heavy circles under

139

her eyes. "Life is serious," she says, and sighs, then returns to reading, leaving me staring at my hands.

I could so use a manicure.

* * *

The whole bronzed family is waiting for us at the train station.

"Aloha!" Jennifer and my dad say.

I need a pair of sunglasses: my dad's blue and red flowered shirt is *that* bright. And, oh, no, Jennifer is wearing a lei. I give their honeymoon glow another week, tops. Then they'll get back to being as miserable as the rest of us.

I'm confused. How did Prissy, otherwise known as Priscilla, who was stuck here with Jennifer's parents on Long Island, get so much color? She quickly clears that up when she says, "Am I pretty? I want to be pretty like Mommy and have brown skin too, so I used self-tanner!"

"No, you did not," I say in disbelief. She's five. Is that legal?

She nods happily.

We all shuffle into their Mercedes. Prissy climbs into her booster seat and quickly puts her tiny tanned finger up her nose.

I try to catch Miri's eye so we can secretly make fun of the entire scene, but she's lost in her saving-the-world thoughts.

* * *

" 'You will soon discover a treasure!' " Jennifer reads, after breaking open her fortune cookie. "You know what that means," she says, winking at my dad across the booth at Happy Palace, our favorite Chinese restaurant.

"What treasure?" I ask Jennifer as I chomp on an almond cookie. "You buried money in the backyard?" Can I have some?

"No," she says, and then smiles. "I meant the new addition."

"You're adding another wing to the house?" I ask. Now Miri and I won't have to share a room when we stay over.

Jennifer looks at my father. "Well, no," she says.

No? "So what kind of addition?" I ask. And then it hits me. Smack in my face. I choke on the cookie, start coughing, and grab my glass of water.

Miri finally snaps out of her reverie. "Already?" she asks disbelievingly.

She's pregnant? But . . . but . . . but I'm still not used to Prissy. And . . . where are they going to put the baby? Won't they need a nursery? Does that mean we'll have to bunk with Prissy? "When's the baby due?"

"What baby, Mommy?" Prissy asks, sucking on a cookie. "What does *due* mean?"

My dad and Jennifer giggle. "We're not pregnant!" she says, still laughing, her blue-green eyes twinkling.

Then what is she talking about? "Are you getting a dog?"

"Do you know how much work a dog is?" Jennifer says, flipping her gorgeous silky blond hair over her shoulder. "No way. We're *trying* to have a baby. We're just not pregnant yet."

Is that really an image I need?

Prissy slams her small fist on the table, face puckered. "No more babies."

Silence.

"Babies are fun!" Jennifer promises in her chirpiest voice. "You'll get to be the big sister!"

"I don't want to be a big sister," she insists, shaking her pigtails. "I want to be the little sister."

I decide to attempt to help. I can certainly relate: rumor has it when I was first told about Miri's upcoming arrival, I spit up in protest. "You can be a big sister and still be a little sister," I explain. "You're so lucky. You get to be both! I wish *I* could be both."

How awesome would it be if I had a big sister? Someone to tell me what to wear, help me with my makeup. Hmm. I've kind of been my mom's big sister lately.

"I don't want to be a big sister," Prissy says calmly.

Miri laughs. "Too bad it's not up to you."

142

"No more babies!" Prissy screams at the top of her lungs, and reaches for her third cookie.

Everyone at the restaurant turns to stare.

"No more sugar," Jennifer says, moving the cookie plate out of her reach.

*

The subject comes up again the next morning.

We're sitting, sleepy eyed, in the kitchen, lazily enjoying our poached eggs and toast, when Prissy's question lands flat on the table like a pancake. "Where do babies come from?" Her blue-green eyes are wide with innocence.

Miri starts coughing.

I take a long sip of my orange juice and try to see to the

bottom of the glass. Would it be weird if I climbed under the table?

"Well . . . ," my father begins.

Oh, God. Oh, no. Don't say it. He's not going to tell her, is he? I can't think of anything more painful than having to listen to my dad discuss the birds and the bees. I remember when I first heard about the facts of life: Jewel's older brother told us when we were in the second grade. I went home and asked my mom if the rumors were true. I remember feeling truly appalled. It goes in *where*? Anyway, I have never discussed this subject with my dad, and I certainly don't want to start now. As far as I know, he doesn't even know I know.

"Well . . . ," my father begins again. I look at Miri, and her cheeks are the same cherry red as I imagine mine are.

Jennifer makes a stab. "When mommies and daddies love each other . . ."

Miri and I sink lower into our chairs.

". . . they sleep in the same room, alone together," she continues. (The detail on this plate is just amazing. Nice plate. Pretty plate. Pretty white square plate.) "That's when they make a baby."

"Oh," says Prissy. Then her eyes squint into small commas. "But *how* do they make a baby?"

Silence.

"Out of love," my dad says.

Could this get any more painfully embarrassing? I'd rather be writing an exam while a dentist fills my cavities. (Not that I have any; I have perfect teeth, unlike my sister, who must brush her teeth with Kool-Aid. I wonder if Will has any cavities.

143

He does eat a lot of licorice. I bet Raf has perfect teeth. . . . No thinking about Raf! Better to listen to Jennifer's sex talk!)

Prissy considers the new and extremely vague explanation and slowly nods. Then she shovels a forkful of egg into her mouth and the subject is forgotten—by her. I think I may be scarred for life.

We go to the mall in the afternoon, because Prissy has inexplicably painted Liquid Paper hearts on her black patent leather party shoes. Dad tells Miri and me that we can each pick out one new item for ourselves.

"New jeans! New jeans!" I beg inside Macy's, leading them from the kids' shoe department to the juniors department.

"You have jeans," my dad says. "You're wearing them."

True. I could even use the multiplying spell for more if I wanted to.

144

"A girl can never have too many pairs," Jennifer says, coming to my defense. I almost pass out from surprise by my new and unexpected ally. Honeymoon Jennifer is awesome! And so smart. I pile ten pairs over my arm and retreat into the dressing room.

Jennifer acts as commentator as I model each one. "Too big. Can we get her a smaller size?" And then, "Too dark. Lighter is really in style this season." She's right! London's groupies are all wearing light jeans.

By the time we've whittled it down to two pairs, Miri, my dad, and Prissy are all asleep on the couch. "Which should I choose?" It's like asking me to pick a favorite parent. I love them equally.

"Ring them both up," Jennifer says. "Let's hang ten! That means go for it."

Viva Hawaii.

If Jennifer keeps this up, I may pick her as my favorite parent.

It's not until we're back in the car that I realize that Miri didn't buy anything. "Where's your one item?" I ask.

"Yeah, honey," my dad says, reversing the car out of the lot. "I said you can have anything you want. And since we bought Rachel two pairs of jeans, you can have two anythings."

"I don't need anything material," she answers. "But you could take my assigned money and donate it to the charity of your choice on my behalf."

Oh, brother.

Jennifer whips her head around. "What?"

My feelings exactly. What a goody-goody.

My father also turns around (which probably isn't that safe). But he smiles at my sister as if she said she'd been accepted to Harvard. "I'd be happy to do that. You choose the charity and I'll double what I spent on Rachel's jeans."

That's not fair. Sigh. I'm horrible. Of course it's fair.

"Thanks, Dad," Miri says.

She's so donating that to the prom.

145

*

I prepare to call Will before dinner. This will be the first time I call him; he's phoned me every day for the last week. I close the door, sit on the bed, and pick up the receiver.

". . . bought her the most adorable jeans. I think I might go back and get a pair," I hear Jennifer saying. "Hello? Did someone pick up?"

Foiled! "Sorry. I'll hang up."

"Do you need the phone, Rachel?"

"I can wait."

"Don't worry, I'll get off. Irma, I'll speak to you tomorrow, 'kay?"

I don't know what's come over her. First new jeans, and now she's getting off the phone with her friends so I can use it? We must have put a spell on her by accident. Nah. Is it possible the fairy tales are all wrong? Once a Soon-to-Be Step-Monster officially joins the family, she becomes nice? I should enjoy it as long as it lasts. It could fade along with her tan. "Thanks."

I wait for the dial tone. Then, palms all sweaty, I punch in the number. I don't know why I'm nervous. He likes me. He told me to call. There's absolutely no reason for me to be—

"Hello?"

Heart. Exploding. That's why I should be nervous. It's Raf. I should hang up. No, I can't. He definitely has caller ID. Not that he'd recognize the Long Island number. But he knows that my dad lives out here. And he might call back. But what should I do? I can't ask the boy I secretly still like if I can speak to his brother! This is so awful. Exponentially worse than my dad talking about sex. Why didn't I block my number?

"Hello?" Raf repeats.

Although . . . maybe it's not Raf. How do I know? Their hellos sound identical. It's probably Will. Of course it's Will. "Hello!" I say, attempting to sound optimistic. I

146

try to use my nonexistent powers of persuasion. *Be Will! Be Will!*

"Hello," the voice says again. "Who is this?"

It's not Will. Will would know it was me. Wouldn't Raf know it was me too? I should hang up. *Don't hang up!* I could claim I got disconnected. *Be mature!* My palms are now so sweaty that the receiver slips out of my grasp. "Rachel," I squeak, pressing it firmly against my ear.

"Rachel who?"

Is he (whoever he is) joking? Which one of them doesn't know me? "Rachel Weinstein."

"I'm just kidding you, Rachel. It's Mitch."

"Oh, hi." I slap my sweaty hand against my forehead. I forgot about brother number three. He's not on my daily radar since he's at NYU. But I thought he didn't live at home. Why is he answering the phone? Just to make me feel like an idiot?

"So who do you want to speak to?" he asks, laughing. "Raf or Will?"

"Raf, please. I mean, Will. Will!" Now I'm confused.

He laughs again and hollers, "Will, phone!"

Glad to be an amusement.

Seconds later Will picks up. "Hello?"

They all sound the same! "Hi, Will."

"Rachel! How you doin'?"

"Headachy." As of now. "You?"

"Good. Kat and I went site hunting and we found some cool places. I'll bring pictures and prices to show on Monday."

147

"Great. What are you doing tonight?"

"Wishing I was hanging out with you, but going to some party with Jerome and the boys. Hey, on Friday? I was thinking Patsy's."

Yum. Only the best pizza place in the city. "Sounds delicious." And romantic. I can already see a string of mozzarella stretched between us like the spaghetti in *Lady and the Tramp*.

"Great. My parents love it there, and they want to meet you."

"Your p-parents?" I'm not ready for a meet and greet. Doesn't that happen much later on? Like when we're engaged? What will I wear?

"Don't worry. It won't be just them. My brothers, too."

Really foiled this time.

148

"Time for all of us to hit the hay," my dad says, turning off the TV. I stand up and stretch.

"I'm not going to sleep," Prissy says, still firmly planted on the couch.

Jennifer laughs. "Oh, really? You certainly are."

"No, I'm not," Prissy says again. She turns around and stuffs her head between two pillows.

Jennifer picks her up by the waist and carries her toward her room. "Yes, young lady, you are."

Prissy begins kicking and screaming, "I want to sleep with you!"

"What is wrong with you tonight? Big girls sleep in their own beds."

Miri and I quickly say good night, leaving them to the parenting trauma, and after washing up, we head to the privacy of our lemon-meringue room. "We have a lot to talk about," I say.

"I know. But let's wait until everyone's asleep."

I don't know why she wants to wait, but I'm too tired to argue. Might as well get in a few winks.

I nod off into dreamworld, and the next thing I know, Miri is shaking me awake. "Are we ready to talk about prom?" I ask groggily.

"Yup," she says. "But let's do it in France." She waves two batteries and some sort of purple potion in front of me. "I found a clean-water spell."

So that's why she wanted to wait. But do we have to do this now, when I'm feeling like a zombie? "Are you kidding me? Don't you think you're going a little overboard on this helping thing?"

She squats on the ground. "Get on. We'll discuss this once we're there."

I sigh and climb aboard the Miri express. I wonder if I'm accumulating any airline points. I'd like a free trip to the Bahamas, please.

A few seconds later, we land on a soft beach. The sunrise is casting shades of pastel pink and orange on the water—if only I had a camera—and the air smells salty and delicious. Excuse me . . . *délicieux*.

Miri goes to work on the oil issue. I make a snow angel in the sand. "I'll be here if you need me," I say.

"Yeah, thanks."

A few minutes later, she's done and I'm in heaven. The

149

lull of the surf is sweet music to my ears. Can I move to France?

"All right, whales saved; let's go home," Miri announces, crouching down beside me.

Already? I pat the spot beside me. "This piece of beach has your name on it, missy. What's the rush?"

Miri shrugs and plops onto her back. "Two minutes. And then I have to get back to work."

I groan and flick a grain of sand toward her. "Stop being such a freak. And speaking of which, I can't believe you didn't get new clothes today."

She sighs. "How could I take home clothes when there are people in the world who are freezing?"

I don't want to sound selfish or anything, but what she just said makes absolutely no sense. "Whatever. What charity are you going to give your money to?"

"I don't know yet! That's the problem. There are so many causes. The homeless, peace in the Middle East, AIDS, animal rights . . ."

Wrong answer. "The prom! We need the money for the prom! Remember our discussion about how we had to help earn money? This is it! So help!"

She props herself up on her elbows. "The prom is not a charity."

"Actually it is. JFK alumni have shelled out thirty thousand dollars for school repairs. Because of the cows. Your cows. The school is using the prom money to fix the gym, so we need to raise money to rent a ballroom."

"I'm not giving up peace in the Middle East for a stupid prom."

Hello? Does she feel no accountability here? "But you ruined prom! You should feel responsible!"

Miri bursts into tears.

Oops. I sit up and put my arm around her. She starts sobbing silently, as though afraid that any sound she might make will . . . scare the whales?

"What's wrong?" I ask.

"I feel"—sob—"so"—sob—"awful. That I ruined p-p-prooooooooom." Snot dribbles along her upper lip. "And I"—sob—"don't know how"—sob—"to fix it. And there are so many bad things in the world. And I have to fix them, too. And I know I'm supposed to be happy that I'm a witch and that I have all these powers, but I feel so"—sob—"responsible for everyone. There's this huge weight on my chest, like someone's sitting on it all the time."

My poor, sweet sister. I need to make her laugh. Not knowing what else to do, I sit on her stomach. "Like this?"

She giggles but quickly starts crying again. Then snorting. "You're hurting me," she says, and I roll off. I got sand all over her shirt.

"I know what will make you feel better," I say.

"What?"

"The Eiffel Tower! Let's go to Paris!"

She shakes her head. "I'm tired. Can we just go home and go to sleep?"

Party pooper. "All right, but can we at least get a baguette?"

She squeezes the batteries in her little hands and motions to her back. "Another time."

When we return to Long Island, I climb straight back between my sheets.

"What are we going to do about the prom?" Miri asks, getting into bed.

I think for a minute before I answer. "We need to raise money. And we can definitely use your help with that. So stop worrying. We'll figure something out. Now, about your feeling responsible for the entire world—"

Suddenly, we hear the door next to us open, followed by little feet scampering down the hallway, then my dad and Jennifer's bedroom door opening.

"Prissy?" my dad says. "What are you doing in here?"

"No more babies!" she declares. "From now on I'm sleeping with you. I don't want a sister."

Miri and I start laughing. After a few minutes of debating with my dad and Jennifer the merits of her staying, Prissy tires them out and wins the argument.

My eyelids feel heavy. "Let me just rest for two seconds and then we'll continue talking." I close my eyes for two seconds, but the next thing I know, the light is streaming through the blinds, Miri is at the desk making lists, and it's morning. All this globe-trotting is definitely exhausting.

152

"Hello?" I say, turning on the hallway light. "Mom?"

"It doesn't look like she's home," Miri says, dropping her weekend bag onto the floor.

Huh? She's always here when we get back. Always. "Maybe she's sleeping," I say. I open her door and flick on her bedroom light. Nope. Her unmade bed looks a lot like mine, covered with clothes.

"This is weird," I say. "It's eight o'clock and she's out? Did she have a date tonight? It's Sunday! She should be home to greet us." With cookies and milk and . . . Oops, been watching too many retro shows.

We decide to watch TV until she gets home. By ten Miri is asleep on the couch. "Go to bed," I say, nudging her. "I'll wait up."

I'm starting to worry. What if something happened to her? What time should I start panicking? Why hasn't she called? I try her cell phone, but it goes right to voice mail.

At ten-thirty I'm pacing. At five to eleven I'm about to start calling—well, not the police, but at least the fireman downstairs—when I finally hear my mom's key in the door.

"Hi, hon," she says, casually hanging her jacket on a hanger. She notices my scowl. "What's wrong?"

"Where," I spit out, "have you been?"

"I am so sorry," she says, unzipping a pair of stunning new leopard-skin high-heeled boots. Where did those come from? "I didn't realize how late it was."

"Next time, Mother, you call home when you're going to be late." I'm about to add that I'll have to ground her if she pulls a trick like this again.

She hangs her head. "I am really sorry, honey." She gives me a hug. "Where's your sister?"

"Asleep. It's *eleven*," I say.

She gasps. "I really didn't realize it was so late. Want to tell me about your weekend? I'll make some tea."

153

Sighing, I follow her to the kitchen and slump into a chair. "How was *your* weekend? Busy?"

"Oh, boy, yes. I went out—a lot."

"How many dates did you have?"

She smiles as she fills up the kettle. "Four."

"Four!" I didn't even know she knew four men! Who are they? "There's the fireman, Adam, Geriatric Lex . . . Who else?"

She shakes her head. "I had to reschedule with Lex. By the time he called on Friday to confirm, my weekend was booked."

I raise an eyebrow.

"I fit him into the schedule for cocktails next Saturday from five to seven." She unwraps two herbal tea bags and drops them into two chipped mugs. She picks up the wall calendar to confirm. "Yup, five to seven." The entire month is covered with red scribbles.

"Pass that to me, please." I don't believe it. There are men's names and locations written down for every night of next week. Two on Friday. Three on Saturday. Yes, three. Has my mom gone crazy? When did she become Crazy Dating Mom?

How can I get my calendar to look like hers?

154

My Mother, My Headache

11

On our way to homeroom, Tammy stops me in the middle of the stairwell, looks around to make sure no one can hear, and whispers, "Bosh called me last night."

"What? No way."

"Way." Her eyes sparkle mischievously. "We spoke for three hours. I told him I have a boyfriend, but he wouldn't let me off the phone!"

"Tammy, what did you possibly have to discuss for that long?" I wonder how many times he said *dude* during their conversation.

"Everything. Life. Movies. The diving in France. He went with his family last year, and he's so relieved that the oil spill didn't damage any of the sea life or underwater wrecks. Can you believe that story? That the oil just disappeared? I mean, one day it was there, and the next day there's no trace of any—"

Enough with the stupid oil! "But back to Aaron," I interrupt. The results of our France adventure have been all over the news. Every possible explanation and conspiracy theory has been suggested, my favorite involving Oprah,

Bill Gates, and a vacuum cleaner–like submarine. "What are you going to do about Aaron?"

"Can you stop clogging the stairs?" I hear.

I look up to see Melissa glaring at us.

I roll my eyes and lead Tammy to class, to two empty seats in the back row. I wave her on to continue. "So? Your current boyfriend? Go on."

She slides into her chair and her shoulders slump. "I spoke to him, too. For two minutes. I don't think we have as much in common as I thought we did."

"What do you mean?"

"Well, he doesn't like movies, or diving. All he seems to care about is fantasy baseball. He got off the phone so he could make a trade or something."

What is it with guys and baseball? "But do you still like him?"

She hesitates. "I mean, he's a nice guy. I like him . . . but as a friend. Not like . . . you know. The stomach butterflies are gone."

"It's not fair of you to lead him on if you don't feel the same."

"I know, I know. But how can I dump someone who's sick in bed? It's too mean." Her eyebrows droop. I never noticed what expressive eyebrows she has. "When I bring over his chicken soup, do I just blurt out 'By the way, I'm dumping you'? I don't think I can do it."

She knows how to make chicken soup? Impressive.

*

It's four-thirty and I'm in Raf's living room.

Impossible, you scream. How can that be?

156

Will made the shocking decision to move the soc meeting from lunch to after school at his town house in the West Village.

Obviously I had a total panic attack when he casually mentioned the development.

"I won't leave you," Tammy said, trying to reassure me, which didn't work, because it's not being alone that's making me hyperventilate. It's seeing where Raf lives. And sleeps. And eats.

Unfortunately, Raf doesn't seem to be home. Perhaps he's out gallivanting with Melissa. Or more likely, he's at Stromboli's or whatever locale the A-list has decided to make today's after-school hangout.

Besides us, the town house is empty, since Will's parents aren't home yet either. I was kind of hoping to meet them— then maybe we could cancel Friday's Get to Know Each Other Dinner, otherwise known as Sure to Be the Worst Night of My Life. What if I can't hide my true feelings for Raf? And then the entire family hates me?

Will and I are sitting on the white carpet in the center of the living room. Hotel and club brochures are spread in front of us.

"These are the only places that still have our date available," Will explains.

"Can't we change the date?" Bosh asks, on the couch with his head on Tammy's lap. Someone's moving in quick, dude.

"Unfortunately no," Will says. "The caterer is already partially paid for, and the band is all booked up. Actually, we're lucky JFK always has prom on a Thursday, because the

157

places are *mucho* more expensive on the weekend." A JFK tradition—seniors get the postprom Friday off. "Anyway," Will continues, "I think we found the right place. I just wanted you guys to run the numbers. It's called Penthouse Fifty and the room will cost us four thousand dollars. But as opposed to hotels, they'll let us bring in outside food. And there are wraparound terraces with panoramic views of the city, since it's on the fiftieth floor of a tower uptown. Kat and I thought it was cool."

Bosh nods. "Sounds good, dude."

"Fine with me," River says. "Jeffrey?"

Jeffrey peeks over from behind the couch. Where did he even come from? I swear he didn't walk over with us.

"All right," he mumbles.

We begged Amy to come too, but she just laughed at us. Way to go, head of prom.

Will calls Penthouse 50 to confirm. "We're in," he says after hanging up. "I'm going to delay giving them a deposit as long as possible. But we seriously need to come up with some fund-raising ideas. Any suggestions? We only have a few weeks. Rachel, Raf said you're like a human calculator. How much money do we have to raise to pull this off? Exactly?"

I know my heart should not be swooning, but . . . Raf still talks about me? I am so pathetic. Now, let's see. "Twenty-seven thousand five hundred was what it cost before, plus four thousand for the room. Minus the profit if we keep the ticket prices at fifty dollars a head . . ." Now I'm just showing off. You can just add four thousand to the missing ten thousand. "Fourteen thousand." Of course, if there were more cool guys like Will and Bosh, guys who date nonseniors, we'd get more kids to come to the prom. Nah. Scratch that idea. I'm looking forward to my special status.

"What do you think, Rachel?" Will asks. "Can we raise that kind of money in time?"

I cannot ruin the prom. I cannot ruin Will's reputation. I look deep into his eyes. This boy is so in love with me that he will listen to anything I say. "Yes," I answer in my most assuring voice, "we can."

"All right," he says. "Let's brainstorm."

Kat twirls her purple pen in her fingers. "Open prom up to nonseniors?" she asks hopefully.

"No way," River says. "Our class will revolt. We don't want a bunch of freshmen cramping our style."

I give him the evil eye.

"It wouldn't help," Bosh adds, head still in Tammy's lap. "We'd have to order more tables and more food, and our costs would go up."

Kat shrugs. "Sell chocolates?"

"That's a whole lot of chocolate," River says. "Why don't we have another fashion show?"

Please, no. I've barely recovered from the last one. "Car wash? That's what people in the movies always do," I say. I envision water fights and lots and lots of suds, Raf wiping a smudge of soap off my cheek, looking deep in my eyes, kissing me . . . I mean Will. Will, Will, Will.

"That's a lot of cars," Bosh says, popping my fantasy

159

bubble, "considering most people in our school don't drive. This is Manhattan."

"We need to leverage the skills we have," River says, fingering an eyebrow piercing.

What do I have that no one else does? A sister for a witch, that's what. How can I best use Miri's magic? Maybe we can sell oranges? Maybe Miri can whip up something even better to sell, and all the money can go to the school. Like a flying broom! Okay, not that, but something more feasible. And then we can have—"An auction!"

Will lights up. "That's a great idea. We can ask people for donations. Theater tickets, gift cards, that kind of stuff. Get parents to donate."

"I bet I can get free CDs from MTV," River says.

"I work at Borders," Kat says. "Maybe they'll donate some books."

"Cool!" Will rubs his hands together like he's starting a fire. "I'll try for some leather coats. My dad's in the leather business. We can put up signs all over school asking for donations. And we can ask local businesses. I'll ask Konch if we can hold the auction after school one day so all the underclassmen can bid too. We'll even invite parents. It'll be wild."

"I like it," Kat says, "but we need some big-ticket items. We're not going to sell fourteen thousand dollars' worth of books and tattoos."

Will looks concerned.

"I can come up with a big-ticket item," I blurt out with a confidence I don't feel.

Tammy's eyebrows go nuts.

"Like what, dude?" Bosh asks.

"I—I don't want to say yet. But I have some pretty incredible resources. So don't worry," I say vaguely, and then instantly feel queasy. "Where's the restroom?"

"Up the stairs, then follow the hall to the third door on your left," Will says, and then starts writing out ideas.

I excuse myself and begin my journey down the hall. Or down the museum. Every space of wallpaper is covered in family photos of the three boys at every stage of their development. Will dressed as a pirate for Halloween. Think it's Will. Could be Raf. Or Mitch. I take another step. Raf as a five-year-old. Shock of midnight hair (in a bowl cut, haha!), adorable dimple in his left cheek, big grin with missing baby teeth. Tiny plaid jacket, mini corduroy pants.

And this must be—

Raf's room. I stifle a gasp. I know it's Raf's room, because the door is open and from my position outside I can see our fat green freshman *Biology: Understanding Organisms* textbook on the desk. I wonder what the rest of his room looks like. Is he messy? Neat? Does he have any pictures up? Any photos . . . of me?

I shouldn't.

I should!

I mustn't.

I must!

I do. I take a deep breath and plunge straight into Raf's room. All my senses are overwhelmed at once. Blue paint! Boy smell! Walls of books! Silver laptop! Gray bedspread that has sailboats and . . . Raf on it!

Oh, no. Please no.

161

"Hi?" says a voice. Raf's voice.

Raf is sprawled on his stomach across his bed, writing in a notebook. I am a deer frozen in an SUV's headlights. If only I were a witch. If only I could zap myself back downstairs. Or zap myself into a fly on the wall. Or fly around the world like a superhero and turn time back three minutes. Then I could calmly find my way down the hall and not be caught in this more-painful-than-a-needle-in-the-eye situation.

Heart. R-r-racing. Calm down, calm down. "Oh, hi, Raf," I say in my most composed voice. "This isn't the bathroom."

Please tell me I didn't just say that. *Please*. Now he's associating me with a toilet. How is it possible I managed to make this impossibly bad situation worse?

He places his notebook facedown on the bedspread and arches his left eyebrow. "It's on the other side of the hall."

I begin backing out immediately.

"Rachel, hold on," he says suddenly.

I stop in my tracks. The tingles that have been rushing down my spine are already in my toes. "Um, yeah?"

He spins around so he's now sitting up against the headboard. "How's . . . you know . . . everything going?"

In life? In love? I miss you, I think before I can stop myself. I lean against the doorjamb. "Good."

"Yeah? What are you guys busy doing down there?"

"Trying to save prom."

He nods and looks at his hands. "Are you going? Did my brother ask you?"

My cheeks burn. "Yeah."

"Whatever," he says, and shrugs. Then he looks back up at me. Our eyes lock. "Have fun."

"Right," I say. "Thanks. I should get back." No! Wait! I want to stay with you!

"Can you close the door?"

I back out of the room, confused, feeling like I've been slapped. Does Raf still have feelings for me? Does he care that I'm dating Will? Why does he seem upset? He's the one who broke it off. I said yes to Will only because Raf wanted nothing to do with me.

So why do I feel like I've made the biggest mistake of my life?

* * *

"I'm just off to MOMA with Jordan," my mom declares as I walk into her room when I get home. "Finish your homework before you watch TV. And make sure Miri finishes her reading in A^2. She's been falling behind in her training. I left you money to order Chinese food on the kitchen table—"

Again? And who's Jordan?

Mom slaps her hand against her open mouth.

"What?"

"I forgot the laundry in the washing machine. Do you think you can— Oh, never mind."

She closes her eyes and purses her lips, and the next thing I know, a heap of our clothes is dry and folded into neat piles on her bed.

All the folding and sorting I've done over the years becomes a distant cruel memory.

163

"How do I look?" she asks, twirling. She's wearing chocolate-colored pants (new), a white blouse (new), and her heart-shaped necklace.

"Gorge. Have fun," I say, and kiss her on the forehead.

She takes off in a flutter, and I try to block out my Raf-induced confusion and focus on the task at hand—figuring out what I'm going to auction off. I find Miri at her desk. "I'm really busy," she says without looking up. "Did you hear about the bushfires in California? What are we going to do?"

"Not much," I say, lying down in my usual position, my feet propped up on her wall. "Can we take a few secs to discuss the prom debacle?"

She closes her notebook and turns to face me. "Go ahead."

"So it seems that alumni have donated most of the money to repair the school, right? But since this whole screwup is partially your fault, I still need your help. Like you promised. To raise prom money instead. And we're having an auction. So I need you to poof up something that I can donate. Something that we can sell. Something cool and expensive."

"Such as?"

"I don't know. What can you whip up? Let's brainstorm."

She heaves a sigh, then opens her notebook to a clean page. "What do teenagers want?"

No more acne, no more rules. "To be older."

"Not sure I can do that." She scratches her nose with the wrong side of her pen and draws a blue line across the bridge. I try not to laugh; I don't want to interrupt the flow of this brainstorming session. "What about a trip some-where?" she suggests.

"How would we do that? Fly the person plus guest there on your broomstick?"

"Ha-ha. Maybe I could zap up some airline tickets to Cancun."

"Yeah? That sounds more like computer hacking than witchcraft." I take her pillow and balance it on my feet.

"Can you stop? I sleep on that, you know."

"It helps me think. Maybe we could get Mom to help."

"Are you kidding? She's way too busy lately."

"No kidding. She needs a clone of herself just to meet all these guys. Hey, that would be cool. Can you make clones?" I would get mine to go to school for me. What would her name be? I think of London and grimace. Definitely not Rochelle.

"I don't think so."

"An iPod?" I could really use one. I kick the pillow over to Miri and she catches it in her lap.

"A laptop?" She tosses back the pillow.

"A TV?" I kick it right back to her, like we're playing hot potato.

She throws it right back. "A flat-screen TV? Lots of flat-screen TVs!"

I catch it with my hands and then lie down on it. "Per-fect! A fancy TV will get us at least a few grand. We poof one up, then use the multiplying spell, and presto, the prom is saved! Is there a spell for TVs?"

"I doubt it, no. But I have a ton of stuff to do this week.

165

I'm going to try that cleaning spell on the Hudson River, and maybe the Mississippi. So let's make Saturday spell day. And we'll figure it all out."

"Perfect! I have nothing to do Saturday anyway. Will is working and Tammy is babysitting Aaron." I realize how selfish that sounds. Here I am asking Miri for a favor and expecting her to fit it into my schedule. Still, there's no reason we can't be efficient with our time, is there? And as far as the prom is concerned, time is of the essence!

"I thought she didn't like him anymore."

"She likes him as a friend, but that's it. But because he has mono, she feels too guilty to break up with him." I really shouldn't gossip with Miri so much about my friends. She never tells me anything about hers. Hmm, I'm not sure she has any. "So Saturday will be a sister day. Maybe we can watch a movie on the new TV!" Maybe I should stay home and watch TV on Friday, too, instead of going out with Will and Raf. How can I deal with both—correction: *all*—the Kosravi brothers simultaneously?

I need a clone. Rochelle, where art thou?

"Oh, will you do me one more favor?" I ask. "I need you to extend the love spell on the glove."

"Extend?" Miri says, shaking her head. "You can't renew a love spell. It isn't a library book, you know."

"What?" I scream. "Are you kidding me?" What am I going to do? Will's feelings for me are going to wear off and I'll be left with nothing! Unless Raf starts to like me again . . . Yeah, right. It looks like I've lost Raf for good.

Miri leans back in her chair again, laughing hysterically. "I'm just kidding. Of course I can do it again. You can sleep

on it tonight. Wow, you should have seen the look on your
face. It was so funny."

Hilarious.

※

Operation Save the Prom, aka the Auction, has been approved by the principal and scheduled for Monday, May 24,
which is only three days before the prom.

I'm in the school bathroom trying to get the no-touch
auto-dryer to work when Jewel and Melissa saunter in. They
start flicking their hair excessively when they see me.

"Hi, Rachel," Jewel says, catching my eye in the mirror.
I feel the familiar tug of my heart. We used to be best friends.
Before she joined the dark side.

"Hey," I respond, and stop waving my hands like a
weirdo. I wipe my hands on my new fabo jeans. This room is
too small for the three of us.

"So, Rachel," Melissa says, sliding up next to me. She
reapplies her lipstick. "Looking forward to dinner tonight?
Patsy's is my fave. Love that white pizza."

What?

Not only do I have to deal with my boyfriend, my quasi
ex-boyfriend and love of my life, and their parents, I also
have to deal with my archenemy? Are Melissa and Raf *that*
serious? Are they a full-fledged couple? Maybe I'll stab her
with the pizza slicer. Maybe I'll stab myself. Waiting for
hours in the ER waiting room has got to be better than en-
during an entire evening at the restaurant, as fave as it is.
(And I know about waiting for hours in an ER. A person has
to be run over by a steamroller before a doctor will see her.

When I was five I got my finger caught in the car door, and I had to wait six hours before someone finally came out from somewhere in back, and then all he gave me was one lousy stitch and a lollipop.)

Melissa's green eyes are twinkling with evil.

You know what? I'm not going to take her intimidation any longer. She should be nicer to me; I'm practically her sister-in-law. So what if Raf and Melissa are an item? It doesn't matter. Raf doesn't want me? Well, I don't want him. I'm dating someone older and wiser. Someone who *wants* to date me. Fine, maybe his feelings are a bit enchanted, but that's irrelevant. I have a boyfriend. Raf is history. "I am," I say in my loudest, bring-it-on voice. I stretch myself up to my full five foot one. "See ya." With that, I exit the bathroom.

168

Not my best closing line, but at least this time I didn't trip over a bike rack.

It's Friday night, and once again my mom and I are acting like wound-up toy cars, running all over the apartment. She's in a bathrobe, blow-drying her long, perfectly blond hair, as I struggle to find the right outfit for my potential night from hell.

When the buzzer goes off, I kiss Miri on the forehead and go into my mom's room to say good-bye. "Have fun tonight!" I say over the sound of the blow-dryer.

She's tilted upside down and smiling, so it looks like she's frowning. "You too! Where are you going?"

It smells like smoke in here. That had better be her hair burning and not a cigarette. "Patsy's!" I say.

"What?"

"Patsy's!"

"Barbequing? Have fun! Can you open the . . ." The blow-dryer drowns out her words.

"What? I can't hear you."

"Never mind!" she says, and with a purse of her lips, she opens her bedroom window with a bang.

I grab my purse and I'm out the door.

This is a disaster.

No, really. I know I've called things disasters before, but this qualifies as an eleven on the Richter scale. Here is the seating arrangement at our round table: Will is on my left. Next to him is Mitch. Next to Mitch is Louise, his girl-friend. Next to her is Mr. Kosravi ("Call me Don, sweetie," he says). Next to Don is Mrs. Kosravi (who keeps giving me the evil eye, most likely for ditching her baby boy and then promptly taking up with her middle child). Next to Mrs. Kosravi is Melissa. Which means guess who's sitting to my right? (Drumroll, please.)

Raf.

How did this happen? It was like a game of musical chairs gone wrong. And now anytime Raf or Will moves his legs, his shoes accidentally bump against mine and shock waves go through my body. My left foot—Will. Right foot—Raf. My brain sensors are in overdrive. And Melissa is

169

ignoring me entirely, laughing and joking with Mrs. Kosravi (she calls her Isabel) and Louise. Melissa's parents, Louise's parents, and the Kosravis go way back. How quaint.

Isabel and Louise let out peals of laughter and my back stiffens. Who knew Melissa had anything funny to say? I stare into my plate of Caesar salad.

Okay, it's not *all* a disaster. The fried calamari is pretty awesome. And the truth is listening to the three boys tease and joke with one another is pretty adorable.

"Do you wanna play some ball tomorrow?" Mitch asks Will. Mitch is, not surprisingly, as hot as his younger brothers. The three of them all have the same sexy dark hair, dark eyes, and lean athletic bodies. Mitch's hair is the longest, his face the most angular. Will's hair is the shortest and I think he's the tallest. Raf has the widest smile. And a curl to his hair that the others don't have.

170

"I can't," Will says. "Unlike you, I have a job on Saturdays."

He is so responsible, my boyfriend. How many eighteen-year-old boys work just to be independent?

"Why do you work so hard?" Mitch asks.

Raf rips a roll in half and dips it into his bean soup. "It's called money. You know, that green stuff you keep milking from Mom and Dad?"

Funny. Fine. But *he* doesn't have a job. So there.

But he does have a drop of soup on the corner of his mouth. He licks it off. Must stop staring at Raf's lips. Must stare at Will's instead.

"You're a comedian, Lobes!" Mitch reaches clear across

the table and tugs on Raf's ear. "Doesn't he have the floppi-est ears? Raf, does your girlfriend give you mooshies?"

Me? What? Oh, right. I'm *Will's* girlfriend.

Raf squirms and turns a deep shade of red.

Melissa stops her conversation to beam a smile across the table, as if she's accepting an award. The Snob of the Year Award.

"You should have seen him when he was younger," Mitch says. "He had the biggest ears in the world. Dumbo ears. Will and I used to tape them to the back of his head. We still think you should have had that surgery." He pol-ishes off the remainder of his salad.

"He was freaky looking," Will says teasingly.

"Lucky he grew up to look more normal," Mitch says. "More like us than Dumbo."

Raf winks at Melissa. "If I looked like either of them, I'd never leave my room."

Why doesn't he wink at me?

"Oh, tough love from Lobes!" Will says, and laughs.

I give Will a wink. He winks back. Ha!

"What's a mooshie?" annoying Melissa asks.

"Pulling his earlobe," Will explains. "Go ahead, try it."

Raf is still blushing, but he's smiling, too. Adorably. And the little-brother thing is so cute.

Not cute! Not cute!

Melissa pulls on his earlobe and the entire table cracks up. "Very soft," she says.

The waiter comes to clean off the table, interrupting the love fest and saving me from intense stabs of jealousy.

171

"Any news on the Columbia scholarship?" Don asks Will.

"What scholarship?" I ask.

"No big deal," Will says dismissively. "The political science department is considering giving me entrance money. Nothing major—just some money for books."

My boyfriend is modest, too! Take that, Raf. And political science! My boyfriend probably wants to be president—which means, one day, I could be the first lady. If I kept the spell up that long, which I wouldn't, of course. But he might have fallen so deeply in love with me by prom that even without the spell he will still adore me—and I him—and we'll live happily ever after, or something like that. That is so cool. *So cool.* I would make the best first lady ever! I could wear tailored suits and say, "Air Force One, fly me to Bermuda!" And I'll have bodyguards. And, of course, do lots of charity work and stuff. Fix health care and social security . . . Would I have to cut my hair short? All the first ladies have Grandma Hair. I wonder if that's a requirement. I could always cut it and then grow it out as soon as he's elected. First lady for thirty seconds and I'm already shirking my duties.

Anyway.

"I should have gotten a scholarship to NYU," Mitch says.

"For what?" Will asks.

Mitch grins. "My good looks?"

The whole table groans. "I think your head might need its own chair. It's getting fat," Raf says, smirking.

I stifle a laugh.

172

"I thought the youngest one was supposed to be the ham," Melissa says.

Isabel smiles at her three sons. "Not mine. My baby is the introvert. My oldest can't stop talking, and my middle one is on a quest to run the world."

Melissa touches Raf's hand. "Raf? Are you going to run for student council president too?"

He shakes his head. "Not interested."

"Really?" Her face drops in disappointment. Someone wants access to the soc lounge. "You'd be so good at it."

"I doubt it. I can't suck up to so many people."

"Hey!" Will says, obviously offended. "I didn't suck up to anyone."

"Kidding, kidding."

How rude. "If you're such an introvert," I blurt out, "why did you try out for the fashion show?"

Our eyes lock. "I didn't," he says. "Will signed me up."

"I knew it would be good for you," Will says. "You needed to make friends besides T. S. Eliot and Dylan Thomas."

Oh. I tear my eyes away from Raf and smile at Will. How sweet is he? Worrying about his little brother.

"Are you going to be in the show again next year?" Melissa asks Raf.

He shrugs. "Maybe."

"And what about you, Rachel?" Melissa asks, the evil glint back in her eyes. "Are you going to try out for the show again too?"

"I might," I say, and pick up my glass of water. Maybe I should dump it on her. How could Raf like someone so

173

awful? It shows poor character. Will is definitely the better brother.

"Mom," Mitch is saying, "will you sew on my camp labels for me?"

Camp? What camp?

She nods and takes a sip of wine. "Sure, dear. Bring over whatever you want labeled."

"Don't you think twenty-one is time to get a real summer job? Or at least sew your own name on your T-shirts?" says Will.

Isabel smiles patiently. "Oh, come on now. There's nothing wrong with a little help from Mom. I'm helping Raf with his camp labels again this year. And I'm happy to help you, too, Will."

The tips of Raf's floppy ears turn pink. I resist the urge to give him a mooshie.

174

"I didn't know you worked at a camp!" I say to Will. I've never understood what the appeal is. Tents? Mosquitoes? Forced swimming lessons? Not my cup of tea. If my parents had been inclined to send me somewhere for the summer, I would have opted for Club Med.

"Yup. Wood Lake. It's up in the Adirondacks. Didn't I tell you I was going back this summer? My *last* summer," he says to Mitch.

"You're just jealous of all the power I'm going to have as a section head," Mitch says.

"I can't believe they're making you the boss of anything." Will makes a face at his brother and puts his arm around my shoulders. "Rachel, what are you doing this summer? Why don't you come too?"

I almost spit out my water. "No thanks, camp's not for me." As much as I like Will, I'm too much of a city girl.

Raf nods. "I can't really see you there," he says.

Excuse me? I stew silently. How dare he comment on my camp potential!

"May I take that plate?" asks the waitress, and our pies are suddenly in front of us. Who does Raf think he is? From now on, I'm all about Will. Raf who?

After Don pays the check (Will tries to pay for our share, but his dad laughs him off), Melissa suggests that the six of us go to a movie.

"I've already seen it," I say quickly. This painful night must end. I've never felt more confused. I *can't* stop thinking about Raf.

Melissa laughs snarkily. "We haven't decided on one yet."

"I've seen a lot of movies lately. And it's already ten-fifteen, and I told my mom I'd be home by twelve. Maybe another time."

We push our chairs back and head toward the door in a single line. And that's when I can't help staring at the world's best cleavage.

I don't often stare at cleavage. But the woman's dress is so low cut and her cleavage is literally spilling over and—

That silver heart necklace looks familiar. That neck looks familiar. That chin. That face. Oh. My. God. It's my mother. My eyes whip back down to her cleavage. That is not my mother's cleavage. Well, it wasn't my mom's

175

cleavage yesterday. My mother is sitting at a table for two, wearing a low-cut black dress I've never seen before, chewing on a piece of crust. Across from her is Adam.

Mitch bumps into me from behind because I've stopped short. He follows my line of vision. "Sweet," he says, and then whistles, which causes my mom to look up.

At first she smiles, but then awareness washes over her face and her cheeks drain of color. She folds her arms across her chest. Too late! Then she pretends she didn't see me and looks back at her date.

My mouth opens but no sound comes out. Did the woman who gave birth to me just ignore me? "Mom?"

She doesn't look up. Is this not my mother? Maybe my mom has a doppelganger too.

The woman bites her thumbnail. Oh, it's my mother all right. "Mom?"

She looks up, feigning surprise. "Well, hello there!" Is she kidding me? "Adam, you remember my daughter Rachel."

"Nice to see you again," I say weakly.

"I thought Rachel just called you," Adam says, looking confused.

"Did I say that?" my mom asks. "I meant Miri. I'm always doing that. It's Miri who needs me to come straight home after dinner."

Huh? What? "There's nothing wrong with Miri. When we left she was—"

My mom gives me a please-shut-up look and I realize that she used my suggested make-your-cell-phone-ring-magically-when-you're-bored trick. And I just totally busted her. Oops.

"That's your mom?" Mitch says, poking his head over my shoulder. "Nice."

Will, who's already a few tables ahead, comes back. "Hi, Mrs. Graff. We were thinking of going to a movie. Is it cool if Rachel's home a little later tonight?"

I try to shake my head without actually shaking it. Why can't I project my thoughts? Why why why?

"Of course, Will!" she says with a great big smile, obviously thinking she's doing me some sort of favor. "And I told you to call me Carol."

Will takes my hand and squeezes. "Thanks."

"Terrific," I mutter, giving her and her breasts the evil eye all the way out the door. I wanted a friend for a mother. When am I going to learn to be careful what I wish for?

177

It's One A.M. Do You Know Where Your Mother Is? 12

Miri's light is still on, so I pound on her door. "You up?"

No answer. I open the door to find her room empty. Where in the world is she? Oh, no. She might actually *be* anywhere in the world.

I'm about to panic when there's a blast of cold and light, and a soaking-wet Miri materializes in the middle of her room. "Hi," she says, blinking furiously, startled to see me. "When did you get home?"

"Two minutes ago. Where *were* you?"

"Arkansas. De-polluting the Mississippi. How was your night?"

"Lame." I could not concentrate on the movie. First of all, it was one of those action extravaganzas consisting of seven car chases, one after the other, which made me dizzy. My larger problem was that we were all sharing one super-sized popcorn, which Raf was in charge of. So even though I wanted nothing more than a handful of buttery deliciousness, I couldn't exactly reach my hand into my ex's lap. How would it have looked?

Melissa was giggling and whispering to Raf the whole

time, which I found annoying and infuriating. How could a guy who liked me like her? But the most distracting part was Will's fingers, which were drawing circles in my palm. See, I'm so over Raf. Will is just amazing. Smart, handsome, ambitious. A senior. What more could I want in a boyfriend?

Miri strips out of her wet clothes and leaves them in a lump by her door.

I cover my eyes. "Mom isn't home yet, is she? I ran into her at the restaurant. Can you say *embarrassing?*"

"Nope, she's still not back." We both silently mull this over.

I sit down on her desk. "Do you think she's gone a wee bit off the deep end? She used magic to do laundry."

Miri sighs. "Yesterday she pretended she made those Mexican tofu tacos from scratch. But I so saw her zap them up."

179

"What is up with her?"

"She's been acting weird ever since Dad got married. Dating, letting me do magic. And then you convinced her to use a spell or two. Or a million. And I found an empty pack of cigarettes in her room. On top of everything, she's smoking again."

She has gone a bit overboard. My mother obviously doesn't know the meaning of moderation. Speaking of which, the waistband of my pants is digging into my stomach. I ate too much pizza. And tiramisu. And Will's licorice at the theater. Good thing I didn't partake in that popcorn; I wouldn't be able to breathe. A yawn escapes my lips.

"You look exhausted," Miri says. "Why don't you go to sleep?"

"I will. What about you?"

"I just have one more spell to find tonight. The bushfires are seriously endangering lives in California," she says. "Remember last year? How many people were hurt? I need to stop them now."

I pat down her soggy and tangled hair. "Moderation? Hello?"

She gives a small shrug. "At least I know where I get it from."

"Ready to work?" asks my irritating sister as she yanks the covers off my half-asleep body. This is known in our apartment as the Wake Up by Freezing Technique. She discovered it way back when she was three and has been using it to torture me ever since. I mumble a very bad word into my pillow.

"We have lots to do today!" she sings.

I pull the covers back over my head. "Come back later. Go bother Mom."

"Get with the program, deary. Mom is already long gone on today's breakfast date. And from there she goes straight to her lunch date. It's just you and me. All day."

I groan. Think fast. "I have to—"

"Don't go making things up."

I roll into a sitting position. "What are your plans for us, precisely?"

"First we're making a TV for your auction. Then we're making rain in California."

Sounds fair. "One project for me and one for you?"

"If you mean one for the pathetic prom and one for the betterment of humankind, then yes."

After a shower and a bowl of cereal, I'm ready to work. I sit myself down on her desk, swinging my legs. "Zap it up, baby. Give me a whopper of a TV."

She pushes me off her notebook. "I found the perfect spell. It's called the incarnate spell."

"Creepy sounding. How does it work?"

"We need a picture of what we want to create, a half cup of broken mirror, a half cup of crushed peanuts, and two cups of dirt."

"I can find that."

"Good," she says. "Go to it while I work on the rain spell."

My first stop is the apartment building's mail room off the lobby downstairs. There I search through the recycling bin for one of the millions of flyers and catalogs that get tossed out daily. Win a Million Dollars! Yeah, right. Free CDs! Sure. Carpet Cleaning! No, thanks. Circuit City electronics! Ding, ding, ding, we have a winner! I carry the catalog back upstairs, plop myself onto the couch, and search for the perfect TV. Hmm. There are an awful lot of terms that sound like a foreign language. Like plasma. Composite video. S-Video. Aspect ratio. And many acronyms that I don't know the meanings of. Like LCD. HDTV Non-CRT. RGB+H/V. How about T.I.V.C? This. Is. Very. Confusing.

"Miri, what kind of TV should I chose?" I scream.

"Busy saving California!"

I flip and flip and flip through pages. Finally, I find a TV

181

I like: 50" HDTV Plasma Display Wide-screen. It looks larger than our apartment. Possibly the size of Times Square.

I like this one the best because the image on the screen is a scene from *The Sound of Music*, and most of the others feature football. In the picture, Maria (aka Julie Andrews) is sitting on the green grass with her guitar, singing to the dressed-in-curtains von Trapp children. I love that part! This must be a good omen. And the blue of the Austrian mountains and the green of the grass are quite vivid; I bet this TV is top-of-the-line. "Doe, a deer, a female deer," I sing happily. "Ray, a drop of golden sun. Tee, a television, I found myself"—ha-ha—"far . . ."—hold the note, you can do it!—"a long, long way to run . . ." I run, giggling, into my sister's room. "Found it!" I say, shoving the catalog under her nose. "You like?"

"Well done. Now find the other ingredients."

No fun. "How do you solve a problem like my Miri-a?" I sing all the way back to the couch. Next! A half cup of broken mirror. That sounds sketchy. Am I supposed to break a mirror? Won't that give me lots of bad luck? "Miiiiiiiiiiiiiii-rrrrrriiiiiiiii?"

"I'm wooooooooooorking. Figure it out!"

What is luck, anyway? I bet my mom has a hand mirror somewhere. Ten minutes and a large mess later, I find a small one under the sink. Now, where best to break it?

Kitchen table? Nah, don't want to eat glass shards by mistake. Bathtub? Don't want to bathe in them either. Hmm. I'd better do it out in the hallway. (Though if anyone comes off the elevator as I'm in midshatter, they might have me arrested; is this vandalism?) I lay out the remaining catalog papers on the floor and place the mirror on top. I'm about to give it a good heeling when I realize I'm not wearing shoes. Brilliant. Back inside I go.

Oops. A key would be so helpful. Ring. Ring. *Ring! A drop of golden sound* . . .

Miri opens the door, scowling.

"Sorry. Just need a shoe. And a key. Wanna watch me break the mirror?"

She hands me a pink sneaker and grumbles, "Fine."

"Not that shoe. Give me one of Mom's." She hands me a high heel (another new shoe? Mom is unbelievable), and I slip it on. Very nice. I should wear these things more often. They're so glam. "Ready? Set . . . go!" I smash my foot down. Crunch. "Yay! See? I have everything under control; no need to give me that look." I bend over to pick up the large shards. Oh. "Can you pass me something to put these pieces in too?"

183

By three o'clock, I have collected all the necessary ingredients. "Operation Wide-screen TV for the Auction, known in TV lingo as OWSTVA, is primed and ready to be turned on. Tuned in. Booted. Energized. Channeled . . ."

"Can you stop with the bad TV puns, please?" Miri begs as she dumps the soil I harvested from the dead kitchen plant into the cauldron.

"But it's fun. Try it. Are you ready for prime time?"

She throws a peanut at my arm. "Why don't you help?"

I sit cross-legged next to her. Tigger rubs his face against my knee. "What should I do?"

"Crush the peanuts, shred the image, and mix 'em together with the mirror pieces. Then plant that concoction like a seed in the earth. Then I'll add water, say the spell, and wait for the TV to grow. And can you take Tigger out so he won't attack our TV tree?"

Wow. "That is the coolest spell I have ever heard. Will it grow *anything*?"

"I guess."

The possibilities are endless. Where to start? What are my favorite things? *Raindrops on roses?* I lift Tigger up and try to carry him out. He tries to scrape my chin with his need-to-be-cut claws. *Whiskers on kittens?* Those I can do without. "Can I have a new prom dress?"

"Can't you wear the dress you bought for Spring Fling?"

Duh. "It's not fancy enough."

184 "Why don't we raise money for the prom first and then worry about what to wear to it?"

I drop Tigger outside, slam the door shut before he can sneak back in, stick out my tongue at Miri, and start crushing peanuts. This is going to be so awesome, as long as we don't somehow screw it up, which I'm sure we won't. The spell seems pretty straightforward. What could go wrong? I'm about to give the page a solid rip in half when I freeze. If the spell creates whatever is in the image, I should check what's on the back! I am so clever that it kills me. I flip the image over to find a picture of a man's hand holding a remote. Good save, Rachel! Imagine if we grew someone's hand! And what if it attacked us? Strangled us? Tickled us? "I'm going to color this hand in with black marker, to avoid conjuring up severed body parts."

Miri giggles. "Nice catch."

Nice catch, indeed. What would she do without me? I find a permanent marker in the kitchen, and then as well as getting ink all over my fingers, I manage to cover up the hand. "Let's do it," I say. I rip up the image, drop the pieces into a plastic bowl, and add the shards of broken mirror. Then I crush the peanuts with a tablespoon and add them to the bowl. Using the same spoon I mixed the stuff with, I scoop up the mixture and dump it into the cauldron of earth.

"A mirror's reflection
For your own detection
Planted in the depths of the earth
Solidify, congeal to a birth."

Miri sprinkles a few drops of water on top and I feel the familiar rush of cold.

Yes! Wide-screen TV! When we do the multiplying spell, I'm so keeping one for us. "Hey, why don't you split the lump into two so we can have one for the living room?"

She considers the idea, then shakes her head. "What if that only makes half a TV? Or two twenty-five-inch ones instead of a fifty?" She carries the bowl to my room, places it carefully on the floor under my window, and opens the blinds. "It needs sunlight," she explains. "And I think we should let it grow here, because your room is bigger."

Yeah, sure. She's trying to avoid a repeat performance of what happened with the oranges. Her room still smells. "Never mind," I say. "One will do." For now. I poke the cauldron with my big toe. "How long does it take to grow?"

"Two moons. Forty-eight hours."

"Then on to the next spell!" I wiggle my fingers in the air. "Rain, rain, go away, come again some other day."

"Rachel, we're trying to create rain in California, not banish it. And we have to concentrate. This one's hard. It's a five-broomer."

Rolling up my sleeves, I follow her back to her room. I'm ready to rumble. "What do we need?"

Miri flips to her sticky note in A^2. "A glass of water, pepper, and a pot. As soon as the water starts to boil, we say the spell."

That's it? Puh-lease. "No problemo. That's all it takes to make it rain? We could do that one with our eyes closed."

"Except we have to do the spell in California. We'll have to build a bonfire."

"I'm bringing marshmallows!"

Miri frowns. "At least we won't be taking a toaster oven for you to burn down the entire state."

I hoist myself onto her back. "Where exactly are we going in California? Can we go to Rodeo Drive? Wait! Let's go to the Kodak Theatre."

"Where?"

"Where the Oscars are! Maybe we'll see a star!"

"Can you be quiet?"

Humph. I cling to Miri as she does her stuff, and the next thing I know, we're in—

The sky is blue. The air is hot. And I smack my elbow against a red minivan. Are we in a parking lot? "Where are we?"

"Disneyland," Miri says sheepishly. "It was the only place I could think of in California."

"We couldn't go to Rodeo Drive, but we could come here?"

"It has to be something I can picture!"

"But how are we going to light a fire in a parking lot?"

"We'll have to find an empty spot. I brought along a reflective shield we can use so no one can see us."

We walk around aimlessly until we find the most deserted area. Miri pulls a newspaper out of her bag, shreds it up, and lights it with a match. When the flame catches, she fills the pot with the glass of water and pepper, puts on an oven mitt, and holds the pot by the handle over the flames.

Her technique concerns me on many levels. "Let me hold it," I say, grabbing it from her and holding it far above the flames. "Put up the shield!"

She reaches into her bag, then pulls out and opens what appears to be an umbrella. An enchanted one, I'd guess. Four seconds pass. Miri stands on tiptoe to peer into the pot. "Is it boiling yet?"

I don't see any bubbles. "Nope."

Thirty seconds pass. "Now?"

"Nope."

Twenty seconds. "Now?" she asks, exasperated.

"Miri, if you keep asking, it won't boil."

"That makes no sense. It's going to boil regardless. And I have to say the spell at the sign of the first bubble."

"Get ready," I say, watching the water. "I think it's about to pop."

She jumps closer, picks up the book, and recites the spell:

"*Sweet expansive sky,*

187

Dress yourself in clouds that cry.
Let the heavens shower a tear,
Over yonder by and near."

Cold blows against my cheeks. Yes! "I felt it; it must have worked."

She peers into the blue sky. "But I don't see any clouds."

"It probably takes a few minutes."

"But most of the weather spells work immediately," she says. "We should have brought those marshmallows to pass the time."

"Whoops. But I have a better plan. Let's go on Space Mountain! By the time we're done, it'll be pouring."

"Well . . ." She hesitates. "Okay. Since we're here."

Wahoo! "Can you zap us to the front of the line?"

Miri shrugs. "I can try."

188

Two Space Mountains, three Mad Tea Parties, and one Big Thunder Mountain later, it still hasn't rained, so we decide to monitor the weather from home.

While I study for a bio test, Miri writes an English essay, taking breaks every few minutes to check AccuWeather. But so far—nothing. The sun is proudly beating over California, fully mocking us.

"I hope I didn't mess anything up," she says nervously. "It *was* a five-broomer. Maybe it sent the rain somewhere else?"

I open the blinds. It's a gorgeous day. "It's not raining here, either."

"I have to pee," Miri says, and disappears into the bathroom.

"I'm going to check on the wide-screen!" Unfortunately,

the cauldron of dirt and broken glass hasn't morphed into an electric appliance yet. "Nothing?" Miri asks when she joins me.

"Nope. Now I have to pee."

"Me too," Miri says.

"You just went!"

"I didn't get it all out." We size each other up and then race to the bathroom. Luckily, because I'm taller and therefore have longer legs, I make it there first.

I don't notice the hot steam until I'm sitting on the toilet. The shower sounds like it's on full blast. Did I leave it on? Is my mom inside? "Hello?" I squeak.

No answer.

I pee quickly, wipe, flush, and open the flowery shower curtain.

The water is on with no one in the stall. Weird. I must have left it on by accident. Ouch, it's hot.

189

I reach to turn it off and attempt to revolve the handles. And attempt.

Hmm. The water is off. But then . . . why is it on? "Did you do something to the shower?" I yell.

She pounds on the door. "Don't shower! You are so mean. I said I had to pee again so you take a shower? What do you want me to do, pee in the sink?"

A splash of hot water scalds my hand. Ouch. I unlock the door. "I'm not showering, you doofus. The water is stuck. Did you not notice how hot it was in here?" How can someone with so much power be so clueless?

"Are you sure?" She pushes me out of the way and proceeds to burn herself on the handle. "Owwww. The shower is busted."

No kidding. *Let the heavens shower a tear* . . . Oh, man. "I think the spell worked. It just took the word *shower* literally."

Miri's fingers go straight into her mouth. "Uh-oh. I knew it was a tricky one. I can't believe I screwed it up! What do we do? We're going to use up all the hot water in the building!"

"Call the super?" I suggest.

"What for? It's not like he can fix it."

It's getting seriously steamy in here. "Do you have any clothes you want de-wrinkled?"

"Very funny."

"Rain, rain, go away, come again some other day?"

She sits on the closed toilet lid and rests her head in her hands. "I don't think that will work."

"I thought you had to pee."

"It got scared away." She looks at me miserably. "Maybe we should just let the water run out. It isn't going to rain for-ever, right?"

"Can't you do a spell reversal?"

"Perhaps, but I told you, it's a five-broomer. Plus I don't have any of the materials. . . . I guess I can if I have to."

"Let's give it a few minutes. Eventually the sun comes out again." It feels like the sun is beaming in here right now, it's so hot. "I have to get out of this room; I'm sweating up a storm."

I close the door behind us. "What do we do now? More homework?"

"I guess."

We open our respective assignments and take our respective places (me on Miri's bed, Miri at her desk) and are about to dig in when Miri sprints back to the bathroom.

"Still running," she says, sitting back in her desk chair. "Or raining."

The downstairs buzzer goes off. Miri jumps up again. "Expecting anyone?"

"Nope."

We both approach the buzzer. "Hello?" she says.

"Hi! It's Lex! I'm here to pick up Carol."

Too bad Carol is MIA (Mom in Absentia). And it's not like Lex has time to waste. He's already, like, a hundred.

"What do we do?" Miri whispers.

"Why are you whispering? He can't hear you. Audible range lowers with age. And you're not pressing the buzzer. Call Mom. I'll buzz him up."

"Hi, Lex!" I say a few seconds later, opening the door.

He's holding a bouquet of daisies. "For you and Miri."

"Thank you!" As I gather the flowers from his arms (second bouquet in less than a month! New record!), I notice that he has nice hands. Long fingers, filed nails. Big palms. I would have expected them to be old and wrinkled, but they're not. Last year I bought my dad leather gloves for his birthday. When he put them on, he was swimming in them. They were at least two sizes too big on him, but on Lex? I bet they would have fit like a glove. Oh, yeah, they *are* gloves. Lex is taller than I remembered too. Although maybe his cowboy hat gives him an extra few inches.

"So how've you been, Rachel?" He gives me a warm smile. "How's school?"

"Great, thanks." My sister and I destroyed the gym, but now I'm dating the soc president, so all is good. "And you?"

"It's been a busy few weeks. Baseball tourism kicks up again in the spring, so I've been leading a whole lot of tours."

Miri returns from the phone call and crosses her arms in front of her chest. "She's not answering," she says, ignoring Lex.

He gives her the same warm smile and tips his hat. "You must be Miri."

She rolls her eyes. "Brilliant assumption."

Terrif. My mom's not answering, so I have to dump Lex for her. I've never dumped a guy myself, so how am I supposed to dump one for someone else? I rack my brains for the excuses I've heard in the movies. It's not you, it's me. Can we be friends? It's not a good time emotionally for me right now.

Not that my mom deserves my creative excuse-making. Forget her; I'll just be honest. "We don't know where my mother is," I explain. "I don't know what to tell you. She could be on her way home. You're welcome to come in and wait."

Lex's brow wrinkles in concern. "Did she have to go into the office this morning?"

Yeah, right. The office of love. "I think so," I say instead.

"I can hang out." He looks from Miri to me. "As long as you two don't mind."

"Not at all." My heart sinks in sympathy. He brings us flowers and my mom can't even bother to show up? "Can I get you something to drink?"

He removes his shoes, lines them up, hangs his hat on the coatrack, and follows me into the living room. "Water would be terrific."

That's something we have lots of. Lots and lots and lots of. Would he like it boiling? As I'm fetching a glass, I hear, "Is it all right if I use the bathroom?"

"Of course," I say over the running water in the sink. As soon as the words leave my lips, I realize my mistake. "Wait!" I scream. Too late.

The door is open and the steam is rushing out. "Is someone inside?" he asks, obviously confused.

I'm about to say "Miri" when she appears next to me.

We're putting in a spa? Trying ashtanga yoga? "Shower's broken."

He squints into the haze of steam. "Do you want me to take a look at it?"

That could be a recipe for disaster. On the other hand, "Why not?"

He steps inside, and his face is immediately dripping with sweat. I hope he's not too old for this type of activity. A heart attack would be very bad. I don't even know CPR. But I have always wanted to learn it. I've also always wanted to learn the Heimlich maneuver. I once saw a woman pop a chicken bone right out of a man's constricted throat. I bet Miri would be up for that since she's so into lifesaving these days. "Mir," I start, but then stop myself. Maybe this is not the time.

Miri is hitting me in the thigh with the back of her hand. "What if he realizes that the shower is cursed?" she mouths.

193

I wave her away and step into the bathroom after Lex. Come on. It's not like he's going to make that leap. Shower's broken, one of these girls must be a witch!

"Just watch him, please," Miri grumbles, and returns to her room.

"This is odd," he mumbles from somewhere in the steam. "I'm going to try taking apart the valve handle. If that doesn't work, I'll try the water source in the basement. Do you have a wrench?"

Blink, blink.

He laughs. "Where's your toolbox?"

That we have. Somewhere. I return a few minutes later and carry the toolbox into the sweatbox. "You know what you're doing?"

"Yup. Don't worry about me."

"Don't burn yourself." We don't want a lawsuit on our hands.

"The hot ran out. It's just cold water now, which makes it easier."

"Good." I'm sure everyone preparing for Saturday evening plans appreciates it.

"So what are you up to? Entertain me with stories while I fix this."

"We're having an auction to raise money for the prom. My boyfriend is the president of our student council . . ." I go on and on, and he actually seems interested, nodding and asking questions. After ten minutes his shirt is totally damp and what's left of his gray hair is all wet.

"This should do it," he says as he makes one quick turn of the screwdriver. And then, the water stops coming.

Oh. My. God. He's like a magician. Okay, not exactly, since his skills have successfully reversed magic, not provided more, but still. Wow. "Thank you so much," I say, quite amazed. "Miri! He did it!"

Miri comes into the foggy bathroom. "That's imposs—" She stops talking when she sees that the water is no longer running. "Oh. Thanks."

How did he do that? Maybe magic *was* involved. Maybe he's a witch too. Or a wizard. Warlock? Weirdo? Nah. If he were, he wouldn't have two massive sweat stains under his arms. How cute is that? Mortal, anyway. And nice. Even though Mom is MIA, he still messed himself up to help us.

Perhaps encouraging Mom to date other guys was not my best plan.

Lex glances at his watch. "It's been a real pleasure, girls, but it seems your mother has forgotten our plans, so I guess I'll take off. Please tell her I stopped by." He heads to the door, steps into his shoes, and plants his hat firmly on his head.

Awwwwwww. He's so nice! Much nicer than Adam or the fireman. They're cute, but they've never given us anything or acted remotely interested in us. Why did I butt into Mom's private business? And he's so handy. If I had only encouraged Mom to date Lex exclusively, by now they'd be practically engaged. And that hard-to-reach bedroom lightbulb would be long changed. And Mom wouldn't be running around like a chicken with five heads.

"Hope to see you soon," Miri says, her voice sounding sad. Apparently, even my I-want-Mom-to-be-miserable-and-alone-and-all-ours sister has been charmed by Lex.

He reaches for the door handle and gives us his warm smile. "Take care of yourselves, girls."

"Thanks," we say, choking back tears. Okay, not really, but almost.

The closing of the door echoes throughout the apartment. I sigh. "Mom just stood up the nicest man in the world."

Miri shakes her head in disgust. "I know! What are we going to do with her? Do you think she's having a midlife crisis?"

"Yes."

"She should just zap herself up a Corvette and get it over with."

When she finally calls us back at seven-thirty, I'm furious. "Where are you?" I can barely hear her, she's surrounded by so much noise.

"Everything all right, honey?" she yells.

"You missed your date!" I yell back.

"What? I can't hear you! I'm on my date!"

"No, you missed it! With Lex!"

"I can't hear you, hon. Reception is terrible. I'll try not to be home too late. I left money for takeout! Make sure you do your homework!"

This. Is. Absurd. Miri and I spend the rest of the night pacing. And complaining about our mother. And pacing some more. We take a break for *Saturday Night Live* but continue pacing during the commercials.

We fall asleep on the couch. When the clock says two a.m., I'm awakened by the clink of a key in the door. Then the lights zap on. Yes, zap. Miri is still unconscious, but I'm quickly on my feet, ready to attack.

"What is wrong with you?" I growl, hands on my hips. Sniff. Sniff, sniff. And Mom reeks of smoke. Like she was *bathing* in cigarettes. "You're smoking again."

Her face falls. "Bars," she mumbles. "People smoke in them."

Gasp. She just lied right to my face. There's no smoking in bars in the city! "Mother, you're smoking again. You're using magic like crazy. You're going on more dates than you can handle. You're home too late. You stood up Lex."

She grimaces.

"Are you having a midlife crisis?"

Her face cements into an unreadable expression. She slowly removes her shoes and leaves them in a mess on the floor. She walks past me and into the kitchen. "I forgot about Lex."

197

I follow her. "I know. It was rude."

She waves me away and pours a glass of water. "You didn't even want me going out with him!"

"I was wrong. I admit it. He's very nice and you've probably ruined your chances with him. I hope you're happy."

She shrugs. "There are lots of fish in the sea. But frankly, Rachel, I don't appreciate being told what to do by a fourteen-year-old."

"Well, someone has to tell you. You're acting crazy." I make a cuckoo motion with my finger. "Why do you have to be so extreme? You went from *no* magic, *no* dating, and *no* smoking to drowning in magic, dating, and smoking. Don't you know how to ease yourself in? First a pinky toe, then a foot, then a leg—"

She slams the glass onto the table, sending water flying everywhere. As if I haven't had enough waterworks for one night. "Are we not clear? I'm the mother. You're the daughter. I tell *you* what to do."

I feel like I've been kicked in the stomach. "Then act like my mother," I snap. I run into my room, slamming the door behind me. She'd better come apologize. She always comes to talk to me when I slam the door. Slamming the door = I need to talk.

Five minutes pass. What is she doing? I peek into the hallway. The nerve of her! She's taking a shower. I hope the water is still cold.

At Least My Middle Name Isn't Lucretia 13

My mom and I ignore each other on Sunday. Not that she's around to be ignored. She has a lunch date with Nick, pops home in the afternoon, takes a nap, and decides to make us a cheese soufflé for dinner (out of remorse, I bet) but then forgets it's in the oven while she showers and lets it burn to a crisp. She zaps up a new one for us, along with a salad and apple cider, and then goes out with Tony for dinner. I refuse to eat her guilt dish out of principle, and make macaroni and cheese instead. The microwave kind. I accidentally add too much milk and it ends up being macaro-mush.

Miri spends most of the day trying and failing to find a better rain spell. I spend most of the day on the phone with Tammy.

Her: "Bosh invited me to prom!"

Despite my sympathy for poor Aaron, I shriek with joy, "We can double!"

Tammy: "I can't go to prom with someone while I have a boyfriend! And anyway, there might not even be a prom."

"There will be," I say. "I'll worry about that. You worry about dumping poor Aaron already."

Meanwhile, I stare at the potted TV, which still looks like a bowl of dirt and nothing like a television. "Shouldn't it be growing?" I ask for the sixteenth time.

Miri pokes it with a pencil. "It takes time."

"But it hasn't done any developing." And I know. I've been lying on my carpet watching for the last eight hours.

"Give it till tomorrow."

"It had better work. I have no backup plan."

She opens the window to let in some fresh air. "You have to think positively! If you don't believe in it, it won't work. Like the tooth fairy."

"You sound like Mom."

"Well, she was right, wasn't she? As soon as I said that I didn't believe in the fairy, that I knew it was Mom, she stopped putting money under my pillow. And where did that leave me?"

"Five dollars poorer?"

"Exactly. So don't worry. Until tomorrow, anyway. Then you can freak out. Has my magic ever let you down?"

Uh, yeah. The phone rings, distracting me.

"Hi, dear!"

"Hi, Dad," I say, and stretch out on my bed. "How are you?"

"Long week. You know. Getting back to the office after so much glorious time off." He yawns in my ear.

"Tired?"

"A little."

We chitchat for a few seconds and then he passes the phone to Jennifer. "What's up?" I say.

"It's a madhouse around here," she says. "You wouldn't

believe what my daughter is doing. She refuses to sleep in her own bed. Absolutely refuses. How are we supposed to conceive if she won't leave us alone?"

Ew. I'm not sure why she thinks I'm the appropriate person to discuss this with. Gasp—does she think we're friends? Buddies? Does she think I'm someone who wants to hear about her marital relationship with my dad? That is so gross. I can't stand it. I close my eyes, trying to shut out the repulsive images—which makes it worse. "I don't know what to say." Except, please stop talking.

"I am so depressed! I don't have time to waste. I'm already thirty-six. And Priscilla is acting like a child."

"She's only five."

"Almost six. It's her birthday next weekend, remember? She's too old for this! I'm too old for this!"

"I'm sure she'll snap out of it."

A loud sigh. "I know. You're right, Rachel. You know exactly what I'm thinking."

What is going on here? Why am I her new best friend? She's my stepmom! She should be acting her role—mean and bossy. And my mother should be acting like a mother. Why can't everyone behave properly?

"It's just that I spent so much time worrying about the wedding that now I'm behind on all my other projects. Like finding a summer rental in the Hamptons. And my car has been giving me trouble—"

Beep!

Thank goodness, it's my call waiting. "One sec," I say, and click off. "Hello?"

"Hey, gorgeous," says Will's deep, manly voice.

201

Ah. See? No role confusion on his end. Me = girlfriend. "Hi! How was the rest of your weekend?"

"Cool. You? What did you do last night?" he asks.

"Oh, I wasn't feeling so hot," I say. I can't exactly tell him I stayed home doing nothing on a Saturday night, can I?

"Are you better?"

A concerned boyfriend. Cuteness. "A-okay. What's up?"

"Penthouse Fifty needed a deposit. So I gave them two thousand dollars."

Don't panic. "Where did you get the money? From ticket sales?"

"No, I had to use the advance ticket sales to give the caterer a deposit. I just took it out of my savings."

My stomach free-falls. "Are you kidding me? The money you've been saving for college?" Doesn't he know the first rule of business: never use your own money?

"No worries. You said you're bringing in a big-ticket item, right? Any hints as to what it is?"

He's basing his future on my promises? What if I can't deliver? "It's, um, a secret. Until tomorrow." I forgot about Jennifer! "Will you hold on? I'm just getting off the other line." Click. "Jennifer?"

"—you know? And my tan is already fading. And all the good rentals are gone."

I don't think she realized *I* was gone. "That's awful, Jennifer. Really. But I have to go. Will and I have to work on the prom auction. We have to raise fourteen thousand dollars."

"I love auctions! Are you selling any good stuff?"

Gulp. "Hopefully."

"Can I come?"

"Sure, parents are invited." Did I just use the word *parent* in association with her? "Can I tell you more about it next weekend?"

"Sure, sorry. Have fun with Will. Are you going to invite him to the Hamptons for a week?"

"I thought you didn't have a house yet."

"I'll find one. So will you?"

My finger is eagerly hovering over the Flash button. "No, he's going to camp for the summer."

"He is? What camp?"

"Wood Lake," I say.

"Really? Hey, that's an idea."

"Jennifer, I have to go. Emergency school stuff, re- member." I say good-bye and switch back. "So where were we?" Eight days till the auction, and eleven days until prom, that's where. And I still don't have a TV or a dress.

By Monday morning, the TV has yet to grow even an an- tenna. I walk to school with a heavy heart. At lunch, I buy a muffin in the caf and head straight to the lounge. Will and Kat are already there, sitting on the floor, cutting out pad- dles for the auction.

I plop down beside Will and he kisses me on the fore- head. "So are you going to tell me the big secret? What are you bringing in?" He looks at me with those puppy dog please-feed-me eyes.

"Wide-screen TVs," I blurt out. Oops. Think positively, don't speak positively. "I'm working on it," I add quickly.

The puppy dogs light up. "They go for like four grand! That would be so cool. Where are you getting them?"

"Family connections," I say as nonchalantly as possible. "I'm still working out some of the details."

Kat nods. "Awesome. When do you think you can bring them in?"

"I . . ." That's an excellent question. Even more excellent, how am I going to bring them in? Am I planning to carry them on my back? No worries. Miri must know a moving spell. Maybe she'll put them on her back and do the transport spell. Not.

Will smiles at me. "We should send out an e-mail with a list of the stuff that's being auctioned off, so students know to bring lots of green. Or their parents' credit cards."

"I'm thirsty," Kat says, putting down her scissors. "Anyone want a drink?"

"No, thanks," Will and I both say.

"See you in five." Kat removes her wallet from her backpack and closes the door behind her.

Will immediately wraps his arms around my waist. "Finally, we're alone."

My heartbeat speeds up like I just ran to class. He gives me one of those perfect kisses. Soft, sweet, warm. How lucky am I?

After a couple of minutes, I pull away. "We need to get

back to work," I say, smiling. "These flyers aren't going to make and hang themselves."

"Very true. But we need more paper. Can you check in Kat's binder? She said she brought orange cardboard."

"Sure." I skip over to the pink couch and take Kat's binder out of her backpack. "Here we go," I say, pulling out the paper. And that's when I see the neat blue ink writing on the inside wing. First her address and then:

Kat Kosravi

Kat Postansky-Kosravi

Mrs. Katherine Kosravi

Mrs. Will Kosravi

Mrs. Katherine Lucretia Postansky-Kosravi

I slam the binder shut. Without the proof staring me in the face, it's easier not to care that Kat likes Will. Is it possible that beneath the spell Will has feelings for Kat? "Will," I say, handing him the orange paper, "if we hadn't gotten together, who would you have asked to the prom?"

He lies on his stomach and pulls the cap off a black marker. "Probably Kat."

Oh, no. "Really? Did you two ever go out?"

The apples of his cheeks turn red. "Me and Kat? No. She's, like, my best female friend."

"And you never thought about asking her out?"

He shifts on the floor, starting to look uncomfortable. "I thought about it. But then you came along, and I realized that it was you I wanted to go with. And be with." He blows me a kiss. "Don't be jealous."

It's not jealousy that's creeping up my spine. It's guilt. I feel bad for her. Not only is her middle name *Lucretia*, but I stole her boyfriend. As soon as prom is over, I have to set him free.

I head straight to my room when I get home. Mom's out, of course. And there's still no TV.

Miri is already sitting in front of the cauldron, staring. "If it's not there by morning, we'll try something new."

"Uh-huh."

I spend the night tossing and turning, and turning and tossing. Every time I turn toward the bowl, I can't stop myself from opening my eyes and staring at its barrenness. I don't even remember falling asleep, but the next thing I know, the sunlight is spearing my eyelids. I open them slowly. Please let there be a TV. Pretty please?

Omigod. Right in front of my eyes is the largest TV ever. It stretches across my window, from my bed to my desk. I don't believe it. The spell worked! I am overwhelmed with awe. It's gorgeous. Amazing. A metallic fixture of true beauty. Long, rectangular, black, and sleek.

"Miri! Come look!" I scream. But a quick peek at the clock tells me that it's only six a.m. Oops.

A second later, she's at my door, dressed in shorts and a tank top—and covered in soot. "It grew?"

"Where were you?"

Miri yawns. "Back at the bushfires, trying to blow them out. But it didn't work."

She's really starting to worry me. "Do you even sleep anymore?"

She rolls her eyes. "I can't waste time sleeping, Rachel. I have too many important things to do." She approaches the TV and taps her fingers on the screen. "This is cool."

"Isn't it? Let's do the multiplying spell right away! Let's make five for the auction, then one for you and one for me!"

She raises an eyebrow. "Mom doesn't get one?"

Humph. "Not these days." I haven't spoken to Mom since our fight. "I can't wait to show the soc. Can we do the multiplying spell right after school?"

"We could. But I have to figure out how to control it. If we make a few hundred, like we did with the oranges, we could have a real space issue." She stands on tiptoe, as though measuring its length. "I'm not sure where even two are going to fit. We don't want the TVs to break."

"We can do it in the living room." Whatever. We'll figure it out. Cha-ching! Even if for some inexplicable reason the multiplying spell doesn't work, I have one TV to donate. A TV that's worth at least four thousand dollars! I rock! I want to test it out immediately. I find the plug and squeeze between the TV and my bed to locate the socket. "And now," I say in my radio-announcer voice, "the moment of truth." I insert the plug and squeeze back onto my bed, where my sister has already made herself comfortable.

"We probably have to turn it on," the know-it-all says.

I have to get up again? "Is there a remote?"

"I've got it," she says, and presses Power.

And nothing. "Press the Power button on the TV," I instruct.

She does, and still nothing. "Maybe it's warming up,"

207

she says. "I bet you it will work by the time we get home from school."

I yawn. "Maybe. I'm going back to bed."

"And I'm going to pop over to Antarctica. You wouldn't believe what's going on with the ozone layer down there."

I sigh. "You'd better put on something warm."

*

"Rachel, where are you getting the TVs? And when are they coming?" Will asks during lunch. We're all sitting around the soc lounge, finishing the paddles for the auction.

I ignore the first question. "They're almost ready. I just have one *tiny* problem left to fix." Which I'm sure we'll be able to do.

Bosh gives me a high five. "Awesome, dude. Let's make up a new poster advertising them!"

"Whoa, wait," I say, suddenly nervous. "You know, in case I can't get them to work."

Tammy raises an eyebrow.

"They'd better work," River says quickly. "We need some expensive stuff. Otherwise the auction is going to be a wash."

Oh, God. He's right. I push the concerns out of my head. It will turn on. It has to.

"Don't worry. The TVs are new, right?" Kat asks.

"Yeah." Brand-new.

"Then they'll be fine. And if not, my uncle has an electronics repair store on First Ave. He can fix anything."

I doubt that.

"Um, guys?" whispers a voice from the back of the room.

"What was that?" River asks.

"Guys?" the voice says again. Ah, it's Jeffrey. "I was thinking," he mumbles. "If it's all right with you, on the big day, I'd like to be the auctioneer."

Will scratches his head. "Do you know how?"

"Yes," he answers.

Will looks to me for advice. I shrug. "All right, then," he says. "If you know what you're doing."

I hope I know what *I'm* doing.

* * *

I run straight back to my room after school and holler, "Let's take our baby out for a spin!"

"Huh?" asks Miri from the other side of the wall.

"Let's watch some high-definition television!" I drop my jacket onto the floor and dive onto my bed. Miri joins me on the bed. I pick up the remote and press the Power button. Come on, come on.

209

Suddenly, there is a jolt of color, and the blankness on the screen morphs into a swirl of blues and greens.

Yay! Pretty! There are mountains and hills and grass . . . and Julie Andrews singing to the von Trapp children.

"*Far . . . a long, long way to run . . .*"

"It works! It works!" Miri cheers. "I rock!"

It does work, but it's Julie Andrews who's rocking. Uh-oh. "It's *The Sound of Music.*"

"I know!" Miri squeals. "I love that movie!"

"But that's the exact scene that was on the image I cut out from the catalog. Isn't that odd? What channel is this?"

"Three." Miri chomps her thumbnail. "Let me change it." She squints at the TV and presses the Channel Up button. A church comes into view.

Thank goodness. I exhale. "At least it's not—"

"How do you solve a problem like Maria?" the nuns on the TV screen are singing.

Right now, Maria's not my problem. "Change the channel again," I order.

"I am sixteen, going on seventeen . . ."

Beads of sweat drip down my forehead. "Again?"

Miri flips through ten more channels and all are showing various scenes from *The Sound of Music*. Eventually we return to channel three, back to "Do-Re-Me."

I flop my face onto the comforter and moan. Wait a sec. I lift myself up on my elbows. "Do we need cable?"

Miri nods. "Let me get a hanger." Miri is a cable superstar. Seriously. Before we got cable she hooked us up with many channels. Now that she's a witch, maybe we can hook up to every station in the universe.

When she returns, she unravels the hanger and adjusts it on the television. A few minutes later, she sits back on the bed. "Let's give it a try." She changes the channel.

The Sound of Music.

The Sound of Music.

The Sound of Music.

"Just turn it off; it's too freaky," I say. I feel like spiders are creeping up my back.

Miri presses the Power button. But it doesn't turn off.

"What's wrong?" I ask.

210

"I don't know. It isn't working," she says, panic seeping into her voice.

"That will bring us back to Do, oh, oh, oh," the TV tells us.

Before I'm the second person in this apartment to have a nervous breakdown, I squeeze behind the TV again and yank the plug out of the wall. I exhale with relief. That should do it.

"Doooooe!" Maria and the children sing.

I close my eyes in pain. "What do we do?"

Miri shakes her head in bewilderment. "I have *no* idea."

"Maybe you should do a reversal spell."

"I'm scared of that spell. Maybe it's like paint and needs time to dry."

That's true. It might just need to set. Like a cake. We check on it again after dinner, but it's still singing away. "Okay, let's let it sit for the night, then." I grab my pillow. "Sleepover at Miri's!"

211

She groans. "If you steal all my covers, you and the von Trapp children can sing duets all night, you hear me?"

"I don't think it's a duet if there are seven of them."

"You know what I mean."

The next morning, I open my door with trepidation. Unfortunately, I find the hills still very much alive. Guess we won't be doing the multiplying spell just yet.

* * *

"Dudes, we're running out of space here," Bosh says.

It's after school, and we're trying to make room for all the loot we've collected. There are CDs, books, dinner certificates, a cactus (no clue who brought that in), designer clothes, spa visits, airline miles, rounds of golf, gift cards, shoes, dishes, and iPods, all new. It's amazing how much stuff people are willing to give for a good cause. And it's amazing how hooked up JFK students are.

"I'm trying to figure out the best place to put all this stuff. Maybe in the cupboard," Bosh says, pointing to the massive storage area on the left side of the room. "Tammy, you want to check it out with me?"

River, Will, Kat, and I laugh. Tammy turns a deep shade of red. Bosh has been using every technique in the book to put the moves on Tammy, but she's not budging. She IMed me last night that she absolutely can't break up with Aaron. He's still home sick in bed. And when he does get better, she still won't dump him. She's been doing a lot of research and she read that stress suppresses the immune system, and if he gets too upset, he could have a relapse. And if he has a relapse, he won't be able to take his exams, and he'll have to retake the entire year.

TamTam: I can't be responsible for that!

PrincessRachel: You're never going to break up with him? Are you going to get married?

TamTam: I just have to wait till he finishes exams in June.

PrincessRachel: But UR gonna miss prom! It's next week.

TamTam: It's just the prom. Not the end of the world.

Tammy is way too nice. Anyway, it's driving Bosh crazy. Every time she turns him down, he seems to want her more. He decorates the outside of her locker with pictures from his last scuba trip. He brings her seashells. Tells her she's prettier than a tropical fish.

"Rachel," Will says, snapping me back to reality. "How

big are the TVs? Are they going to be delivered? Where do you think we should put them?"

In a fun house? "Um, I'm not sure yet. I'll let you know tomorrow."

Evade, evade, evade.

I almost pull out my hair on the way home from school. With the auction, stress, and my recent frequent sightings of Relissa (that's what the kids are calling Raf and Melissa these days), in addition to my mother, I'm surprised I'm not bald yet.

Oh yes, my mom and I are *still* not talking to each other. It's been four days! We've never been mad at each other for this long. She hasn't even commented on the singing TV. And I know she's heard it. How could she not have?

At home, I find the TV still singing, and with a sinking feeling, I head to Miri's room, which is a mess. There are papers all over the floor, notes and lists are taped to her walls, and Tigger is lounging in her still-unmade bed. She's sitting in the center of the disaster, dumping the contents of her backpack onto the mess.

"What happened here?" I ask.

"I'm just figuring something out."

"What are we going to do? Do we get rid of the TV? Can you find a new spell that will work? Am I supposed to sleep in your room forever because that movie will always be playing—" The phone rings, and I grab it. "Hello?"

"Is Miri there, please?" squeaks a tiny voice.

Miri has a new friend! Finally! "Sure. Who's speaking, please?"

"It's Ariella from school."

213

"Hold on one second." I smile and pass Miri the phone. "Ariella?" I say.

Miri shakes her head violently. "Tell her I'm busy," she mouths.

"Why?" I mouth back.

She shoves the receiver away.

"Can I take a message?" I ask, perplexed.

"Yeah," Ariella says. "I wanted to know if Miri wanted to come over this weekend. I'm having a sleepover."

"I'll let her know. Does she have your number?"

"Well, I've given it to her before, but she never calls me back."

As she recites her number, I glare at my sister. "Why won't you call her back?" I ask after hanging up.

"I don't have time for sleepovers," Miri says. "You know that. I can barely keep up with my homework and saving-the-world stuff. I haven't even been to Tae Kwon Do in weeks."

I wondered what happened to Tae Kwon Do. "You're being crazy. And why are you wearing one white sock and one black sock?"

She eyes her mismatched feet. "Oops. I told you, I have a lot going on." Now back to my questions. "No, you cannot sleep in my room again. You sleep with your mouth open and your breath stinks. And I haven't found a new TV spell. I'm working on it, but I also have to figure out how to make it rain, and I need to get back to Antarctica to work on the ozone problem. And my head hurts."

"Tell me about it." I sit next to her and hear paper crumpling.

"Careful!" she says, annoyed.

"Sorry." I pull the paper out from under me and am about to hand it to her when I see the red writing in the top right-hand corner: *D-*. What is this?

1. 8x - 2 = 14

And underneath Miri wrote: $x = 1.5$

Which, of course, is wrong. It's 2, Miri. The answer is 2! I don't believe it. "You failed a math test?"

She grabs the paper from my hand. "I did not. *D-minus* isn't failing."

"Miri, what happened? Didn't you study?"

"I didn't have time, okay? What's more important, a math test or the ozone layer?" She opens her mouth to say something else but yawns instead.

I start rummaging through her papers. "Are you having problems in all your classes?"

"Stop it. I'm fine." She tries to lie across her papers so I can't get to them.

I grab what looks like a book report. "C-plus? Miri, you've got to be kidding me." I find a French test. An F. "Oh, Miri, come on. You have got to promise me you'll start paying attention in school."

She waves her hands above her head. "I'm trying. But I have a lot to do!"

"Miri, an educated witch will solve more global problems than a middle school dropout witch."

"I'm not going to fail, all right? I'm doing my best. But I'm tired! So can you stop wasting my time? You're in my way and I have lots to do."

She has lost it.

We hear my mother's key in the front door. So nice of her to come home.

"Girls?" she calls. "Can you come to the kitchen, please? I'd like to talk to you."

Terrific. Now what? Miri follows me silently to the kitchen, where we find our mother already sitting at the table.

"Girls," she begins, "I know that seeing me move on with my life is scary for you. Watching a parent date can be difficult for kids of any age."

Just what I need on top of all my troubles: the Divorced Parent's I Have a Life Too Talk. Well, at least she's talking to me again.

Click, click. Click, click. My mother is tapping her fingernails on the table. My mother is tapping her long red fingernails on the table. When did my mother get long red fingernails?

I grab her hand to take a good look. "What *are* these?"

"My nails," she says, coloring.

"No, you bite your nails. Like Miri." I hold up my sister's left hand. "It's disgusting. But it's you. So where are *your* nails?"

She pulls her hand away. "I fixed them, all right?"

"You went to a salon and got acrylics, or you poofed up a new set of hands?"

"Rachel, what does it matter?"

Doesn't she get it? "It matters to me. You're turning into a crazy woman."

"I am not," she says, and then, right before my eyes, she zaps up a cigarette and an ashtray. "I understand that my dating scares you. But I need you two to grow with me. I'm still your mother." She taps her claw against her forehead. "There was something else I was supposed to talk to you about. But I can't remember what. I have too much on my mind these days. It was something to do with your father—"

"At least he acts like a parent," I mumble, squeezing Miri's hand. "More than you, anyway. Do you know that Miri is failing school?"

Miri takes back her arm and scowls at me.

My mom leans over to Miri while magically lighting her cigarette. "Honey, I guess that's your way of getting back at me for my dating—"

"It has nothing to do with your dating!" I say. "Miri has also gone crazy. I'm living with two loons!" And with that, I storm out of the kitchen and into my room. I don't leave until I hear the front door slam two hours later. Guess my mother has another date. Miri's door is closed, so I make myself a grilled cheese (I'm all egg-rolled out), do my math homework, and get into bed.

What am I going to do? My mother and sister are going crazy, and there's no way we're going to make enough money at the auction to save the prom. If we don't make enough, my boyfriend's reputation and savings account are officially ruined. And—sob—if there *is* a prom, I don't even have a dress.

I blink back tears and try to fall asleep.

A difficult feat when my lullaby is a thunderous rendition of *The Sound of Music*'s "The Lonely Goatherd."

217

14

Aaron is back. Now that he's healthy, and around, Tammy can no longer spend her entire day with Bosh.

"Just dump him!" I beg her during bio.

"I can't!" she says miserably. "He's very fragile. Did you see him? He's so pale and skinny."

She's right; I spotted him before homeroom and he looked pretty waifish. "But prom is in one week! And you don't even like him anymore!"

"I know, I know, but I can't do it. It's just prom. Bosh understands."

Again with the *just prom*? What an oxymoron.

When I get home from school, I find Miri right back in the center of her disaster, dressed in a tank top and earmuffs. She must have done a Cali-Antarctica combo. I decide to forget about our fight. "How was your day?"

No answer. Apparently, she's decided not to forget.

"Hel-lo? What are you doing?"

"I'm not talking to you. You called me a loon."

Because you've been acting like one? "I'm sorry. But I want you to do your homework. And study for your tests."

"What, now you're my mother?"

"Well, someone's got to be." I sit down next to her. "Do you have any tests coming up that I should know about?"

"No."

I tickle under her arms. "I don't believe you."

"Get off. Stop it," she says, laughing. "Fine, I have a math test tomorrow. Happy?"

"Yes. Did you study?"

"I will, as soon as I finish doing this global—"

"Enough saving the world," I say sharply. "For tonight, anyway. Right after dinner, we're working on equations and inequalities."

She sighs. "We're on our own for dinner again. Mom has another date. She zapped us up a pizza, but it looks a little rubbery."

"Surprise, surprise."

She leans back, smiling. "But I'll let you help me. You owe me anyway."

"What for?"

"Do you hear anything?"

I listen intently. "No. Should I?"

"Yes. The sound of silence. I did the five-broomer reversal spell to get rid of your TV. So it's gone."

I throw my arms around her neck. "Awesome! You figured it out! Thank you! I only slept for five minutes last night."

"No kidding. I heard every toss, turn, and sigh," Miri says. "Rachel, the spell-reversal charm was so cool. I had to buy a clear crystal and bury it in a tub of salt for an hour. Then I put it on a silver chain and wore it around my neck while I circled the TV backward. And finally, the TV disappeared." She snaps her fingers. "Just like that."

"Thank you, thank you, thank you!" But panic creeps back in. "What am I going to bring for the auction? I have nothing. Nada. Zilch. Zip."

Maybe we could try one of the football TVs. At least that wouldn't be a musical. Although I'd have to listen to annoying sportscasters all night.

"Don't worry, I'll find a new spell so you can make a TV. I just need some time."

"We don't have time! We're going to Dad's tomorrow and the auction is on Monday! We need to get cracking."

"I don't really need to study for math anyway," she says, looking relieved.

I remember her D-. "I think you do. Math tonight, the spell tomorrow." Sigh. What's another day? It's not like we're cutting it close or anything.

*

"I found a transformer spell," Miri whispers on the train to Long Island. "You basically change something into something else of the same family."

"Huh?"

"Like a radio into a big TV."

I heave a sigh of relief. "Sounds perfect."

"So what do you want to zap? A TV again?"

"I guess. And then, if it works, we'll use the multiplying spell to make a whole bunch. We need to raise fourteen thousand dollars, remember?"

When we get off the train, we can't find my dad's car.

"Where is he?" I wonder aloud. And that's when I spot Jennifer in the driver's seat of a brand-new Mercedes-Benz convertible. It's slinky. It's silver. And Jennifer is honking like a deranged woman, smiling and waving. Guess she's feeling better. Funny how a brand-spanking-new car can do that. "Hi, girls," she sings. "A present from your dad. You like?"

I like.

"Shotgun!" Miri screams. She climbs into the front, and I slide into the small backseat. It smells yummy, like a hundred new leather purses. The seats feel soft, like the skin on the inside of my arm.

Jennifer reverses and pulls onto the road. And even though the wind has a field day on my hair, blowing it every which way, making me look like a singer in an eighties cover band, I don't care.

Because I have a new plan. Who needs a TV? We're going to zap up a car.

221

"*Happy birthday to you, happy birthday to you! Happy birthday, dear Priscilla! Happy birthday to you!*"

Prissy takes a big breath and blows out all seven candles (one for good luck) perched on her chocolate cake. "Do you want to know what I wished for? I wished not to have any more sisters or any brothers. Do you think it'll come true?"

Jennifer and my dad squirm in their dining room table seats. "We hope not," Dad says.

All I want is for this dinner to be over already. Miri and I have *lots* to do tonight.

Jennifer smiles across the table. "Do you want your birthday present now?"

Prissy claps excitedly. "Yes! What did I get? A Princess Barbie castle? Is that what you got me? Please, please, please, please. Where is it?"

"Here it is!" Jennifer says, and hands Prissy a fancy envelope with a pink bow in the corner.

What on earth is that? A restraining order?

Prissy shakes it and then rips it open. She pulls out a photograph. "Huh?" she says, staring at it. "What is it?"

The photo is of some kids canoeing. Across the sky in bubble letters, it says *Wood Lake*.

Excuse me?

"For your birthday, we signed you up for two weeks at sleepaway camp! It's a very special place for girls and boys. You're going to get to sleep in a bunk and play all day!"

Prissy looks confused.

"What about visiting Daddy?"

Jennifer smiles. "You'll get to spend a few weeks with him in L.A. this summer. But first, camp!"

"Are you going to be there too?"

Jennifer shakes her head. "I won't, but your sisters will! We signed Miri and Rachel up too! And they're going for the whole summer!"

"What?" Camp? Hello? *Raf and Will's camp?*

My father walks over and kisses me and Miri on our heads. "I remember how much you two always wanted to go to sleepaway, so I figured this would be the perfect birthday gift for all of you."

"But my b-birthday isn't until December," Miri stutters.

"And mine's not until August," I protest.

"It's an early present. Surprise!" Someone wants Prissy out of the house. Badly.

"But I never wanted to go to camp. Club Med! That's where I wanted to go." On the other hand . . . moonlit sailboat trips and campfires with Raf? I mean *Will*. Moonlit sailboat trips and campfires with *Will*. My boyfriend. Raf . . . and Will?

My dad looks momentarily confused. "Oh. Well, you should have told me that before we paid in full. And wasn't it you who suggested the idea to Jennifer? Anyway, I promise, you'll love it there! Even your mom thought this was a good idea."

What? I bet that's what she wanted to talk to us about but was too busy to remember. My back stiffens. I guess she wants us out of the house too.

Dad lifts his wineglass. "You three are going to have the best summer ever!" He takes a big gulp and starts cutting the cake. "Small piece or big piece?" he asks me.

I can't believe my mother would okay this without even mentioning it to us. But you know what? I don't even have time to properly worry about this. My plate is that full. Although it could use a piece of cake. "Big, please."

223

✳

"Do you have everything?" I whisper.

"I hope so," Miri says. "We're so going to get caught," she adds.

"No, we're not! Think positively."

If anyone on my dad's street opens their blinds, we will

definitely be spotted. Somehow I think two girls flying on a tricycle might attract attention, even though it's three a.m. on Sunday.

"Ready?" Miri asks.

"Yup." Before I know it, we're airborne.

"I can't believe they're forcing us to go to Wood Lake," Miri says as we pass over a neighbor's roof. "How am I supposed to save the world if I'm at camp?"

Tell me about it. "I don't understand where we're supposed to go to the bathroom. Are they outside the tents? Are we supposed to pee in the bushes?" Grossness overwhelms me, as does guiltiness. I was planning on stopping Will's love spell after prom, but now I'll have no choice but to extend it through the summer, will I? How much would it suck to be stuck at camp with two ex-boyfriends? And anyway, dating Will has been fun. And it's not like Raf wants to get back together with me anytime soon.

"What I can't believe is that Dad asked Mom, and she allowed it," Miri says.

"She probably just wants us out of the way so she can date twenty-four seven."

"No kidding. Okay, no more talking; I need to concentrate."

Our new plan is slightly adventurous, if I do say so myself. We've decided to zap up a new Mercedes with the transformer spell. This way we won't need to worry about controlling the multiplying spell. So that's why we're on my tricycle (which I handed down to Miri, which she handed down to Prissy), which we've discovered flies just as well as a broom. That is a good thing, because we couldn't find a single broom in the house—Jennifer is far too glam—so instead we would have had to use her high-tech vacuum cleaner, which weighs at least a hundred pounds.

We're flying all the way to JFK. The school, not the airport, although we will pass the airport. I hope they don't pick us up on their radar. We don't want to get arrested for breaking the no-fly zone. We tried to use the transport spell, obviously, but for some reason it refused to move the tricycle with us (perhaps it has a weight maximum?), which is an integral part of our plan, so we had to use the more primal technique of flying. It's not the most comfortable for me, I'll admit, since I'm squashed in front of Miri between the handlebars and the seat. *E.T.* made it look much more fun. Anyway, we're wearing all black in an attempt at camouflage. (Not that the canary yellow bike will give us away or anything.) Once we get to JFK, we're using an open-door spell to get inside. The spell totally works. We tested it before dinner on the garage. It's made of oil and—wait for it—sesame seeds. The spell actually includes the phrase *open sesame*. I'm not kidding.

After dinner, we tested the transformer spell. How? We made me a prom dress. A beautiful, long, emerald green silk gown. We borrowed/stole one of Prissy's Barbie outfits and transformed it into a perfect prom dress. And the best part of the spell is that it works immediately: the cloth stretched itself into a size four and grew taffeta right before our eyes. The dress fit me perfectly. If I were ever in another fashion show (which no one would ever let me do), I would want to wear this.

This plan might actually work. The lights of the

225

Queensboro Bridge are twinkling below us; the full moon is glowing overhead. The wind in my face is warm, the helmet itch is minimal (Miri packs these babies wherever we go), I have the best prom dress ever. . . . I think I might be happy. I know I complain a lot, but the truth is, I'm one of the luckiest girls in the world. I live in an amazing city, I have two (plus one) parents who love me, and I have a younger sister who not only adores me but is also a witch. I do well in school, and I have a boyfriend and a fantastic best friend. So I have to spend the summer as a mosquito snack. I'll deal. At least Miri will be with me.

Suddenly, the tricycle swoops a few feet, and my stomach shoots into my throat. But then we stabilize.

Did I mention I'm happy I have my health?

As we fly high over the city and above the buildings, I peer down at the miniature taxis and people, who look like game pieces on a Monopoly board. And then, before I know it, the ride is over and we're landing on the home plate of the JFK baseball field. (It's a miniature field; we're in Manhattan, after all.) No matter how much fun flying is, it's always nice to feel the grass under my shoes. By the time I take off my helmet and shake out my hair, Miri is already at the door working her magic.

I roll the tricycle and meet her at the gym entranceway, just in time to watch her toss the sesame seeds at the door handle and say,

"Slack to slick,
Talk to tick,
Believe and see,
Open sesame!"

The door springs open. "Good work!" I say, and happily skip into the building, the tricycle trailing behind. It's very dark in the hallway. We don't want to turn on any lights for fear of attracting attention. Why did I take off my helmet? I could really use the night vision.

"Where should we put it?" Miri wonders out loud.

"In the auditorium. Follow me." As I creep through the empty hallway, every sound makes me jump. Being in the school alone at night is super creepy.

I open the doors to the auditorium and see the rows and rows of seats. Now, where do we put the car? "Let's do the transformation on the stage," I say, and climb up the steps and pull back the curtain. It'll be the grand finale! This is really the best plan I've ever had. From the Mercedes Web site, we learned that Jennifer's car cost sixty thousand dollars. So even if the highest bidder offers only a quarter of the money, fifteen thousand, I save the prom almost single-handedly (with the help of Miri and her magic, of course).

Miri climbs onto the stage and removes the ingredients from her satchel: sunflower seeds, raisins, flour, and lemon juice. She tosses them into the purple plastic container we borrowed/stole from the house. Once the ingredients are mixed, she says, "Ready? I have to pour it on the tricycle."

"Go for it!" How cool is this going to be? She's going to whip up a Mercedes. And some lucky person is going to buy it and drive the car right out of the— "Wait!"

She stops in midpour. "What?"

"How will someone drive the car outside?" I point to the four walls. "There's no garage door."

227

She places the container back on the creaking stage floor. "Oops. I guess we have to do it outside."

"We'd better wish up a car alarm, or the Mercedes will be gone by Monday."

A few minutes later we've dragged the tricycle and the ingredients back through the hallway and outside and set up the bike in the outfield next to the school gate. Miri then begins to pour, chanting:

"Transform this being,
With the cycle of life,
To become its destiny.
Like a caterpillar into a butterfly
("This is the part I added," she says, smiling.)
A Mercedes from this tricycle."

Her lips purse, the air gets cold, and I take a giant step backward so I won't get run over. Good-bye, sweet bike! You served me, Miri, and Prissy well. We had a fantastic time together in Central Park. But now you're being turned into your destiny. Or at least something that could get a higher price at the auction.

Nothing happens for the first few seconds, but then my front tire expands, like gum being blown into a bubble. When it's fattened to car-tire size, it suddenly splits in two and separates. With an earth-shattering squeak, the metal frame of the bike starts expanding into the body of a car. Cool! The small triangular seat transforms into five seats of plush black leather, and the handles grow into a steering wheel. As the interior completes itself, the car's exterior grows upward in liquid form and then hardens into finished, shiny steel.

Thirty seconds later, a complete canary yellow Mercedes roadster convertible is assembled in front of us. "It worked! It worked, it worked, it worked!" I can't stop myself from jumping up and down.

Miri jumps up and down with me, equally amazed. Wow. A prom dress is one thing, but *this* is a car. My baby sister just built the world's coolest car from practically birdseed. The hood glistens in the moonlight, and I give the side mirror a pat.

"Let's make sure it works before we get too excited," Miri says with caution. "I don't want this to be another fiasco."

She's right. We've had a lot of fiascos lately. I'm barely able to contain my excitement. I hop toward the front seat. "I'm driving!" I've always wanted to say that. "But you can have shotgun," I add.

I jump over the side window, like they did in the fifties. Ouch. They must have made the cars shorter in the fifties. Yes! The keys are lying on the seat. Magic is so clever.

"Where are we going?" Miri asks, opening the passenger door. "You know you don't know how to drive, right?"

I fasten my seat belt. "Back to Long Island?"

She starts biting her fingers.

"I'm kidding! I thought we would just spin around the field. How hard can it be? Millions of morons do it." Now if I can only figure out how to start the engine.

"Put the key in the ignition," Miri advises.

Obviously. I lean toward the ignition and insert the key. Done. Still not on. "Do you think it's broken?"

She laughs. "You have to turn it."

Right. I turn the key and the car roars to life. Fun! Now,

229

let's see. Hit the gas? How do I know which is the gas? I press down my right foot. The engine revs but nothing happens. "It must be broken," I say, deflated.

"I think *you're* the moron," Miri says, still laughing. "You have to take the car out of park. Put your foot on the other pedal." I do as I'm told. "Now move your foot back to the first pedal. Gently. I said, gently!"

We tear a few feet forward before I slam on the brakes. Yikes. "I declare the car working!" We check the reverse, the air-conditioning, the heating, the windshield wipers, the convertible top, the power seats and windows, and of course the CD player. Céline Dion's voice blares from the speakers.

"It's perfect!" Miri says. "And it smells so new and leathery. Just like Jennifer's car. Too bad she already bought hers, or we could have made her one for free."

"Oh, how you've grown, little tricycle," I say, like a proud parent.

We get out of the car, taking the keys with us. (I'll leave them in the student council lounge on Monday morning.)

"Perfect," Miri says. "Let's get back to Long Island."

I climb on her back, and away we go.

*

"It's gone! It's gone! We have to call the police!"

That's what wakes me up the next morning.

Miri and I both jump out of bed and run to the two-car garage, which is where my dad, Jennifer, and Prissy are standing.

My father's car is still there. But in the spot where Jennifer's car used to be is my old tricycle. At least, I think it's my old tricycle. It looks exactly the same except it's . . . silver?

Tears are streaming down Jennifer's cheeks, and her hands are flailing above her head hysterically. "Someone stole my car! Right out of"—she lets out a loud wail— "my garage!"

My eyes lock with Miri's. This is not looking good. If my bike is here and Jennifer's car is gone, does that mean that on the school baseball field is Jennifer's car?

"Did anyone hear anything last night?" my dad asks, scratching the bald spot on his head.

"No," Miri and I say simultaneously.

Jennifer sobs, shaking her head.

"I did!" Prissy chirps. "It was after I climbed into your bed, and you were both sleeping. There was a noise, and I tried to wake you up, but, Mommy, you told me I was being a big baby and I should go to sleep. When am I going to camp?"

"I'm calling the police," my dad says.

"At least I hadn't put a car seat in yet," Jennifer says.

"Was anything else in the car?" Dad asks.

"Just my Céline Dion CD," she sobs. "I love that CD."

It's official. We stole our stepmother's car. And to add insult to injury, the spell reversed the colors.

Miri and I retreat back into our room as our father files a complaint.

"I knew it looked like her car," Miri says.

231

"How did that happen?" I murmur. "We have to transport ourselves back to school right away and switch it. Now."

"We can't disappear in the middle of the day," Miri says. "Don't you think Dad will wonder where we are?"

"So we'll tell him we have to go home. *Now.* I'll pack up. You tell Dad that you forgot about an assignment due tomorrow and you have to get back to the city. And that I've offered to go home with you. Go."

*

Six hours later, we've taken the train back to the city (Dad insisted on making sure we were on), stopped at the apartment for the spell reversal, snuck back onto the school baseball field, and reversed the spell. By the time the police arrived at my dad's, the car was back in their garage, causing, I'm sure, much confusion.

The thing is, it's Jennifer's car—they could tell by the serial numbers—but it's still canary yellow.

"I kind of like it this way," Jennifer said.

I didn't dare ask about the tricycle.

At the moment I'm pacing up and down my room. I failed. All I had to do to save the prom was come up with something to auction off, and I have nothing. And now we won't make enough money on Monday and Will is going to lose his deposits and there won't be a prom and it's all my fault.

But that's not what's bothering me the most. What's scratching at my brain is how Jennifer's car ended up at JFK. Isn't magic creating something from scratch? What about all the other stuff we zapped up? Like the oranges?

I pace right into Miri's disaster of a room. "Have we been stealing?" I ask.

She continues writing without looking up. "I screwed up a spell. Get over it."

"Nothing comes from nothing, you know? Remember when you zapped the cows to safety? And they ended up in the gym? If everything has to go somewhere, it's only logical that it has to come from somewhere."

She adamantly shakes her head. "You're wrong. Can you stop wasting my time, please? I have real people to help. Starving people." And with that, she stands up, pushes me out of her room, and slams the door in my face.

I turn on my computer. I type *orange shortage* into the search engine. Two hundred and thirty thousand hits.

I click on the most recent. Maybe no one would notice a few oranges missing.

"Tristate Grocery Stores Missing Fruit." Oh, no. It's dated Saturday, April 24. The same day we zapped up the oranges. How weird. And reportedly, all the crates of oranges in the tristate area inexplicably went missing. Did we cause the shortage? I feel sick to my stomach.

Funny that the oranges went missing from the stores and not a grove. Maybe because Miri's an urban witch?

What about the clothes we gave away?

I type in *clothing disappearance* and am horrified to read that after a hundred shirts disappeared from Bloomingdale's Soho on Saturday, May 1, a staff member was fired, even though she claimed she hadn't taken them.

Is magic just stealing from someone else?

If I went to Circuit City, would a salesperson tell me that

a fifty-inch wide-screen TV had disappeared one day and then reappeared shortly after?

Instead of saving the day, are we taking from the rich to give to the poor? Are we not Batman and Robin, but Robin Hood and a merry man?

Going Once, Going Twice, Going
Fourteen Thousand Times 15

I am hiding in the student council closet.

The first bell just rang and there's no way I can be seen in the hallway, because then everyone will ask me where my TV is and I will have to admit failure. Admit that there is no TV. No car, no *anything*. I have nothing to auction off. Will is going to dump me, spell or no spell. We're going to raise only a measly few hundred dollars, and Will is going to lose his deposit and be known as the worst JFK soc president ever. And I'll be known as the worst girlfriend ever. No wonder I've never had a boyfriend before. I am a hazard to men.

He will probably be so upset that he'll need to spend some time rethinking his life, and he'll put off going to college for an entire semester. And in that time he'll get some random job. Like as a limo driver. Every day he'll pass the Columbia campus and feel a heaviness in his heart, and then one day he'll pick up some crazy client who will yell at him for no reason, and he'll get distracted and veer into a pole and then spin the other way, drive straight off the Brooklyn Bridge, and plunge to his death.

Sob. I've killed my boyfriend.

I came in early today with the hope of being inspired by the donations. Unfortunately, the donations are thousands short of true inspiration. If only we could auction off broom rides. Although, after what I discovered on Sunday, I'm not sure I ever want to use magic again.

I stiffen at the sound of the door opening. Clomp, clomp, clomp. I'm about to be found out. Discovered. The person is opening the closet. He/she must smell my desperation. The light spears my eyes and I blink twice.

"What are you doing here?" asks Kat. "What's wrong?"

Terrific. She'll expose me to Will as a complete fraud and he'll dump me. I know she's always acted nice, but surely she'll use my failure to her advantage. Before I can stop myself, I burst into tears. "I don't have the TV!" I snivel. "I have nothing to sell. The auction is going to be a big flop and it's all my fault."

Kat's creamy vanilla forehead wrinkles in concern. "It's *not* your fault. You didn't put the cows in the gym."

I hiccup. Little does she know. "But I promised Will I would have something to auction off."

She climbs into the cupboard beside me. "Let's brainstorm. What do you have that's sellable?"

Doesn't she listen? "Nothing, that's the problem."

She pulls her purple pen out from behind her ear and taps it against the closet. "Aren't you a math genius? Exams are coming up. Why don't you sell blocks of tutorial time?"

Well.

Why, that's a good idea. I could tutor. I realize something else: there are lots of smarties at JFK. I'm not the *only* one. What about help in essay writing? Biology? My heart races with excitement. "We can ask all the smart people to auction off tutoring!"

"There you go," Kat says, smiling. "Problem solved."

My mind is whirling. "And not only tutoring. There are a million things we can auction off. Like . . . a date with the hottest senior?"

Kat's pen is tapping in overtime. "Locker cleaning? Slave for a day? Tennis lessons?"

I reach over and give her a big hug. "You're a genius!"

She backs her way out of the closet. "I'm going to beg Konch to let us take the morning to prepare. You start making a list of all the services." She tosses me her pen. "Let's hope this works."

I'm already scribbling as the final bell rings.

237

"I can't believe she said no," Tammy says, shaking her head. "We're trying to save *her* prom!"

"She's horrible. What did you expect?" I ask.

It's freshman lunch, and Tammy and I are washing our hands in the girls' bathroom before returning to the lounge. London has refused to auction off dance lessons. And it's not because she can't—her cast came off at the beginning of last week—it's because she just doesn't feel like it. (Who knows? Maybe she doesn't have a date!) Not that it matters; we've lined up fifty students who are willing to volunteer their services.

We're so busy complaining about London that we barely even notice Jewel, Melissa, and Doree spilling into the bathroom.

You know what? I'm no longer afraid of them. In fact . . . "Guys," I say bravely, "I have a favor to ask you."

The three of them freeze in shock. "What?" Melissa snarls, crossing her arms.

"I was wondering if you three, and Stephy, would be willing to be part of the senior auction today and sell a dance lesson. Since you four were so good in the show. What do you say? We would really appreciate it."

Tammy, Doree, Jewel, and Melissa are all looking at me as though I should be institutionalized.

Melissa shakes her head. "Have you not noticed that Stephy hasn't been here for, like, a month?"

Oh. Not really. I lean against the sink. "What's wrong with her?"

"Duh," Doree says. "She has mono."

Tammy snaps to attention. "She does?"

Melissa gives her evil grin. "Yup. She got it from your boyfriend. They had a little make-out session over spring break."

"What?" Tammy and I both scream.

"Sorry to be the one to break it to you." She smirks. "But your boyfriend's a cheater."

At first Tammy doesn't speak. Her lips form a shocked O.

"You're not going to start crying, are you?" Melissa says, thoroughly enjoying this.

Tammy's O slowly turns into a huge smile. "Fantastic! He's so history!"

I laugh. Melissa, Jewel, and Doree give each other a what-weirdos! look.

"So how about the three of you, then?" I ask. Might as well.

Melissa tosses her long red hair behind her back. "As if."

Oh well. Didn't hurt to ask. I shrug and am about to head out the door when I hear: "I'll do it."

I turn back and realize that it was Jewel. She's looking me right in the eye. "You will?" I ask. My heart skips a beat. Is it possible? Is this Jewel's way of . . . making amends?

Doree and Melissa are scowling at her.

"Yeah," she says, smiling hopefully at me. "Why not?"

"Sixty, do-we-have-a-sixty-five? Sixty-five to the young man in the red sweatshirt. Do-we-have-a-seventy?" says Jeffrey. I've never seen an auctioneer, but I bet Jeffrey is the best one ever. Who even knew he could talk?

The auditorium is packed with students, teachers, and parents. We've raised more than eight thousand dollars so far, which is great but not nearly enough. We've gone through most of the items—clothes, books, CDs, picture frames, dinners. We're almost done auctioning off the students' services. Kat and I are sitting on plastic chairs off-stage, keeping track of the income. Bosh and Tammy are suspiciously absent. I'm pretty sure they're making out in the soc lounge. Right after we left the bathroom, Tammy found Aaron in the finally fixed cafeteria and dumped him.

"Last call at seventy dollars for ten hours of biology tutoring? Come on, boys and girls, chemicals are confusing! If

239

you fail bio, you're not getting into a good college. Seventy to the guy with the goatee in the back row. Do-I-hear-seventy-five? Seventy-going-once-going-twice-going-three-times. Sold!"

Hah. My five hours of math tutoring went for eighty. Never mind. Jewel's dance lessons went for two hundred.

Jeffrey holds the next item above his head. "Two prom tickets for nonseniors. Price starting at a hundred dollars for both. Do I hear a hundred?"

Where did those come from? Will must have slipped them in.

A sophomore raises her paddle.

Kat nudges me with her foot. "Maybe I should buy them," she jokes.

"Do I hear a hundred and twenty? A hundred and twenty to the girl in the back! Do I hear a hundred and thirty?"

"You're going to come for a bit, aren't you?" I ask.

She shakes her head. "I can only go if a senior asks me."

"That's insane. You worked on it all year. The prom wouldn't be happening without you."

She shrugs. "That's the way it works. Don't look so horrified," she adds, giving me her big smile. "It's not the end of the world."

"A hundred and thirty. Do I hear a hundred and forty?"

"Buy the tickets!" I urge. "Then you can go."

"I don't have anyone to go with," she says. "Really, it doesn't matter. I'll go next year." Her head stays straight, but I can't help noticing that her eyes trail to the other side of the stage—where Will is now standing, holding four jackets.

I feel a dipping in my stomach. Will would have asked Kat if it weren't for Miri's love spell. As with the oranges, and the clothes, and the car, I stole his affection.

"Sold for three hundred dollars to the pretty redhead!"

My head snaps up at the word *redhead*. I peer out from behind the curtain to see who's cheering. Melissa. Groan. Melissa is going to prom? That means Raf will be at prom too.

"Maybe the four of you can double," Kat offers.

Double groan.

"Next up, donated by the generous Kosravis from Kosa Coats and Goods, we have classic men's high-grade leather jackets, in the color camel, sizes small, medium, large, and extra large. Retail value six hundred and thirty-five dollars each. We're starting off with size small. Do I hear a hundred?"

241

My heart lurches. Now I'll be thinking I'm seeing Raf everywhere. Definitely a potential problem.

But not the only problem. Will's jackets are our last items. That means that after these products, we're out of loot to auction off. And we've raised only ten thousand dollars. We're still four thousand dollars short! Even if the coats earn their retail value, that's only two thousand five hundred and forty dollars!

I watch with a sinking feeling as the size small goes for four hundred and fifty, the medium and large go for six hundred apiece, and the extra large goes to Mr. Earls for only three hundred fifty. We're two thousand dollars short.

We didn't make it. After all that, we're still going to have to cancel prom.

I'm about to cry when Will walks over to River with a final bag. More coats?

"And for our final item tonight, also from Kosa Coats & Goods, we have a brand-new limited edition Izzy Simpson leather hobo bag, retail value one thousand five hundred dollars."

Yes! One more item to go! A gorgeous item, if I do say so myself. Izzy Simpson is my all-time favorite designer. Not that I would *ever* spend so much money on a bag. But if someone buys it, we're almost saved.

"Bidding starts at five hundred! Do I have a bidder?"

At this point, both Kat and I have pushed the curtains aside and are eagerly watching to see if there are any buyers. Even *I'm* biting my nails. Come on, come on.

A paddle goes up from Ms. Hayward.

"Five hundred dollars to the math teacher in the front row. Do I see seven hundred? Come on, people, it's for a good cause!"

Wow, go, Ms. H! Who knew she was a fashionista? You so wouldn't be able to tell from her boring gray pants and sweaters.

Amy Koppela raises her paddle. So nice of her to show up.

Then Ms. Hayward raises hers again.

London Zeal raises her paddle. Boo!

"One thousand three hundred dollars," Jeffrey says. "Do I see fifteen hundred?"

The room is silent. Please don't tell me we're going to be short by seven hundred dollars!

Come on, Amy, you're the worst soc member ever! Can't you at least buy the purse?

And that's when a paddle goes up in the back of the room. "Two thousand dollars," the person says in a familiar voice. Who is it?

All of us backstage are in shock. Is it possible?

"Two thousand going once. Twice. Sold to the blond woman in the back!"

I step on tiptoe and see Jennifer waving at me. Oh my God!

As soon as the crowd begins to disperse, I run right up to my stepmom. "I can't believe you bought it."

"Why not? It's gorgeous and a fantastic deal. It's a limited edition, you know. I'm already on the waiting list at Henri Bendel. Plus, because I bought it here, it's tax deductible."

"But how did you know that we needed two thousand dollars?"

She shows me a notepad that's covered in numbers. "I was keeping track. You said you needed to raise fourteen thousand, right? So that's what you had left."

"Wow" is all I can say.

"I was an accountant before I had Prissy, you know."

I didn't, actually.

She pays for her purchase and then waves good-bye.

"We did it!" Will says, picking me up and spinning me around. "We raised fourteen thousand dollars! Prom is going

243

to be amazing. And it's all because of you, Rachel. This auction was your idea."

He puts me down and looks into my eyes. "I really love
you," he says.

And you know what I wish? At this moment, what I
wish more than anything is that I never used the love spell.
I wish that his words were real.

All anyone can talk about for the next two days is prom,
prom, prom. It's on! After school on Tuesday, Tammy and I
go shopping to get her a dress and me some shoes. When I
get home, I spend an hour walking around the apartment,
hoping to break in my new two-inch heels. At least neither
my mom nor my sister is around to make fun of me: Miri is
locked in her room doing God knows what (she'd better not
be ignoring her schoolwork), and my mom is out as usual.
Not that we're talking. When she arrives home at nine,
looking tired and out of it, she zaps her shoes off and goes
straight to bed. I go to bed less than an hour later, counting
the hours (forty-four!) till prom.

By the time I get home on Wednesday, I can barely contain my excitement. I slip on my new heels right away
to continue breaking them in. When I hear my mom's
television, my good mood convinces me that it's time to
make amends.

I hop over to her room. The door is ajar, and I gently
push it all the way open. I find her in her bed, surrounded by
a huge mess. Clothes and food cartons are piled on the
sheets, and the room stinks like an ashtray.

244

"Are you sick?" I ask.

She shakes her head but doesn't move. I sneak over to her bedside and see that her bed isn't the only thing that's a mess. Her hair is in knots, her skin looks pasty, and her nails have been bitten down to the quick. I immediately climb into bed beside her, pushing over a wrinkled cashmere sweater. "What's wrong?"

"I'm fine," she says, and zaps on the light. "It's the men. I've gone on all these dates, and I know they all like me, but I don't really like them. Do you want some cheesecake?" she asks, and then zaps one up. "Or pie?" and then zaps that up too. "I want a cappuccino." Cappuccino appears on a tray on her bed. "Never mind. I think I want a cup of tea." The cappuccino is replaced. "Or maybe—"

"Stop. Just stop," I say. "Are you feeling okay?"

She shrugs. "Actually, I'm a little depressed."

No kidding. "Why don't you go fix yourself up?"

Mom nods and does a little waving thing with her hand.

"No!" I say, sternly grabbing hold of her wrist. "I meant, take a bath."

She blinks. "Oh. But it's easier this way."

"I know it's easier. But a bath feels good."

She considers the possibility and decides to do it. As my mom runs her bath, I start cleaning up her room. A sweater here, a jacket there . . . What is all this stuff? Why did she zap it all up? Because it was easy? Maybe that's why she's so depressed. When you get what you want so easily, it doesn't mean anything.

Like an empty I-love-you, I realize sadly.

After I finish cleaning, I check on Miri, who looks

equally exhausted. She's sitting on her floor, surrounded by three binders with labels: *Saving the Whales, Bushfires,* and a new one, *The Evil Circus.*

Another head case. But one problem family member at a time. "Mom is having a crisis," I say.

At first she looks confused, and I'm worried she's going to say "Mom who?" but then the clouds clear and she says, "What's wrong with her?"

Do these people live in the same house? I'm beginning to wonder if anyone pays attention besides me. "Just back me up," I say. And a half hour later, when we hear the bath draining, Miri and I are waiting on my mom's bed.

"What's going on?" my mom asks.

"This is an intervention," I say. "Mom, you shouldn't be using magic at all if you can't use it in moderation."

"But I . . . ," she begins, and then trails off. She sinks onto her bed. "I can't believe this is happening. Again."

Huh? "Excuse me?"

"This is why I stopped using magic. Why I became a nonpracticing witch. When I was a kid, your aunt and grandmother and I used magic for everything. Clothes, tests, school, boys, friends. But I was never happy. Nothing meant anything. And it wasn't just me. My mom and sister were never truly happy either. So I decided I would stop using magic. Just stop. In college, I studied for my own exams, bought my own clothes, and met my own boyfriend. Your father. And it made me happier."

"Not for long," Miri says. "He left you. It didn't work out."

"If I hadn't married your father, I wouldn't have had the

two of you. I wouldn't trade my situation for anything in the world. I'm not saying everything was perfect, but I experienced life."

"I get it," I say. "Keep going."

My mom takes a deep breath. "When your grandmother saw how at peace I was, she decided to do the same. We both realized that our powers were more of a curse than a blessing. We vowed that we would never use magic again. Of course, when Sasha realized what we were doing . . . when I let it happen . . . when I didn't use magic even when . . ." She chokes up, and tears spill over her cheeks.

I lean toward her. Is she finally going to tell us why she doesn't speak to Aunt Sasha? "When what happened?"

She shakes her head.

I guess not.

"I should have realized that this would happen this time," my mom says finally. "That I couldn't just dip my toe in. That it's not in my nature. I can't live like this. I have to quit." She nods slowly. "Cold turkey."

"Are you sure you need to cut it all out?" Miri asks.

"Yes," she says. "I didn't plan on being so extreme this time. But I'm an all-or-nothing kind of witch. I'm sorry, girls."

I hug my mother tightly. "I promise to support you any way I can. We both do. Right, Miri?"

But my sister is already lost in her own thoughts. I elbow her in the ribs, and she quickly snaps out of it and nods. "What? Oh, yeah, I'll support you. But I don't have to give it up too, do I? I have a lot of stuff I need to take care of. Important stuff."

247

"We all have to do what we all have to do," my mom says. "It's your decision."

Miri looks relieved. "Good. Because I'm still working on that rain spell for California. And, Rachel, I just found out that the circus is in town, and I absolutely have to take care of that first. Do you think—"

How insensitive is she? "Miri, I think Mom has enough to be concerned about without worrying about your next scheme." I mean, come on. Do you smoke a cigarette right in front of someone who's trying to quit? I give my sister my best stop-being-an-idiot eyebrow lift and say, "Why don't we get Mom into bed and make her dinner?"

"But I'm really—"

I give her my don't-mess-with-me look.

"Oh, okay."

My mom touches my cheek. "When did you become so mature?"

Mature? Me? "Good question."

After we tuck her in, make dinner, and clean up, I follow Miri to her room and close the door. "Okay, what's all this about a circus? You planning to become an acrobat or something?" Now, that's a cool job. I've always wanted to try a real trapeze. When I was younger, I pretended the curtain rod was one, and I'll admit that didn't end happily for me, Miri (she was the catcher), or the living room.

She thrusts a flyer at me. "The Faher Family Circus is in New York!"

I read the photocopied yellow paper. "So? You want to go?"

She grabs the flyer back, rolls it, and hits me over the head. "No, I don't want to go. Don't you know how cruel circuses are? They chain the animals to the ground! Lock them in cages! Make elephants, lions, and monkeys perform acts that are totally unnatural!"

"I like the circus," I say. Our parents took us when we were kids. Hmm, now that I think about it, I remember that Miri spent most of the trip crying while I spent most of the time eating cotton candy. Yum.

"We have to save them! It's our responsibility! Animal circuses are already illegal in most other countries. Sweden, Austria, Costa Rica, India . . ."

"Let's sit down and discuss it." I make myself comfy on her bed.

"I don't want to sit down!" she screams, sounding a wee bit hysterical. "We need to go. Now."

249

"Now? As in tonight?" My plan for the night involves lots of sleep. "It's been a stressful few weeks, and prom is tomorrow, and now I'd really like to chill."

She narrows her eyes. "The elephants don't get to relax. They're too busy having metal hooks slammed into their feet."

Gross. "That's pretty graphic."

"You can't just pretend these things don't happen." She disappears from the room and returns with the lithium batteries. "I'm going. Are you coming or not?"

She's out of control. "Let's just take the night to think this through. We'll make a plan. Why don't we have a rally? Or a protest? We don't have to do it tonight. I did lots of research on the Internet and the consequences of our spells have been—"

"I said, I'm going. Guess you're not." She puts her fists together, scrunches her eyes shut, and says, "Transport to the place inside my mind."

Oh, drat. I jump on her back.

"The power of my fists shall ye bind!"

I close my eyes in preparation for the screaming light.

"It didn't work!" Miri says angrily.

I open my eyes. Indeed, we are still in her bedroom. I slip off her. "What happened?"

She places her fists on her hips. "Did you gain weight?"

"No!" The nerve. "Maybe the batteries died. Do you have spares?"

She pouts. "Noooo. Guess we'll have to fly. I'm changing into camouflage!" she says, stripping. "And bringing the reflective shield in case."

"Can we just pause for a second and discuss this like rational people?"

"There's nothing to talk about. I have to help. It's my responsibility."

"Not everything is your responsibility!"

"You don't understand," she says as she pulls on my black sweatpants. "You're not a witch."

Ouch. "You're right, I'm not." Maybe she has a point. I don't understand how she feels. I don't know the pressure of having the capability of doing so much good. Of feeling like the entire world's health and happiness is in my hands. I don't know the fear that comes with magic. I don't know anything.

She fetches our broom, then pulls a black sweatshirt

over her head and fastens her helmet. "Are you coming?" she asks.

The only thing I do know is that it's my job to support my sister. "I'm coming," I say, and dash back to my room to change. "Do I have a choice?" I scribble a note for our mom.

Miri joins me in my room, the broom in tow. She yanks open the window and the cool air breezes in.

"Time is of the essence," she says, straddling the broom. "Hop on!"

I fasten my helmet, climb on behind her, hold up the umbrella shield, and duck as the broom jolts toward the open window.

Here goes nothing.

251

Should Have Taken a Taxi

16

"What's your plan exactly?" I say over the sound of the wind.

"Huh?"

"Plan? What? Is? Yours?" I yell directly into her ear.

"I can't hear you!" she says back, obviously ignoring me. Funny, I can hear *her*.

We're flying high over the buildings in Chelsea, my two-inch heels dangling beneath me. Unfortunately, in my rush I forgot to put on something a little more appropriate.

Miri does a few circles over the massive convention center as she scouts a landing. When she sees a side entrance that appears empty, she nose-dives toward the pavement and quickly lowers the broom to the ground. We topple onto the cement. I wish she'd learn to land this thing better; one day I'm going to break an arm for sure.

This is obviously the worst plan she has ever had. We're in a sketchy part of the city, all the way on the West Side. We could easily be mugged. By the time I regain my balance, Miri is already at the convention center's side door, chanting her open sesame spell. I hand her the broom and she props it against the brick wall.

The door opens, and Miri rushes inside. I'm reluctant to follow. "There are going to be trainers here," I whisper. "What are you going to do? How are you going to save the animals exactly?" I'm afraid to lose her, so I step inside.

"Don't close the door," Miri tells me. "In case we have to make a quick exit," she explains. Not exactly encouraging words.

Great. My heart speeds up as I enter the dark building. At least we have on our night-vision helmets. I hurry to catch up with Miri, which isn't easy in these heels. Maybe tonight isn't the best time to break them in.

"ROWRRRRRRRRRRRRRRRR!" A wild, animal noise echoes through the room. I'm pretty sure that was a lion. Or a tiger. Very possibly a bear. Oh my.

We both freeze. "Miri. This. Is. Not. Safe," I hiss through a clenched jaw.

"Don't worry. It'll be fine."

And that's when I see it.

A massive lion licking her massive paw.

And she sees us.

I jump back about twenty feet before realizing she's in a cage. A locked cage. There are two lions in there, and they're both beige and maneless and lying in the corner. It's kind of sweet, actually. One of them is resting her leg against the other's leg. They're kind of cuddling. I wonder if they're sisters and—

"ROOOOOOOOOOOOOAAAAAAAAAAAAAAAA AAAAAAAAR!" The cranky younger sister, obviously. I jump back about ten feet.

How secure is that lock?

253

"Poor little lions," Miri murmurs, tiptoeing toward the animals. Little? "See how claustrophobic they look in that tiny cage?"

I grab her shoulder so she won't get any closer. I like my sister in one piece, and those lions look hungry. Fine, they look sleepy. But maybe that's just a trick.

"We should start here," she says, reaching into her satchel.

I begin to panic. "Start what?"

"Freeing them, what else?"

That's it, she's losing it. I'm losing it. I shake her by the shoulder. "Are you insane? What are you going to do? Open the cages and set the sister lions loose on New York? They'll have us for appetizers and then chomp down all of Manhattan for the main course!"

You know what? It smells in here. A lot like JFK after the cow invasion.

She struggles to remove my hand from her shoulder. "Do you think I'm stupid? Manhattan is no place for them. I'm sending them home. Where they can run free. Now, let me go!"

I step back and take a good look at my angry, red-in-the-face, disheveled-haired sister. She's definitely out of her mind. I think my entire family needs a vacation.

She removes a Tupperware container from her satchel, opens it, then sets the spell book in front of her and chants:

"Be free of reins
And drop your chains,
By tomorrow's morn

You'll be back where you were born!"

She tosses the concoction on them, and I feel the familiar rush of cold as I ask, "Can't you just get them to click their heels together three times?"

The two lions begin to fade. They get lighter and lighter, and then they're gone.

"Cool," Miri says.

I really hope they're not going to reappear behind me. I carefully turn my head. Nope. I let out a long breath. "Where do you think they went?"

"Duh. Africa. Let's see who's next," Miri whispers. But she stops walking when she spots a trainer at the end of the room rattling about outside a cage. "Wait for him to go," she whispers. We freeze, and I start to panic. What if we're caught? How would we explain the animal disappearances? Would we be arrested for animal-napping? Even if they couldn't find the evidence?

As the trainer comes our way, we duck behind a pole. "Don't move," Miri whispers.

About five minutes later, the trainer disappears into a back room out of view, and we move on to the next cage. Camels. I love camels. How cool are they that they don't need any water? How cute is that hump? Not that I would want a hump like that or anything. I snap back to attention as Miri chants the spell.

And away they go!

Next we hit the tigers, elephants, zebras, horses, alligators, and llamas, which takes forever. Finally we're at what I think is the last cage.

255

Where there are two goats. A mama goat and her baby.

Once again Miri goes through the whole spell, the throwing, yada, yada, the cold, the fading. Well, the big goat fades, but the little one doesn't budge.

Miri approaches the cage. "What's wrong, baby goat?"

"Try again," I tell her, already bored. I'm now sitting on the floor, too tired to care about what's been on the floor before me.

Miri tries again. *"Be free"*—blah, blah, blah—*"born!"*

The goat still doesn't budge.

"Something's not working," Miri says. "I'm going to check it out." She looks around for a lock, finds it, recites the open sesame spell, and opens the cage. "Isn't he cute? Hello, adorableness. Why won't you go home?" She gently pats his head.

I approach the door. He *is* cute. Small, too. He's all white, with a small wet gray nose and two triangular floppy-looking ears that are pointing to the high ceiling. I bet he'd be great to mooshie. He looks like a teddy bear. Teddy goat. Billy the Teddy Goat. He looks so cuddly, probably only a few weeks old. "Maybe he was born here," I say. "That's why he didn't disappear."

Billy looks up at us and widens his big dewy eyes.

"Aw," Miri and I both murmur.

And that's when it happens.

Billy bolts. Right out of Miri's arms, right between my open legs, and out of the cage, galloping at a speed I would never have believed possible for a goat. A baby lion, maybe. But a goat? This one is faster than a speeding bullet. As Miri and I watch him in disbelief, Billy the Supergoat runs straight for the door. The open door.

"Get that goat!" Miri screams, and we take off. Fine, I'm laughing a bit. I can't help it. But I run after the goat anyway, right through the convention center, until I'm outside, wondering which way he went.

"Billy's gone," I tell Miri.

"Who's Billy?" she says, panting. "We should fly. That will make the goat easier to—"

The broom is no longer where she left it. "What the—"

"What did you expect to happen on an isolated street in the city?" I scream. Someone is in for a rude shock when they try to sweep their floor. "There's Billy!" I say, pointing at the small creature currently licking his hoof.

We bolt after him. And he runs. And we chase. We chase him all the way down Thirty-ninth Street, cringing every time he crosses an avenue, praying he doesn't end up goat cheese. We continue chasing him right to Forty-second and Eighth, and then right into the—

Oh, no. Not the subway station!

Miri freezes at the landing. "We're not allowed to take the subway so late at night," she whimpers.

We're allowed to go hightailing over Manhattan but not to take the subway? Does this make sense? I ignore her and take the stairs two at a time, trying to catch up to Billy the Bolting Supergoat. "Come here, Billy," I call, but he doesn't stop. Instead, he runs right under the turnstile. Of course I don't have my MetroCard. Why would I? It's two in the morning!

257

"Zap it around," I tell my ashen-faced sister. She's almost the same color as Billy, who's now calmly licking himself in a very inappropriate way on the other side of the turnstile.

Miri does as she's told, and I push through and lunge after Billy. He's faster and takes off as soon as I'm an inch away from grabbing him. Luckily, there're only two other people waiting for the train.

And then Billy the Supergoat takes a flying leap—"No, Billy, no!" we shriek—directly onto the subway tracks.

Our jaws drop in horror, and we peer over the edge. Billy seems to have realized that he might have made a mistake, because he is now bleating loudly, and his little legs are quivering.

"We have to get him," Miri says, and takes a step toward the track.

I give her a power block with my arm. "Over my dead body are you stepping onto a subway track."

"But . . . but . . ."

And then we hear it. Oh yes, the rumble of the swiftly approaching train.

"Oh, no," Miri whimpers. My heart races almost as fast as the oncoming car. As the headlights glare toward us, I see poor Billy, eyes wide and wet, begging us to help.

Miri shrieks, reaches her hands toward the train, and yells, "Stop!"

Her lips purse, I feel the rush of cold, and the subway grinds to a sudden halt.

The station is silent. Until Billy bleats.

The conductor pops his head out his window. "What the

258

hell?" he says. "We just lost power." He spots Billy. "All this because of one little goat?"

"One little goat," I say. "That my father bought for two *zuzim*."

Miri starts to cry.

I lead my blubbering sister and the sleeping goat she's cradling up the pitch-black stairs. It seems Miri blew out the power in the whole station. Thank goodness for our night-vision helmets. "I almost killed you," Miri tells the goat between sobs.

"Yes, you did," I say as I finally step into the night. I'm furious. We have no broom, no batteries, no money, and no working subway, and my feet are killing me. Not only are my shoes broken in, but my feet feel broken too. "You have to think about the ramifica—"

Oh, no. I look around.

The entire city is dark. As in cloaked in darkness. As in all the sparkling lights that normally illuminate the city have either burnt out simultaneously, or—

"Uh, oh," Miri squeaks. "Did I . . . ?"

"Yes, Miri. Apparently you did. Apparently your little stopping-the-train tactic blew out all the power in Manhattan." I am so mad, I'm fuming.

"Well, what else could I do? What about poor little Billy?"

We arrive home two hours later. I won't even discuss the bloated, deformed shape of my feet. I'm too angry to talk to my sister, so I leave her and Billy to figure out their sleeping arrangements. I throw the itchy helmet onto the floor and feel my way toward my mom's room. After making sure that she's sleeping soundly, wrapped in her covers, oblivious to the world, I kiss her on the forehead and feel my way back to my room, drop my camouflage outfit on the floor, and slip under the covers. I need to get some sleep! Prom is tomorrow and I'm going to be so tired and I'm going to look exhausted and there's no power and I don't even know what time it is because my clock isn't working and please, please, please let everything be better in the morning.

Blackout

17

I'm awakened by Miri's screaming, "No, Tigger, no! Leave Billy alone!" and realize that maybe everything does not always seem better in the morning. I look at my alarm clock, but it's black. Please don't tell me that the power is still out.

And then I remember the goat, so I get out of bed to see how our houseguest is doing. I find Billy on the kitchen table, bleating like crazy, Tigger hissing on a neighboring chair, and Miri failing to manage the ménage.

"What time is it?" I ask, rubbing the sleep from my eyes.

"Eight-thirty," Miri answers.

I groan. "I'm going to be late for school!"

"There is no school," she says, pulling Tigger's chair across the room to the sink. "Power is still out."

She points to the radio next to the sink. I carry it to the kitchen table and turn the volume up. Hmm. Good thing we're out of lithium batteries and not AAAs.

The voice coming from the radio is loud and crisp. "At 2:09 a.m. eastern time, the entire island of Manhattan was hit by an unexplained blackout. Subways stopped midtunnel, streetlights went out, and electricity consumers are still waiting to have service restored. The cause of the blackout is still unknown. All schools are closed today, and most businesses are expected to remain closed until power is restored, hopefully by tomorrow morning. The bell on Wall Street will not be ringing. . . ."

You've got to be kidding. Oh. My. God. "Miri! Are you listening?"

Billy bleats. The cat hisses. I sigh.

Instead of listening, or caring, Miri watches Tigger as he leaps off the chair and onto the countertop, and she scoops him up before he attacks the table. I sink into Tigger's vacated chair and cradle my suddenly pounding head in my arms.

"What do you think *bleat* means?" Miri asks.

"I think it means 'I miss my mother,' " I say.

262

"In other news," the radio announcer continues, "exotic animals have been appearing in unexpected places all across the country. This morning, a dance troupe in Birmingham, Alabama, found a seven-thousand-pound elephant on the stage of the BJCC Arena."

That's it. I've had enough. "Sit down, Miri." I must look serious, because she slithers into a chair, holding Tigger tightly on her lap. "Do you realize what you've done? By trying to save the circus animals, you caused a citywide blackout. Plus you've endangered the animals you tried to save! They just found an elephant in Alabama! There could be a alligator in Maine!"

"An alligator wouldn't have been born in Maine," she says, reddening.

"How do you know? Stranger things have happened! My

point is, you have to realize that all your spells have consequences. You have to think, and I mean *really* think, about each and every action before you end up ruining everything!"

"B-but I thought the animals were b-born in the wild . . . ," she stutters.

"I'm sure some of them were, but you didn't do your research and lots of people—and animals—are going to get hurt."

Her eyes fill with tears. "I just wanted to help."

"I know you did, and that's very honorable. But you're not helping! You're making things worse! What do you think is going to happen to that elephant? They're not going to fit him with tights and ballet slippers and give him the starring role in *The Nutcracker*! He's going to be tranquilized and could be hurt. Is that what you wanted?"

"No," she whimpers. Billy bleats.

"Don't you see? Everything comes with a price. The cows had to go *somewhere*, so they went to the school gym. The oranges had to come from somewhere. The Mercedes had to come from somewhere. Nothing comes from nothing. You're not making something appear from nothing, Miri. Your magic just moves things from one place to another."

"Stealing," she says, and starts crying all over again. "You're right. Helping just made everything worse. I'm the worst superhero ever!"

Finally, my message is getting through to her. "And I still haven't figured out what happened to the oil you zapped. I'm hoping it ended up in a gas station or some lucky guy's

263

backyard. But don't you see? You're just like Mom. She's a magicoholic. You're a do-goodoholic."

She nods. "From now on I'll mind my own business. Keep my nose in my own books."

Good. Well, not exactly. "That's not what I meant—"

"Stop trying to make the world a better place," she says sadly. "I'll never help anyone again."

Now she's just going to extremes. "Miri, you don't have to stop helping *anyone*. You have to stop helping *everyone*."

"Huh?"

I walk over to the table and sit on it, facing my sister. "You have to learn that doing a hundred things partially means you're not doing anything a hundred percent. In the past two months, you've tried to feed and clothe the homeless, stop the bushfires in California, fix the ozone layer, and save circus animals, among other things. It's too much. You need to try to make a difference one issue at a time so you can give each issue your all. Every action has costs, even every nonmagical one. What you have to do to make a real, positive difference is plan. Map out your potential actions so you can figure out what the consequences are ahead of time. That way, you'll do good, not damage."

She dries her eyes with the backs of her hands. "That makes sense."

I pat Billy on the head. "I know. I'm very smart."

The phone rings and we both jump. I grab it before it wakes my mom. She needs her rest.

"Rachel? Are you okay?"

"Hi, Will. I'm fine. How are you?"

"Not so good. I just called Penthouse Fifty and the prom is officially canceled."

What now? What else could possibly have gone wrong? Why is this prom so cursed? Why, why, why? "Because of the power?"

"Yup," he says, sighing.

"But we still have the space, right? Can't the band sing without a microphone? We could light up the room with candles. It would be really romantic!"

"We could, but the room we rented is on the fiftieth floor. So everyone would have to walk all the way upstairs."

Oh, right. No elevator. "Don't they have any rooms on the ground floor?"

"They do, but the other problem is that the doors all have key cards that don't work without power." His voice cracks. "I just can't believe this."

"But can't they move the date?" I ask, feeling desperate. "We can have it tomorrow, or next week—"

"Rachel, everyone's booked. The band and the rentals can't make it another day and they won't return the deposits unless it's tonight. So unless the power comes back on, it's over."

Not only have Miri and I caused a major blackout in the metropolitan area, we've ruined the prom. Again.

I hang up with a depressed Will and recount the latest news to Miri, Billy, and Tigger.

"We have to wake up Mom," Miri says.

"No," I say firmly. "She's recuperating. We're not asking for her help. We have to deal with this on our own. Let's try the spell reversal."

265

"But the animals—"

"The *animals* will be better off. If we reverse the go-home spell and the animals return, maybe this whole chain of events will unravel. Billy wouldn't have run into the subway, you wouldn't have had to save him, and the power wouldn't have gone out. I know it's a long shot, but it's worth a try."

"Okay." Miri sighs, and I follow her into her room. "But I need to recharge the crystal in the salt for an hour. And I can't promise it will work."

"I know. But let's give it a go."

By noon we buy new batteries and transport ourselves back to the convention center. Luckily, the goat is light, and Miri is carrying him in a satchel over her shoulder while I'm on her back wearing the crystal necklace and holding up the umbrella shield.

Bright light!

We pop up behind a police car. Good—no one seems to have seen us. Bad—there is a police car. Four officers and a crowd have surrounded the front door to the convention center.

"Damn animal rights groups," someone says.

We head back to the side entranceway. "We're actually going to circle the entire building backward?" I ask in amazement.

"Since the crystal is already enchanted," she says. "Can you do it? I'm a jinx these days."

I would, but I know that I'd be doing more harm than good. She has to learn to pay the consequences. I shake my head, and hand her the crystal necklace, and she passes me the goat satchel with a sigh.

"This had better work," she says. "Billy misses his mommy. Ready?"

"Yup," I say, and begin leading Miri around the million-square-foot block-long building, reflective shield hiding us from prying eyes.

Twenty minutes and six stumbles later, we're back at the side entrance. As she takes the final step, we hear an explosion of roars, bleats, and howls from the animals now inside. A little cranky, are we?

A trainer throws open the side door and yells to a nearby policeman, "The animals are back! It must have been some sort of publicity stunt!"

I remove Billy from the bag and set him free toward the door. "Run, little goat, run! Let's get out of here," I say as a policeman and onlooker approach the door. We sneak back toward the street, hoping to see working traffic lights. To our disappointment, they're still not on. So much for the great spell unraveler.

267

Miri sighs. "Next plan?"

We find a five-broomer light spell, but before we try it on the city, we test it on the apartment. Our curtains catch on fire.

My mom is now awake in her room, chatting on the phone, oblivious to our role in this catastrophe.

So we listen to the radio, which tells us that they've located the problem. Reportedly, a power blockage around Times Square caused a surge, which made the lights go out on the entire island. Who caused the blockage isn't, of course, on the news. The newscaster also reports that the power is expected to be back up and running by early tomorrow morning. I give Miri a dirty look.

"Great," I say. "One day too late."

"Should I try another spell?" Miri asks.

"No," I say, resigned. "It's too risky. What if it goes wrong? They say they'll have it fixed by tomorrow morning, so we'll have to wait."

"But your prom is tonight."

I shrug. "It's just a prom." I try to smile.

"I feel awful," Miri says. "If only you could have it someplace out of the city."

"Like where? Disneyland?"

"Very funny." Then she jumps up. "I know! I know! Didn't you say the theme was Oscar night?"

"Yes. But I doubt we'll be able to have it in L.A. Unless the entire class is going to climb on your back."

"What about the drive-in? You know, the one we flew over? It's only about forty minutes away. They're not in the city, so they'd have power."

"How would we even get there? We can't fly everyone out there on brooms, and the subways aren't running. It's not like we know anyone who owns a car, never mind a bus."

She sighs. "That's true."

We hear my mom's door open and she comes out in a bathrobe. Her roots are back to normal (dark), her nails are back to normal (ragged), and her breasts are back to normal (small and saggy). But she's smiling. "Morning, girls!"

"You seem happy," Miri says gloomily.

"I slept very well, thank you. And I just had a very nice conversation with Lex. Remember him? He called to see how we three girls are holding up in the blackout. Wasn't that sweet of him?"

Aw! That *was* sweet of him. "Lex is a really nice guy, Mom. You should definitely go out with him." Wait a sec. Lex is a tour guide. And a tour guide definitely has bus access. I start jumping up and down and I'm so excited that I can barely talk. "Call him back! Lex! Bus!"

As comprehension dawns on Miri's face, she starts jumping up and down alongside me.

"We need to get to prom! Upstate! Because of the power failure! Do you think Lex will help us?"

My mom looks confused. "It doesn't hurt to ask. Um, girls, you didn't have anything to do with the power problem, did you?"

269

* * *

The next four hours are a bit of a whirlwind. First we have to explain it all to Mom, which we do, and luckily she doesn't freak out. Instead, she gives Miri a big hug.

"Like mother, like daughter," she says, smoothing Miri's hair back. "We forgot about the importance of moderation, didn't we? And we both paid the consequences."

"If I had powers," I say longingly, "I would so use them carefully and sparingly."

My mom and sister take this as a cue to begin laughing uncontrollably.

When she calms down, Mom warns us that now that

she's *back*, she'll be monitoring our shenanigans far more closely. And that, yes, Miri is still allowed to use magic but not unconditionally. Then Mom helps us *non*magically track down the drive-in (hello, phone book) and then the owners, who live just down the road from the theater. They're a sweet elderly couple who only charge a thousand dollars. Plus they offer to play any movies we want in the background all night. *Pretty in Pink! Grease! Carrie!* Okay, maybe not *Carrie.* I'd be happy to see any movie at all, except *The Sound of Music.* But anyway, Mom calls Lex back, and he agrees to pack his bus with eager prom-goers. He also asks some bus driver pals of his to help us out.

Then I call Will to share the good news.

"You are the best," he says. "I'll get Kat to start calling all the seniors. Bosh, River, and I will head out early to lead the setup committee. Is it okay if I meet you there? Or do you want to bring your stuff and come with me and get ready at the drive-in?"

"I'll get ready here. I need lots of time to beautify." I don't even want to think about my under-eye circles.

"You're beautiful as is."

He's the best boyfriend ever. I mean, really, what else could I ask for?

As I get ready, I can hear Mom and Miri chatting it up in the kitchen. Mom is making homemade veggie egg rolls ("I'll try to cut down on the tofu overload, I promise!") as she helps Miri with her homework.

The phone rings as I'm towel-drying my hair. "It's me!" screams Kat. "I can't believe you saved prom! You are a star.

Honestly. It's too bad you're only a freshman, otherwise you could so run for president next year. Just wanted to say you rock! Have a great time tonight."

And that's when it hits me, and I know what I have to do.

Pretty in Pink . . . Sneakers

18

I pull my hair back into a ponytail, put on one of my new pairs of jeans, and slide my swollen feet into my sneakers.

"You sure?" Miri asks.

"Yup." I hang the garment bag over my left arm and lift the two smaller bags with my right.

She gives me a hug. "Have fun. If you need me, I'll be here not saving the world."

"Good," I say. "You need to relax. Why don't you read?"

"I thought I'd watch *The Sound of Music*."

"Ha-ha."

She laughs and returns to her room.

There's a knock on the door. Who's that? "Hello?" I ask.

"Hi. It's Lex!"

What is he doing here? "I thought I was meeting you at the school."

"He's coming to get us," says my mom, sashaying out of her room in an old pair of jeans and a cotton blouse, looking like her old self. "Miri, come say good-bye and give us a hug!" she hollers.

Huh? "You're coming?"

She blushes. "Lex asked me to keep him company on the trip. If that's all right with you. He thought he'd pick us up first and then we'd stop by the school. If you'd let him in." She eyes my outfit quizzically. "You're planning to get dressed at the drive-in?"

I open the door to find Lex flushed, sweating, and smiling. He's also holding a corsage. "For you," he says to my mom. Aw. "Ready, ladies?" he says, and tips his hat.

"Yup," I say, picking up my bags. "I just need you to make one quick stop before going to school."

He takes the bags from my arms. What a gentleman, I think, thoroughly impressed.

Kat unlocks her front door and throws it wide open. "What are you doing here?"

"I've come to pick you up," I say.

She laughs. "What? Why? I'm not going anywhere."

"Yes, you are." I hand her the garment bag. "This is your prom dress."

"W-what . . . ," she stutters, surprised. "I can't go. I don't have a date."

"Yes, you do."

"Who?"

I smile. "It's a surprise. What size shoe are you?"

"Six."

I toss her the second bag. "It's your lucky day. They're even broken in."

She's holding up both bags, looking at me like she just woke up on a different planet. "I don't understand."

I hear Lex honking outside. "Now, hurry up and get dressed. Your pumpkin awaits."

*

As we pull into the drive-in, I can already see the rainbow of girls in their prom dresses dancing on the cobblestones with their tuxedo-clad dates. The massive screen is playing an old black-and-white movie I don't recognize, and the band is singing one of those songs that's always on the radio. Under one of the rows of glowing lanterns are the dinner buffet and beautifully set tables. The party is in full swing. Two empty buses, some cars, and a few limos are parked in front of us.

"Are you sure you're okay?" Tammy whispers to me as we join the line to get off the bus. "I don't get what's going on." She peeks at Kat, who's a few people behind us. "Why is she wearing your dress?"

I give Tammy's arm a squeeze and ignore the question. Luckily, she spots Bosh through the window and goes into giggle overdrive, forgetting all about me.

"Look how cute he is in his tux," she gushes, straightening her strapless red dress.

As I climb down the stairs of the bus, I spot Will in *his* tux, and my throat feels dry. My heart pounds faster, louder, until I can feel it in my neck and fingers.

He's talking to the photographer, smiling and nodding at something he's saying. When he looks up and sees me watching him, the smile lights up his eyes.

He doesn't even notice that I'm wearing jeans. Gripping my final bag, I walk down the red carpet toward him. "Hi," I say when he's only a foot away. I remove the crystal necklace from the bag and slip it over my head.

He's going to make some girl very happy, I think as I circle him. Just not me.

"What the . . . Why did you do that?" He blinks repeatedly, not knowing what just hit him. As I take my final backward step, he opens his mouth. He closes it. He opens it again.

Okay, I'll admit it. A fraction of me, my ego, is thinking that he'll still love me. That his feelings for me have grown stronger than any spell.

He blinks again.

Oh well. A girl can dream. But the truth is, while what he felt for me wasn't real, what I felt for him was just as illusory. I was enamored with all he represented, his hotness, his social status, his never-ending supply of licorice. But there was never any *real* magic between us.

275

I take a deep breath. "Listen, Will, we have to talk. You're a terrific guy, but I don't think we're right together. I didn't want to leave you stranded tonight, so I got you another date." I point to the bus just as Kat is stepping off the last step.

His eyes follow my finger. And light up. Kat looks beautiful. The dress flatters her figure in a way that capris and hoodies never could, and her hair is wavy around her shoulders. She and Will smile shyly at each other.

"Hi," she mouths.

"You look amazing," he mouths back, not losing her gaze for a second.

Kat walks toward us and looks at me quizzically. "We broke up," I tell her. "Would you mind being his date tonight?"

Kat's head swivels between the two of us. "Are you sure?" she asks incredulously.

I nod, smiling, and walk away. He takes her hand and they head toward the dance floor.

So.

What to do for the next four hours until I can hitch a ride back to the city? I guess I'll wait in the bus. Or maybe in my tree?

I climb to the spot where Miri and I once watched *Spider-Man* and get comfortable. A slow song begins and echoes through the night. From my perch, I see Will and Kat in each other's arms, moving to the music. Behind them, Lex and Mom are also dancing, totally oblivious to everyone around. Under a lantern, Tammy and Bosh are looking deeply into each other's eyes. All the couples are back where they belong. Just like in the end of *A Midsummer Night's Dream*. If we witches have offended, think but this, and all is mended.

Almost all. I swallow the lump in my throat when I spot Raf and Melissa slow-dancing, her head on his shoulder, his arms around her waist.

My heart races at the sight of him. Even though I've tried to convince myself that I don't care, that old feeling comes back with a punch. Or maybe it never really left me in the first place. All is back to normal, including my feelings for Raf. If only he felt the same way about me.

Suddenly, he lifts his gaze into the tree and our eyes lock. And he smiles at me. Is it possible? Could he feel the same way I do?

And that's when a raindrop lands smack on my forehead. Two drops. Three, four. I look up through the branches to see the sky disappearing behind angry black clouds. Suddenly, the clouds crack open. Within two seconds, the entire senior class is shrieking and searching for nonexistent cover.

Oh, no! Prom will be ruined after all!

I lift my face to the downpour. Good thing I'm not wearing mascara.

I close my eyes, pulling all the energy I can muster from every pore of my body, until I can feel it imploding inside me, and wish with all my heart:

Rain, rain, go away,

Go instead to help L.A.!

I feel a wave of cold and then . . . nothing. I open one eye. And then the other. It stopped raining.

Huh? Did I . . . ?

I watch as the dark clouds swiftly disappear, leaving a gorgeous starry night over the prom once more.

And as I realize what just happened, my body tingles with electricity.

I did that.

I. Did. That.

Omigod.

OMIGOD.

Yes!

277